FUGITIVES OF HELHEIM

Heroes Of The Nine Realms

BOOK 1

ALEX E. MARTIN

Copyright © 2025 by Alex E. Martin

All rights reserved.

No portion of this book may be reproduced in any form without written permission from the publisher

or author, except as permitted by U.S. copyright law.

ISBN: 979-8-89694-029-6 - eBook

ISBN: 979-8-89694-037-1 - Paperback

ISBN: 979-8-89694-038-8 - Hardcover

This is a work of fiction. All characters, events, and places portrayed in this book are the product of the author's imagination or used fictitiously. Any resemblance to actual persons, living or dead, or to real events, locales, or organizations is purely coincidental. The views, thoughts, and opinions expressed in this book do not represent the personal views or beliefs of the author and do not necessarily reflect the views or positions of any individuals, entities, or organizations referenced herein. This book is not intended as historical or factual representation, nor does it reflect real-world circumstances, practices, or beliefs.

To my teacher Matt, mentor Joe, artist Metakosmian, and Self-Publishing.com,
who helped me complete this book.

—◆—

BEFORE YOU BUY

Before You Begin...

To thank you for joining me on this journey, I would like to offer some gifts: free colored copies of Helheim's First Level and the World Tree. Click Here to tell me where to send them or scan the QR Code.

Helheim's
First
Level
Valley of Shadows
Gjallerbru
Gnipa Cave
Garm
Bridge of Judgment
Hringhorni
Eljudnir
Hræsvelgr, the Corpse Eater
Helheim's Lower Levels
Náströnd, the Shore of Corpses
City of the Lost
Yggdrasil's Roots
River Gjöll

Yggdrasil

Gullinkambi
& Vedrfolnir
Asgard
Vanaheim
Alfheim
Svartalfheim
Midgard
Jotunheim
Ratatoskr
Niflheim
Helheim
Muspelheim

NOTES ON PRONUNCIATION

The following notes are intended to clarify some of the pronunciations of key names in this series and are by no means exhaustive. Readers can pronounce the names however they choose, but this is how the author pronounces them.

AESIR (Pronounced "A-Seer")

ALGIZ (Pronounced "AHL-giz")

ÅNDSROSTAVEN (Pronounced "Ands-roh-stah-ven")

ANGANTYR (Pronounced "AHN-gahn-teer")

ANGRBODA (pronounced "An-gru-boda")

BRYNHILD (Pronounced "Brin-hild")

DAGR (Pronounced "DAH-Ger" like the word "Dagger")

DRAUG (Pronounced "DrahG")

DRAUGIR (Pronounced "Drah-Geer")

EINHERJAR (Pronounced "EYN-hair-yahr")

EYLIMI (Pronounced "AY-lee-mee")

ELUDNIR (Pronounced "e-lud-near")

FAFNIR (Pronounced "FAHF-near")

FENRIR (Pronounced "FEN-rear")

FREKASTEIN (Pronounced "FRE-kah-steyn")

FREYJA (pronounced "Freya" [silent j])

FREYR (Pronounced "Frey-ER")

GJALLERBRU (Pronounced "Ya-ler-brew")

GJUKI (Pronounced "GYOO-kee")

GJUKUNG (Pronounced Ga-YOO-koong")

GJÖLL (Pronounced like "Joel")

GUNNLQÐ (Pronounced "GOON-lohth")

GUTTORM (Pronounced "GOOT-torm")

HÁMUNDR (Pronounced "HA-mun-der")

HÁVARD (Pronounced "Ha-vArd"

HELHEIM (Pronounced "Hell-Hime")

HERMONDR (Pronounced "Hermond" [silent r])

HJORDIS (Pronounced "YOUR-des")

HLJOD (Pronounced "yold")

HODR (Pronounced "Ho-Der")

HÖGNE (Pronounced "Hog-KNEE")

HJALPREK (Pronounced "HYAHL-prek")

HRÆSVELGR (Pronounced "Ha-roth-el-gar")

HREIDMAR (Pronounced "HRAYD-mahr")

HRINGHORNI (Pronounced "Ring-horn-E")

IDUN (Pronounced "EE-doon")

IVALDI (Pronounced "EE-vahl-dee")

JONAKR (Pronounced "YON-nah-kr")

JÖRMUNGANDR (pronounced "YOUR-mun-gand-er")

JOTUN (Pronounced "Yo-tun")

LITR (Pronounced "Li-tur")

LYNGVI (Pronounced "Ling-vi")

MÓÐGUÐR (Pronounced "Mod-gu-dur")

MUSPELHEIM (Pronounced "Moose-pel-Heim")

NÁSTRÖND (Pronounced "Na-strond")

NIFLHEIM (Pronounced "Nif-ill-Hime")

NJÖRD (Pronounced "Nyord")

OTTR (Pronounced "O-Ter")

RAGR (Pronounced "RAH-gr")

REKR (Pronounced "REH-Kur")

RERIR (Pronounced "Re-rear")

SIGGIER (Pronounced "Sig-gear")

SIGI (Pronounced "Sig-E")

SIGYN (Pronounced "Sig-In")

SIGNY (Pronounced "Sig-knee")

SIGRÚN (Pronounced "SIG-roohn")

SIGURD ("Sig-urd")

SINFJOTLI ("Sin-fot-LEE")

SKADI ("Ska-Dee")

SUTTUNGR (Pronounced "SOO-ton-ger")

SVARTALHEIM (Pronounced "Svar-ta-Hime")

TABLUT (Pronounced "TAH-Bloot")

TÝR (Pronounced "Tier")

TYRFING (Pronounced "TEER-fing")

VANIR (Pronounced "Van-ear")

VÖLSUNG (Pronounced "Vol-sung")

YNGLING (Pronounced "EEN-gleeng")

YGGDRASIL (Pronounced "IGG-drah-seel")

YMIR (Pronounced "EE-meer")

PROLOGUE
The Lone Shield-maiden

The frigid air stabbed the valkyrie's lungs as she blindly trudged forward.

She'd spent nine grueling days traveling the Road to Hel through valleys so dark that she saw nothing at all. It had taken her years to break through Helheim's barriers and infiltrate the underworld. Yet now, her only reward was traveling down a dark canyon. The World Tree's colossal roots snaked through the sky above, plunging the canyon into such total darkness with its shadow that she began forgetting what color looked like.

Many wouldn't be able to handle it. Some would lose their minds. But she'd come to the underworld with a purpose, and wouldn't be deterred no matter what it cost her.

Eventually, the pitch-black valley brightened as she emerged from the giant root's shadow into an open-air valley illuminated by Helheim's emerald sky. The light reflected off her golden metallic wings and body armor, giving her a green tinge. She took a moment to admire the sight, drinking in the colors as her muscles ached, and then she spread her angelic wings and surged forward.

As she glided south, she passed many bronze and stone statues sculpted in ghastly poses lining the Road to Hel and carved into the canyon walls, each capturing a moment of deep sorrow. A bronze woman tilted her head back in a silent scream, with tears carved into her metal visage pooling at her feet. Beside her kneeled an old man, gnarled hands clutching a shattered sword. A young couple stood in an eternal embrace while an old woman looked skyward, snow-covered hands outstretched in an unresolved plea for lost loved ones.

Those statues were not just decorations; the valkyrie took them as a message to all spirits to abandon hope and a warning to all living beings to turn back.

She ignored them and kept flying. No statue, scarecrow, or monster would stop her.

As she journeyed to Gnipa Cave, she heard Garm's baneful howl in the distance and realized something was amiss. Landing to catch her breath, she sensed an absurd number of undead creatures amassing in front of Gnipa Cave. At first, she thought the undead hoard was laying siege to Gnipa Cave and attempting to escape Helheim. But as she sensed their movements from a distance, she realized they were not trying to escape or bypass the Hound of Helheim. They were moving *away* from Garm and heading south toward the Bridge of the Dead.

That made no sense. The restless dead usually tried to escape Helheim. It was in their very nature. Blinded by their anger, they always longed to return to Midgard and exact vengeance on those who had killed them. That was why Odin and Hel tasked Garm to guard the realm to keep these violent souls from escaping. But these draugirs seemed to be headed *toward* the City of the Lost instead of away from it!

Why? She thought.

Suddenly, the ground vibrated. With a flap of her wings, she soared to safety as a cluster of sharp stalagmites erupted from the ground beneath her.

Hovering sixty feet in the air, she turned and noticed a massive statue of a woman in armor sitting on a throne carved into the canyon wall. The giant figure was made of stone, but its hair and nails were pure gold. The statue's hair was arranged in five elegant, varied braids, the longest of which fell over her right shoulder and reached her knees.

The ground shook as the statue's massive ruby eyes opened. The giantess stood up from her throne, towering over the valkyrie at hundred ten feet tall. The giantess grabbed a huge hoplite shield leaning against the throne, adorned with an intricate design and a large ruby crystal at its center.

"You're a stone giantess." The valkyrie noted. "Why are you getting in my way?"

"I am Móðguðr," the giantess said in an earthy voice. "I ensure that those who walk the Road to Hel are dead. You shall venture no farther toward my mother's domain, valkyrie. Your kind isn't welcome here!"

The giantess slammed the rim of her shield against the ground. The ravine quaked and rumbled as giant stone barriers erupted from the earth and walls of the canyon. The valkyrie watched as Móðguðr altered the topography of the stone canyon, sealing it shut to block the way south.

Móðguðr's flashy provocation and display of power did not impress the valkyrie. She redirected her attention to the swarm of draugirs amassing farther south beyond these earthen barricades. She sensed millions of restless spirits rising from the ground around Gnipa Cave and converging around the Gjallerbru.

"What's happening?" The valkyrie demanded. "Why are so many draugirs and restless spirits amassing around the Gjallerbru?"

"Two gallant souls are valiantly attempting to escape Helheim," Móðguðr explained with a hint of grudging admiration. "They are powerful and resilient. They defeated many warriors. But their rebellion ends now. My mother and my cousin, Garm, will bring the full might of Helheim upon them and prove once and for all that none may leave her realm."

"Hel summoned her army to deal with just two escapees?" The valkyrie questioned. "That seems excessive. Who are these warriors?"

"You know one of them very well," Móðguðr said in a deadpan tone. "One is Sinfjotli, the bastard son of Sigmund and Signy, and the other is Sigurd the Dragon Slayer."

Upon hearing Sigurd's name, the valkyrie drew her swords. The quills of her wings calcified into sharp metallic feathers.

"Let me pass, giantess," the valkyrie demanded, pointing her weapons at the giantess.

Móðguðr studied the valkyrie with her giant ruby eyes in a literal stone-faced expression that conveyed no emotion.

"I know who you are… daughter of Buthli," she noted. "You've caused the deaths of many heroes and even the fall of house Gjukung. Why do you come here looking for another woman's husband? Haven't you caused enough suffering?"

"I don't have to answer to you," the valkyrie declared.

"True enough," Móðguðr agreed. "But are you sure you want to continue traveling this path? Once you pass Gnipa Cave, you won't be able to leave this realm. Garm will never let you leave without my mother's permission. Whatever your intentions, Sigurd and Sinfjotli will be long dead by the time you reach them. The army of death will soon tear them to pieces."

"I will not let them!" The valkyrie brandished her swords. "Sigurd is mine. No one will come between us. Now sink down, giantess!"

Chapter One

THE FORSAKEN CITY

A gentle sensation filled Sigurd's body. It was like a hand was trying to drag him from deep water.

A garbled voice whispered: *"Awaken...walk the path..."*

The warmth subsided, and he felt a deep, all-consuming cold that seemed to penetrate his entire being. He lunged from bed, gasping for air. The frigid air stung his lungs and throat with every breath, like a knife inside his chest.

Sigurd Snake Eyes felt fatigued. His innards felt like a sack of clay. Even blinking felt exhausting as he struggled to open his heavy-lidded eyes.

There was no light source, but he could see in the pitch blackness with his snake eyes.

He was inside a sealed, dark room. The unfamiliar bed beneath him was an elevated slab of dark, oily stone instead of the usual softness of his own bed's feathers. Its texture felt like basalt, yet this stone was unlike anything he had ever encountered. The oily stone, cold as a clammy corpse, felt alive, as if it were siphoning all of his body's warmth the way a leech sucks its host's blood. As he walked around, he found that the walls, ceiling, and floor were all made of this same strange material, adding to the eerie, frigid atmosphere.

"Gudrun?" He called out.

Silence. His wife wasn't there. He was alone and naked in this cold, dark room. There wasn't even a blanket to cover himself with.

Sigurd wasn't sure where he was or how he got here. He thought he was still dreaming, but he wouldn't feel cold in a dream, would he?

He tried to recall the last thing he remembered... but nothing came to mind. His head felt fuzzy, as if parts of his brain hadn't woken up yet. But he didn't have the luxury to ponder this. He had to escape this freezing room and find warmth.

A neatly folded pile of wool clothes and his trusty sword, Gram, lay on the floor beside the stone slab, along with his golden hauberk, a padded black tunic, and other armaments. His trusty enchanted helmet was missing, but Sigurd was unconcerned. He was just eager, desperate to put something warm on.

Sigurd wasted no time getting dressed. As he adorned the hauberk made of intricately woven golden rings, he couldn't help but shiver. Though lighter than linen and stronger than steel, it felt like ice. The rest of his armor felt just as cold as if he were now wearing an entire robe made from solid ice. But Sigurd didn't care. He had worn the armor so often that it felt like a second layer of skin. It had protected him well in many battles, and he had always worn it through harsh weather or challenging terrain.

Finally, dressed and ready for action, Sigurd searched for an escape. The only exit in this pitch-black room was a doorway walled off by some strange barrier. When he pressed his hand against it, he realized it was made of thick, compacted snow. It was so packed that Sigurd had to draw Gram and jab the sword into several spots, carving holes to dig his way out.

As Sigurd sheathed Gram and shoveled his way through the snow barrier with his gloved hands, a slight opening emerged near the top of the doorframe. A sickly green light shone through the gap, cutting through the shadows of the dark room with its ethereal hue.

Curious, Sigurd thought. But now wasn't the time to get distracted. He had to escape this freezing room. He dug until the gap was wide enough to wriggle through the tight space, and he tumbled down a large mound of green snow onto a cold, hard stone pavement.

As he lifted his body from the frosty ground and gazed around, Sigurd was taken aback by what he saw. He stood in the center of an ominous stone city, trapped in a raging blizzard. The clouds and sky enshrouding the city were tinted green, giving the snowflakes an otherworldly tinge. A faint green sun glimmered in the west through the clouds, but it provided no warmth to the forsaken city. It was so cold it hurt to breathe, as if a hundred icy shards traveled down his throat and scraped his esophagus and lungs every time he inhaled. The blizzard had been raging for a long time, and the amount of snow and ice accumulated around each building was a testament to that.

As Sigurd looked up at the building he'd emerged from, he couldn't help but feel dwarfed by the towering skyscrapers made of that strange, oily black stone. The buildings soared to dizzying heights, some stretching up to thirty stories tall. And the designs were breathtaking—pointed arches, ribbed vaults, flying buttresses, and otherworldly shapes that defied explanation and gravity. Every building was made of a mysterious black stone that seemed to shimmer in the green sunlight.

The colossal snow and icy mounds surrounding their bases only added to their imposing presence. Yet, as he looked up toward the sky, he noticed the severe damage some buildings had sustained, as if the wind had slowly but violently eroded their peaks.

A shiver crept down his spine as he gazed around him. Seeing those long, sharp icicles swinging from the roofs of the buildings was daunting. And then there were those icicles that seemed to defy gravity, sticking horizontally from the walls and sides of the buildings, serving as a testament to the harsh force of the winds that ripped through the city.

But what took Sigurd's breath away were the people appearing in this strange city. After following a paved street eastward, he discovered what looked like countless human-shaped silhouettes shuffling along a broad paved road that cut through the center of the city. To his amazement, none seemed to leave any footprints in the snow. Upon closer inspection, he discovered why.

"They're all ghosts!" Sigurd gasped. Their bodies were dark, featureless wisps of green and black miasma that lacked any physical form of their own. He started waving and talking to them. But despite his attempts to get their attention, they remained indifferent to his presence. They didn't even react when he walked straight through them! Their bodies faded like smoke when he tried to touch them, only to rematerialize a few feet behind him. But the ghosts continued walking down the road as if nothing had happened.

Based on the green sun's position, he judged they were heading south. He watched spirits continue their journey, shuffling onward as if on a mission to reach an unknown destination at the end of this wide, paved road. They appeared oblivious to their surroundings, consumed by their strange purpose.

A powerful gust of wind blew from the north, the same direction these ghosts originated. The cold, relentless blasts arrived at random intervals, creating a strange humming sound as they traveled between buildings. Sigurd felt like he was getting stabbed by hundreds of icy knives whenever the frigid air blew against his skin.

Sigurd's first instinct was to head north to uncover the source of the mysterious spirits and icy wind that plagued the city. But that plan crumbled when he stepped north and felt short of breath. Although the city's topography was flat, Sigurd tired whenever he took even a single step north, as if trudging up an endless mountain. However, when he turned around and tried moving south, everything became easier, as if he was walking downhill. Sigurd didn't know how to explain it, but it was as if everything in this strange city was *compelled* to follow the road south.

But Sigurd refused to be deterred. He was a man who made his own decisions, forged his own path, and wouldn't succumb to the whims of fate. Instead of traveling north or south, Sigurd crossed the road and headed eastward, curious to explore this enigmatic city and uncover all its secrets.

He wandered through the city's eastern section, his eyes darting from one towering skyscraper to the next. Amidst the imposing structures, the cityscape changed, and he spotted quaint houses, market stalls, and even a modest palace. But there was something strange about this place—an eerie stillness that hung in the air like a thick fog. A vine-like plant snaked up the sides of the buildings, the only sign of life in this vast metropolis.

Whoever built this city put a lot of time and effort into its construction. It was so big it could house over a million people, maybe more. But there wasn't a single living person anywhere in sight. The spirits traveling along the long road lacked corporeal bodies, meaning they couldn't touch or interact with anything in this city, unlike Sigurd. It begged the question—Why go to such great lengths to build a city its citizens couldn't even inhabit?

However, it soon became apparent that he wasn't alone. Something caught Sigurd's eye as he explored a desolate bazaar alongside the winding road running through the city. A trail of footprints in the snow piqued his interest. The spirits traveling on the nearby roadway didn't have physical bodies and, therefore, couldn't leave footprints. Footprints meant there was another live person nearby.

Sigurd studied the footprints and deduced that someone had traveled west toward the central road. However, upon reaching the long-paved road, they turned around and headed east to wherever they'd come from. The deep imprints in the snow and the longer strides between each footprint suggested they began running. Had they been chased by something sinister? Perhaps they got spooked by the spirits and ran away? Or maybe they succumbed to the biting cold of the blizzard and sought refuge?

Regardless, Sigurd saw an opportunity. If another human was out here in this desolate city, maybe he could find some answers. Perhaps they could tell him where he was and why he was here. And if nothing else, he could at least find shelter from the unforgiving cold.

As Sigurd trekked through the snow-covered streets, his heart thumped with excitement. The footprints led him to a massive plaza on the city's eastern fringes. This area was filled with deserted houses, buildings, and fountains adorned with frozen bronze statues of people sculpted in states of grief and terror. The condition of the buildings was dismal, having been ravaged by the elements for centuries. Because the plaza was on the city's outskirts, the structures here were more exposed to the elements, resulting in their dilapidated state. The narrow paths and alleys between the buildings were choked with tons of ice, making the area seem even more desolate.

The plaza was also covered in giant blocks made from the same oily black stone as the buildings. Some blocks were remnants from the tallest buildings that had collapsed because of the wind. But many others lay scattered around the plaza like massive puzzle pieces that had fallen from a table and been left unmoved for centuries. Sigurd estimated that moving a single one would require at least eight hundred men.

As he gazed into the distance, Sigurd's eyes fixed on the cloudy skyline framed by an impressive eight-foot-tall curtain wall enclosing the entire city. Curiosity tugged at him, urging him to peek over the barrier. With a deep breath, he leaned forward and caught sight of a tremendous green river flowing hundreds of feet below. He could discern support columns to the side as he tilted his head. He realized this section of the dark city was built atop a colossal bridge suspended hundreds of feet above the vast emerald waters.

Sigurd resumed following the trail of footprints that brought him to the large fountain pool in the center of the plaza. The tiered fountain was about twenty feet high, surrounded by a circular pool that spanned ninety-six feet wide. The pool's water had frozen a long time ago, and the entire base of the fountain was encased in ice. Perched on top of the fountain stood a striking bronze statue of a hooded woman standing eight feet tall. Her back was adorned with long, curved icicles resembling icy wings. The wind and elements had eroded the statue's features, leaving only vague hints of a mouth, nose, and eyes beneath its hooded mantle. But something ominous about its half-human face made Sigurd feel uneasy.

As Sigurd surveyed the area, he couldn't help but notice something peculiar: a broad, rectangular patch beside the fountain where the snow was shallower. Upon closer inspection, he observed four deep imprints on the ground. Curious, Sigurd looked around and noticed three benches surrounding the fountain. From this, he deduced that there used to be a bench where the patch was.

Sigurd whistled as he noted no drag marks scarred in the snow leading away from the tiered fountain. Considering the size of the other three benches, this missing one must have weighed at least three hundred pounds! Whoever stole the bench possessed serious strength to carry it away single-handedly. Sigurd couldn't help but feel impressed by whoever had done it.

He now followed the trail of footprints to a large two-story stone building. This building was in better shape than the others, but the architecture was unremarkable. The simplistic design suggested that someone had carved an eighty-ton stone block into a crude two-story building. The windows and door were missing. Nine-foot-long icicles hung from the roof above, and the snow around the house was piled six feet high. The ebony stone pathway leading to the steps was clear of snow, allowing Sigurd to approach the entrance unimpeded.

Sigurd peered through the doorway. The empty interior of the building was devoid of furniture, decorations, or any signs of long-term habitation, just like in the building Sigurd had woken up in. Patches of snow and ice covered most of the floor around the entryway and the stairway leading to the next level. But Sigurd ignored that as he found who he'd searched for.

In the center of the room, Sigurd saw a muscular man wearing a fuzzy fur outfit attempting to light a fire. Next to him was the dismantled bench. The man was trying to start a fire using a makeshift bow drill, using one leg as the spindle, one of the seat boards as a hearth board, and a thick black, vine-like thorn plant as the nest. The stranger seemed experienced in starting fires this way. But his efforts were in vain. Sigurd knew the wood from the bench was too wet to ignite.

As he stood on the stone steps, watching the man inside desperately try to produce an ember, Sigurd shivered. It felt like the ebony stones beneath his feet were sucking his bodily warmth.

That shivering feeling compelled Sigurd to act. He didn't want to startle the stranger, so he tried to think of a graceful way to announce his presence before entering.

Suddenly, the burly man perked up his head and sniffed the air like a hunting dog catching a scent in the wind. Without turning to look over his shoulder, he grabbed the remainder of the bench with one hand, hoisted it over his shoulder, and chucked it behind him.

Sigurd dodged left as the bench slammed into the wall beside him and splintered into pieces. Sigurd noticed the stranger rushing toward him as the pieces fell to the floor. The savage expression on the man's face suggested he intended to tear out Sigurd's throat with his bare hands and teeth. He slammed Sigurd against the wall, but Sigurd seized the man's arms and prevented him from doing anything drastic.

"Take it easy!" Sigurd urged. "I'm not here to hurt you!"

The burly man snarled. But his demeanor changed when he noticed Sigurd was holding his wrists and keeping him at bay. He stopped struggling and looked Sigurd square in the face.

"You're real?" the man asked, though it wasn't a question. "You're not one of those ghosts?"

"I'm real." Sigurd nodded.

The man's body relaxed. Sigurd gambled and released his wrists, hoping the burly man wouldn't try to tear out his throat again. Thankfully, he had calmed down enough to engage in civil discussion. The stranger stepped backward, and the two sized each other up.

The man was bull-like, with heavy shoulders, a thick neck, and beefy arms. His biceps and triceps were as wide and thick as tree trunks. He measured about six foot four, just a few inches shorter than Sigurd, who was six foot eight inches tall.

The man wore a shaggy outfit made from various animal furs. His arms and chest were very hairy, and his face was covered in stubble. Long, textured, wavy dark brown hair touched the base of his neck and shoulders and parted down the middle. His handsome face seemed incongruous compared to his sharp eyes and the unkempt stubble covering his chin and neck. One look at his blue-gray eyes made it clear this was not a man you wanted to cross.

He was covered in old battle scars, some of which were peculiar. The ragged scars on his wrists looked like someone had flayed his forearms. The teeth marks and scars around his neck and shoulders hinted that he'd been mauled by a feral animal long ago.

The burly man studied Sigurd and then looked askance at his golden hauberk and sneered. "It's quite conceited to wear gold armor. I once knew a proud jarl who went into battle wearing an entire suit of gold armor. It broke after a single blow from a sword, and he died instantly."

"Don't underestimate mine." Sigurd thumped his chest. "This enchanted armor is ten times stronger than steel, despite its golden appearance, and the chain links are comparable in design and durability to carbon nanotubes."

"Is that so?" The man raised an eyebrow and looked Sigurd square in the face to see if he was bluffing. But he flinched and backed away when he noticed Sigurd's golden eyes.

"By Freyja, what's wrong with your eyes?!" he exclaimed. "They look like the eyes of a serpent."

"Indeed," Sigurd grinned. His eyes had black, vertical pupils and golden sclera like a serpent's. Long ago, he had devoured a dragon's heart, causing his eyes to assume this unusual appearance. It came with several perks. Their color complemented his shoulder-length golden hair and enriched his comely features. Plus, he could peer across great distances and see in the dark.

"My comrades used to call me 'Sigurd Snake Eyes.'"

"A fitting moniker, I suppose." The burly man nodded in approval. "Those slitted eyes match the color of your armor and..."

He trailed off, and his eyes widened as he noticed the sword hanging from Sigurd's waist. His shock turned to fury as he balled his fists and shouted, "Thief!" He stepped forward and socked Sigurd with a solid right hook across the jaw before Sigurd could react.

Pain exploded across Sigurd's face and nose as his feet lost contact with the ground. Sigurd soared out of the building and tumbled across the snowy ground.

Sigurd lifted himself off the ground and spat blood. He glanced up and realized the stranger had punched him hard enough to send him flying several yards outside the building. An ordinary person might have had their skull caved in from such a powerful strike. But Sigurd was no ordinary man.

And neither was this stranger. Before Sigurd could fully stand up, the burly man appeared before him, and he gripped Sigurd's throat and hoisted him off the ground with a single hand.

"Where did you get that sword?" he growled.

"What are you...?" Sigurd struggled to ask.

"That's my father's sword!" The stranger pointed at Gram. "I'd recognize that hilt anywhere. Where and how did you get it? Did you murder him and steal it from his corpse?!"

"Your father's... sword?" Sigurd repeated in disbelief, unsure if he'd heard him right. Gram was an heirloom left for Sigurd by his father, Sigmund, who died before he'd been born. And Sigmund had no other surviving sons, aside from Sigurd.

Unless...? A chilling possibility flashed through Sigurd's mind.

"Wait...who... are...?" Sigurd tried to ask.

"Enough prattle, *thief*. I'll just kill you and take it back." The burly man tightened his grip on Sigurd's throat as he reached for Gram's hilt with his free left hand.

"I...said...wait!" Sigurd knocked aside the stranger's left hand, grabbed the man's right wrist with both hands, and yanked hard, throwing him off balance. Without letting go of his right arm, Sigurd jumped up, wrapped the man's arm and shoulder between his legs, and twisted his body midair, causing them to fall to the snowy ground. Before the man could recover, Sigurd repositioned himself. He pressed his hips against his attacker's armpit, extended his legs across his chest, and crossed his feet around the man's left shoulder, leaving his attacker trapped in an armlock.

"Speak!" Sigurd ordered, while tugging the stranger's right arm. "You just said, 'That's my father's sword.' What did you mean by that? Who are you?"

When the stranger refused to respond, Sigurd yanked his arm and dislocated his shoulder. The stranger grunted but didn't cry out in agony. Whomever this man was, he was tough and no stranger to pain—as if the scars weren't proof enough of that.

"Talk!" Sigurd yelled while yanking even harder on the now dislocated arm.

"I am Sinfjotli," the stranger answered, "son of Sigmund."

It took Sigurd several moments to recognize that name. But when he did, his fighting spirit came to a screeching halt, and his resolve crumbled.

"Sinfjotli?" Sigurd repeated in disbelief. "How can...Argh!"

A sudden sharp pain ran up Sigurd's left leg, and he bellowed. While he was astounded, Sinfjotli sank his teeth into his left calf. As Sinfjotli bit harder, Sigurd winced in pain just enough to loosen his grip on Sinfjotli's right arm. Sinfjotli capitalized on the opportunity by grabbing Sigurd's right ankle with his free left hand, wrapping his freed right arm beneath Sigurd's waist, and chucking Sigurd's body right over him like a catapult.

Sigurd tumbled across the snowy ground and bumped into the stone wall of the building he'd just emerged from. As he stood, his left leg erupted in pain. Sinfjotli had bitten with enough pressure to dent the metal plate of Sigurd's shin guard. Sinfjotli's teeth hadn't drawn blood or pierced Sigurd's skin, but it felt like the tibia in his left calf had cracked under the intense pressure.

"Impressive," Sigurd remarked as he examined the dents Sinfjotli inflicted on his left shin guard with his bare teeth. However, what really impressed Sigurd was Sinfjotli's immense physical strength. Sinfjotli had sent Sigurd soaring several yards out of the building with a single punch earlier. And now he'd tossed Sigurd over ten yards while lying on the ground with the strength of a single dislocated arm. Sinfjotli possessed the sort of strength and vitality found only in legends. That made Sigurd even more convinced that he was telling the truth.

Sinfjotli was already on his feet, examining his dislocated right arm. Without hesitation, he approached one of the nearby, massive stone blocks and rammed his shoulder against the edge with a loud crack. After setting his arm back into its socket, he pivoted on his heel and marched toward Sigurd.

"Wait!" Sigurd raised his hands. "Please, just hear me out! My name is Sigurd, son of Sigmund and Hjordis. If you are *the* Sinfjotli... then you're my older half-brother!"

Chapter Two

Brother vs. Brother

Sigurd anxiously watched as Sinfjotli studied him with shock and suspicion, initially appearing like he was about to call Sigurd a liar and attack him anyway. But then he seemed to notice something familiar about Sigurd's features. Sinfjotli leaned his head back and sniffed the air.

"You do smell like Sigmund," Sinfjotli noted.

"That's... good," Sigurd replied, relieved and confused. Could Sinfjotli sense they were related just by Sigurd's musk? Was his sense of smell that powerful? Or was Sigurd's stench truly that pungent?

"I'm sure you're just as confused as I am," Sigurd began. "So, let's just talk..."

"Fight me." Sinfjotli interrupted.

Sigurd blinked. "Excuse me?"

"Fight me," Sinfjotli repeated calmly. "You claim to be a son of Sigmund, wielding his sword and a scent reminiscent of his. But that alone won't convince me. I want to see how you fight. Prove that you are a genuine son of Sigmund through your martial prowess."

"But I don't want to fight you!" Sigurd protested, raising his hands.

"You don't have a choice. Now prove that you're worthy of wielding that sword. Or I will kill you!"

Before Sigurd could say anything else, Sinfjotli landed a powerful uppercut beneath Sigurd's sternum, sending Sigurd clear over the two-story building behind him. He landed on the snowy ground behind the building with enough force to knock the wind out of him.

He's stronger than he looks! Sigurd realized while rubbing his throbbing chest. *That punch sent me flying over that building!*

Sigurd rose in a panic and looked upward to see Sinfjotli standing on the roof of the building. Sinfjotli jumped from the roof, somersaulted midair, and swung his heel down in a falling axe kick. Sigurd dive rolled out of the way. Sinfjotli's heel struck the ground, decimating the surrounding area. Cracks and crevices spread through the stone street as his foot burrowed deep into the stone.

"He's a lot heavier than he looks, too," Sigurd remarked, looking at the deep crater and the devastation Sinfjotli had caused to the street and bazaar.

Sinfjotli withdrew his foot from the cleft in the stone ground and wasted no time attacking Sigurd, inciting a brutal fistfight. As Sigurd suspected, Sinfjotli was even stronger than he appeared and attacked with powerful blows that could kill an ordinary man. But Sigurd matched his vicious strength blow for blow by relying on skill and technique. Whenever Sinfjotli threw a punch Sigurd couldn't block, Sigurd would redirect the strike using his opponent's power and inertia against him.

For almost thirty minutes, the two warriors brutally beat the tar out of each other, neither gaining the upper hand until Sigurd scored a lucky punch to Sinfjotli's throat, causing Sinfjotli to gasp and stagger backward. But before Sigurd could capitalize on this opportunity, Sinfjotli surged forward, wrapping his arms around Sigurd's waist and pushing him back into the building where they'd first met. They crashed through the stone wall of the building and collapsed on the floor. Cracks spread throughout the walls and ceiling of the stone room as Sinfjotli tried to straddle and pummel a dazed Sigurd. A moment later, the entire edifice collapsed on top of them.

Sigurd was the first to recover and dig himself out of the rubble. But Sinfjotli, who took the full brunt of the collapsing debris on his back, had a harder time making his way out.

Sigurd rushed forward, locked his hands together, and swung them down at the nape of Sinfjotli's neck. But he hesitated after realizing that such a mighty blow might kill him. That slight hesitation cost him his chance.

Sinfjotli jumped to his feet, knocked aside Sigurd's hands, rushed behind him, wrapped his arms around Sigurd's waist, and suplexed him onto a pile of rubble. Pain exploded across Sigurd's upper back and neck. Before Sigurd could recover from the devastating suplex, Sinfjotli sprang to his feet and kicked Sigurd square in the chest, sending him tumbling twenty feet before slamming into the fountain at the center of the courtyard.

Pain raced throughout Sigurd's body as the tiered fountain cracked from the impact. Sigurd collapsed like a puppet whose strings had been cut. He couldn't breathe, and his left leg and upper back were howling in pain. Through sheer willpower, Sigurd forced himself back to his feet.

Sigurd was barely on his feet for three seconds before Sinfjotli lunged at him again. But this time, Sigurd was ready. He instinctively sidestepped out of danger, grabbed Sinfjotli's torso in midair, and redirected his opponent's inertia to send him hurtling toward the curtain wall at the plaza's edge.

Sinfjotli slammed face-first into the wall with enough force to send tremors throughout the plaza. Amidst the quaking, every icicle hanging from the rooftops of the surrounding buildings came crashing to the ground. Sinfjotli crumbled to the ground, dazed and clutching his bleeding forehead.

Sigurd used this brief respite to recover his stamina and assess his injuries. His body was covered in bruises, and his face felt swollen from Sinfjotli's many punches. His upper back and neck still ached from the suplex he'd just received, and his left calf howled in pain with every step. The sharp stabbing pain in his chest and sternum from the kick he'd received moments ago proved the worst.

Sinfjotli looked just as injured. Sinfjotli had struck Sigurd in a blind rage, mainly aiming for his face and torso, but Sigurd's attacks had been more precise and surgical. He couldn't match Sinfjotli's brute strength, so he focused his attacks on key pressure points and other vital areas along Sinfjotli's body, like the elbows, kneecaps, ribs, shoulders, and throat. His strategy had paid off; Sinfjotli struggled to get up.

As Sinfjotli clutched his bleeding forehead, Sigurd noticed that the plaza and courtyard around them were just as damaged and battered as they were. The building where they had initially met was now a heap of rubble. As Sinfjotli staggered to his feet, Sigurd noticed the curtain wall behind him was still intact, without a single crater or crack. Unlike the building, which crumbled under duress, the curtain wall encompassing the city was as rigid and unmoving as a mountain.

"That was a brilliant move." Sinfjotli hawked and spat blood from his mouth. "It seems we're evenly matched in hand-to-hand combat. But I notice you haven't drawn that sword yet."

"I don't want to risk killing you." Sigurd's hand slipped down to grasp his sword's hilt. "If you are familiar with Gram, then you should know it can cut an anvil in half with one swing. Do you understand what I'm saying, you daft fool? I don't want to harm my brother! There's no honor in harming your kin, especially in a pointless duel like this."

Sinfjotli's eyes narrowed, and he snarled. "It remains to be seen if we *are* brothers." He glanced at the curtain wall behind him and noticed a nearby flagpole swaying in the wind. The flag had a ghastly coat of arms sown into the cloth, depicting a silver scythe on a black field. The silver flagpole had a black iron spear tip at its top.

Sinfjotli reached up and snapped the flagpole from its hinges. He tore off the flag, which fluttered away with the wind.

"Not my weapon of choice," Sinfjotli noted as he examined the flagpole and its spear tip. "But at least the point is sharp. I will make you draw that sword one way or the other."

Sinfjotli charged toward Sigurd and used the flagpole like a makeshift spear. Sigurd still refused to draw Gram and only resorted to defending himself as Sinfjotli viciously attacked him in a whirlwind of impressive but pointless strikes. Sigurd's golden hauberk was enchanted and ten times stronger than steel, and there was no way a paltry iron spear tip could damage it. Thus, Sigurd was never in any danger. He defended himself from Sinfjotli's attacks more out of habit and instinct than actual necessity.

However, when it became clear that Sinfjotli had no intention of stopping, Sigurd decided he'd had enough. As Sinfjotli prepared to swing his makeshift weapon again, Sigurd drew Gram and slashed in a downward strike. The blow was so fast that Sinfjotli didn't initially realize that his flagpole had split in half. He glanced down at his chest and discovered that Sigurd had inflicted a severe but shallow laceration across his chest and abdomen with that same lightning-quick strike.

Sinfjotli stared at the wound with an unreadable expression. He dropped the broken pieces of his makeshift weapon and doubled over to the ground on his hands and knees.

"That was me holding back," Sigurd warned. "Now yield! I don't want to harm you further."

As he waited for a response, Sigurd realized something was off. Sinfjotli's body language did not resemble that of a wounded man doubled over in pain. Instead, he was crouched on his hands and knees like a leopard waiting to pounce. Even more alarming, Sinfjotli was grinning!

Suddenly, Sinfjotli's body spasmed. Sigurd instinctively retreated to a safe distance. Sinfjotli cackled maniacally as his body underwent a horrific transformation. His bones snapped, lengthened, popped through his skin, and moved back in place as necessary. Thick black fur sprouted rapidly from every inch of his body. His hands became mangled, and the skin below his knuckles peeled away as clawed fingers burst through his skin. A slimy dog-saliva-like substance oozed out along with blood as the clawed digits sprouted from his joints. In an instant, his hands and feet were replaced with a beast's large, hairy, and clawed paws. Unable to withstand his expanding body, his clothes burst into slithers of rags dangling from his black fur. And as his pants ripped apart, a long, bushy tail sprouted from his buttock.

"I haven't used this against a worthy opponent in a long time." Sinfjotli snarled giddily. "I wonder how long it's been."

As he spoke, his face pushed forward and lengthened into a snout. His jaw dislodged to make room for a massive, deadly maw as his teeth elongated into fangs. It was as if someone had grabbed his face and yanked a new one straight out. His ears elongated into furry dog ears. His eyes dilated as the irises and pupils turned as black as coal, and the sclera became blood-red. The glowing red orbs of a predator now radiated from his eye sockets.

When the ghastly metamorphosis ended, Sigurd stared in horror at an enormous ten-foot-tall black wolf.

"Oh, yes!" The wolf licked his chops. "It's been a long time since I fought as my *true self*."

"You're a skinchanger!" Sigurd gasped. "By the gods!"

"Let's keep them out of this, shall we?" Sinfjotli quipped. "They have nothing to do with our duel. Now fight!"

The wolf lunged forward and swiped its paw at Sigurd. Sigurd attempted to block the strike with Gram, but the force behind the hefty blow sent him spiraling backward through the air and crashing into the second floor of a three-story building.

"That...hurt." Sigurd groaned as he rose from the rubble. One of Sinfjotli's claws had torn a gash through the chain links in armor and scratched him just below his right shoulder. It wasn't a severe wound, but it stung.

Sigurd clutched his throbbing chest as he examined the gash in his armor, marveling how Sinfjotli had torn through metal stronger than steel. He tried to catch his breath, but Sinfjotli wasn't finished. The giant wolf sprinted across the plaza and leaped at him. Sigurd dashed toward the hole in the wall he'd crashed through and jumped outside into a deep snowdrift. Half a heartbeat later, Sinfjotli slammed into the building, smashing the dilapidated edifice to pieces.

Such monstrous strength! No wonder he punched me so hard earlier. As Sigurd stood up and rubbed his bruised face, he noticed that his left hand felt moist and sticky. He held up his hand and saw his entire palm covered in wet, sticky blood.

Where did all this blood come from?! Sigurd glanced at his chest and discovered that his undershirt and golden hauberk were soaked in blood. But it wasn't fresh. The dried blood stains looked to be about an hour old. Sigurd pulled open the collar of his shirt to examine his bare chest.

What he saw made his blood run cold. His entire chest and abdomen were covered in dried, crusted blood. There was a gaping hole in his chest, barely an inch away from his heart. Sigurd touched his back and felt an exit wound only an inch away from his spine.

"How did this happen?!" Sigurd panicked. "When did I get stabbed?"

Piercing pain flared behind his eyes, and his head erupted in excruciating pain. Sigurd dropped his sword and doubled over, clutching his head as his brain beat against the walls of his skull like a drum. His vision became blurry and static. His brain felt on fire, but this didn't feel like a concussion. It felt like his brain was being assaulted on a psychic level, as if long-buried memories were forcing their way to the surface and overwhelming his mind. Amidst the throbbing pain, Sigurd saw images of a distant memory play out through his faded and static vision.

Sigurd remembered waking up in bed in the middle of the night with a sword impaled through his chest. He recalled his killer fleeing after his wife, Gudrun, screamed. He remembered using the last of his strength to draw Gram from their bedside and hurl it at his assassin. The sword cleanly bisected his murderer in half before he could reach the doorway. Sigurd recalled looking at his murderer's severed torso as the blood congealed in his throat, and Sigurd began losing consciousness. Beneath the spot Gram had embedded in the wall, his youngest brother-in-law, Guttorm, lay in two bloody pieces. Then Sigurd's world dissolved into blobs of light and shadow before plunging into an all-encompassing blackness.

"Guttorm!" Sigurd gasped as his vision returned to normal, and the pain behind his eyes subsided. "*You* murdered me in my bed?! I...I died?!"

Sigurd froze as he realized what he just said. "I died... in my bed," He reiterated, dismayed. He glanced up at the emerald clouds. Terror gripped his heart as he realized where he was and the full gravity of this situation. "But then that means... I'm in..."

"Pay attention!" Sinfjotli roared.

Sigurd snapped back to reality just as Sinfjotli rammed into him. The giant wolf bit down on Sigurd's chest and left shoulder. Then the wolf lifted him off the ground, swung his head to the side, and hurled his body like a rag doll through the air. Sigurd crashed through the walls of three dilapidated buildings before slamming into something rigid, cold, and unmoving.

Sigurd almost blacked out from the pain. But he desperately clung on. He couldn't afford to lose consciousness. Not now. Especially not *here*.

As he struggled to breathe, Sigurd's vision cleared. He noticed he had crashed in a glacier in an alleyway next to the last building he'd crashed through.

"How *incredibly* disappointing." The giant wolf bared its fangs and growled as it made its way across the courtyard. "I expected more out of you! You claimed to be a son of Sigmund, yet this is the best you can do?!"

"Stop," Sigurd croaked weakly as he tried to dislodge himself from the ice. "Please... stop. This fight is meaningless. Don't you realize... where we are right now? We're in..."

"The time for talk has passed." Sinfjotli snarled. "Now, FIGHT!"

The giant wolf jumped in the air, lunging at him again. Sigurd had only moments to pull himself from the human-shaped crater he'd made in the ice and roll out of the way before the wolf slammed into the glacier. Loud cracks and fissures erupted from the glacier, and an instant later, the whole thing shattered and came crashing down.

That was close. Sigurd thought. He stood up and instantly felt pain flare in his left side and shoulder. He grasped it, and when he removed his right hand, he saw it was now covered in blood. But this wasn't from the old sword wound Guttorm had given him. His left shoulder and torso had been punctured when Sinfjotli bit him. Thanks to Sigurd's armor, his teeth hadn't sunk that deep, but it was enough to cause concern.

He hurt me. Sigurd thought in astonishment. *He actually hurt me!*

Sigurd had a very justifiable reason to be so shocked. Besides his enchanted armor, Sigurd had another secret defense. Long ago, he bathed in the blood of Fafnir, the dragon he had famously slain, on the advice of an old sage he encountered. This ritual made his skin invulnerable to most mortal weapons in Midgard. After that literal blood bath, no weapon made by mortal men could leave a scratch on him. But there were a few exceptions. This must be one of them.

Sigurd didn't have long to ponder how Sinfjotli had injured him because the giant wolf lunged at him again. But this time, Sigurd was prepared. He sidestepped out of danger, wrapped his arms around Sinfjotli's neck, and used the wolf's weight and inertia to flip him onto his back. Sinfjotli tumbled across the courtyard and crashed into a three-story building that collapsed on top of him.

Sigurd stared at the rubble, amazed by what he had just done. He shouldn't have been able to flip a creature that big through raw strength alone in his injured state. That's why he had resorted to a unique technique that used the wolf's momentum against it. But he knew a trick like that wouldn't be enough to incapacitate a dangerous foe like Sinfjotli. As if on cue, the mound of rubble shifted as the beast roused itself from the wreckage.

"You're still holding back!" Sinfjotli snarled as he rose from the rubble. "You've had plenty of opportunities to kill me already. You could have pierced me in the head with that sword as I lunged at you just now. You could have hacked off all my limbs and then inflicted a coup de grâce while I lay on the ground helpless. Instead, you've only been resorting to defense; even in that regard, you've held back! You could have sliced off my paw when I attacked you earlier. Instead you blocked my strike with the flat of the blade. Why must you continue to disappoint me?"

"Because I don't want to hurt you," Sigurd insisted as he retrieved Gram from where he had dropped it earlier. "Do you understand me, you fool? I don't want to harm my half-brother! No man is as reviled as a kinslayer, and I have no desire to become one."

The wolf's eyes narrowed, and he snarled. But for once, Sinfjotli didn't attack. Perhaps Sigurd's remark had struck a nerve? Regardless, Sigurd didn't waste this opportunity to continue speaking.

"Please listen to me," Sigurd pleaded. "This fight is meaningless. We have bigger things to worry about. Don't you realize where we are right now? We're in Hel..."

"I already told you, the time for talk has passed." Sinfjotli interrupted. "Now, *FIGHT!*"

Sinfjotli began attacking Sigurd much more viciously than before. Sigurd tried to resist, but Sinfjotli was relentless.

The wolf swiped at Sigurd with its clawed paw, sending him flying through the air and crashing through four buildings. The fifth and final building collapsed, dropping a ton of rubble on top of him. Sigurd dug himself out of the wreckage and clutched the side of his now bleeding neck.

That was too close! Sinfjotli would have ripped out a chunk of my neck if I hadn't turned my head at the last second. And I would have been crushed beneath all this rubble.

Sigurd looked down and found Gram lying amidst the rubble. Sigurd noticed his reflection in the shiny blade and saw what a pitiful mess he looked like. His face was bruised, battered, and swollen. His armor had taken several notches, and his chest was soaked in his own blood.

It's been a long time since I've been this wounded in battle, Sigurd thought as he examined his blood-soaked hand. *Sinfjotli won't listen to reason. I'll have to attack him like I mean to kill. Otherwise, I have no chance of surviving.*

"Fine," Sigurd sighed as he retrieved Gram from the rubble. "If violence is the only language you'll understand, then I'll speak your language."

CHAPTER THREE

EUPHORIA

Sigurd felt lost in a trance of pain and euphoria as he and Sinfjotli viciously fought. Sinfjotli swiped and snapped at Sigurd with vicious strikes, but Sigurd matched his alleged half-brother's savagery blow for blow, inflicting dozens of grievous wounds with Gram. After about ten minutes, they had leveled every building in the plaza into rubble during their titanic fight.

"Yes!" Sinfjotli yelped after Sigurd slashed his shoulder with Gram. "More! More! Show me more!"

Sinfjotli swiped a paw at Sigurd, who was becoming too weak to dodge every attack.

Sigurd flew backward, the power behind the blow sending him spiraling through the air toward the curtain wall at the city's edge.

He slammed into the curtain wall with enough force to knock the wind out of him. Although the other buildings were weak and dilapidated, this curtain wall surrounding the city remained solid and undamaged as Sigurd crumbled to the ground.

"Can't believe...I'm related...to this beast!" Sigurd wheezed. He was on his knees, clutching Gram desperately in his hand. By force of will alone, Sigurd rose *again* to his feet.

He stepped forward, grimaced, and clutched his throbbing chest. Besides the gaping sword wound in his chest, dozens of other injuries from Sinfjotli were taking their toll. His face was battered and swollen, and he barely had any feeling in his left shoulder. His left calf erupted in pain with every step, and his neck was bleeding. Worst of all, he'd already lost a substantial amount of blood. If he were to guess, Sigurd wagered he had lost about two or three pints of blood throughout this intense battle. He didn't know how long he could continue fighting. He felt as vulnerable as a falcon that had fallen from the sky.

Meanwhile, Sinfjotli was too injured to attack him right away. Sigurd watched as the giant wolf licked the wound Sigurd dealt to his shoulder. Besides that deep slash, Sigurd had inflicted dozens of other injuries on Sinfjotli. Most opponents or savage beasts would have collapsed and gone into shock from the number of grievous wounds Sigurd had inflicted, but Sinfjotli almost seemed to take sick, masochistic pleasure from them.

But the wounds *were* hindering him. Throughout the fight, Sigurd targeted pressure points and other vital areas along the giant wolf's body, such as his shoulders, elbows, kneecaps, and back. Although these wounds weren't deadly, they were grievous enough to weaken Sinfjotli. The wolf couldn't move as fast, and his attacks lacked power.

Yet even in their battered and bloody states, Sinfjotli wouldn't relent. The giant wolf finished licking its wounds and stared at Sigurd, eager for more.

I'll have to finish him with this next strike. Sigurd squeezed his eyes shut. *Forgive me, Father. Even if he is your son, I must kill him.*

Sigurd raised his sword and charged with a booming war cry. Sinfjotli responded with a blood-curdling howl and rushed forward. The gilded warrior and the savage wolf barreled toward each other, prepared to kill each other in a final strike. But a bright light appeared between them as they were about to attack. Sigurd, blinded at that moment, swung his sword with all his might.

CLANG!

The ominous sound reverberated throughout the courtyard as Gram wobbled while striking something impenetrable. Sigurd howled in pain from the recoil. His palms felt like they were bleeding as he held the vibrating hilt. The metallic noise ringing in his ears sounded eerily human, as if the sword itself was screaming in pain. A moment later, his ears registered a new sound.

"Hello there!"

When Sigurd's eyes adjusted to the bright light, he discovered a mysterious and incredibly handsome man standing before him.

The stranger, about seven feet, six inches tall, had a muscular but lithe build, and his body was enveloped in an aura of white light. Despite his radiant and divine-looking features, he wore simple leathers, garb fit for hunting or riding, with only a studded jacket to protect him from the cold. He wore no other lavish garments aside from a red cloak strewn over his shoulders. His long brown beard was bound with golden rings and bands. His incredibly long, straight brown hair touched the backs of his kneecaps.

Somehow, his absurdly long hair and simple garments complemented and enhanced his already immaculate appearance. His perfectly chiseled face included an impish, almost beatific smile, radiant, pristine teeth, and lips and eyes that were somewhere between feminine and masculine. Sigurd felt like he was staring at the most handsome man in the world. His gorgeous face could make any woman swoon with joy and any lesser man green with envy and admiration.

More important than his handsome features, Sigurd noticed the stranger appeared completely unharmed. Sigurd had swung Gram with enough force to split his palms open from the recoil, but the legendary blade pressed harmlessly against the man's neck.

Sinfjotli's charge had been just as ineffective. The dazed giant wolf lay sprawled on the ground behind the stranger. Sinfjotli had slammed headfirst into the stranger's back, but the handsome man hadn't budged.

"I take it you two are the source of all this commotion I've been hearing?" The handsome man asked in a cheerful, reedy voice, oblivious to the danger he had put himself in and unconcerned about the sword pressed against his throat.

Sigurd was too thunderstruck to respond, still baffled that Gram was pressing harmlessly against the man's throat. This was the first time Gram failed to cut something. Sigurd took pride in the fact it couldn't be parried or blocked. And yet, his legendary sword couldn't cut through even a single strand of hair in the stranger's long beard.

Sinfjotli finally recovered his senses, stood up, and glared murderously at the newcomer.

"How *dare* you disgrace and embarrass me like this!" Sinfjotli snarled. "How dare you intrude in our battle!" The wolf rose on its hind legs and chomped the stranger's left arm. But like Gram, his teeth could not pierce the stranger's skin. Sinfjotli kept gnawing uselessly at the man's arm in anger and frustration.

"All right, that's enough," the stranger urged calmly as he pushed Gram away from his neck with his bare right hand. "Brothers shouldn't fight each other like this. Take a moment to breathe and clear your minds."

His aura glowed brighter. A sudden wave of calmness and tranquility seeped into Sigurd's bones. His hostility, anger, bewilderment, and negative thoughts vanished in a state of bliss. Sigurd's pain ceased, and his neck injury and the sword wound in his chest stopped bleeding.

Sinfjotli was also affected. The wolf ceased gnawing at the stranger's arm and stepped backward, the sclera of his eyes turning white again. He looked calmer and more amenable to reason.

"Now, inspect the man before you," the stranger commanded. "What do you see? Is he an enemy? A thief? A monster? No. He's your brother. He said so himself. He smells like your father, doesn't he? And any warrior who fights as resiliently as you did must be your brother."

Sinfjotli listened to the stranger's words in stony silence and glanced at Sigurd. The wolf closed his eyes and began morphing back into human form. His fur receded into his skin, and his snout receded into his face. His body shrunk, and his bones emitted an unnerving crunching as they contracted to a humanoid size.

Normally, Sigurd would have winced at those sickening sounds and turned away in disgust, but the stranger's aura kept him in a bizarrely calm and blissful state as he watched the grisly transformation unfold.

"That's better," the stranger muttered when Sinfjotli finished reverting into a humanoid form. "Now, let me have a good look at you both."

He took a step back and scrutinized them. "Yes... I can see the physical similarities between you. You share the same blood. You are indeed brothers, albeit from different mothers." His eyes widened. "Interesting...I also sense Sigi's blood flowing through your veins." He clapped his hands together. "Wonderful! I suppose that makes us distant relatives!"

"Sigi," Sinfjotli frowned. "That was the name of my ancestor, the renegade son of Odin and the founder of my family's dynasty. But how could you possibly be related to him? He died centuries ago."

"Indeed," the stranger affirmed. "Sigi died almost three centuries ago, if I remember correctly."

"Three centuries?" Sigurd sheathed Gram and stared blankly at the stranger. He couldn't possibly be that old. "Who are you?"

"Who am I?" The stranger cocked his head to the side. It evidently wasn't a question he was accustomed to being asked. After a moment, he clapped his hands again and chuckled. "Oh, that's right! I haven't introduced myself yet. I sometimes forget social trivialities when I'm excited."

He took a step backward and curtsied respectfully. "I am Baldur, son of Odin and Frigga, the god of goodness, joy, and light."

Sigurd's jaw dropped. *He's an Aesir!* Sigurd was face-to-face with an actual Aesir!

"And who might you be?" Baldur inquired.

"I am Sigurd the Dragon Slayer, the son of Sigmund and Hjordis."

"And I am Sinfjotli, the son of Sigmund and...and the son of Signy."

"Well then, Sigurd and Sinfjotli, let me be the first to welcome you to Helheim, the realm of the dishonorable dead," Baldur announced with his arms outstretched.

Sigurd found the cheerfulness of Baldur's voice both disturbing and curious. Baldur seemed to take joy and interest in everything without malice or enmity. His infectious joy and euphoria caused Sigurd and Sinfjotli to forget all hostile and negative thoughts. Even the soul-crushing revelation that they were trapped in the underworld would not bother them so long as they remained under the effects of his aura.

"Come with me," Baldur requested. "I have a place where you can find refuge from this bitter cold. You can share a meal with my family and me. You two must be quite famished after such an intense fight. And we'd better get those wounds looked at. Oh, and you need some new clothes, Sinfjotli."

Sinfjotli looked down and realized he was standing naked in the blistering cold, his old clothes torn to shreds amidst his earlier transformation.

Baldur unfastened his cloak and handed it to Sinfjotli, who wrapped it around his body. Then, without question or a word of protest, they followed Baldur away from the devastated plaza.

CHAPTER FOUR

A CHILLING TRUTH

They followed Baldur as he made his way west through the city, arriving at the massive icy black road Sigurd crossed earlier. The smoky figures, which he now realized were the souls of the dead, continued marching on their sojourn south.

"This paved road is called the Path of the Dead," Baldur explained. "If we follow it south through the City of the Lost, it'll take us to my home."

And so, they joined the souls of the dead as they marched south. Although heavy snow and the chilly winds lashed across their backs like icy whips, Sigurd noticed that the air near Baldur didn't feel as frigid. His wounds had stopped bleeding, and his head felt clear and devoid of negative thoughts.

Now that he had a clearer mind thanks to Baldur's aura, Sigurd studied the city's architecture as they traveled the icy road. Helheim's architecture consisted mainly of elevated bridges, gates, and tall buildings, all made of oily black stone. The buildings in the center of the city along the Path of the Dead were the most elevated. They were in better shape than the ones in the plaza they'd fought in, which lay on the city's outskirts. This was likely because the buildings were closely grouped, providing better wind protection. Only the tops of these skyscrapers showed any sign of damage or age. The rest of the buildings appeared as sturdy as the day they had been built. Each structure was composed of oily black blocks, and the moisture from the falling snow made the damp stone walls appear coated in viscous black oil.

Many metal statues were scattered throughout the city and along the Path of the Dead, depicting humans in various states of lamentation, agony, and despair. Many were severely damaged, missing limbs, or frozen in ice, giving them an even ghastlier appearance. The ever-present arctic wind had slowly whittled them the same way it had whittled away the buildings in the plaza where Sigurd had encountered Sinfjotli.

One silver and bronze statue depicted a man shivering in the cold as he trudged south. His face was awash with despair, icicles jutting sideways from his head, shoulders, and legs.

If not for Baldur, I might've ended up in that frozen state with my face awash with despair, Sigurd realized.

The only sign of life in this dark city was a thick, black, vine-like thorny plant that crawled up the sides of several buildings and areas sheltered from the wind. The plants looked dried and flammable, and Sigurd wondered if fire could exist in Helheim.

Helheim's most distinguishing feature was the thousands of deceased souls Sigurd and Sinfjotli walked alongside as they followed Baldur down the Path of the Dead. But traveling with the deceased was not as exhilarating as Sigurd expected. They appeared indifferent as they allowed Sigurd and Sinfjotli to move past them. The ghosts didn't respond when Sigurd accidentally walked through them a second time. They kept following the road south to an unknown destination.

However, a curious phenomenon occurred whenever Baldur walked by a spirit. When he neared a ghost, its body solidified into physical form, allowing Sigurd to glimpse the soul as it looked when they were still alive. But they'd fade back into humanoid smoke when Baldur walked further away. Baldur seemed vaguely aware of this, but paid it no mind as they continued south.

However, what Sigurd found most intriguing wasn't the spirits, Baldur's effect on them, the black vine-like plants, or the damaged statues. It was the strange material that composed the entire city. Every building and road in this city was composed of a bizarre, oily black stone. At first glance, the material resembled basalt. But the stone featured distinctive rippled patterns, like the type someone might see in a tempered or an enchanted steel blade. The curtain wall in the plaza where he'd fought Sinfjotli had also been made of this substance. Sigurd knew from that painful experience that it was rigid.

Sigurd curiously stepped off the Path of the Dead to examine one of the tallest buildings. The granite-like stone structure was so shiny that he could see a twisted likeness of his own features in its depths. He reached out and slowly ran his hand over the oily black stone. Sigurd felt a familiar chill in his spine, like the current in a flowing river. He knew what this was. Magic. All the black stone in this city was imbued with magic.

The absurdly powerful magical current flowing through these stones overwhelmed Sigurd into an inviting trance. The longer he touched the stone, the more he felt drawn toward it, as if his hand and arm were sinking into a whirlpool. It felt like his entire being would soon get absorbed into the stone's current when someone seized his shoulder, snapping him out of the trance.

Sigurd snapped out of the trance when someone grasped his shoulder.

"Listen, brother. I... I'm sorry I got carried away during our fight," Sinfjotli apologized. "It's been so long since I faced an opponent of your caliber, and I guess I got too excited."

"It's all right," Sigurd assured as he removed his hand from the stone. He paused and smiled. "So, you've accepted the truth that we're brothers?"

"Definitely," Sinfjotli affirmed proudly. "Only a son of Sigmund and a true descendant of Völsung could have put up a fight like that." He crossed his arms and glanced at the sky, deep in thought. "Let's see... That makes you Sigmund's fourth son after me, Helgi, and Hámundr."

As Sinfjotli stared at the dark emerald sky, shock and soul-crushing terror washed over his face as it finally dawned on him that he was in the underworld. But the fear vanished because of the effects of Baldur's aura.

"So, this is Helheim?" Sinfjotli asked calmly, in a voice sapped of fear and angst. "But isn't that the realm of dishonorable dead? Why are we here?"

"Oh, that's simple," Baldur assured. "You're here in the underworld because you both died dishonorable deaths outside of combat. Tell me, Sinfjotli. What's the last thing you remember before you woke up here?"

"I was at a feast," Sinfjotli recalled after a moment. "I had just returned after helping my brother, Helgi, win a bloody and brutal war to marry the love of his life, Sigrún. Father proudly hosted a grand feast to celebrate our victory and honor our fallen comrades. Helgi's mother, Borghild, personally served me three cups of wine during the feast. Father insisted on drinking the first three, but he got inebriated and insisted I drink the third. I did as I was told and drank deeply. And then... next thing I know, I woke up in that plaza you found me in, surrounded by glaciers and buried beneath a blanket of snow. I explored the city but fled back to the plaza when the cold became too much to bear. And then I met Sigurd."

"I see," Sigurd muttered sadly. "Then the rumors were true."

"What do you mean?" Sinfjotli asked.

"Your stepmother poisoned you at that feast."

"She poisoned me?!" Sinfjotli exclaimed. "Why?"

"I can't tell you the complete story because I don't know all the details," Sigurd admitted. "It happened many years before I was born. But from what I understand, you purportedly murdered your stepmother's brother in a quarrel over a woman you both desired right before Helgi's epic battle against Sigrún's family. So, she avenged his death by poisoning you at Helgi's victory feast."

"That hateful bitch!" Sinfjotli snarled. "I didn't '*murder*' her brother! I gave Brynjar a chance to draw his weapon and slew him in honorable combat, giving his soul a chance to ascend to Valhalla! How is that murder? Father and I even paid the blood price for his death, and she repaid us by murdering me at a feast?!"

Sinfjotli ran off the Path of the Dead and punched a glacier sandwiched in an alleyway between two buildings. He struck the ice so hard his fist bled. Cracks spread throughout the ice, and the entire glacier broke apart. Sinfjotli stood in front of the crumbling chunks of ice, trembling with anger.

"Father banished Borghild after that," Sigurd added. "Our other brothers, Helgi and Hámundr, her own sons, disowned her. On one of my voyages, I learned she died in poverty, a broken woman shunned by all."

"Am I supposed to find comfort in that?" Sinfjotli snapped. "I should have died a glorious death in battle, fighting for a meaningful cause. Instead, I'm trapped here in Helheim because she murdered and robbed me of the chance!"

"All right, that's enough lamentation." Baldur decided. His aura glowed brighter, and Sigurd once again felt a wave of calm bliss wash and seep into his bones. Sigurd calmly watched as Sinfjotli's anger and frustration were washed away by the effects of Baldur's benevolent aura. There was no resisting it. It was impossible to stay angry or give in to despair while in Baldur's presence.

"You can bemoan your death along the way, Sinfjotli, but we've got to keep marching," Baldur insisted with a sense of urgency.

Sinfjotli obeyed without protest, and they resumed walking down the icy road. Sigurd mulled over everything they had discussed as they walked alongside the spirits.

"Did you really kill your stepmother's brother in a duel over a woman?"

Sigurd blinked in shock at what he had just blurted out. Under normal circumstances, Sigurd would have thought twice about asking a violent man like Sinfjotli such a dangerous and intrusive question, but Baldur's presence negated any ear, caution, or trepidation. Baldur's aura also made him unable to keep his thoughts to himself.

Sinfjotli stared at Sigurd. There was no anger or shame in his gaze, just absolute calmness.

"That's only half the reason," he admitted. "During one of my raids with Helgi leading up to the bloody Battle of Frekastein, I encountered a beautiful woman I fancied. But Borghild's brother Brynjar desired her as well."

"So, you killed him in a duel over who could claim her as a war prize?" Sigurd inferred.

"No, she wasn't the sole reason," Sinfjotli insisted. "In fact, I let her run away after the duel was over without ever laying a hand on her. The real reason I killed Brynjar is that during our argument over who could claim her as a prize of war, he... called me a 'bastard born of incest unfit to be called Sigmund's son.' When he said that, something turned within me. Something dark. I told him to draw his sword then and there if he wanted the woman so badly. Brynjar agreed, and I killed him in the ensuing duel."

"So, you killed him because he offended you?" Sigurd surmised.

"You have a problem with that?" Sinfjotli asked with a hint of irritation.

"Not really," Sigurd admitted. "I've known men who were killed for less. But why would he call you a 'bastard born of incest?' And why did it offend you so much?"

"Because it's the truth." Sinfjotli looked up at the emerald clouds and took a deep breath. "My...my mother...my mother's name was Signy, and she was... our father Sigmund's twin sister."

CHAPTER FIVE

THE SHIP OF THE DEAD

Sigurd reeled in shock. While growing up, he had heard several vile rumors about his father's and aunt's alleged relationship. But he dismissed them as calumnies that Sigmund's old enemies concocted to besmirch his father's good name. And yet his long-lost half-brother Sinfjotli had just confirmed his parents were indeed siblings. Sigurd would have retched if it wasn't for Baldur's aura. Feelings of disgust soon dissipated as Sinfjotli continued his story.

"When Helgi and I returned to Hunaland after the war, my stepmother Borghild learned what happened on that raid and became livid," Sinfjotli recalled. "She demanded our father exile me as a criminal. But our father became furious when Helgi and I told him what her brother Brynjar had said to me. He pardoned me, paid Borghild her brother's weight in silver, and ordered her to never speak of the matter again. Borghild seemed placated, telling him: 'You shall decide, sir, as is fitting.' But it seems it was an act. In the end, I guess we both underestimated her fury."

Sinfjotli covered his face with his hands and groaned. "Bah! I knew something was amiss when Borghild insisted on serving me those drinks at the feast. Borghild was a proud noblewoman who would never carry out a servant's work at a feast without reason."

36

"Sinfjotli, you mentioned your father drank the first two drinks she offered you," Baldur interjected. "Why didn't Sigmund die from poisoning as well?"

"Father had a stomach of iron, which was immune to poison. He must have suspected that the ale was poisoned and tried to save me. But it seems Borghild planned for that and spiked the brew so that even his liver couldn't handle it." Sinfjotli frowned. "Now that I think about it, she was the one who suggested I have that third drink, and Father drunkenly agreed I should have it. And since he was the host of the feast, I couldn't refuse, or he'd…"

"Are you all right, Sigurd?" Baldur interrupted. "You're looking very green."

"I just can't accept it," Sigurd muttered, still in shock. "I still can't believe our father committed, with his twin sister no less!"

"It's not what you think happened," Sinfjotli assured. "He had no idea it was even her. What happened between my parents… had nothing to do with love, lust, or desire. She *used* him."

"Just what the hell is that supposed to mean?" Sigurd demanded.

"It's a long story, and I don't enjoy telling it," Sinfjotli replied. "It brings back too many painful memories."

"Then let's change topics," Baldur suggested. His aura grew brighter and, once again, sapped them of their negative thoughts. "What about you, Sigurd? How did you die?"

Sigurd winced and clutched the wound in his chest. He wasn't feeling any physical pain now because of Baldur's aura. But he could still remember the feeling of Guttorm's sword driving deep into his flesh. Those phantom pains were something even Baldur's magic couldn't dispel.

"I…I think my brother-in-law, Guttorm, murdered me in my bed," Sigurd managed. "He ran a sword through my chest while I slept."

"Why the hell would he do that?" Sinfjotli asked, raising an eyebrow. "Did you offend him somehow?"

"I... I'm not sure," Sigurd admitted. "The memories of my final days are fuzzy. I can't think of any reason my brother-in-law would want to murder me."

"So, your brother-in-law killed you?" Sinfjotli threw his head back and burst into a fit of laughter.

"What's so damn funny?" Sigurd demanded. "Do you find my death amusing somehow?"

"Sort of," Sinfjotli chuckled. "I've just realized a tragic trend among our family. Your brother-in-law murdered you. I got poisoned by my stepmother, and our grandfather, our uncles, and our ancestors all got killed by their in-laws. It seems our family's greatest enemies were almost always our in-laws."

"That amusing coincidence aside, how did Guttorm even manage to kill you?" Baldur asked. "You bathed in dragon blood and made yourself invulnerable to conventional weaponry, right? I can tell because that flagpole Sinfjotli used couldn't leave a scratch on you, even though the spear tip was as sharp as obsidian. So how did Guttorm overcome that invulnerability?"

"Guttorm used an enchanted sword named Mimung," Sigurd explained. "I gave him that sword on his sixteenth birthday. As you deduced, Baldur, I'm invulnerable to any manmade weapon from Midgard. However, any cursed or enchanted weapons from another realm are the exception to that rule."

"Did you say Mimung?" Baldur blinked. "Unless I'm mistaken, that sword was forged by the famous elf, Volund the Smith."

"How'd you come across an elfish sword?" Sinfjotli asked, intrigued.

"That is another long story," Sigurd replied dismissively.

"Well, you'll have plenty of time to talk about it soon," Baldur promised. "I look forward to hearing both of your tales in copious detail. But for now, we've arrived!"

Sigurd glanced past Baldur. They had reached the southern end of the city. In front of them was a seven-mile-long bridge suspended hundreds of feet over a green river that led to the largest palace Sigurd had ever seen. The fortress-like castle was so tall that Sigurd had to bend his head back to his spine to see above it, even from this distance. Its colossal curtain walls were sheer and high as mountain cliffs. It looked like a palace more suited to housing giants than humans. Based on its colossal size, Sigurd estimated the fortress was at least six miles high and covered over two hundred fifty thousand square miles.

Although it was gargantuan, the giant palace wasn't immaculate. The walls and towers of the palace were windswept and showed heavy signs of damage and erosion from the wind and elements. Icicles the length of skyscrapers draped from the sides of the walls and roofs. Coupled with the gothic architecture, the ice gave the windswept palace a chilling, foreboding appearance. Two massive iron doors opened slightly at the castle entrance. The dead souls they had been walking alongside continued traveling across the bridge and passing through the gates of that foreboding fortress.

"That's your home?!" Sinfjotli exclaimed.

"Good heavens, no!" Baldur laughed. "That rain-lashed palace is Hel's palace of Eljudnir. I have a special place reserved for me inside that palace, but I rarely stay there. It's such a dreary, gloomy, and dreadful place. I prefer to stay on my ship instead."

He pointed over the side of the bridge. The largest ship Sigurd had ever seen was moored next to the palace and bridge. A big city sprawled along the deck of the absurdly long vessel. The hull was covered in elaborate gold and silver decorations. The ship displayed at least five different masts, with the mainmast in the center stretching two miles tall. Every city in the world could have fit on the deck of that ship. The ship was so large that it was a miracle it didn't sink into the green river under its weight.

Baldur clapped his hands. "Excellent, Sigurd. I'm impressed you deduced its length from a mere glance. That is Hringhorni, my private home here in Helheim. And that green river it's moored in is the River Gjöll. And this bridge we're standing on is called the Bridge of Judgment. Come on! It's almost time for supper, and I'm sure my wife, Nanna, will prepare something special for us."

Sigurd looked back at the towering palace, his eyes drawn to the expanse of land looming behind it. The enormous green river flowing beneath the bridge seemed to demarcate this dark mass of land, which stretched farther than even his eyes could see. It was a vast and expansive continent in every sense of the word. Sigurd was about to use his snake eyes to survey the land's interior when Baldur thrust a hand in front of his face.

"Don't," he cautioned, urgency dripping from his words. "Some things aren't meant for mortals like you to see."

Sigurd's curiosity piqued. "What's that dark land over yonder?"

"I dare not utter its name. Never venture there. Some things can't be unseen." Baldur's voice was steady, but the gravity of his words sent shivers down Sigurd's spine. Following their guide's advice, he averted his gaze, glanced over the side of the bridge, and frowned.

"Lord Baldur, how are we supposed to get down there? I don't see any stairs or anything connecting the ship to this giant bridge."

"I don't need stairs!" Baldur laughed merrily. "I prefer to jump."

"Wait, what?" Before Sigurd could say anything else, Baldur scooped him and Sinfjotli in his arms and leaped over the side of the bridge.

Sigurd's heart pounded like a drum inside his chest, and his mind experienced a sensory overload as they rocketed toward the ship. With only air between him and the vessel below, Sigurd could see everything in picturesque detail. A crisp, clean smell overwhelmed his nostrils. The loud rush of wind deafened his ears as they rocketed downwards. He felt the overwhelming wind resistance from their freefall speed against his skin. Sigurd worried what would happen if they missed and splashed into the River Gjöll. All his instincts warned him to avoid those sickly green waters.

Thankfully, they avoided the river and landed on the ship's bow with a mighty THOOM. When the cloud of dust settled, Sigurd discovered he was unharmed. Baldur had taken the full brunt of the impact. Judging from the many craters on the deck, Sigurd assumed Baldur performed this stunt often.

Baldur gently deposited them on the deck, straightened his back, and burst into a jovial laugh. But Sigurd and Sinfjotli crumbled to the ground, panting and trying to control their heart rates. Even under Baldur's aura, they could not recover from the shock of falling hundreds of feet through the air and nearly splashing into the River Gjöll.

"Ha, there's nothing like falling hundreds of feet through the air to make you feel alive!" Baldur chortled. "What's with that angry look, Sigurd? You were never in any danger."

"That's not the point!" Sigurd snapped, still short of breath. "Warn us next time before you do something crazy like that!"

For a moment, Baldur looked perplexed. Then he burst out laughing. "Ah, I apologize about that. I often forget how fragile it is to be mortal and how terrifying it must be."

Sigurd wanted to say more, but Baldur's aura enveloped him in another wave of euphoria, washing away his anger and calming him. Sigurd decided just to let it go. It was impossible to stay upset at Baldur when he could literally make his anger disappear with his presence.

When he recovered from the shock and excitement of falling hundreds of feet through the air, Sigurd stood and examined the ship's deck. And what he saw disappointed him. Upon closer inspection, the "city" sprawled across the deck was more like a shanty town. Although the architecture was impressive, the buildings were composed of old, cheap wooden planks and other makeshift materials salvaged from the ship itself. Whoever built these structures had done a remarkable job. But the architecture couldn't disguise the fact that the buildings were made from salvaged materials, giving them an ugly, though admittedly unique, appearance.

"Have you both finished recovering?" Baldur asked. "Good. In that case, let's get moving. My family should be waiting at the stern of the ship."

They followed Baldur through the lofty city of wooden and stone buildings sprawled across the deck. The *Hringhorni* wasn't as impressive up close. The giant ship was elegant, but not immaculate. The ship's deck was heavily damaged, covered in scorch marks, and parts of the deck had rotted from the snow and rain. The towering masts looked like melted candles, and their sails were little more than burned tatters. The ship looked as if it had burned inside a massive bonfire.

The ship's atmosphere felt different from the rest of Helheim. It was not warm, but the temperature here was less chilly than in the city. It seemed brighter here, and there was no trace of snow or ice anywhere on the deck. And although a heavy blizzard raged over the bridge and city above them, no snowflakes fell upon the ship.

Despite its unsightly and shoddy appearance, this ship was a paradise compared to the dark, cold, and scary city above them. And it was very lively thanks to its many denizens. As the trio traveled to the stern of the ship, they passed by many spirits engaged in various activities. Children played tag, women wrung laundry, men read books, and a group of elders engaged in a symposium. And there weren't just humans—dwarves, elves, and even a gentle giant and giantess moved amongst the spirits. As a fifty-foot male giant lounged against one mast, some children playfully competed to see who could climb up to the top of his head first. The giant patiently let the children climb up its body and tug at his hair. He even caught anyone who fell with his enormous hands.

These spirits differed from those Sigurd had walked alongside on the Path of the Dead. They all had corporeal forms and physical attributes, and whenever Baldur walked near the spirits, their bodies became brighter, taking on a more lifelike appearance.

At first glance, one might think the denizens of this ship were ordinary people. But there was a dead giveaway that they were spirits. Sometimes, a group of children would run over to say hello to Baldur or ask him to play with them. But they spoke in a raspy and guttural language Sigurd couldn't understand, but Baldur could. He would ask them how they were doing and what happened on the ship while he was away, and he promised to play with the children another time.

Sigurd smiled. After everything he had seen in the City of the Lost, finding a vibrant, peaceful, and lively place like this in Helheim felt strangely comforting. Despite its crude and imperfect appearance, this city and the rest of the ship were like a paradise compared to the dark City of the Lost and the rest of this ghastly realm.

Sigurd's only complaint was how absurdly long the ship was. It took an hour of walking before they reached the vessel's stern. In front of the captain's quarters was a large dining pavilion. Many long tables and benches were arranged across the deck, reminding Sigurd of the typical setup inside a longhouse. A grand golden throne sat on an elevated dais where a jarl might sit in front of the captain's quarters.

Two tall, conspicuous figures played a board game with golden and silver pieces in the center of the dining pavilion. The buxom woman to the left was about seven feet two inches tall with long golden hair that reached the small of her back. She wore a simple red dress complete with a green belt and shroud. She was gorgeous, and Sigurd got the impression she was as pleasant and good-natured as Baldur.

The man she played against looked like Baldur's opposite. If Baldur was the god of light, then this man must be the god of darkness. He was an inch taller than Baldur. His skin had a grayish, icy tint, long, smoky black hair reaching his pectoral muscles, and a long-braided black beard. He wore an impressive suit of black leather armor and a pitch-black cape woven from living shadows draped over his shoulders. The shadowy cloak pulsated every few seconds in rhythm with his heartbeat.

However, the man's most distinguishing and unnerving feature was his eyes. They were clouded and lacked pupils, indicating blindness. The man looked handsome and amicable, but his shadowy appearance, pale skin, and milky white eyes were enough to make one cautious.

But despite his blindness, he wasn't helpless. He seemed to grasp the situation around himself from sound, touch, and presumably another sixth sense the Aesir possessed that allowed them to sense things imperceptible to humans. Baldur claimed he'd "sensed" Sigurd and Sinfjotli's battle from afar. It stood to reason that this man and woman possessed the same sense.

Another spirit sat next to the blind man, studying the board and describing the layout of the pieces in his ear. Based on his short and stocky, muscular appearance, this spirit was a dwarf. Like the other spirits on this ship, this one had a more condensed form than the ones they'd seen in the City of the Lost. He had red hair, brown eyes, and a massive rust-colored beard that reached his waist. He was about four feet six inches tall and stood on a bench to whisper in the blind man's ear.

Seeing the dwarf reminded Sigurd of another dwarf named Regin, who had served as his mentor and foster father. He'd taught many valuable lessons to Sigurd, tutoring him in languages and the art of writing runes. He had even reforged Gram, which had broken before Sigurd had been born. Watching this dwarf whisper into the blind man's ear stirred up many nostalgic memories for Sigurd. But it also made him feel slightly guilty as he remembered what had happened to his mentor.

Sigurd cast aside those bitter memories as Baldur cautioned him and Sinfjotli to wait until the game finished before announcing their presence. They watched and waited as the blind man and woman clashed wits. It looked like they were playing a game of Tablut with silver and gold pieces carved in the likeness of the Aesir. Sigurd recognized a few of them. There was Odin, the All-Father, on his high throne. Another one was carved in the likeness of Thor holding his hammer. Another piece holding a horn to its lips was presumably Heimdall. There were even several pieces cut in the likeness of Baldur. The players had been playing for a while, but there was still no clear winner.

After the woman moved one of her golden pieces, the blind man leaned over to the dwarf and listened as the little fellow described the board's layout. The blind man smiled as he moved a silver piece and won the game. Baldur cleared his throat and stepped forth as the comely woman conceded defeat and complimented her opponent on his victory.

"Nanna, Hodr!" Baldur called. "Come here! We have proper guests!"

Nanna glanced toward him and squealed with joy. She lunged at Baldur, wrapping him in a fierce embrace and shouting, "Baldur!" She kissed him...long enough for it to become awkward for Sigurd, though he said nothing.

When Nanna pulled away, she buried her face in Baldur's neck, sobbing, "I missed you so much. I was so worried!"

"Nanna, I'm overjoyed to see you, too." Baldur laughed. "But there's no reason to weep tears of joy. I've only been gone a couple of days."

"Actually, you've been gone for over a month, brother," Hodr informed.

"Really?" Baldur blinked. "It's been that long already? Where does the time go? Well, I'm happy to see you both. But as you can see, we have important guests now."

"No, brother! I can't '*see*' anything!" Hodr exclaimed in a nettled tone. He pointed a long, thin finger at his milky white eyes. "How many times must I remind you I'm *blind*?"

"Oh, don't mind him." Nanna giggled as she wiped away her tears. She untangled herself from Baldur and turned to Sigurd and Sinfjotli. She revealed the warmest smile Sigurd had seen and extended her arms as if she were expecting a hug.

"Welcome aboard the Hringhorni! I am Nanna, Baldur's wife and the goddess of joy and peace. And the glum man over there is Baldur's brother Hodr, the god of darkness and winter. And the dwarf next to him is Litr."

Hodr perked up at the mention of his name. He glanced in their general direction and gave a welcoming smile. The dwarf stood on the bench and curtsied respectfully.

"It's a pleasure to meet you." Hodr smiled. "What are your names?"

"I am Sinfjotli."

"And I am Sigurd, son of Sigmund and...argh!"

Before he could say his mother's name, Sigurd's chest erupted in pain, and he collapsed. He opened the collar of his armor and undershirt slightly and discovered that the gaping wound in his chest had started bleeding again. A moment later, Sinfjotli also collapsed, clutching his bleeding arms and neck. All of the injuries that Sigurd had inflicted on his body during their titanic duel reemerged and began painting the deck red with blood. Whatever magic Baldur had used to stave off their injuries had just worn off. Now, they were bleeding so much Sigurd feared he would perish from blood loss.

"What's wrong?" Nanna asked worriedly. "Let me have a look at you... Good heavens! How in Ymir's name did you get so injured?"

"Oh, they had a little sparring match and got a bit carried away." Baldur chortled. "Can you patch them up?"

"Of course," Nanna sighed, rolling her eyes. She pressed her hand against Sigurd's chest.

"Sunnan," She whispered. A moment later, Sigurd's chest wound and other abrasions stopped bleeding, and his left leg stopped howling in pain. He was still too injured to move on his own. But it felt like his wounds had stagnated, giving him a reprieve from the overwhelming pain. Nanna then cast the same spell on Sinfjotli. His injuries weren't as life-threatening as Sigurd's, and he managed to pick himself off the deck.

"Sinfjotli, was it?" Nanna asked. "Help me carry your brother over to that table. Then, put on a pair of pants, sit on that bench, and wait a bit. I'll treat your injuries as soon as I finish with Sigurd."

Sinfjotli nodded and carried Sigurd to the nearest table. At Nanna's instructions, he removed Sigurd's golden hauberk and armor and handed it to the dwarf Litr, who she promised would repair all the damage. Then Sinfjotli picked up a pair of wool pants from a wicker basket and sat down at a nearby long table.

The table creaked next to Sigurd as Nanna sat down on the bench. Placing a bowl of water and other supplies she needed on the table beside her, Nanna made herself comfortable and leaned forward, inspecting Sigurd's wounds.

"I can heal much of this with magic, but I need to clean the wounds to see what I'm working with." She admitted. "It's going to sting."

"I'm no stranger to pain." Sigurd drawled. "Go ahead."

There was a quiet trickle of water as Nanna wrung out a cloth before the first touch met his shoulder. Sigurd grimaced at the feeling. Even the gentle touch of her fingers was enough to send spikes of pain through him.

"Only a beast can inflict these kinds of wounds," Nanna noted. "How did Sinfjotli...?"

"He's a skinchanger," Baldur surmised. "They had a... brotherly spat and got too carried away."

The cloth stilled, and there was silence next to Sigurd. Nanna looked at her husband and sighed as she dropped the rag back into the bowl.

"Hell and bloody damnation," she chided. "You should have brought them here at once, Baldur, not let them batter each other within an inch of their lives."

Sigurd couldn't agree more.

"I couldn't help myself." Baldur shrugged. "I was mesmerized by their fight. I haven't seen a duel like that in years."

Nanna looked like she wanted to say more, but she held her tongue and continued treating Sigurd's wounds. She disinfected Sigurd's injuries and then deposited the cloth back in the bowl. She then examined his more severe wounds. Her gentle fingers touched the edges of the lacerations, careful not to cause more pain than necessary.

"Sinfjotli did quite a number on you. These wounds are deep. I can heal them, but…"

"It's fine." Sigurd consented. "Do what you must."

Nanna pressed her hands against Sigurd's left shoulder. He saw a warm orange glow from her fingertips before the skin on his shoulder tingled strangely. It felt warm and comforting, unlike the magic he'd felt coursing through the stones of the City of the Lost. The feeling of magic on his skin flickered momentarily as Nanna moved on to his other wounds.

Eventually, Nanna wrapped his shoulder in linen and put his left leg in a splint. She then rose from the table and gathered some of her supplies.

"I'll come back and finish patching you up soon." She promised. "I have to treat your brother now. Try not to move too much, Sigurd. You've lost a lot of blood."

As Nanna left to treat Sinfjotli's injuries, Sigurd sat up and examined the dining pavilion and the rest of the ship.

The dwarf Litr was busy repairing Sigurd's hauberk at a forge near the captain's quarters housed beneath a purple tent. The workshop and smithy were not very impressive. It had a furnace, a grindstone, and some rudimentary tools scattered across several tables but not much else. Despite the setback, it looked like Litr knew what he was doing and could compensate for his lack of equipment and materials with his masterful forging skills.

Nearby was a stable with a six-legged horse inside. Judging from the many elegant trappings covering its body, it was Baldur's horse. There were other interesting sights around the dining pavilion, including a pet dragon sleeping above them on the mainyard of the mast! The dragon wore custom-designed armor, most likely of Asgardian craftsmanship, which covered most of his body and sported two horns in his helmet. As it dozed leisurely on the mainyard, smoke billowed from its nostrils like a chimney.

However, what really captured Sigurd's attention was the many spirits shuffling about the deck. Unlike the other shades in the City of the Lost, the dead souls on this ship all had physical attributes and corporeal forms, and they looked the same as when they died. Some even had open wounds, missing limbs, and split heads, indicating violent deaths.

Some spirits huddled around braziers, staring absentmindedly at the fires, which Sigurd knew were just for show because he hadn't felt any genuine warmth from the flames earlier. Many sat around tables conversing in a guttural language Sigurd couldn't understand. Perhaps they were discussing the events of their past lives? Overall, they had one thing in common.

"These spirits seem...different from the ones we passed by on our way here," Sigurd observed. "They all have physical attributes and forms, and they look...kinder...gentler even. But they also seem sad and...well, just plain bored."

"Indeed," Baldur agreed. "There isn't much they *can* do here. But we do our best to entertain them and lighten their mood."

Before he could say anything else, Nanna finished patching up Sinfjotli and returned to finish treating Sigurd's wounds. *She works fast,* Sigurd thought as she laid him back on the table. As she worked, Sigurd thought about how many spirits they'd passed by on their way here. And a depressing thought crossed his mind.

"Lord Baldur..." Sigurd called.

"Just call me Baldur," he requested. "There's no need to be so formal."

"Ah... all right. I was wondering... were all the souls we passed by on our way here wicked?"

"Not all of them," Baldur assured. "There were surely some evil spirits among them. But not every soul sent to Helheim is wicked. Many souls on this ship died of sickness, old age, or didn't get the chance to die bravely in battle. You could say I've made it my solemn mission here in Helheim to help these poor souls and raise their spirits."

"What do you mean? Ow!"

"Hold still, dear," Nanna advised as she sowed the abrasion on his neck shut. "I'm nearly finished."

"Sorry," Sigurd grunted. "What were you saying about sickness and old age?"

"My, you must have taken too many hits to the head in your tussle with Sinfjotli!" Baldur laughed. "I'm sure you already know this, but I'll still explain it. Since time immemorial, only righteous warriors who die glorious and heroic deaths in combat can enter Valhalla or Fólkvangr. Unfortunately, this means everyone else who dies of sickness, old age, or doesn't get the chance to die bravely in battle winds up here in Helheim."

"Virtuous souls are condemned to Helheim along with the vile ones because of the circumstances of their death?!" Sinfjotli objected incredulously. "How is that fair?"

"I realize that seems harsh, but it's how things are." Baldur sighed. "But I understand how you feel. I also thought that the law was too draconian. When the three of us first arrived here on this ship, thousands of poor, unfortunate souls were being tortured in the City of the Lost simply because they hadn't died in battle. Many of the souls you see on this ship never spilled a drop of blood before or harmed another living creature when they were alive. Yet they were all sent here to Helheim because they hadn't died bravely in battle. I took pity on them and made a pact with Hel, the Queen of Helheim. We agreed to divide the dishonorable dead between us just like how my father Odin and Freyja split those who die heroic deaths between them. From now on, all the continent and incontinent souls who don't die gloriously in battle come here and find sanctuary on my ship. Here, under Hodr, Nanna, and my watchful care, they're protected from harm and Helheim's brutal torment.

Meanwhile, Hel retains all the wicked and vicious souls and can torture them as she pleases."

"So, every soul sent to Helheim makes their way to Hel's palace to receive judgment?" Sigurd inferred. "She keeps the wicked souls, and you receive all the virtuous souls?"

"Yes, but I'm afraid it's not that simple," Baldur admitted. "Many innocent and virtuous souls are still lost in the City of the Lost. Many have been there since before I arrived. And many souls who walk the Path of the Dead don't even make it to Hel's palace to face judgment. They lose heart, step off the path, and get lost in the city before they reach the palace of Eljudnir. I often wander around the City of the Lost, grant my protection to any lost souls I take pity on, and escort them back to my ship. You could say I've made it my solemn mission in Helheim to offer sanctuary to every continent soul whose only crime was not dying bravely in battle along with any other soul I take pity on."

"That's how you found us, isn't it?" Sigurd inferred.

"That's right," Baldur nodded. "I happened to be nearby when your scuffle started. And I stopped it before it went too far."

Nanna sighed and rolled her eyes as she treated Sigurd's sword wound with magic. "If you had intervened even earlier, they wouldn't *be* this injured."

Baldur laughed at Nanna's subtle scolding. Then he glanced at the spirits huddled around a nearby brazier, and for a moment, his smile faltered. "They're all safe from Helheim's brutal torment on my ship, though there is little we can do to alleviate their boredom. We try our best to brighten their mood. Nanna and I do our best to entertain them. Litr builds houses for them to inhabit, and Hodr strives to improve the ambiance of this ship. As the god of winter, he can manipulate the weather to ensure it never snows upon this ship. He also uses his powers as the god of darkness to dispel all the darkness on this ship and brighten the ambiance. But even he can't change this gloomy and melancholic sky above us."

Baldur stared at the pale emerald sky. For a moment, an emotion other than joy appeared across his face. "I'll be the first to admit this ship may be a far cry from the mighty feasts of Valhalla or the vibrant fields of Fólkvangr. But this ship is still a paradise for these spirits whose individualities and identities had nearly been stripped away because of Helheim's brutal torment."

"There, I'm finished," Nanna announced as she bandaged Sigurd's chest in linen. "Sigurd, that sword wound on your chest requires further treatment. But we can deal with it later. For now, come and join us for dinner. You two must be famished."

"That's a splendid idea," Baldur agreed. "It's been so long since we dined with family!"

CHAPTER SIX

DREADED MISTLETOE

Sigurd and Sinfjotli sat beside Baldur and Hodr around a long table on a raised platform near the captain's quarters. This was evidently a spot reserved for Baldur and his most honored guests. Many spirits assembled in the dining pavilion and sat around the trestle table rows.

Once everyone was seated, Nanna and the dwarf Litr disappeared below deck and soon reemerged, carrying plates full of freshly cooked meals. Sigurd felt his jaw drop at the sheer amount of food she laid on the table. Nanna served suckling pig, which was well peppered and served with onions and mushrooms. She then served vegetable wedges coated in a batter made with brown ale, then fried until golden and crispy. Nanna also brought a bowl filled with dough balls, dropped into hot oil, fried until golden, and dipped in honey. She also served a peacock roasted in its plumage, a great pike with crushed almonds, honey-glazed root vegetables, nettle soup, fermented fish, boiled lambsquarters, and many other succulent dishes fit for kings. She also rolled out a barrel of mead and invited Sigurd and Sinfjotli to come and drink their fill, which they gladly did.

"This food is so delicious!" Sigurd exclaimed as he gorged himself on a platter of roasted beef. *This may not be Valhalla, but I could learn to like this hell.*

"My wife is an excellent cook." Baldur boasted. "And Nanna has plenty of ingredients to work with since my family packed enough food on this ship to last us until Ragnarök."

"I'm also an excellent seamstress." Nanna reached into a basket, pulled out a pile of woven clothes, and handed them to Sinfjotli. "You can put these on when you're finished eating. Baldur mentioned that you're a skinchanger, Sinfjotli. So I enchanted the fabric so you don't rip them to pieces. These clothes will magically disappear and reappear whenever you transform."

"T-Thank you," Sinfjotli managed between messy mouthfuls.

"You're welcome." Nanna smiled, doing her best to overlook his poor table manners. "Oh, and Litr finished repairing your armor, Sigurd. It should be as good as new. Feel free to put it on whenever you're ready."

"Thank you," Sigurd said as the dwarf laid the hauberk and armor in a neatly folded pile on the table beside his clothes.

"Velbekomme," Litr replied cheerfully before drinking an entire horn of mead a servant handed him.

Sigurd frowned. "Excuse me?"

"He said, 'You're welcome,'" Baldur translated.

"Ah," Sigurd muttered. It was easy to forget that despite his corporeal appearance, Litr was a spirit like all the other people on this ship. And he spoke in that guttural language that only Baldur and his family could understand.

They continued feasting. Nanna played her lyre as they ate, performing a sad and beautiful dirge that made both Sigurd and Sinfjotli tear up. Her voice was as beautiful as she was, and the melody sounded magical. Sigurd couldn't understand the words, but the song sounded plaintive and bittersweet, as if she were describing a home she could never return to. The music reminded Sigurd of his best memories: training with his mother, going on adventures with the Orphans, watching sunsets with Gudrun, and playing with his children. It made him miss home.

Nanna stopped singing and looked up. Sigurd followed her gaze and saw that the sleeping armored dragon above them had awakened. It spread its wings and swooped down to the main deck. The drake was at least one hundred fifty feet long from snout to tail, yet it carefully made its way through the dining pavilion to their table as delicately as a cat. It momentarily eyed Sigurd and then leaned its long serpentine neck toward Baldur. To Sigurd's astonishment, the dragon nuzzled Baldur's hand with its snout like a dog rubbing its owner's leg. Baldur petted the dragon he called Twilight and chucked twenty pounds of meat into its gullet. The dragon ate its dinner and then swooped back up to its perch on the mainyard of the mast to resume its nap.

Midway through the feast, Baldur called everyone's attention.

"If you've both had your fill, I'm eager to hear a story, Sigurd," Baldur announced excitedly, rubbing his hands. "Now then, could you please tell me...?"

"Baldur, there's something I've been meaning to ask," Sinfjotli interrupted as he shoveled in a sloppy mouthful of fermented fish. "We're in Helheim, which is the realm of the dead. If you're here, does that mean you're dead, too?"

A sudden hush enveloped the deck as if the air had been sucked out of their lungs. After a tense few moments, Hodr broke the silence, muttering, "That was blunt."

Nanna had an altogether different reaction. "How *DARE* You!" She rose from the table, and a wave of hot air blasted Sigurd and Sinfjotli as harsh light radiated from her eyes and mouth. "You *DARE* ask my husband such an insolent question after we have showered you with such magnanimous hospitality?!"

"It's all right, Nanna," Baldur urged calmly. His aura glowed brighter, and once again, Sigurd was overwhelmed with a wave of euphoria and tranquility.

But most of that energy was directed at Nanna. After a few moments, Nanna calmed down and sat back in her chair.

"Thank you, darling." Baldur smiled as his aura dimmed. When he looked back, Sigurd noticed that Baldur's demeanor had changed. His eyes were warm and welcoming but didn't look as merry. He almost looked sad, if he was even capable of that emotion.

"Yes, Sinfjotli, I died long ago. It's a genuine tragedy. A story even I would enjoy...if it sadly didn't end in my death."

Baldur sat back on his throne and took a long sip from his drinking horn, suggesting this would be a long story. When he finished drinking, he handed the horn to Litr and leaned back on his throne.

"I was once the most beloved and handsome of the Aesir." Baldur began. "Goddesses and giantesses all vied to make me their husband. Some rivals would even fight each other to the point of death just for the right to accompany me on a pleasant afternoon stroll. I was loved by all. Even the pranks that Loki pulled on me were harmless fun...at first.

"But one night, I had a dreadful nightmare. I dreamed I had died and was seated here in Helheim, beside Hel herself, in that ghastly wind-lashed palace high above us. When my mother, Frigga, also had the same dream, I became immensely depressed. Even my wife, Nanna, couldn't cheer me up."

"Why?" Sinfjotli blurted. "What was so disheartening about a bad dream?"

"Dreams are very powerful," Baldur explained. "My father, Odin, realized long ago that dreams can shape reality and even glimpse the future. My nightmare that night had been a precognitive dream, a glimpse of what was to come. The realization that I would soon die depressed me. But my mother, Frigga, was determined to prevent it. She traveled across the Nine Realms and made every object in creation vow never to hurt me. Pregnant mothers swore on behalf of their children, and every man and beast swore for their future progeny. All objects made this vow, even inanimate objects like stone and metal. As a result, I became invulnerable to all threats, physical or magical."

"I see," Sigurd remarked. "So that's why Gram had no effect against you earlier."

"Are you saying you struck my husband?" Nanna asked in a threatening tone.

"Not intentionally," Sigurd admitted. "He appeared between me and Sinfjotli when we were about to strike each other. I swung my sword before realizing what had happened and was baffled afterward. Gram has never once failed to cut something, yet it couldn't cut through a single strand of his hair. That spell must be why."

"Indeed." Baldur chuckled while stroking his long beard. "However, I'm afraid the spell has a slight drawback. Since no object or person can harm me, no instrument in the Nine Realms can cut my hair. So, to my wife's eternal chagrin, I'm afraid I must keep my hair and beard this long."

"But putting that slight inconvenience aside, my brothers and sisters found this divine protection so amusing that they made a game of it." Baldur continued. "They began throwing sticks, rocks, furniture, and weapons at me and laughed as everything richocheted off my skin. Even my older brother, Thor, joined in the fun. He swung Mjolnir at my head with enough force to smash a mountain to dust. But even that mighty hammer bounced harmlessly off my skin.

"Well, Loki became jealous of all the attention I was getting. Through some snooping and shapeshifting, he tricked my mother into revealing that only one thing in creation hadn't sworn the oath: mistletoe. My mother thought it was so small and innocent that she felt it superfluous to ask it to make such a serious oath."

Baldur paused and glanced unhappily at Hodr. "Armed with that knowledge, Loki then committed a truly despicable act. He noticed my brother Hodr was feeling left out of the fun. Because he is blind, he couldn't aim accurately to throw anything at me. So Loki gave him a mistletoe spear and promised to help guide his hand. And then...well, you can infer the rest."

"I've told you a thousand times, I'm sorry for what happened," Hodr admitted. "I never dreamed it would kill you."

"And I have forgiven you a thousand times, brother," Baldur assured. "But our family was not so forgiving. Our brother Vidar was so angry that he killed Hodr in a fit of rage. My beloved Nanna was so heartbroken over my death that she died on the spot."

Baldur paused and took another deep sip from his drinking horn. "Afterward, my family gave me a hero's funeral. They laid me, Nanna, Hodr, my horse Léttfeti, my pet dragon Twilight, and all I possessed on this ship and set it ablaze. After it burned, the ship magically appeared here in Helheim, where it traveled down the River Gjöll and moored itself next to the palace of Eljudnir. And we made it our home, preferring it over Hel's palace.

"Thus, the three of us have remained here in Helheim as esteemed guests of Hel herself ever since. I honestly don't know how long we've been here." For a moment, Baldur had an uncharacteristically sad expression. Sigurd couldn't help feeling pity for Baldur. It was clear time passed in different ways for different beings. And though Baldur did not age in Helheim, immortals like the Aesir felt the weight of years as heavily as mankind.

"What about him?" Sinfjotli gestured to the dwarf seated at their table. "Why is he here?"

"Oh, Litr had an unfortunate mishap." Baldur's sad expression vanished as he resumed his jovial, carefree attitude. "During my funeral, my family summoned a giantess named Hyrrokin from Jotunheim to use her strength to launch my massive ship out to sea. With a single push, she set it afloat, but the violent motion sparkled fire from the rollers, and the ship caught fire. My brother Thor was incensed that she had boorishly launched the ship and set it on fire early without ceremony or reverence. He wanted to crack in her skull, but our father stopped him from smiting her, mindful that they had invited her, and thus she was under the protection of guest right. Thor was still seething when he stepped forward to consecrate my funerary pyre. And when Litr got in his way to better view the pyre, Thor angrily kicked him into the blazing ship where he burned alongside us."

Sinfjotli glanced at the dwarf with pity. "You got sent to Helheim just because you got kicked into a pyre and died outside of combat? Harsh."

Litr shrugged. "Meh, það er það sem það er."

"Litr had the misfortune of running afoul of our brother on one of his bad days," Hodr admitted. "But he keeps us company and helps us fulfill our tasks. He also does his best to keep the ship in good shape and builds homes for the spirits to inhabit."

"Anyway, that's enough about us." Baldur smiled eagerly. "Tell me all about *your* lives. It gets quite boring here in Helheim. And it's been *so* long since I listened to heroes recount their adventures."

CHAPTER SEVEN

THE HONOR BOUND WOLF

"I'll go first," Sinfjotli volunteered. "The story of my life…well, it began many years before I was born. My parents were Sigmund and Signy. They were twins born to our grandfather, Völsung, and his wife, Hljod, and they also had nine younger brothers. In time, all of Völsung's children distinguished themselves in battle, but none more so than my parents. Thanks to his children's efforts, Völsung's kingdom of Hunaland doubled in size."

Sinfjotli paused and took a deep drink from his drinking horn. "One day, Siggeir, King of Gautland, visited and asked Völsung for his daughter's hand in marriage. Everyone called him 'Siggeir the Beast.' They say his mother was a she-wolf who was so besotted with his father that she took on the guise of a human just to become his bride. He was one truly demented individual. As a lad, he took sick pleasure in maiming animals and the helpless and watching the life fade from their eyes. And in battle, he was a true sword demon. He couldn't care less for the lives of his subordinates or others and would do whatever it took to achieve victory.

"He was my father's first and greatest enemy. But at that time, he had been a friend and ally of my grandfather. Siggeir had fought alongside Völsung in many battles and helped him expand the borders of his kingdom from the Rhine to the Neman River. In gratitude, my grandfather agreed to let Siggeir marry his daughter Signy. Mother disapproved of the marriage, knowing he was a treacherous and murderous king, but she reluctantly did as her father commanded. Although the marriage would prove stormy and later bloody, the wedding feast hosted at Völsung Castle was one for the ages. Mead and meat flowed plentifully. My father once told me that the wedding feast at Völsung Castle lasted five straight days, and the celebrations continued even after the marriage had been consummated!

"That evening, while everyone sat near flaming hearths drinking themselves stupid, a mysterious guest arrived. The tall, barefooted stranger wore a hooded, mottled cape with linen breeches tied around his legs. Wordless and without welcome, the old man walked toward Barnstock, our family's ancestral tree. He drew a magnificent sword from his cloak, held it high for all to see, and thrust the blade hilt deep into the tree trunk. The tall stranger placed the scabbard next to the trunk and announced, 'Whosoever can draw this sword from the trunk shall have it for his own, and he shall never find a better sword in all the world.'

"With that, the mysterious old man left the hall, leaving the guests captivated by the sword and wishing to try their luck at dislodging the blade from Barnstock. Siggeir, our grandfather, nine uncles, and everyone else tried removing it, to no avail. But when it was Sigmund's turn, he easily pulled it from the tree. When Völsung decided they should put it back in the trunk a second time, just to be certain that only Sigmund could remove it. It was as if the sword itself yearned to be his. He held it high for all to see, and everyone in the hall roared with approval...all except Siggeir. He was smitten with envy and desire for the sword and offered three times the sword's value. But Sigmund refused. 'You heard what the old man said,' Sigmund told him. 'Only he who is worthy may draw this sword. You tried and failed five times to draw it. That must mean you're unworthy.' Siggeir, offended that Sigmund had brazenly denied him a gift on his wedding day, returned home to Gautland with Signy the next day, plotting revenge.

"Three months later, Siggeir invited our grandfather and all his sons to a feast at his castle in Gautland. My mother sent messages warning her father that it was a trap, but Völsung treated it like a challenge. He wasn't the type to walk away from a fight, no matter the odds stacked against him. And so Völsung arrived with his sons and forces and died fighting in Siggeir's ambush. My father and his nine brothers were captured alive, but Gram was nowhere to be found. Sigmund had been the only one to take Signy's warning seriously and had hidden the blade before the battle. Enraged, Siggeir was about to execute them all then and there when my mother pleaded with her husband to spare her brothers. Siggeir agreed to show mercy...in his own sick way. He cut down a tall tree, laid the trunk over our father's and uncles' legs like a bilbo, and left them in the castle's courtyard. Then he had his mother, a woods witch and skinchanger, shapeshift into a wolf and devour one brother each night. My mother tried in vain to save her brothers, but the log was too heavy. One by one, our uncles were devoured until only our father remained. Desperate, my mother ordered a loyal servant to smear honey all over her brother's face and inside his mouth and deliver a message to keep his mouth open when the time came. That night, when the wolf arrived, she licked the honey from Sigmund's face instead of biting him. As my mother predicted, the she-wolf stuck her tongue inside Sigmund's mouth, at which point he bit down hard and refused to let go. The wolf jerked back in pain, pulling so hard that she split the log in half. Freed at last from his stocks, Sigmund ripped her tongue off from the back of the beast's throat and crushed its teeth into jagged, useless pieces, killing her. He then retrieved Gram from where he'd stashed it before Siggeir's ambush and fled into the deep woods of the Tiveden Forest, where he vowed he would not leave Gautland until he had avenged his father and brothers."

Sinfjotli sighed. "Unfortunately, it would be many years before justice could be served. When Siggeir discovered his mother's corpse the next morning, he knew Sigmund would one day come for him. He strengthened his castle's defenses and refused to leave the fortress unless at least twenty men guarded him. He sent hunting parties led by his best general to scour his entire kingdom, searching for Sigmund.

"He also kept a close eye on my mother, Signy. He wouldn't even sleep in the same room as her without a dozen men standing watch, fearing she might slash his throat. My mother wore the mask of a meek, subservient wife for many years. She endured his beatings and sexual abuses, kept her mouth shut when Siggeir boasted at feasts about how he had killed her father and brothers, and reluctantly bore him two sons. At the same time, she secretly sent aid to Sigmund as he recovered from his wounds and remained on the run from Siggeir's persistent hunting parties.

"How awful," Nanna gasped.

"It gets worse," Sinfjotli warned. "My childhood was filled with hate. Growing up, my mother would tell me all about how Siggeir had betrayed and murdered my grandfather and uncles, and I came to believe it was my sole purpose in life to punish him for his sins. She made me undergo many brutal trials to test my resolve and harden me. And when she decided I was ready, she sent me to live with my father when I was eleven. Neither of us knew the truth about my parentage at the time. But he took a liking to me all the same. After I arrived in his secret hideout, he handed me the flour sack with a venomous snake hidden inside and told me to make bread with whatever was inside the flour sack like he had done with my older brothers, Ragr and Rekkr. When he returned with firewood that evening, I reported that something was slithering in the sack, but I pounded it and kneaded it into the bread dough.

"My father was pleased and announced that I showed promise. However, he claimed I was still too young to exact revenge against King Siggeir. So, to harden and train me, we spent four years roaming through the wilderness and waging guerilla warfare against Siggeir's men. I even became a skinchanger to ensure that Siggeir could not escape justice when the time came.

"When the day of reckoning arrived, we stealthily entered the palace. Since everyone thought I was Siggeir's son, nobody questioned me when I entered the castle armed alongside a man that I claimed was my teacher. We met up with my mother in an outer room and started discussing how best to deal with Siggeir. But our plans came undone when her youngest children, Aurora and Hansel, walked in on us.

"Since my parents were twins and looked very similar, ten-year-old Hansel deduced that this was his uncle Sigmund and the man his father had been hunting. He cried out, warning the guards that his father's arch-enemy had infiltrated the castle. My mother reprimanded them, gave them one of her rings to play with, and told them to leave. Then she turned to my father and ordered him to kill them both. But my father refused. He still felt guilt-ridden about executing my older-brothers Ragr and Rekkr at Mother's behest years prior and refused to kill any more of his sister's children. But I had no such compunction and slew them myself.

"Unfortunately, the damage had been done. The guards heard Hansel's cries and raised the alarm. Since our cover was blown, we were forced to readjust our strategy to catch Siggeir off guard. When we settled on a plan, my father entrusted my mother with Gram and urged her to leave before the guards arrived.

"Afterward, we fought and hacked our way into Siggeir's main hall, dragging Aurora and Hansel's corpses behind us. We entered the great hall and threw their corpses at the feet of my stepfather. Furious, he ordered his men to capture us alive. We put up a good fight, but we were outnumbered and eventually overwhelmed.

"Once they subdued us, Siggeir's advisors urged him to execute us immediately. But when I told Siggeir I was the one who had murdered his remaining children, he vowed to subject us to the slowest death possible. The next morning, he had me and Father bound and entombed alive inside a large stone mound. That night, Siggeir held a massive celebration, certain that he was finally rid of the Volsungs. Little did he know that he had played right into our plan. Our entire strategy revolved around tricking Siggeir into lowering his guard and catching him when he was most vulnerable."

"So, how did you escape the grave mound?" Baldur interrupted.

"It was thanks to Gram," Sinfjotli explained. "My mother had smuggled the sword into the grave mound inside a bundle of straw and pork before the barrow was sealed off. Siggeir allowed her to do it, thinking prolonging our torture with some nourishment would be ideal. My father used the sword to cut through our bonds. Then I turned into a wolf, dug our way out of the barrow, and we reunited with my mother in the woods to set the last step of our plan in motion.

"We hued many trees with Gram and laid the logs around the castle. We blocked off all the exits except one and set fire to his fortress while everyone celebrated our deaths inside. My mother and I took our positions at the only remaining door and cut down everyone who tried to escape. Meanwhile, my father fought and slew Siggeir in a final duel, finally avenging his father and brothers after thirty years.

"Afterward, my mother revealed the soul-shattering truth. I wasn't Siggeir's biological son, but Sigmund's. Because she had ordered the deaths of her own children, she returned to the burning palace to die alongside her hated husband. I nearly committed suicide that night out of shock and despair, but my father stopped me and convinced me to come with him.

"Afterward, we returned home to Hunaland, where we had to drive out the king who had set himself as ruler and punish the other vassals who had carved up our kingdom in the years since Völsung's death. It took us less than a year to reestablish complete control over Hunaland. Sigmund then married a noblewoman named Borghild, and she bore him two sons: Helgi and Hámundr."

Sinfjotli smiled. "I came to love my half-brothers. They were both natural protégés, especially Helgi. He fought many wars and won his own kingdom at only fifteen years old. Helgi later fell in love with a beautiful princess named Sigrún following a bloody battle at Logafjöll. But her father, King Högne of Östergötland, had already promised her hand in marriage to Hothbrodd, the son of King Granmar of Södermanland. Neither was willing to let Helgi marry her, which ultimately led to war. I fought alongside him in the epic Battle of Frekastein, where we clashed against King Högne, King Granmar, and all their allies."

Sinfjotli shuddered. "That was the single bloodiest battle of my entire life. The battlefield was a swamp of steel, arrows, and gore. On that day, over one hundred thousand men viciously fought. Ultimately, only Helgi, Sigrún, her younger brother Dagr, and I survived. Afterward, our father hoisted that grand and fateful feast during which Sigurd claims Helgi's mother poisoned me to avenge her brother, whom I had killed in a duel. And then I woke up here."

"My goodness, you've lived quite a checkered life, Sinfjotli," Baldur remarked. "Well, Sigurd, it's your turn. Won't you tell us your life story?"

"Of course," Sigurd nodded. "But before that, there is something I'd like to know." He turned to Sinfjotli. "How exactly did you become a skinchanger? You never mentioned that detail."

Sinfjotli winced. He touched the scars on his neck and shoulder. "It was because of wolf skins."

Sigurd arched an eyebrow. "Wolf skins?"

"When I was thirteen, Father and I came across a cabin in the forest," Sinfjotli explained. "Two bandits were sleeping inside with wolf skins hanging over them. Father and I took the pelts, put them on, and they turned us into wolves. We were then struck with a sudden blood rage and ran into the forest. We spent eleven days rampaging through the forest, killing many animals and men. On the last day, Father attacked me and tore out my windpipe, nearly killing me. I have no idea how I survived that horrific attack. But when the sun set on the eleventh day, we were able to remove the pelts and turned back into humans. We burned the pelts, but the experience had turned us into skinchangers able to transform at will."

"So our father was a skinchanger, too?" Sigurd asked.

"Yes, but he detested the power he had gained. He was horrified that he had almost killed me and swore he would never use the power again. As far as I know, he kept his vow. His new physiology made him stronger than the average man and enhanced his senses, but he never transformed into a wolf again."

"I don't blame him," Sigurd muttered. He glanced around the table and noticed Baldur and Nanna were giving Sinfjotli curious, suspicious looks. But Sigurd couldn't fathom why.

After a moment, Baldur sighed and took a long sip of mead. "Well, Sigurd, I believe it's your turn."

CHAPTER EIGHT

THE IRON SHIELD-MAIDEN AND THE LUSTFUL KING

"Like you, Sinfjotli, the story of my life began many years before I was born," Sigurd began. "It started right after you died. After Borghild was banished from Hunaland for poisoning you, our father Sigmund ruled over his kingdom with the bitter resignation of a man with nothing left to lose. Even his other sons, our half-brothers Helgi and Hámundr, could not bring him much joy. And things worsened when Helgi died under mysterious circumstances, leaving Hámundr as the heir apparent."

"Wait, what happened to Helgi?" Sinfjotli interrupted.

Sigurd shrugged. "I have no idea. There were so many rumors and speculations by the time I was born over how Helgi died that the circumstances of his death have remained a mystery to this day. Only a handful of people, including our father and half-brother, Hámundr, knew the truth. But they kept it secret, probably to preserve Helgi's reputation and avoid a scandal."

"Anyway," Sigurd continued, "although Hámundr was the heir and had it in him to become a promising king like our father and forebears, many of Sigmund's advisors urged him to take a new wife to secure the succession of the throne. Helgi's sudden death had been a grim reminder that any man could die at any time, even healthy and mighty warriors like Helgi. Should anything happen to Sigmund and his last living son, who would follow them as the next ruler?

"In hindsight, their fears were well founded. But Sigmund proved surprisingly reluctant to take a new wife. Although he was very handsome and many comely women still vied for his attention, he was an old man close to sixty years. Borghild's betrayal had hardened him, making him stern and untrusting. Although he was charming, courteous, and treated women as equally as men, he viewed the many noblewomen vying for his affections as little more than vipers seeking to poison his last son to see their children put on the throne. Thus, he spent the remainder of his reign grooming Hámundr and ruling with the bitter resignation of a man with nothing to lose. Meanwhile, his council spent years of his reign silently praying that nothing happened to him or Hámundr, fearing a succession crisis may break out.

"But everything changed when Sigmund embarked on a fateful tour of his kingdom. While traveling, he stopped to pay a visit to his old ally, King Eylimi, who ruled over a client kingdom on the borders of Hunaland. And it was there where he fell in love with Eylimi's daughter Hjordis."

"Eylimi?" Sinfjotli interrupted. "I faintly recall someone by that name. I believe he was one of our first allies to rally to us when Father and I returned to retake power in Hunaland."

"That's right," Sigurd affirmed. "And after the throne of Hunaland was secure, our father rewarded Eylimi with the right to set up a client kingdom on the outskirts of Hunaland, trusting him to defend the kingdom from invasion."

"He granted many of our closest allies such a right." Sinfjotli pointed out, sounding unimpressed. "There were many client kingdoms on the borders of Hunaland, even when Helgi and I were still alive. Helgi himself governed his client kingdom on the frontier of the kingdom. Your grandfather may have been a loyal vassal, Sigurd, but I don't recall him accomplishing many great deeds."

"My grandfather's life wasn't particularly remarkable," Sigurd admitted. "But as for my mother...ah... now her life was the stuff of legends. In the fullness of her life, my mother, Hjordis, became a wise and beautiful queen and the love of Sigmund's life. But she was also a tomboy, a free, adventurous spirit who could never be tied down by the restrictions of her gender. And she proved to be quite a rebellious princess in her youth. Rather than take on sewing, play with dolls, or live the life of a typical courteous princess, Hjordis preferred to spend her time with boys. She proved to be as strong as them and excelled in their activities at a young age. By the age of ten, she had learned archery. At eleven, she mastered horse riding. At thirteen, she mastered swordsmanship at an age when most boys are still learning the basics of blocking and parrying from older, more seasoned warriors.

"My grandfather Eylimi accepted he could do nothing to rein her in. If he tried to take her sword or lock her in her room, she would just run away and find more mischief. Once, he confiscated her sword, locked her in her room, and refused to let her leave until she had taken up needlework and sewn a quilt like the other girls. The next day, he discovered she had escaped by trading clothes with a faithful washerwoman and walked out the front gate with her sword hidden within a laundry basket. Three days later, she returned riding a horse and pulling a chain gang of bandits, scoundrels, and ruffians. She announced that these were the bandits that had been raiding her father's lands for years, and after an entire day of fighting, she defeated them all. She had even slain their leader, Harmund the Black, a cruel man almost seven feet tall who claimed to be the son of a giantess from Jotunheim. He had been feared as one of the fiercest warriors of his day and a bitter enemy of my grandfather Eylimi. Yet Hjordis nevertheless triumphed over him in single combat.

"With this show of skill and fortitude, Eylimi accepted he could do nothing to reign in his daughter's restless spirit. Moreover, he couldn't threaten to disown her because her younger brother, Grípir, had a pious, reclusive, and bookish nature and would make a poor leader if made king. So, whether Eylimi liked it or not, Hjordis was his heir. Reluctantly, he invited the finest tutors and swordsmen to teach her all they knew to keep her out of trouble.

"By the time she was fifteen, she had become a master swordswoman and had mastered every form of combat known at the time. She later taught me everything she knew, every skill she possessed, and made me into the skilled warrior I am today.

"But even this wasn't enough to satiate her restless spirit. When she became a woman at sixteen, Hjordis felt the call of adventure. She cut her hair short and served incognito in her father Eylimi's army as they raided foreign shores. She dressed like a man and fought, killed, and pillaged under the alias Alfhild. She was so proficient at fighting that her comrades did not realize they were serving alongside a woman until they spied her bathing naked in a river one day.

"Still, by then, her father's warriors had grown to love her as a comrade and respected her skill at arms and valor enough to overlook her sex. She drank with them, ate with them, sailed the seas with them, gambled with them, wagering coin and sometimes clothing, raided with them, and fought alongside them.

"The plunder she and her comrades accumulated brought enormous wealth and prosperity to Eylimi's kingdom. At their zenith, they amassed so much food and spoils of war that no one in the kingdom needed to farm for an entire year.

"Eventually, she grew tired of her adventures and retired home at the age of twenty-six to finally live the quiet life of a princess. She spent her time reading the memoirs of past generals and writing about her own exploits. She started sewing and embroidering like other women and was considered a beautiful, good-mannered, but very strong-willed woman."

"Unfortunately, that's when the *real* trouble started." Sigurd sneered. "One day, a king named Lyngvi visited my grandfather's kingdom and became smitten with my mother. When Lyngvi asked Eylimi for his daughter's hand in marriage, my grandfather told him he'd have to address the matter directly with her. Despite being her father and the king, he understood by now he could not force her into anything she did not want.

"Moreover, she swore to Freyja that she would only marry a warrior who could best her in combat. In the past, those who tried were defeated and so impressed by her martial prowess that they never tried again. But Lyngvi refused to back down.

"Lyngvi tried and unsurprisingly failed to best Hjordis in combat. Still, Lyngvi refused to concede, and the besotted king kept wooing Hjordis. But that damn simpleton never understood her true nature. My mother was not some princess to be cajoled with pretty words, gifts, and grand promises, nor could she be bought and sold like a broodmare. To her, Lyngvi was a failure of a man who'd had everything handed to him, coasted by on his familial prestige, and would rather hide behind the strength of his army than fight himself. He had already proven what kind of man he was through combat, and she rejected his every advance.

"When wooing Hjordis proved fruitless, Lyngvi began courting her father. He figured that if he could convince Eylimi to give Hjordis an ultimatum threatening to disown her, she would have no choice but to marry him. Lyngvi spent months tempting Eylimi with promises of riches, power, and the vast empire they would rule if they joined their houses. After a year, it seemed like Eylimi was on the verge of agreeing when my father unexpectedly arrived.

"As I mentioned earlier, he had only come to pay a courtesy call and renew his old friendship with Eylimi. But when Sigmund and Hjordis saw each other, it was love at first sight. Despite being three times older than her, Hjordis fell in love with the grizzled warrior king. He had lost everything he had ever known as a youth and worked hard to regain it threefold, carving out a kingdom twice the size his father Völsung had at the height of his reign. Moreover, Sigmund was a legendary warrior whose honor was without question. To many, Sigmund was a man who had earned his right to be called a king through right and deed. To Hjordis, she had finally found a man whom she could call her equal.

"Sigmund and Hjordis spent the entire day together in deep conversation, each recounting their many deeds and adventures well into the night. The whole time, Lyngvi watched jealously from the shadows.

"That night at the feast, Sigmund asked Eylimi for Hjordis's hand in marriage, and Lyngvi objected, pointing out that he had been a suitor in waiting for a year. Unwilling to risk offending either king, Eylimi announced that Hjordis should decide on the matter herself. When asked whom she would marry, she responded, 'Meet me in the courtyard at dawn.'

"The following day, the three kings awoke to find Hjordis dressed in full battle armor, brandishing her sword, Lady Misery. She announced she would marry whichever king bested her in combat.

"Lyngvi was the first to take up the challenge...and lose. Hjordis disarmed and knocked the overconfident king on his back in just three moves, humiliating him for everyone to see.

"When Sigmund stepped forward, he unfastened Gram from his belt, handed it to a servant, and asked for a new sword, claiming it wouldn't be a fair fight if he used Gram. The duel that followed was a sight to behold. My mother was a master swordswoman, but Sigmund proved her equal and matched her blow for blow. For nearly an hour, the two fought, whirling and slashing around. My uncle Grípir told me their duel seemed more like a dance than a fight.

"Eventually, Lady Misery faltered, and Sigmund disarmed Hjordis and knocked her to the ground. As Hjordis lay defeated, her back having touched the ground during combat for the first time, Sigmund held out his hand. 'May

I have your hand, my lady?' he asked. 'Yes,' Hjordis accepted, smiling. The two clasped hands, and as soon as she was back on her feet, Hjordis pulled Sigmund in for a passionate kiss for all to see. 'King Sigmund may be very old,' Hjordis announced. 'But he is the most famous of all kings and the greatest warrior I have ever faced. I choose him.'

"Everyone in the assembly roared with approval...save Lyngvi. Not only had he lost the chance to marry Hjordis to a man twice his age, but he had also been publicly beaten by a woman. Thus, the jilted suitor invaded Hunaland a year later, intent on destroying the Volsungs once and for all.

"Although Sigmund commanded a mighty army, Lyngvi had invaded without warning, and Sigmund was forced to rely on the limited forces he could muster up to meet him. Lyngvi had Sigmund outnumbered three to one, but Sigmund and his forces fought valiantly and exacted devastating losses. But the tide began turning. It seemed like Sigmund was on the verge of winning when the unthinkable happened. Somehow, Gram shattered amid the battle."

"Impossible!" Sinfjotli exclaimed. "Gram can cut through anything. How could it have shattered?"

"I've wondered the same thing for years," Sigurd admitted. "I never learned how exactly it happened. But the result was devastating. Without Gram, our father was helpless. He, my grandfather Eylimi, and all their men fell in battle against the invaders."

Sigurd drew Gram and stared idly at the blade. "After the battle, my mother walked across the battlefield until she found her dying husband and cradled his body. She could never forget my father's final moments. He had been stabbed multiple times. His lungs were filling up with blood, and he could barely breathe. Despite that, he endured the pain just so he could speak to her one final time. 'Odin no longer wants me to wield this sword,' he told her, looking at the broken pieces beside him. He handed her Gram's broken hilt, placed a hand on her stomach, and said: 'You are carrying our son...Sigurd.

And this sword is meant for him. It will be called Gram and will serve him well.'

"My mother cradled Sigmund's body until he died. Then she collected the broken shards and escaped into the woods with a faithful bondwoman with whom she exchanged clothing to hide her identity. Normally, my mother would have cut a bloody path to Lyngvi to avenge her husband's death. But for the first and only time in her life, she chose not to fight. She was fighting for two lives now and could not risk her unborn child's life in a meaningless and suicidal last stand.

"Together with her brother Grípir, her closest friends, and some servants, my mother fled Hunaland. As they fled through the forest, they encountered a large troop of raiders who had observed the carnage from their ships and noticed them fleeing into the woods. They captured them and brought them to their leader, Alf, King Hjalprek's son and Denmark's future king. When he saw my mother's radiant beauty, which stood out from the rest of the women, he deduced that she was too beautiful to be a mere bondswoman and demanded to know who she was. Upon hearing her story and Sigmund's last wish, Alf offered to marry Hjordis and care for her unborn child as his own. The surviving women were also treated honorably with all the respect afforded to wives, even though some chose not to marry Alf's men."

"That was how my mother married into the House of Yngling, the oldest and most powerful Scandinavian dynasty." Sigurd grimaced. "Unfortunately, the people of our homeland suffered a dreadful fate at Lyngvi's hands because of it. After defeating my father and grandfather in battle, Lyngvi and his forces scoured Hunaland, searching for Hjordis. After three days of looting and pillaging the countryside, he invaded and sacked King Eylimi's kingdom. He wrongly believed Hjordis had fled to her family's kingdom after the battle and was still hell-bent on finding her. My grandfather and his strongest warriors had died in the battle alongside Sigmund, so his people were helpless without their king and generals leading them. Lyngvi and his savage army spent seven days destroying the kingdom and slaughtering its inhabitants. The atrocities Lyngvi and his army committed were nightmarish and calamitous."

Sigurd scowled. "He had my grandfather's castle torn down brick by brick, stripping it of all its wealth. They looted villages, burned and salted crops out of spite, and set ablaze every building they passed. Every male citizen was put to death, regardless of age. The few nobles who hadn't partaken in Sigmund's final battle or refused to resist the invaders were tortured until they revealed where they'd hidden their wealth. Every woman that survived the invasion was raped repeatedly, even girls as young as ten. All the children and women who survived the sack were taken into slavery, and many were kept as thralls and concubines."

"The worst atrocities were committed by Lyngvi's nephews, the dreaded Sons of Hunding." Sigurd bared his teeth. Even Baldur's aura could not immediately quench the fury his felt as he thought about those vicious whoresons. "They were a monstrous pack of sadistic murderers and rapists who brought ruin and death wherever they went. Those seething rabid dogs attacked half a dozen towns and villages and burned them all to the ground! They left naught but ash and death in their wake. Mercy was a foreign concept to them, and they took great pleasure in tormenting their victims and desecrating their bodies. The few captives they kept alive from their raids were allowed to die only after being subjected to prolonged, agonizing torment. Rumor has it the Sons of Hunding competed to see who could keep their captives alive the longest while dismembering them. They also competed to see who could devise the most creative and sadistic way to kill their victims. I heard one horrific tale story where those vile demons ripped a dozen babies from their mothers' arms, impaled them upon spears, and then laughed as they violated the wailing mothers. In another, they dragged all the men and women from their homes, stripped them naked, set their beards and hair on fire, and watched them writhe in agony as they burned to death. And in an even more horrifying tale, they dragged all the citizens into a town they had captured, separated the children from their parents, locked them inside a barn, covered it with straw, pitch, and oil, and then set it alight. They forced the parents to watch and listen as their children burned alive before putting them to the sword.

"The men who served under them were cut from the same cloth, and they followed the Sons of Hunding's every command and joined them in their dark perversions. King Lyngvi did nothing to stop the atrocities, and he joined in the sadistic revelry, raping so many women that he earned the infamous moniker 'Lyngvi the Lusty.' I heard of one dark tale in which he entertained himself during a feast in my grandfather's ruined castle by watching prisoners get slowly cut to pieces and then boiled in oil.

"But that was just a dark prelude for what came next!" Sigurd gnashed his teeth. "King Lyngvi never realized that my mother had fled to Denmark and married into House Yngling. He concluded she'd died and flew into a black rage. The woman he lusted after and the reason his brother and so many of his men had died was now lost. Most sane men would have conceded and moved on. But King Lyngvi was not like other men. He considered the loss of Hjordis a stinging defeat that tasted like bile in his mouth. Instead, King Lyngvi chose a truly despicable act to abate his wrath and grief. Without warning or just cause, he once again invaded Sigmund's kingdom of Hunaland.

"Never has a village, city, or kingdom in the history of the Norse been subject to as long or brutal an invasion as the ancestral kingdom of the Volsungs. Every village and town Lyngvi encountered as he made his way inland was plundered and razed to the ground. Surrender did not save the inhabitants; many drowned in rivers trying to swim away from the carnage. My people were given no quarter because Lyngvi and his army had only bloodlust and malice in their hearts. When Lyngvi and his bloodthirsty army arrived at Völsung City, the entire land for leagues around was reduced to barren, scorched wastelands. Under the command of our half-brother Hámundr and his sister-in-law Sigrún, the remaining warriors of Hunaland abandoned Völsung Castle and held out inside the famous city their king had built. They resisted Lyngvi's army for six grueling months and made the invaders pay for every inch with a pound of blood. When they were at the point of starvation and realized that they faced annihilation, they vowed to die fighting rather than shame the memory of their king. They killed their wives and children to spare them the fate that had befallen the inhabitants of King Eylimi's kingdom and then threw open their gates and charged at Lyngvi's army in a final blood charge. The fighting lasted an entire day, and Hámundr's warriors seemed to gain the upper hand. If they had been at full strength, they might have been able to defeat Lyngvi. But alas, months of siege and disease had weakened them, and they were inevitably overwhelmed and killed to a man. The last of the Volsungs died bravely with swords in their hands. But King Lyngvi did not show a single ounce of respect for the dead. He and his nephews desecrated their bodies and sacked the famous Völsung City until no stone remained intact. They seized all the wealth of the Volsungs Sigmund had accumulated over the years as their plunder. At the height of Sigmund's power as a king, his kingdom boasted a population of about twenty-five thousand inhabitants. Only about one thousand scattered survivors remained following Lyngvi's wrath. And all the wealth, knowledge, infrastructure, and cultural developments the Volsungs had created over the years was lost."

"How awful," Nanna gasped.

"Indeed," Sigurd affirmed. "But their crimes wouldn't go unpunished because it was around that time that I was born."

CHAPTER NINE

THE BROKEN SWORD REBORN

"As a child, I excelled at everything, especially combat." Sigurd boasted. "My mother taught me how to fight before I could walk. By the time I was seven years old, I was already a master swordsman and besting warriors three times my age. When I was eight, she trained me to swim while wearing a full suit of armor. When I turned nine, my stepfather sent me to be fostered by a refugee in his court: a dwarf named Regin, the son of Hreidmar."

"Hreidmar!" Litr exclaimed. The dwarf said something else in his guttural, incoherent language.

"He said, 'Hreidmar was a powerful dwarf king and one of the few dwarves from Svartalfheim who lived in Midgard with his sons,'" Hodr translated. "Litr also wants to know how Regin ended up in the service of a human king."

"I'll tell you that tale soon," Sigurd promised. "But the short version is that he fled to Denmark after a violent altercation in his family. He'd spent decades wandering until he entered the service of Alf's father, King Hjalprek, and quickly made himself a loyal asset since he was a skilled blacksmith and a jack of all trades. He showed the men of King Hjalprek's kingdom how to forge crucible steel and other valuable metals, build ships that could travel great distances and weather any storm, and maximize their farms' productivity every harvest. Through his teachings, the Kingdom of the Danes prospered, and house Yngling became the most powerful dynasty in Denmark."

"Well, he certainly sounds like a knowledgeable dwarf." Hodr grinned.

"Regin proved to be a sage teacher." Sigurd agreed. "He tutored me in languages, history, physics, and poetry. Regin taught me how to read and write runes, play music, bind wounds, cook and sew, and he showed me how to win at any sport or game. He also taught me about human anatomy and how the body works, more so to teach me how to kill rather than to heal. I often thought of him like a second father."

Sigurd grimaced. "But there was darkness in him. I could sense it, even back then. He always moaned about his lost inheritance, and he'd urge me to take on a fierce dragon named Fafnir and claim the gold hoard he guarded when I was old enough. One day, I got sick of Regin cajoling me to take on Fafnir and seize his wealth. I demanded to know why he knew so much about this treasured hoard and the mighty dragon that guarded it. And so, he told me his family history."

Sigurd paused and gulped a long swig from his drinking horn. "As Litr pointed out, Regin's father was a powerful and wealthy dwarf named Hreidmar. He had three sons: Fafnir, Ottr, and, of course, Regin. Fafnir, a born warrior, was the largest and fiercest of the brothers. Ottr was a capable fisher who could shapeshift into an otter and catch salmon at a nearby waterfall. And Regin became a blacksmith and skilled carpenter. Together, Hreidmar and his sons lived in the mountains in a house of glittering gold and flashing gems built by Regin.

"One day, the gods Odin, Loki, and Hoenir were traveling through Midgard exploring the world's hidden places when they came across Ottr's favorite fishing spot: a waterfall hidden amongst the mountains. They found him dozing on the riverbank as an otter with a half-eaten salmon by its feet. Wanting its pelt for himself, Loki killed the otter with a stone, and the three

Aesir skinned it together. Since the sun was setting, they picked up the otter and salmon and searched for a place to spend the night.

"As fate would have it, they stumbled upon Hreidmar's house just over the hills. The dwarf agreed to show them hospitality, but everything went wrong when Loki proudly displayed his catch, unaware that it was Hreidmar's son. Furious, Hreidmar summoned Regin and Fafnir, and together, they overpowered the Aesir, taking away Odin's spear and Loki's magic shoes. When the Aesir realized what they had done, Odin argued that the murder had been an accident since none of them knew the otter was a dwarf. They offered to pay a wergild for Ottr's death as compensation. Hreidmar agreed and demanded that they fill Ottr's skin with gold and then provide enough wealth to cover the slain dwarf's body completely.

"Since Loki caused Ottr's death, he was sent to collect the gold while Odin and his brother Hoenir remained behind as hostages. Knowing time was of the essence, Loki headed for Svartalfheim, where gold could always be found in vast quantities. When he told Ivaldi's sons about his predicament, they advised him to seek a dwarf named Andvari, who lived underneath a waterfall in Midgard and had the power to change himself into a pike at will. He would challenge wandering travelers to try catching him before he could swim away. If they succeeded, he would bequeath his entire fortune to them. But if they failed, they'd forfeit their valuables, further adding to his wealth. He had winkled many unfortunate travelers over the years and amassed a fortune large enough to cover the gods' debts.

"Loki returned to Midgard and found Andvari resting near the waterfall. Andvari turned into a pike when he saw the trickster and dashed away. Andvari was quick, but Loki was clever. He had already set up a net trap further downstream, and Andvari swam straight into it. Loki dragged Andvari out of the stream and marched back to his cave with his captive. Having been caught, Andvari had no choice but to hand over his wealth. But as Loki gathered the treasure, he noticed Andvari pocket something out of the corner of his eye. He demanded Andvari show him whatever it was. The dwarf reluctantly revealed the golden ring he had just pocketed. He explained it was called Andvaranaut, a magic ring that could help the wearer find wealth. Andvari told Loki to take the rest of the treasure but begged him to at least leave him the ring. As long as he had it, he could restore his lost fortune.

"But Loki was unmoved. He coldly reminded Andvari that the dwarf had promised him 'all of his wealth.' And so, he took the ring, leaving Andvari destitute. As Loki was leaving, Andvari cursed the treasure and magic ring to bring misfortune and destruction to whoever possessed it. But his curse fell upon uncaring ears, since Loki had no intention of keeping the hoard for himself. Loki shrugged his shoulders and went on his way.

"Loki returned to Hreidmar's home, showed Odin and Hoenir the hoard, and they went to work. They stuffed Ottr's skin with gold and buried it beneath a barrow of gold. When they were finished, they noticed one whisker sticking out, so Loki used the now-cursed ring to hide it. Satisfied with the results, Hreidmar returned Odin's spear and Loki's shoes and permitted them to leave. As they left, Loki turned and told the dwarves about the curse Andvari had placed upon the gold and the ring.

"Most sane people would have thought twice about keeping the gold after that. But Hreidmar and his sons didn't care. And what Loki and Andvari foretold came to pass because the dwarves were soon consumed by greed and became irrational.

"Ignoring Loki's warning, Hreidmar locked the entire fortune away in a vault, vowing to keep it under his watchful eye. Soon, Regin and Fafnir confronted their father and demanded part of the wealth. They argued that as Ottr's brothers, they were both entitled to a share of the ransom. But Hreidmar niggardly refused to part with a single coin. He told his sons that the treasure would be his until the day he died.

"But Fafnir didn't feel like waiting that long. The dwarf seized his father, slit his throat, and stole the key to his vault as Hreidmar bled to death. The murder horrified Regin. His instincts urged him to flee, but he didn't want to relinquish his share of the gold. Feeling either brave or mad, he suggested that the treasure be divided equally between them. But Fafnir refused. He had been seized by the same gold fever as their father and told his brother that he'd have to pry it away from his cold, dead hands. Fafnir then put on his magic helmet, Tarnhelm, which can take on the shape of someone's worst fears. Regin wasn't immune to its power, and he fled to Denmark, where he became a loyal servant to the House of Yngling.

"Meanwhile, Fafnir took the fortune to a cavern called Gnitaheath, where he jealously guarded the cursed hoard. Over the years, his greed turned him into a great dragon, and he would occasionally leave his cave to raze and plunder villages to amass even more wealth to slate his lust for gold."

"I told Regin I was sympathetic to his plight." Sigurd continued. "But slaying Fafnir would be no simple task. I'd need several things.

"First, I needed a horse to take me to Fafnir's lair. But no ordinary horse would do. It needed a mount that would be utterly fearless and loyal. And so, on Regin's advice, I went to visit my uncle Gleipnir, who lived as a hermit in the woods near my stepfather's castle and cared for King Alf's horses. Walking through the woods, I met a long-bearded old man I had never seen before. I told the grizzled stranger that I was going to my uncle's home to choose a horse and asked if he could come with me to help me decide. The old man agreed and suggested we drive the horses down to the river Busiltjörn. Whichever horse remained in the water would be my ideal mount. So we drove the horses down into the deeps of Busiltjörn. All the horses swam back to land except for a large, young, handsome gray horse that no one had ever mounted. After crossing the river, he raced around the opposite meadow and plunged back into the river again. He crossed again and returned to his former pasture with no signs of exhaustion. The gray-bearded old man told me this horse was a descendant of Sleipnir, and he promised he would be the best horse in Midgard. I turned around to thank him, but the old man had vanished. I named that horse Grani. As the old man promised, he was the best and fastest stallion in the Midgard. He was utterly fearless. He never got scared when I rode him into battle or when he heard the howling of beasts. I loved Grani like a brother, and he became my closest friend and companion.

"Next, I needed a suit of armor. Regin forged a suit made of crucible steel that put all other suits of armor in my stepfather's kingdom to shame. He warned me it wouldn't be enough to protect me from Fafnir, but it would still prove helpful to me in battle.

"Last, I needed a powerful sword to slay the mighty beast. However, this last step proved the hardest. Regin spent three days and nights forging me a sword. But when I tested it by striking the anvil, the blade shattered. Regin was not one to give up, so he started over. He labored five days and nights forging me a sword that was even better than the first. But this one also broke when it struck the anvil. As I stared at the broken pieces on the floor, an idea formed in my head. I asked my mother if she still had the fractured sword fragments that had belonged to my father, Sigmund. She admitted she did, but wouldn't just give them to me until I proved worthy of wielding my father's sword.

"And so, my mother put me through a grueling training regimen. Every day at dawn, we'd meet in the training yard, and she'd drill me in every form of combat she knew. I was already a master swordsman by then, but she didn't think that was adequate. She believed my father died in his final battle because he had grown too accustomed to Gram. And so when it shattered, he could not fight adequately. She wanted to ensure that the same couldn't happen to me. Therefore, I must first learn every skill she possessed, train with every type of weapon, and master every form of combat she knew before she considered giving me the broken pieces of Gram."

"Those days were tough. Sometimes we'd train with axes, spears, knives, and sometimes nothing but my bare hands. Every day at the crack of dawn, we'd meet in the training yard, and she'd drill me until I could hardly stand.

And at night, Regin and my friends would patch my wounds. Sometimes, she trained me hard enough for me to sweat blood. Her methods were brutal and relentless, but efficient. She made me the warrior I am today.

"After three years of training, Mother decided I was ready for a final test. We met in the training yard, and she promised that if I could defeat her just like my father had, she would give me the pieces of Gram. We fought, and I disarmed her and knocked her to the ground. It had taken my father an hour to defeat my mother. But it only took me twelve seconds to do the same. My mother was speechless. In her eyes, I had surpassed both her and my father. Overjoyed, she embraced me, told me how proud she was, and gave me the pieces. She then recounted my father's final moments and the name he had given the sword with his last breath. I promised her I wouldn't rest until I avenged my father and punished Lyngvi for his crimes against our people.

"I took the fragments to Regin and demanded that he forge a new sword from them. This time, he labored for ten days and nights until it was finished. He presented the finished blade and said: 'If this sword doesn't fit the bill, then I am no blacksmith.' When I tested it by striking the anvil, the blade cut clean through the heavy iron, its oak stand, and right through the floor. Then, to test its edge, I threw a tuft of wool into a river and held the blade downstream. The yarn was cut cleanly in two. Afterward, we went to a waterfall, and I waited in the plunge pool as Regin took a large bundle of logs upriver, dropped them in the water, and sent them tumbling down the waterfall at me. I chopped through each log as they fell. By the end, I had chopped almost thirty logs in half, but Gram hadn't suffered a single nick.

"I told Regin he'd done an outstanding job. He replied, 'I have done my part. Now, you must help me avenge my father's death by killing my brother Fafnir.' I told him I was a man of my word and would do as promised in due time. But before I slew Fafnir, I had to avenge the deaths of my own father, grandfather, and other countrymen."

CHAPTER TEN

A WRATHFUL STORM

"I approached my stepfather and asked him to lend me an army to crush Lyngvi," Sigurd recounted. "He agreed to supply me with all the men and ships I'd need. With his help, I assembled an army of my close friends, second sons, and other colorful characters eager for glory, plunder, adventure, and vengeance. Every one of them was disciplined, well-trained, and ruthless. My stepfather offered his most seasoned generals to help me lead the army, but I politely refused. I had my own candidates in mind to serve as my lieutenants."

Sigurd smiled. "The warriors I picked were my closest and most trusted friends. They were Birna Bloodtusk, Folan the Fletcher, and Vafi the Loon. They were the sons and a daughter of three women who had accompanied my mother when she fled Hunaland. We had all lost our fathers and other family members in Lyngvi's brutal invasion of Hunaland. We called ourselves 'the Orphans' and swore a blood oath that we would one day avenge our families and punish Lyngvi.

"They were each seasoned warriors in their own right. Folan was one of the finest archers in Denmark, second only to me. He could shoot a bird in flight down upon the wing and once shot an elk through the heart from over a thousand feet.

"And then there was Vafi." Sigurd's grin widened. "He was a fearsome, hulking warrior who could shatter an iron sword with a single swing of his axe. He touted himself as 'Vafi the Bear.' But my friends and I always called him 'Vafi the Loon' because his fearlessness went far beyond the pale of bravery, deep into the realm of suicidal madness. He'd earned the nickname when he was ten and accompanied me and my friends on an expedition into the forest. There, we discovered a bear sleeping in its den. Although I wanted to leave it be, Vafi rushed inside the cave and woke the sleeping beast with a hearty kick to the head. The bear slashed his face open, and I had to save him by crushing the bear with my bare hands. Vafi survived the attack without losing his left eye, but his face got permanently scarred. Yet he proudly displayed those scars as a badge of honor and proof of his courage.

"Finally, there was Birna. Her father was one of Sigmund's closest drengr, and her mother was my mother's loyal friend who fled with her to Denmark after Sigmund's final battle. She styled herself 'Birna Bloodtusk' after she famously killed a boar when she was thirteen with nothing but a knife. She was a better fighter and planner than most men and raiders, and she had a sound, patient mind. Birna always considered every variable before committing to a plan. Her strategies often emerged victorious, which was why I made her my second-in-command.

"Anyway, with my stepfather's backing, my friends and I amassed an army of over fifteen thousand warriors and a large fleet of dragon ships to sail us to Lyngvi's kingdom." Sigurd continued. "I captained the biggest and finest of the ships. Its prow was carved in the likeness of a dragon, and the sails were painted in ochre and blood-red so that everyone who saw it would know my purpose. With my fleet, we departed Denmark and sailed straight for Lyngvi's kingdom.

"Our fleet had a good passage at first. We had the sun by day, the moon by night, and a strong wind at our backs. But after several days of sailing east, everything went badly. We lost the wind first. There wasn't a single breeze for two days, and our ships could only move as far as we could row them. The wind finally returned around sunset on the third day. The men had never seen a more beautiful sunset and considered it a blessing. But I considered it an ill omen. The sky was blood red, and it painted the water the color of fresh gore. The wind began howling that night, and then the ocean turned on us."

"It was the fiercest storm I have ever seen. It was as if Thor and Njörd had unleashed their full wrath on us. The waves rose above our masts and washed over our decks with every rise and fall. Lightning crackled everywhere, and the downpour was so heavy that we could scarcely see what was before us. Raindrops the size of eggs washed over my skin so vigorously, it felt like I was standing in a flowing river rather than a thunderstorm. My men began losing heart and begged to turn back. But instead of reefing the sails, I ordered them hoisted higher. I had waited and trained my whole life for this invasion and wouldn't let a storm deter me.

"Perhaps I should have listened because my flagship soon separated from the rest of the fleet. The mast groaned as we plowed through the surging waves. The wind ripped at our sails, and the floorboards beneath my feet creaked and moaned as if the entire hull could split apart at any moment. Grani whinnied as the ship rocked back and forth, and it took every ounce of my strength to keep him from jumping overboard. The wind and waves soon pushed us dangerously close to the shoreline. If we hit a reef or a rocky seabed, our hull would splinter, and that would be the end.

"Then something miraculous happened. As we sailed past a promontory, a loud voice called out to us. It belonged to a lone man standing on the nearby cliffs. His voice was louder than a blast of thunder and could clearly be heard over all the wind, rain, and lightning. He shouted he had recently been marooned in a shipwreck and asked if I could lower my sails and take him aboard. I agreed, and the storm ceased as soon as he stepped aboard. Soon, the sun rose, the sea calmed, and a perfect amount of wind began pushing us.

The waves lapped gently against our hull, and the water was so clear and blue a man might never know that a storm had been raging mere hours earlier.

"The old man proved to be a sparkling conversationalist. He dressed in simple blue robes and had an eye patch over his left eye. He never gave me his name, but I sometimes think of him fondly. If not for him, I'm certain that we would have been dragged to Rán's icy depths that night. We had many long and insightful conversations about history and philosophy as my men rushed about making what repairs they could. And that afternoon, I spotted sails in the distance—it was my fleet, come back to rescue us."

"I held an emergency meeting with my friends and commanders to check the status of our fleet. Amazingly, no one had died or fallen overboard during the storm, but many of our ships had been badly damaged. The sails of Birna's boat had torn to shreds, and Folan's ship lost its mast after a lightning strike split it in half. Vafi's ship was so severely damaged that it had to be towed by three other longships. Thankfully, I had several shipwrights in my army whom Regin had trained. They claimed they could repair the ships within a day, but warned me they'd need an ample wood supply.

"Then the old man spoke up and told us about a nearby bay he had been sailing for before he got shipwrecked. He claimed it was where my ancestor Sigi first set foot in Midgard centuries ago. He also told me there were many trees there we could use to repair the damaged ships. I wasn't about to look a gift horse in the mouth, so we set sail for the bay.

"Along the way, the old man pulled me aside and asked where I was sailing with such a mighty fleet. I told him we planned to invade Hunaland to avenge my father, brother, and all our forefathers who had died at Lyngvi's hands. The old man told me my homeland, Hunaland, wasn't far from the bay we were sailing to. He suggested I visit my homeland while I still had the chance, as I might not get the opportunity again. He added that seeing the ruins with my own eyes would help me understand the full gravity of Lyngvi's crimes and steel my resolve for what needed to be done during the invasion.

"When we reached the bay, the old man walked into the forest and was never seen again. Afterward, I told my army to repair the ships while I journeyed inland to visit my homeland. I promised I would return within a day, mounted Grani, and traveled to the ruins of Hunaland. That trip proved...life-changing. I returned the next day, and we resumed sailing beneath clear blue skies and with strong winds at our backs.

"When we finally arrived in the Lands of Hunding, we got to work and made our intentions clear. We burned and plundered settlements and left scorched earth in our wake. People fleeing the destruction came to King Lyngvi, warning him that a great army was ravaging the land and that at its head was Sigurd, son of Sigmund.

"I can only imagine how terrified Lyngvi must have been then. After almost twenty years, a vengeful ghost from his past had come back to haunt him and bring down justice upon him for his countless crimes.

"Fearing for his life, Lyngvi gathered all his forces and marched against us with over sixty thousand men. He had us outnumbered four to one. He also positioned armies of prisoners and enslaved people from Hunaland as his front line, which proved an efficient yet horrific strategy that almost took the heart out of many of us. But we were battle-hardened and had justice on our side. Our armies clashed in a large clearing littered with trees. The battle was long, brutal, and bloody. Arrows and spears blackened the sky as we fought. Many men fell on both sides. But I was always in the center riding Grani, swinging my sword, and traveling up and down our front lines to prevent us from being encircled.

"After the battle had raged for some time, I decided I'd had enough. I advanced past my men and rode deep into the enemy's ranks. Grani and I blazed across the battlefield in a flash of gold as I cut down fearsome foes with one swing of Gram. I felled countless men and horses as I cut a bloody path through the army. By the time I reached the center of Lyngvi's army, I was covered in blood up to my shoulders. There, I encountered the Sons of Hunding along with all of Lyngvi's sons.

"To their credit, they were the strongest warriors I faced that day. The Sons of Hunding preyed upon the weak. But they weren't weak or craven, like most thugs. Most men in Lyngvi's army fled in terror before me, but Lyngvi's bloodthirsty nephews refused to back down. They didn't know the meaning of fear. They kept smiling as we fought, even after I shattered their weapons with Gram and left them defenseless. The Sons of Hunding laughed as they boasted about all the horrors they would inflict upon Denmark after they killed me." Sigurd's fingers coiled into a fist. "I made sure that each of them died without a smile on their face. I have killed many men on principle, but never have I wanted others to suffer as much as them! Even though I was in the middle of a fierce battle with enemies all around me, I took my sweet time dispatching the Sons of Hunding, making them understand what it is to wail and beg for your life. I made them all experience a small taste of all the pain and misery they had inflicted on others until their smiles vanished, and they died screaming in anguish. Then I turned my wroth onto the other terrified princes. I split Lyngvi's eldest son's head and body in one swift blow and cut down each of the remaining brothers.

"That was what won the day. After seeing their strongest soldiers and princes cut down by a single warrior, Lyngvi's army lost the will to fight and tried to flee. But there was no escape because, at that moment, Birna's army appeared from behind and crashed into Lyngvi's rear."

"Was this part of your plan?" Hodr inquired.

"Yes." Sigurd nodded. "I had already scouted the battlefield the night before the battle and familiarized myself with the terrain. I split my army in half, placed the other half under Birna, and had them discreetly move around Lyngvi's forces and attack from behind. My grand strategy worked perfectly. Trapped in a pincer movement between her fresh army and mine, Lyngvi's entire army was cut to pieces.

"By the end of the day, the field was red with blood. I had lost over two thousand men. But Lyngvi's entire army of sixty thousand had been annihilated. Lyngvi was captured alive by Birna's war party and delivered to me in chains. I had the lustful king tied to a tree stump and carved the blood eagle on his back, avenging my father, Hámundr, and all the people of Hunaland after twenty long years. Then we moved to Lyngvi's capital. We recovered all the treasure he had stolen from Hunaland and liberated all the slaves Lyngvi had taken from my grandfather's kingdom.

"We returned home to Denmark with great wealth and glory. My stepfather held a grand celebration in our honor. He hosted seven days of feasting, hawking, and hunting. During the festivities, Regin pulled me aside. He congratulated me on avenging my father's death. Then he said it was time to fulfill my vow and help him avenge his own father's death. I agreed, and we set out a month later to fulfill my destiny."

CHAPTER ELEVEN

THE DRAGON SLAYER

"Regin and I rode together for months to the rocky heath where Fafnir dwelled," Sigurd narrated. "Regin claimed that the land around Gnitaheath was once a beautiful, lush alpine forest where lush vegetation and fauna thrived. But after years of Fafnir blowing poisonous clouds everywhere, the land had been reduced to great tracts of barren wastelands with dead ash-white trees protruding from the ground like twisted bones.

"We dismounted at a nearby stream and found a well-worn trail where the dragon usually traveled from his cave to drink water. Regin warned me that slaying Fafnir would be no simple task and that the dragon could not be slain conventionally. Whenever Fafnir bestirred himself from his pile of treasure to drink water from a nearby stream or hunt for food, he would always blow a cloud of poison into his path, ensuring he could not be ambushed. This gas was also flammable, so if anyone ventured too close, he'd ignite the poisonous cloud and incinerate the trespassers in a fiery explosion. Only subterfuge could defeat him. Regin instructed me to dig a trench within the trail and hide inside it. Then I could wait for Fafnir to approach and stab him from beneath as he made his way for water. Regin wished me luck and ran away.

"As I started digging the trench, I was approached by a wandering old man with a long beard who asked what I was doing. After hearing my plan, the

93

graybeard cautioned that one trench wouldn't be enough. He warned me that after I stabbed Fafnir, the dragon would bleed so much that his blood would flood the entire valley. I would surely drown in the great deluge if I didn't dig several more trenches, one to hide in and others to channel the dragon's blood so I wouldn't drown. I thanked him, and the stranger went on his way.

"I finished digging the trenches by sunset and waited inside the pit until I fell asleep. I awoke the following day when I felt the earth shake. The birds had stopped singing, and I could hear trees splintering in the distance. I realized Fafnir had finally arrived. I waited until the beast passed above me and plunged my sword upward through the dragon's heart.

"Fafnir's death throes were a sight to behold. As he writhed in agony, his tail smashed the rocks and trees around him to sand and splinters. He tried to take to the sky once, but his body lacked the strength to carry his weight, and he came crashing to the earth. His blood poured from the wound like a gushing river, painting the landscape crimson red and washing over me in a seething hot current. I would have drowned inside that hole if I hadn't dug the extra channels to redirect the blood.

"When the dragon's tremors weakened, I clamored out of the pit, covered head to toe in steaming hot dragon blood. As he lay dying, Fafnir demanded to know his killer. I told him my name, and with his last breath, the dragon warned me to stay away from his golden hoard and to beware his brother Regin.

"After that, Regin emerged from the heather he'd been hiding in. I remember he seemed... surprised when he saw me. And it wasn't because I was covered head to toe in dragon blood. He seemed shocked that I had survived but recomposed himself and congratulated me on my victory.

"I told him we could follow Fafnir's trail back to his lair and then split the treasure between us. Regin agreed, but first, he asked me to remove Fafnir's heart and cook it for him. And so, I cut out the dragon's heart and roasted it over a fire while Regin drank his brother's blood.

"Then something bizarre happened. As I cooked the heart on a spit roast, I pressed my thumb against the meat to check if it was cooked, and the juices burned my thumb. Without thinking, I thrust my thumb into my mouth. The moment my tongue tasted the dragon's blood, I gained the ability to communicate with birds. I overheard a pair of nuthatches speaking in a nearby tree. They were discussing Regin's plan to kill me. When they noticed I could understand them, the birds instructed me to kill Regin and take the gold for myself.

"I thought I was going mad. But when I glanced at Regin, I realized the nuthatches were right. By tasting the juices from Fafnir's heart, I also gained the ability to read the hearts of men. I read Regin's heart and realized that beneath his mask of polite concern, he planned from the beginning to kill me and take the gold for himself once he devoured his brother's heart. He'd schemed to have me drown in the deluge of Fafnir's blood so he could claim his brother's treasure for himself. But since I had survived, he planned to consume Fafnir's heart to gain the power needed to kill me.

Sigurd took a heavy breath. "I told myself my story wouldn't end there in that moribund valley. I drew Gram and cut off Regin's head in a single swing. Then, I consumed the entirety of Fafnir's heart, which caused my eyes to take on the golden appearance of a serpent's. Afterward, Grani and I followed Fafnir's trail back to his lair.

"I'll never forget how awestruck I was when I stepped inside that legendary cave. There were towering mountains of gold, silver, jewels, gemstones, enchanted items, and other treasures beyond price and count spread across the cavern. I attained my golden hauberk, trusty armor, and the infamous ring Andvaranaut. I even found Fafnir's Helmet of Terror and claimed it as my own. Sadly, I don't have it with me now. I can only assume I wasn't buried with it at my funeral. Anyway, I gathered Fafnir's treasure into two magical chests and secured them to Grani's saddle. And then we left Gnitaheath and I... I..."

"Is something wrong, Sigurd?" Nana asked after a period of silence.

Sigurd frowned. "I...I can't remember what happened next."

"Give it some time," Baldur suggested. "Parts of your brain must still be waking up. You'll remember it soon enough."

"I don't think it's that simple." Sigurd demurred. "I'm certain that one of the most important events of my life happened right after I slew Fafnir and took his treasure, but the memory isn't there. It's like there's a mist in my head that's preventing me from remembering anything."

Nanna and Baldur shared a look. Nanna rose from her seat and walked around the table to stand before Sigurd. She pressed her hand against Sigurd's forehead, closed her eyes, and murmured a spell.

Sigurd closed his eyes as a warmness raced throughout his head. His thoughts became murky and fluid, as if he had sunk beneath the surface of a dark river. He had no form or thought, but he could feel everything as if the river were a part of him, an extension of his consciousness. And somewhere in that river, he felt a foreign object he knew didn't belong there, like a massive boulder that disrupted the river's entire flow.

The next thing he knew, his eyes snapped open as Nanna stepped away.

"That's what I thought." Nanna sighed. "You're right, Sigurd. This isn't a simple case of amnesia or forgetfulness. It's magic. Someone placed a magic barrier in your mind."

Sigurd blinked. "Someone...erased my memories with magic?"

"Oh no, all of your memories are fully intact," Nanna assured. "But a select few are being locked away behind this barrier, much like water behind a dam. Hmm...I must say, the spell is exceptionally potent. Someone went to great lengths to make you forget *very* specific events."

"That isn't something any ordinary sorcerer can do," Hodr noted. "Whoever cast that spell must be a powerful practitioner of magic. Sigurd, can you think of anyone capable of such a feat?"

"I'm not sure," Sigurd mused. "I can think of a handful of people, including my uncle Grípir, who *might* be capable of doing something like this. But I can't fathom why any of them would want to erase my memory."

"Hmm... let's address that later," Baldur suggested. "Please continue your story, Sigurd. I'm curious about what else happened."

"Well, after... whatever happened during that gap in my memory, I remember traveling back home to Denmark. My mother, Uncle Grípir, and many of my closest friends had died fighting valiantly in a civil war against my stepfather's brother, Yngvi. And so I returned to attend their funeral. I wasn't the only one. Many great kings and lords from all over the continent traveled to Denmark to attend my mother's funeral and pay homage. I even met two famous princes named Gunnar and Hagen. They were the sons of Gjuki, the King of the Burgundians, who ruled the land of eternal mist. We became fast friends. When I showed them the gold I had taken from Fafnir's hoard, they invited me to visit their family's kingdom. But I declined. The recent civil war had ravaged Denmark. And as my stepfather's adopted son, it was my duty to help him restore order to the kingdom."

Sigurd scowled. "Unfortunately, I soon had a falling out with my stepfather after he remarried a noblewoman named Thora."

"Why did you disapprove of the marriage?" Nanna inquired. "Did you dislike her?"

Sigurd shook his head. "No, that wasn't it. Thora was a virtuous woman whom I admired. She had a good heart and was very compassionate. She hailed from one of the oldest noble families in Denmark. The match between her and Alf was necessary to bind the kingdom back together after the civil war had ravaged it. But the timing... gods, my mother had been dead for barely *two months* before my stepfather remarried! Even an animal would have mourned its mate longer than he did. Given how devastated Denmark was following the civil war and the urgent need to reunify the kingdom, I understand why he was so hasty in marrying Thora. But it felt like he'd spat upon my mother's memory by remarrying so soon. I never forgave him for that. So when Gunnar and Hagen returned to Denmark, seeking my aid in an ongoing war against their family's greatest enemies, I left with them and never returned to my childhood home.

"I helped Gunnar and Hagen win their war against their enemies and helped them win several other battles. Afterward, we swore an oath of brotherhood, and they renewed their offer to bring me to their family's kingdom. This time, I didn't refuse.

"My visit to their homeland proved to be a fateful one. I married their beautiful sister, Gudrun, and we had two children together. My daughter Svanhild, who was born with the same piercing snake eyes as me, and a son I named Sigmund after my father.

"My exploits didn't end there. Afterward, I wandered throughout the great world with Gunnar, Hagen, and Gudrun, having many adventures. Along the way, I even helped Gunnar marry a beautiful woman named Brynhild..."

Sigurd faltered. Something about what he just said resonated with him, especially the name "Brynhild." He felt a vague sadness in his chest, but he couldn't fathom why. Sigurd tried to keep telling his life story and his many adventures with Gudrun, Gunnar, and Hagen. But he stopped when he realized there were even more gaps in his memory.

"What's wrong Sigurd?" Baldur asked, breaking the silence. "Why did you stop?"

"I'm sorry, Baldur." Sigurd apologized. "I can only remember bits and pieces of the rest of my life. Parts of my brain must still be waking up. And my memory becomes frustratingly dimmer and foggier the closer I get to my death. That's the most vivid memory I have."

Sigurd winced and placed a hand on the hole in his chest. "I woke up in the middle of the night when I heard my wife screaming, and I discovered a sword had been driven through my chest. And my killer was Gudrun's youngest brother, Guttorm."

"Why would he murder you?" Hodr asked.

"I don't have a clue," Sigurd admitted. "But regardless of his motive, I know for a fact that Guttorm didn't live to celebrate my death. As he fled the room, I drew Gram from my bedside and hurled it at him, splitting the little bastard in half. Then everything faded into darkness. Next thing I knew, I woke up in the city and found Sinfjotli."

CHAPTER TWELVE

THE MAVERICK AESIR'S DESCENDANTS

"My word, those were some extraordinary stories!" Baldur clapped his hands. "Even when I was in Asgard, I don't think I ever met heroes who have lived such heroic and checkered lives as yours! Then again, I'd expect nothing less from Sigi's descendants!"

"So you knew our ancestor Sigi?" Sigurd asked.

"Of course," Hodr smiled. "He's our younger brother, a son of Odin and Frigga like us."

Sigurd blinked in surprise. "He was Frigga's son? I thought he was...?"

"A bastard Odin sired on some fetching mortal woman who caught his eye?" Nanna finished. She shook her head. "No. Sigi was a full-blooded Aesir like us."

"It's no surprise you assumed Sigi was a demigod," Hodr sighed. "Many kings and noble houses in Midgard claim descent from the All-Father to boost their prestige and glorify their past lineage. But they're all frauds! The number of humans who can authentically claim to be Odin's descendants can be counted with the fingers on one hand."

"How can you be so sure?" Sinfjotli asked. "Doesn't Odin often have children out of wedlock?"

"Our father is not a faithful consort," Hodr admitted. "He often cheats on our mother Frigga with giantesses and occasionally sires children with them. But our father never has these affairs out of lust or love. He sees these dalliances as a way to gain more knowledge and to further his schemes. If a child comes of it, so much the better. It's yet another addition to our family."

"Take our brother Bragi, for instance," Baldur suggested. "He was born from a liaison between our father and the giantess Gunnlǫð. It was a sordid affair, but he hadn't slept with her out of desire. It was to attain the precious mead of poetry she guarded. Her father, Suttungr, had locked her and the mead within a chamber inside Mount Hnitbjörg. Our father had to work for her uncle, Baugi, incognito for an entire summer before he could access the mountain. And he only seduced her to lower her guard so he could steal the mead from under her nose. That the affair also resulted in the birth of our brother, Bragi, was an afterthought. A bonus, if you will."

"I see," Sigurd muttered. He grasped what Hodr and Baldur were implying. Odin used sex and seduction as a means to an end. That was to be expected. The All-Father Odin was regarded as a wise but also mysterious and cunning deity among the Norse pantheon. His insatiable thirst for knowledge often led him to go to great lengths to attain it, even if it meant disregarding communal values such as justice, fairness, and respect for law and convention. He sacrificed one of his eyes to gain wisdom and drove his spear through his own side, and then hung himself from the World Tree for nine days and nights to learn the art of writing. It seemed sex and seduction were other convenient tools in his endless quest for knowledge and power. It made Sigurd sick to his stomach that the All-Father would treat women, even giantesses, as childbearing tools and a means to an end. But he clearly did so for purposes known only to him.

"Having said all that, our father would *never* sleep with a mortal woman," Hodr stressed. "He and our uncles Hoenir and Vé created humans from pieces of driftwood they found on a beach long ago. For him to desire a mortal woman would be like an artist falling in love with a painting he drew. It's utterly beneath him."

"You two should count yourselves fortunate," Baldur added. "The Volsung bloodline is one of the few in Midgard that can authentically trace its descent back to Odin, thanks to our brother Sigi."

"So he was a god, just like all of you?" Sinfjotli inferred.

"Yes, but he was also a renegade." Nanna frowned, wrinkling her nose. "Ugh, that man was the second biggest troublemaker in Asgard after Loki. His antics led to him losing his godly status and being banished to live as a human in Midgard."

"Really?" Sigurd muttered. "What was Sigi like? I've heard so little about my ancestor."

"I'm curious as well," Sinfjotli agreed. "Father always spoke of our ancestors with reverence. But even he knew next to nothing about Sigi."

"Oh, where do we even begin?" Nanna sighed.

"At the beginning, of course," Baldur laughed. "As we mentioned, our father, Odin, has many sons and daughters. But he only had four sons with our mother, Frigga. I was the eldest. My twin, Hodr, was the second eldest. Our brother Hermod, the messenger god, was third. And Sigi was the youngest."

"But he was also a troublemaker and a delinquent," Hodr added. "Despite being our flesh and blood, our brother was more well-known for his free spirit and unconventional ways. Our parents often joked that Baldur, Hermond, and I were so pleasant and well-natured because all of our recklessness, mischievousness, and insubordination were transferred straight to Sigi when we were born."

"In his youth, Sigi often worked with Loki to orchestrate many pranks," Baldur added. "Their antics would often get out of hand, and our parents would force him to perform immense acts of penance afterward."

"Those punishments did little to change his personality." Nanna sighed. "Sigi was extremely brash, confident, reckless, and self-willed. He was swift to anger and would retaliate for anything as simple as an insult to him or any of his subordinates, regardless of how small it might be."

"But he was also honorable, charitable, and extremely compassionate," Baldur added. "He treated men and women as equals. In his later years as a king, he would often travel around his kingdom and invite his subjects to come to speak to him. Everyone was welcome at these events regardless of their status of birth or gender. During these special events, Sigi encouraged them to speak freely and openly about their fears, concerns, and hopes. Afterward, he would vow to do everything within his power to ease their lives. And he always followed through on his promises."

"One time, a large group of peasants and thralls complained they had no land to till for themselves and humbly requested that the nobility donate some land," Hodr added. "When the proud nobles refused, Sigi found an altogether different solution. He traveled to a nearby lake and began digging drainage tunnels by himself. Within a month, he reclaimed over thirty-two square miles of land by draining the lake and then donated it to the exclusive use of the lower class."

"He was also a highly skilled warrior," Baldur added. "Sigi was a boisterous fellow, daring in every respect of the word. While in Asgard, he frequently challenged our brother Týr to duels to hone his skills, as the one-handed god of war was the only one who could best him in combat. He would also challenge Thor to wrestling and drinking contests, which he often lost, and go on many adventures with our older brother in Jotunheim. And he would often accompany Skadi on hunts to hone his hunting skills."

"He sounds like an extraordinary man," Sigurd remarked.

"Indeed, he was," Baldur agreed. "But it seems we've gotten ahead of ourselves. Let's return to the story at hand."

Baldur took a sip of his drink and then leaned back on his throne. "Sigi lived in Asgard as an immortal Aesir like us for many years. He was admittedly a minor god, but was always there in the background. Sigi made a name for himself as a great warrior in the Aesir-Vanir War. He witnessed the binding of Fenrir and spoke out against our family's shameful treatment of the wolf. He attended my funeral and continued living in Asgard long after the three of us were gone."

Baldur's smile faded. "But he didn't remain there in perpetuity. One day, he went hunting in Midgard with Skadi's servant Bredi, who was a member of the Einherjar. When the two hunters laid out their kills that evening, Sigi was flabbergasted to discover that Bredi amassed more skins and proven himself to be the better hunter. Furious at being outdone by a mere thrall, Sigi killed him and buried him in a snowdrift. He thought he covered his tracks well, but Skadi soon discovered the body. Because Sigi had kept quiet about what had happened, it was labeled murder. At his trial, Bredi provided damning testimony against him, as did several others who held grudges against him."

"Wait a second!" Sinfjotli interrupted. "How could Bredi have been at the trial? You said he was murdered and his body buried in snow. Since he died outside combat, shouldn't his soul have been sent here to Helheim?"

"Normally, that would be the case," Hodr admitted. "If someone dies an inglorious death, their soul is automatically sent to Helheim. If they were wicked in life, Hel claims them for herself. But if they lived a virtuous life, they become a denizen of our ship. However, death doesn't affect the Einherjar the same way. Once a warrior becomes a member of the Einherjar, their soul is bound to the halls of Valhalla, and they become exempt from the draconian rules of the afterlife. They can leave Asgard, accompany the Aesir on adventures to other realms, or slay each other in the endless battles that go on in those sacred halls. But regardless of how or where they die, their soul will always return to Valhalla."

"Coincidently, Sigi thought the same thing, Sinfjotli," Baldur admitted. "He claimed Bredi's presence at his trial was an affront and a sacrilege. He argued that Bredi had no right to be there as he had died an inglorious death outside combat. In his indignation, he further insulted other esteemed members of the Einherjar, claiming they had no right to even set foot in Asgard.

"This time, he took things too far. The Aesir and Einherjar cried out for justice. Sigi wouldn't have survived long had our father not intervened and carried him away. They traveled far away from Asgard to a cove in Midgard, where they found a fleet of forty warships and a large troop of warriors waiting.

"While standing on the beach, Odin informed Sigi that the Aesir had endured enough of his nonsense and non-conformist lifestyle. From this moment on, he had been stripped of his divinity, become mortal, and would be banished from Asgard. However, he wouldn't be leaving our brother empty-handed. He gestured to the fleet and army waiting in the cove and told him, 'Do whatever you like with these troops and ships. Carve out a kingdom for yourself. But try not to get into too much mischief. Maybe someday you'll be allowed back into Asgard.' With that, he handed Sigi a golden apple as a last gift and departed.

"With these ships and a large troop of seasoned warriors at his command, Sigi led many successful raids, accumulating vast wealth. With that fleet of ships, Sigi became the undisputed master of the Baltic Sea within a year. He then pushed inland with his mighty army and waged war against the surrounding tribes. He became a king, and within ten years, he had carved out a great kingdom named Hunaland."

The spirits seated around the other tables began chattering in a rasping language Sigurd couldn't understand. Baldur paused as if listening.

"According to the spirits, the territory of Hunaland has since changed hands," Hodr translated. "They are saying your family's former kingdom is now split between two groups called the Franks and the Huns."

"That's not surprising," Sigurd remarked. "When I was alive, Hunaland had already fallen into ruin, and its people and culture had been extirpated thanks to Lyngvi. But I already spoke at length about that topic earlier. Please continue your story."

"Certainly," Baldur said with a smile. "Sigi ruled over that territory for many years. His actions even helped reform the land into something beautiful. The wastelands, dense forests, and swamps around his capital were transformed into a vibrant region full of laughter and prosperity. Sigi had the unnatural ability to draw the worst of humanity to him and then transform them into the best possible versions of themselves. He gave ruffians work as sailors, farmers, builders, and scholars. He dug new rivers, built trading villages, and constructed roads to connect with neighboring regions and people. Thanks to Sigi's charisma and headstrong leadership, his new followers turned their blood-soaked land into a place worth living. However, our brother was still a maverick by nature and wasn't content to just sit back and rule as a king. For all the time he spent building, he also spent at war raiding distant shores, expanding his territory, and bringing rivers of gold and loot to his capital.

"He marveled many with his bravery and prowess and soon became one of the greatest warriors ever known. Whenever he went to war, Sigi would march into the center of enemy territory, plant his standard on a hill, and challenge everyone to face him with a boisterous bellow that could be heard for miles. Once he finished dealing with the brave foot soldiers, he'd challenge their general, king, or leader to single combat. Afterward, the enemy underlings would prostrate themselves and swear fealty. Not out of fear, mind you. But because they had never seen such a great and maverick warrior.

"He married a woman of noble birth and sired a son named Rerir. Your great-grandfather proved to be a strong and capable man, and he was just as fond of war as his father had been in his prime. Everyone agreed he was a worthy heir and would become a fine king."

"But for a long time, it seemed like Rerir would never get the chance to become king," Hodr interjected. "Sigi lived an incredibly long time in Midgard. He sired Rerir when he was ninety years old. That's still quite young for an Aesir, mind you. And he still looked like a man in his forties, even at that age. And when his conquering days were done, he ruled as a king in Midgard for over eighty consecutive years!"

"Unfortunately, after living over one hundred and fifty years in Midgard, old age finally caught up to Sigi. When his brothers-in-law realized his frailty, they saw an opportunity. They had been Sigi's most trusted men, but they all secretly envied him and desired to carve up his mighty kingdom amongst them when he died. Now that Sigi was becoming old, they saw their long-awaited opportunity.

"While his son Rerir was out raiding, Sigi's in-laws mustered an army of over twenty thousand men and marched on Hunaland. They planned to guest at Sigi's castle, kill him in his sleep, then murder his son and carve up the kingdom amongst them. The army was supposed to subjugate the kingdom and confront Rerir when he inevitably returned for vengeance. They had no intention of actually using their army to fight Sigi. His in-laws believed eliminating a man already over one hundred and fifty years old would be a piece of cake."

Baldur beamed proudly. "They could not have been more wrong. Although Sigi had grown old, his strength *never* left him. When the army arrived at the castle, they found Sigi clad in his armor and itching to face the army of twenty thousand men alone."

"Wait, why did he face them alone?" Sinfjotli interrupted. "How did he even know they were coming?"

"Our father, Odin, visited him the night before the invasion and told him," Hodr explained. "And before you ask, we know this because one of Sigi's servants overheard their conversation that night and later told us about it when Baldur found her in the City of the Lost."

"Anyway, Father warned him about his brothers-in-law." Baldur continued. "Sigi countered he had enough men to wipe them out. But our father told him he had a choice: 'In a few days, Hunaland will lose either its people or its king.' He warned. 'If you fight with your men, you will triumph, but many will die, and Hunaland would be devastated. But if you fight alone, you will die, but the kingdom and its people will prosper under Rerir.' Our father left, and Sigi spent the night pondering those words.

"The following morning, he gathered his army, told them about the incoming invasion, and ordered them to evacuate the capital and then find his son Rerir. He would face the traitors himself to give them all plenty of time to escape and gather more forces.

"That evening, his brothers-in-law found Sigi standing in front of the gates of his castle. Clad in armor and brandishing his sword and shield, he faced their army of twenty thousand men alone. The battle lasted for three full days and nights. But on the fourth morning, Sigi succumbed to old age and battle fatigue, and the enemy slew him. But even in death, his body refused to touch the ground, and he died standing proudly on his feet."

Baldur sipped his mead and leaned back on his throne. "Sigi lived in Midgard for over one hundred and fifty years! He carved out a mighty kingdom in ten years and ruled over it for eighty consecutive years. In his final battle, he slew no less than ten thousand, seven hundred fifty-nine men. Sigi was struck by over one thousand three hundred sixty-eight arrows. He was stabbed by over nine hundred eighty-nine spears. He received no less than five thousand, three hundred fifty sword wounds. The haunting image of his battered body, which mowed down his enemies, was a sight to behold. By the end, he was so mutilated that even the valkyries had trouble identifying it amongst the mountains of corpses. And so, Odin himself came to personally collect his son's body and escorted him back to Asgard. There, I imagine our father proudly welcomed his son as one of the foremost members of the Einherjar."

"I'm astonished!" Sigurd exclaimed. "I—I never imagined it was humanly possible to receive so many injuries!"

"It isn't," Nanna confirmed. "But Sigi was no ordinary human. He used to be a full-fledged Aesir like us before he was banished to Midgard. And his strength and vitality never left him. It is no simple task to kill an Aesir, even one that has been stripped of his godly power and become mortal."

"So what happened next?" Sinfjotli asked excitedly.

"Well, Sigi was dead, but it had come at an enormous and bloody cost to his brothers-in-law. They lost more than half their army fighting just one warrior. After their Pyrrhic victory, they gathered the survivors and seized power in Hunaland. But they only held onto it for less than a week. When Rerir heard the news, he was so livid he drew his knife and cut himself to the bone. He swore he would avenge his father's death and gathered all the forces loyal to him into a massive army of fifty thousand warriors. Together, they marched into Hunaland and wiped out the remainder of his uncle's army in a single day. He himself slew all his father's traitorous brothers-in-law, even though they were his uncles."

"I—I've never heard this version of the tale," Sinfjotli admitted. "All I heard was that Sigi was murdered in his sleep by his brothers-in-law, and Rerir avenged him when he came of age."

"I'm not surprised that's the watered-down version that has been passed down through the ages." Hodr sighed. "You've never heard the true details about Sigi's last stand because his son Rerir and his army wiped out all the survivors from Sigi's final battle. In the aftermath of Rerir's bloody vengeance, no one left alive had witnessed or could attest to his father's last stand. The carnage Rerir's army inflicted upon his uncles' army was so savage everyone vowed never to speak of it again. Thus, all knowledge of the events of Sigi's final battle died with Rerir and his men."

"Hang on, how could you know all this if you've been dead the whole time?" Sinfjotli interrupted. "You said Sigi remained in Asgard long after you had died."

Sigurd nervously glanced at Nanna, half expecting her to smite Sinfjotli then and there. She didn't appear upset, but Sigurd worried about his brother's oafish etiquette when speaking with Aesir. Sinfjotli had already enraged Nanna once with his insolence. Sigurd didn't know how much more disrespect she would tolerate.

"We heard all the details about Sigi's banishment, his life in Midgard, his last stand, and Rerir's vengeance from the many spirits here in Helheim, including Rerir's uncles," Hodr explained. "They're all here in Helheim, and his uncles and their minions are enduring excruciating torment as we speak. They told us about Sigi's last stand and the terrible vengeance Rerir exacted upon them afterward. But we won't recount the grisly circumstances of their deaths. Trust me, some things are best left buried and forgotten. Suffice to say, their punishment here in Helheim is a paradise compared to what Rerir did to them."

"That grievous detail aside, I think it's time we got back to the story," Baldur suggested. "After retaking Hunaland and savagely punishing his treacherous uncles, Rerir gained all of Sigi's wealth and consolidated his rule as king. He married Brenda the Iron Maiden, a renowned shield-maiden and a beloved comrade who had accompanied him on many voyages. His many victories expanded the kingdom's borders until he was even more popular and powerful than his father had been. Rerir proved to be a wise, just, but stern ruler over Hunaland for the best part of sixty years."

"However, he quickly encountered a problem," Nanna chimed in. "He couldn't conceive an heir with his queen. Rumors circulated that Rerir's seed had been cursed, and the Aesir would never grant him a living child for the atrocious ways he had killed his uncles. For a while, it seemed Sigi's legendary bloodline would be extinguished right there in its infancy. In desperation, Rerir prayed to Frigga, who was sympathetic to her grandson's plight. She sent a valkyrie named Hljod down to Rerir, who gifted him with a Golden Apple of Idun and a message from Frigga. Following her instructions, he and his queen consumed the apple and then planted the seeds from its core in his courtyard. Soon, Brenda became pregnant. Rerir was overjoyed and dreamed of fishing with his son and teaching him how to fight, raid, and rule."

"But that dream would never materialize because, after a year, there was still no sign that the child was ready to be born," Hodr interjected. "The pregnancy lasted so long that Rerir died fighting in a meaningful skirmish before ever seeing the birth of his child."

"After his death, his queen, Brenda, became the ruler of Hunaland," Nanna continued. "She proved to be a wise and beloved monarch. But although Rerir had gone to join his father in Valhalla, their child was still no closer to being born. After enduring a difficult six-year pregnancy, Queen Brenda decided she'd had enough. She summoned her physicians and begged for the child to be cut out from her womb. It was done, and a fully grown boy was pulled out from her belly. To everyone's surprise, the child pushed himself out of the physician's arms, walked over to his dying mother on his own two feet, and kissed her cheek. With her dying breath, Queen Brenda named the huge infant Völsung."

"And now we come to your grandfather, Völsung," Baldur announced excitedly, rubbing his hands together. "Oh, his life alone was legendary! He had already lost both his parents at birth, but he had quite the head start in life. As Nanna mentioned, he could walk minutes after being born. He was wise and could give sage advice even when he was still suckling at his wet nurse's teats. Völsung grew tall rapidly and possessed strength and vitality that had been unseen since his grandfather Sigi. They say he swam across the entire North Sea and back on his first swimming lesson when he was six years old!

When he was ten, he climbed to the top of Mont Blanc. He marveled many with his bravery and prowess and soon became one of the greatest warriors ever known."

"He rose to prominence when he was fourteen years old and ruled over Hunaland with the same spirit and vigor as his father," Hodr added. "Initially, many vassals scoffed at the idea of being ruled by someone so young, and they seceded or rebelled. In hindsight, this rebellion was inevitable. Many jarls and chieftains had been the sons or grandsons of men Sigi and Rerir had killed, and they still harbored grudges. Many also yearned for the days when they were their own masters and could raid and govern without input from a king. But none of them dared rebel against Sigi. After Rerir brutally punished his traitorous uncles and later crushed a rebellion lead by an ambitious noblewoman, no one dared challenge or speak ill of him, knowing his draconian disposition toward traitors. But with this new prince, they saw their chance to secede."

"Thus, Völsung spent many years fighting battles and securing his lands," Baldur added. "But even after he finished subjugating his unruly vassals, he kept pushing past his borders and subjecting neighboring tribes. By the time he was twenty years old, he had already expanded the kingdom of Hunaland to twice its original size under Rerir. When Völsung first came into the world, Hunaland was a savage place full of warring tribes, unsafe roads, and banditry. When he was finished, he left Hunaland, a mighty empire the Aesir would be proud of.

"With his rule finally secured, Völsung settled down and erected a magnificent palace with a golden roof around a tree his father, Rerir, had planted in his courtyard," Nanna added. "He named it Völsung Castle, which became a symbol of power and was famed worldwide for the enormous tree that stood at its center."

"Barnstock," Sinfjotli interrupted. "You're talking about our ancestral tree!"

"Indeed," Baldur affirmed. "Rerir planted that famous tree from the seeds of the golden apple the valkyrie, Hljod, had gifted him. Speaking of whom, when Völsung was at the zenith of his power, he was visited by Hljod. She married Völsung, and the two had a happy and fruitful marriage, giving birth to eleven children, including your parents, Sigmund and Signy."

"You've already spoken at length about Sigmund, and I'm sure you've heard all there is to know about your father," Baldur concluded. "So, nothing more needs to be said about him."

Baldur stood up from his throne and smiled proudly at Sigurd and Sinfjotli. "We've heard all these stories about your family and forebears from the spirits gathered here. But without a doubt, you both had the most epic, interesting, and colorful journeys of the entire Völsung line!"

"You're right," Sigurd muttered sadly. He gazed up at the emerald clouds and felt his heart sink. "We were the greatest in the Volsung line. But now we're doomed to remain in Helheim for dying inglorious deaths."

"Actually...that might not be the case," Baldur admitted after a long silence. He sat back on his throne and gave Sigurd a strange look. "What I'm about to say will sound strange and incredulous, but... you two aren't truly dead yet."

CHAPTER THIRTEEN

A FATEFUL DECISION

"We're not dead yet?" Sigurd repeated incredulously. "I—I don't understand. I *died*! My brother-in-law murdered me in my bed. I have this gaping hole in my chest to prove it! And Sinfjotli's stepmother poisoned him at a feast."

"True," Baldur conceded. "You're both 'dead' in so far as humans understand death. Your connection to the mortal realm of Midgard has been severed forever. Still, you're not *entirely* dead yet."

"What is that supposed to mean?" Sinfjotli demanded. "Speak plainly."

"Hmm...I suppose it's more accurate to say you are both caught in a state of stagnation between life and death." Baldur clarified. "It's like you're at death's door but haven't fully stepped through."

"How can you be so sure?" Sigurd asked. In hindsight, that was probably a foolish question to ask the Aesir, who served as a lord of the afterlife. But nothing Baldur said made any sense.

"It's because of your shadows," Nanna answered.

"Our shadows?" Sigurd glanced at the shadows he and Sinfjotli were casting beneath the table. There was nothing remarkable about them. But as he stared at the floorboards, he noticed that despite how brightly Baldur and Nanna's auras glowed, neither cast shadows. Sigurd glanced at the other spirits around the dining pavilion and realized that none were casting any shadows despite their corporeal forms.

"If you were 'dead,' then you wouldn't be able to cast a shadow," Nanna elaborated. "You'd be like those poor intangible spirits on the Path of the Dead you passed by on your way here. And the spirits you see on this ship only have a corporeal form because of our magic. The moment they step off this ship, their bodies become intangible, and they lose their physical appearance."

"But why aren't you, Hodr, and Baldur casting any shadows?" Sinfjotli asked. "You all have physical bodies, even when you step off this ship."

"Death affects us Aesir a bit differently than mortals," Hodr explained, shaking his head. "We possess a more tangible form than the other spirits and keep all our godly power here in the underworld. But make no mistake. We are still quite dead."

"That's why none of us can cast shadows," Baldur added. "Our bodies, the vessels of our souls, are long gone. They burned on this very ship during my funeral. However, you two *still* have your original bodies, which is why you're casting shadows."

Sigurd held up a hand and studied the shadow it cast on the table. *Was this all the proof they needed to show they were still alive?* He glanced at Sinfjotli and thought about the grievous wounds they had inflicted on each other during their earlier fight. As Sigurd stared at his brother's bandaged injuries and contemplated what Baldur and his family were implying, a realization dawned on him: How could they harm each other if they were already dead?

"I still don't understand," Sigurd managed. "How could this be possible?"

"It's simple," Baldur assured. "Someone resurrected you inside your original bodies before your souls arrived in the City of the Lost, denying Helheim the chance to assume complete authority over your souls."

"But why?" Sigurd asked. "Who could have done something like that? Who is even capable of such a feat?"

Baldur smiled. "Oh, I have my suspicions. But it's quite obvious *why* you were revived. You've both been given a second chance to prove yourselves worthy of Valhalla."

A second chance at Valhalla? That was unheard of. In the Norse culture, the rules of the afterlife were simple, if admittedly draconian. Those who died brave, glorious deaths in combat earned a chance at Valhalla or Fólkvangr. But the warriors who died cowardly, dishonorable, or inglorious deaths were doomed to Helheim. That had always been the tradition. But could it change? Could Sigurd and his brother get a second chance? Were they even worthy of one?

"Is...is it even possible?" Sigurd asked. "I mean, we both died outside of combat. Is it even possible for us to leave Helheim?"

"It's never happened before," Baldur admitted. "Not a single soul that died a dishonorable death has escaped Helheim. But I think you both have what it takes to become the first. You are skilled warriors. And you have won battles that lesser men have called unwinnable."

"It won't be easy," Hodr cautioned. "Trying to escape the underworld is like scaling a mountain of swords. Every step could rip you to pieces. Hel won't sit idly by while you attempt to escape her realm. She'll stop you in any way she can. But that's no reason not to try. To be a true descendant of Sigi is to walk fearlessly into danger and die smiling in the face of adversity as he did."

"And if you succeed, you will become legends," Nanna embellished. "You'll become a symbol of hope for the hopeless. I believe you have what it takes. And they do as well."

Nanna gestured around the dining pavilion. The spirits rose from their seats and bowed their heads. Their eyes were full of hope and encouragement.

"Vær ikke en kujon!" The dwarf Litr spoke. "Gå efter det."

Sinfjotli frowned. "What did he say?"

"Go for it," Hodr translated, though Sigurd got the impression that wasn't all the dwarf had said based on the brusque tone of his voice.

"As things stand, you have been given a second chance at Valhalla." Baldur surmised. "But you also have another choice. You're more than welcome to stay here on my ship and live in peace if you wish. And if any of your family members are in this realm, I shall do everything in my power to find and reunite them with you. I'll protect all of you from Hel and ensure she can never harm you or punish you for your sins. However, if you wish to do the impossible and aim to be the first to fight your way out of Helheim, then I shall do everything I can to help you succeed."

"I'd take Baldur's offer and stay on the ship if were you," Hodr cautioned. "You've both committed wicked deeds. If you fail to escape and perish, even we won't be able to protect you from Helheim's wrath. You'll be tortured without mercy for your sins and endure unspeakable agony. Worse, you'll get stripped of all humanity and become one of Helheim's minions, sworn to obey Hel's every command. I wouldn't wish that on my worst enemy."

"The choice is yours," Nanna surmised. "You can remain here with us and any family members we locate or stake your souls on a thorny path with everything at stake."

Sigurd leaned back in his chair and stared at the dark emerald clouds, weighing his options. He glanced at Sinfjotli. From the look in his eyes, his brother had already made up his mind. As he stared at his brother's blue-gray eyes, Sigurd remembered something Regin told him long ago: *"You can't choose the circumstances of your birth. Most people don't get to choose how they die, either. But you **can** choose your legacy."*

Sigurd's heart filled with fiery resolve as he decided death wouldn't be the end of his story. He turned to Baldur. "Could you show us the way out of this realm?"

"It would be my pleasure." Baldur beamed, clearly pleased by their decision. When Sigurd and Sinfjotli began to rise, Baldur waved them back to their seats. "Whoa! Hold up! Please don't leave the table just yet. There's still something we must do. Whoever revived you only did half the job. As I mentioned, you're caught in a state between life and death. You each have one foot in the grave and the other in the land of the living. As long as you remain in this state, Helheim won't be able to assume authority over your souls. But consequentially, you won't be able to leave this realm either. To leave Helheim, you must become well and truly alive. Fortunately, we have just the solution for that. Nanna, my love, could you please fetch the apples? It's time they had their desert."

For a moment, Nanna hesitated. She glanced at Sigurd and Sinfjotli with uncertainty. "Baldur, are you certain about this? You'll only be able to use *them* once."

"I'm positive, my love." He affirmed.

Nanna nodded and vanished into the captain's quarters. She soon reemerged with a wicker basket containing two large glowing golden apples wrapped in purple velvet. She handed each one to Sigurd and Sinfjotli.

Sigurd studied the golden apple in his hands. It was three times the size of a regular apple, although it weighed as much as a normal-sized one. Its skin was the color of twenty-four-karat gold. It smelled tantalizingly sweet. But more than anything, it felt powerful in his hands. Great energy radiated through his fingertips like electricity, making the hair on his arms stand up.

"These are the Golden Apples of Idun," Baldur explained. "Personally cultivated by the goddess of youth Idun herself, these apples allow us Aesir to retain our vigor and youth in Asgard. I've had these apples with me for quite some time. When we first arrived in Helheim, my parents sent our brother Hermod to bargain with Hel to release me from this realm and allow me to return to the Aesir. Hel agreed to release us, but only if all creation, alive or dead, wept for me. If anyone refused to cry, then I would remain with her. I'm sure you've heard that sad tale before, so I won't recount all the details. What's important is that Hermod gifted me these two apples before returning to Asgard to order every living creature to weep for me. My mother hoped the apples could release me from Helheim's grasp. But they'll serve you better."

Sigurd was stunned, opening and closing his mouth several times. As a boy, he'd heard stories about the Aesir's golden apples and how they granted the Aesir their youth, vigor, and virtual immortality. And now he was holding one of those legendary apples in his hands. It felt overwhelming, humbling, but also undeserving. He was just a mortal. These apples were meant for gods. Frigga had intended for Baldur to eat these apples to help him escape Helheim. Who were they to deserve such an extraordinary gift?

"Baldur, we cannot accept this," Sigurd refused humbly.

"You must," Baldur insisted. "If you want to leave Helheim, you must eat these apples. There's no way around it. Don't worry, we do not need them. None of us will age here in Helheim, and we can't leave until after Ragnarök."

Sigurd relented and took a bite. His eyes widened. It was the sweetest thing Sigurd had ever tasted. He continued eating slowly, savoring every morsel. But Sinfjotli wolfed his apple down like a ravenous beast afraid someone might steal his meal.

"Oh, I should apologize in advance," Baldur said when they finished eating. "The healing process might sting a bit."

Before Sigurd could ask Baldur what he meant, a seething pain erupted in the center of his chest. He collapsed from his chair and clawed at his sternum while his body violently contorted in excruciating pain. Sigurd couldn't breathe. It felt like someone had poured lava inside the gaping hole in his chest, and the magma was hardening into obsidian. The bones in his left calf burned and itched like buzzing insects under his skin. The wounds Sinfjotli had inflicted upon him earlier started sizzling.

Through his faded vision, Sigurd noticed Sinfjotli had also fallen from his chair and was now doubled over on his hands and knees. All the wounds Sigurd had inflicted on him earlier sizzled as well, and he was vomiting a thick black sludge that was probably the poisoned mead that slew him.

After a few agonizing moments, the burning pain in Sigurd's chest subsided and bizarrely gave way to pleasure. Wave after wave of pure ecstasy raced through his body. After a minute, these feelings of bliss morphed into strength, and he could feel power and vitality coursing through his veins.

When it was over, Sigurd stood up, unwrapped Nanna's bandages, and examined his bare chest. The gaping hole had been replaced with newly grown flesh. In its place was an ugly and conspicuous scar plastered across his sternum. He removed the splint Nanna had fashioned and flexed his left foot without pain.

Sigurd glanced over at Sinfjotli. All the injuries he inflicted on his brother during their earlier duel had vanished without a scar. Sinfjotli's muscles bulged, and his skin glowed slightly. He looked more robust than ever.

"It worked!" Baldur clapped excitedly. "Well, how does it feel?"

"I feel amazing!" Sinfjotli laughed. "I've never felt this energized! I feel like I could level a mountain to rubble with my fists! Or swim across the entire ocean without tiring!"

"And as a bonus, you won't need to eat or sleep for weeks," Baldur added. "Plus, any injuries you suffer will rapidly heal." His smile faded, and his expression turned serious. "But those apples' effects are temporary. Even we Aesir must keep eating them regularly to maintain our youth and vigor in Asgard. You must escape Helheim before the effects of those apples expire. Otherwise, you'll remain trapped here forever."

"I see," Sigurd muttered. He studied his hands. He felt invigorated and alert, as if a liquid fire was pumping through his veins. But power like this wouldn't last in perpetuity.

"How long do we have?" Sigurd ventured.

Baldur leaned back on his throne and stared at the emerald sky in deep thought. "Hard to say. I can't say for certain how long the effects of those apples will last on you. Normally, the Aesir must eat the apples every few days. I remember that when the giant Thiazi kidnapped Idun, my family, and the other Aesir grew old and weak within a few days without access to her apples. Then again, time flows differently throughout the realms, which might prolong or shorten your time limit. But I'm certain the effects of those apples will last far longer for you than they typically do for us Aesir. My brother Sigi lived quite a long time in Midgard before he died. And the spirits told me that Rerir lived two whole years without sustenance after he consumed the apple given to him by Hljod."

Baldur crossed his arms and pursed his lips, racking his brain. "Hmm...If I had to guess, I'd wager the effects of those apples could last anywhere from three to four months."

"*They won't live long enough to find out,*" a shrill voice declared.

Sigurd's heart skipped a beat. That piercing voice sent a sudden chill straight to his bones and almost made him scream. He glanced around, unable to discern where the voice had come from.

One spirit in the dining pavilion shouted and pointed upwards. An unearthly emerald green fog had emerged from the palace of Eljudnir high above them and enveloped the Bridge of Judgment. The mist slithered down the bridge piles like a serpent and then raced across the surface of the River Gjöll and enveloped the ship. It was deadly cold, sapping Sigurd's energy as he stood.

As the fog thickened around them, Sigurd heard a clomping followed by an unnerving crunch. He peered through the emerald fog and saw a hooded figure riding an enormous three-legged black stallion on the deck.

The fog enveloping the ship emanated from the mysterious rider, making it impossible to see their face. The deck froze over in a layer of ice every time the horse's hooves pounded the floorboards. The ice then crumbled beneath the horse's weight with an unsettling crunch.

As the foreboding horse and its mysterious rider cantered forward, nearby baskets full of ripe fruit and food littered across the tables rotted and emitted a putrid smell. All the spirits that Baldur had gathered in the dining pavilion quivered in terror, hid below deck or under tables, or fled before the approaching rider.

As the rider approached, Nanna clenched her fists, and Baldur displayed an unusually stern expression. Hodr perked his head up and sighed.

"A troublesome woman just showed up at a troubling time to start some trouble," Hodr remarked.

The horse stopped in the center of Baldur's dining pavilion. The fog ceased, allowing Sigurd to see the horse and its master clearly. The stallion appeared to be a large, heavy draft horse. Its rider, a tall woman wearing a purple hooded cloak covering her face's left half, carried an enormous scythe strapped to her back. The six-foot-long crescent-shaped ebony blade connected to a ten-foot shaft shaped like a human spine.

"We met at last, sons of Sigmund," the mysterious woman announced. She dismounted, and a large section of the deck froze beneath a layer of ice when her bare feet touched the floorboards.

Sigurd, too scared to look directly at the woman, focused on her horse, who looked just as intimidating as its master. It had a hefty and muscular build, its legs as tall as a full-grown man. Its coat was as black as the darkest night. The hair of its mane, tail, and the feathers of its lower legs were made of smoky shadows, just like Hodr's cape.

Its most remarkable feature was its left hind leg. Unlike its other three legs, which were covered in sinewy black flesh, this leg was a green astral limb. The limb's smoky skeletal appearance reminded Sigurd of the ethereal bodies of the spirits he'd seen on the Path of the Dead.

The stallion's aura was just as intimidating as his rider's. His eyes glowed red with malice, and his muzzle was caked in dried blood. Sigurd inferred this stallion was accustomed to eating something more sinister than oats and hay. The horse eyed him hungrily, pawed the deck, and whinnied.

The rider placed her right hand on the horse's neck and caressed it. "At ease, Helhest," she purred. "I haven't decided what I'll do with them yet. You may still get a *meal* if you behave."

Alarms sounded in Sigurd's head. His arm failed to move when he reached for his sword. He tried to retreat to a safe distance, but his legs wouldn't respond. His limbs felt as if they were freezing up. He tried to turn away, but his neck refused to move. His body felt rigid as stone.

The rider looked at him and smiled. She removed her hood and raised her arms in a welcoming gesture as if she were expecting a hug. But no force in nature could compel Sigurd to embrace her, for she was terrifying to look upon. The right side of her face and body was heart-achingly beautiful. Her sea-green right eye twinkled in its socket like a star. Her hair on the right half of her head was straight and well-combed. But the left side of her face and body was black as a carcass from a bog. The left half of her face was covered in withered skin with membrane-thin lips, a milky white eye, and a part of her jaw exposed.

"Welcome to Helheim, sons of Sigmund." She announced. "I am Hel, daughter of Loki and Angrboda, elder sister of Fenrir and Jörmungandr, goddess of death, Queen of the Underworld, and Mistress of the Dishonorable Dead."

CHAPTER FOURTEEN

THE ONE IRON RULE

The Queen of the Underworld and eponymous ruler of Helheim was a terrifying sight. Hel was quite tall, at least ten or eleven feet; Sigurd had to strain his neck to look at her face. She had quite a contrasting appearance.

The right half of her face looked young, heart-achingly beautiful, yet unsettling. Her body's right side body was as pale as a bloated corpse, and her milk-white skin was almost translucent enough to see the bones beneath. Her sea-green right eye twinkled like a star in its socket, and the teeth and skin on the right half of her face were immaculate. The waist-length black hair on the right half of her head was straight and well-groomed.

By contrast, her body's left half was hideously burned and blackened. The left side of Hel's face was nightmarishly grotesque, covered in withered skin, a milky-white eye, and parts of her jawbone were exposed. Her left arm and leg were covered in patches of blue frost over decayed, blackened flesh and exposed muscles. The waist-length hair on the left side of her head was braided with femurs, tibias, ribs, and other human bones.

Her ominous outfit featured a tattered purple dress with a human spine fashioned into a belt. A warlike crown of black iron points in a band of dark steel sat on her forehead, and she wore a ragged hooded cloak draped over her shoulders that she'd used to cover the left side of her face. She had a large scythe strapped to her back and a knife with a sinister-looking hilt holstered to her belt. Both weapons glowed with an unnerving aura, and every one of Sigurd's instincts warned him to avoid them at all costs.

But her voice was the most frightening thing about her. Whenever Hel spoke, she emitted an awful jangle that scraped Sigurd's bones and hollowed his guts. Yet it also sounded as mellifluous as the lullabies his mother used to sing him. Sigurd felt his soul tremble in fear whenever a syllable escaped her membrane-thin lips.

"I'm pleased to finally make your acquaintance," Hel proclaimed. "I've been waiting to meet you since you arrived in my realm. Though it seems Baldur took you on a brief detour."

She walked a slow circle around Sigurd and Sinfjotli, creating a ring of ice around them as her bare feet touched the floorboards. The bones in her hair rattled like macabre wind chimes with every step.

Hel leaned before Sinfjotli, forcing him to stare at her mismatched eyes. "Let's see...How many sins have you committed? Oh, that's right; *you* murdered your younger siblings, Sinfjotli! And what else? What else?! Ah, and you killed your stepmother's brother in a quarrel over a woman you fancied. You also drove your lover to suicide. And let's not forget all those *poor* Geatish families and civilians you slaughtered in your parents' quest for vengeance. Tell me, just how many innocent souls did you condemn to my realm to slake your parents' thirst for vengeance?"

Sigurd wanted to tell her to leave his brother alone, but no sound escaped his mouth. He tried to reach for his sword, but his arm wouldn't respond. He tried to step away, but his legs refused to move. His entire body was paralyzed by icy primordial fear.

"What about you, Sigurd?" Hel turned toward him. She leaned close to Sigurd, forcing him to stare at her unnatural face. A pale lavender pupil sat jarringly in the center of her milky left eye. Her emerald right eye looked normal, but it was just as unnerving. It twinkled in her eye socket like a green star.

As Hel studied Sigurd with her contrasting sea green and milky white eyes, it felt like she was peering directly into his soul. His limbs trembled violently as if he were having a seizure, and his soul was shaking within his body. Sigurd desperately wanted to look away, but his eyeballs, like the rest of his body, refused to respond.

"Oh my, you also have plenty of blood on your hands," Hel remarked. "I wager you've killed even more people than your brother has. You exterminated the entire Hunding bloodline in the name of vengeance and butchered every loyal vassal who followed them. Then you murdered your teacher and surrogate father Regin after killing his brother Fafnir and took Andvari's treasure for yourself. Oh, and you're an oath breaker as well! How delicious! You broke an oath and betrayed the one you love most, and it led to your demise!"

"That's enough, Hel," Baldur interrupted, rising from his throne. "Why have you come here?"

Hel smiled at Baldur. The moment she stepped away from Sigurd and Sinfjotli, they collapsed to the deck, gasping for air. Sigurd's body had been so utterly gripped by terror that he'd been unable to breathe, as if his lungs had been flattened against his ribcage. He had never felt such sheer terror or power as he had just from standing in Hel's presence.

As Sigurd panted, he glanced over his shoulder and watched Hel casually walk to Baldur's table. She raised her arms as if she was expecting a hug.

"Baldur!" Hel smiled. "How many years has it been? Twenty? Fifty? I've lost count. You've been spending far too much time on this ugly ship. Why don't you come to visit me in my palace anymore? It gets quite boring without you there to lighten the mood."

"We prefer living on our ship than residing in that dreary windswept palace," Nanna said coldly. "The last time we visited your palace, you tortured an entire family in front of us at dinner and called it 'entertainment.' Not even my husband can bring joy to that dreary place you call home."

Hel turned and smiled at Nanna with her half-rotten and half-pristine teeth. "Nanna, still the loving, supportive, and overprotective wife, I see. And Hodr, you're looking well."

"I wouldn't know," Hodr joked, waving a hand before his milk-white eyes. "But I'll take your word for it."

"I'll ask again," Baldur continued sternly. "*Why* have you come here?"

"What a foolish question!" Hel snickered. "You know *exactly* why I've come, my old friend."

A second later, Sigurd blinked and realized Hel no longer stood near Baldur's table. She had vanished! Suddenly, he heard rattling bones directly before him. Ice-cold fingers clasped his chin and gently turned his head forward. Hel was crouching in front of him and Sinfjotli with both hands cupped beneath their chins.

Sigurd's mind reeled in terror and confusion. Hel had moved so fast he hadn't even heard her footsteps!

Hel licked her pristine and rotten lips and smiled. "I came to fulfill my duty as Queen of Helheim and collect my prey."

She grabbed them both by their throats and lifted them high in the air. Sigurd struggled, kicking and flailing in vain as her icy fingers dug into his neck. Her skin, as cold as a glacier, burned his neck like acid, spreading frostbite across his throat.

"Did you think I wouldn't notice you reviving them, Baldur?" Hel scoffed. "Did you think I would stand idly by and let them waltz out of *my* realm? You might have fully brought them back to life, but that can change. I have *so* many creative ways to torment them after I kill them! Or maybe I shouldn't kill them yet. Mortals are much more fun to play with while still alive."

"Leave them alone, Hel!" Baldur demanded.

Hel ignored him as she held them aloft by their throats and stared into their eyes, listening to them rasping for air. She leaned forward, forcing Sigurd and his brother to stare directly into her contrasting eyes as they struggled to breathe. Sigurd's lungs burned as his other organs used up the last bits of air in his body. The world closed in around him until he could only see Hel's face and eyes inches away from his.

"Do you two know the worst sin a warrior can commit?" Hel asked. "Is it murder? Rape? Kidnapping? Fraud? Adultery? Cannibalism? Incest? Kinslaying? Betrayal? No! The greatest sin a drengr can commit is to die outside of combat without honor! Those who die of old age, sickness, or perish outside combat all wind up here in *my* realm! It's what happened to these two. It's what happened to the souls on this ship. And it's what happened to *you*, Baldur!"

"I said that's enough!" Baldur yelled. "Release them!"

"You know the one iron rule of Helheim better than anyone else, Baldur!" Hel sneered. She squeezed their throats even tighter. Sigurd felt the sides of his esophagus press against his spinal cord, and his arms went limp at his sides. "Not a single soul may leave *my* realm unless *I* allow it. And these two sinners deserve to be in Helheim more than *anyone* else on this ship. They slaughtered *thousands* in the name of vengeance, and both died dishonorable deaths. That last fact alone makes them my prey, just like the canaille on this ship."

Hel vanished, and Sigurd and Sinfjotli dropped to the deck like weighted stones. As he clutched his burning throat and gasped for air like a fish, Sigurd heard the rattling of bones to his left. Hel stood before a group of cowering spirits near the ship's port side. Sigurd noticed a trail of icy footprints she'd left behind on the deck and realized what was happening. Hel was moving so fast that his mind couldn't even process it. But he was sure of one thing. The last sound her victims would hear before they died was the rattling bones in her braided hair.

Hel loomed over the trembling spirits, studying each one. "This young woman was a princess who died from a fever. This codger was a village herbalist who died peacefully in his bed from old age. And this young lad died outside combat while cowering behind a haystack as warriors ransacked his village. The circumstances of their deaths may differ, but every single soul on this ship is guilty of the same crime: they all died outside of combat."

One spirit began crying in terror. It was a petite little girl with blond hair and blue eyes.

"Even little children aren't exempt from that rule," Hel remarked. "The young and old, the continent and vile, and the sick and murdered all wind up here in *my* realm. There can be no exceptions. I did not create that draconian rule. But I am the one who enforces it."

Hel tried to touch the weeping girl's cheek, but an invisible force repelled her hand. Through his blurred vision, Sigurd noticed a glowing symbol on the child's forehead.

Hel growled at the glowing symbol. She turned around, unstrapped her scythe from her back, and pointed it at Sigurd. "As Queen of the Underworld, I must ensure every soul that dies outside of combat remains here in my realm and punish the wicked. I agreed to let you keep all the virtuous and continent souls and add them to your little *collection*, Baldur. But these two sinners are *mine!*"

Hel lunged at Sigurd and Sinfjotli, swinging her scythe faster than the eye could see. She moved so quickly that she would, without a doubt, have killed them both right where they lay on the deck if Baldur hadn't intervened. He stepped before them, and the scythe ricocheted harmlessly off his chest.

"Stand aside, Baldur," Hel warned. "These two are *my prey*. They've sinned on a scale reserved for monsters. They have no right to be on this ship. Did you not hear me? I demand..."

"Nothing," Baldur interrupted defiantly. "You demand *nothing* of me. Helheim may be your sovereign realm. But this ship, Hringhorni, is my kingdom and mine alone. You have no authority here."

"I told you to move!" Hel seethed. She swung her scythe at Baldur's neck. But the blade once again bounced harmlessly off his skin. The frustrated Hel slashed uselessly at Baldur in a vicious whirlwind of strikes. Baldur withstood the onslaught, standing as still as a statue as the blade ricocheted off his skin.

"Have you forgotten, Hel?" Baldur asked as he snatched the spiny shaft of her scythe mid-swing. "Like all creation except mistletoe, you swore an oath at my mother's behest to never harm me. Even though I'm dead, you are still bound by that oath."

Baldur thrust out his other hand. A massive, invisible force blasted Hel, sending her tumbling backward across the deck toward the captain's quarters.

"Now, Hodr!" Baldur shouted.

Hodr rose from his chair and wrapped Hel in his arms under her armpits, locked his hands behind her neck, and locked her in his arms.

"Unhand me, Hodr!" Hel threatened. "Release me this instant, or I will tear open your belly, rip out your intestines, and shove them down your throat!"

"Sounds painful," Hodr noted. "But you're wasting your breath on empty threats, Hel. You heard Baldur. You can't harm anyone on this ship."

Just then, Sigurd noted a glowing blue symbol on Hodr's forehead. It was the same one he had seen on the other spirits. It reminded him of a trident, but the middle prong was shorter than the other two. The mark looked familiar, but Sigurd was too busy recovering to remember.

Hel raged and struggled so violently that the ship began rocking in the water. Although Hel cursed and fulminated, the blind god of winter restrained her.

Meanwhile, Baldur dropped Hel's scythe to the deck and helped Sigurd and Sinfjotli to their feet.

"Are you all right?" he asked.

"I—I think so," Sigurd croaked as he rubbed a patch of frostbite shaped like a handprint on his throat. But he could feel it quickly healing. He glanced at Sinfjotli and noticed that the hand-shaped burn mark on his neck had already faded without a trace.

This rapid healing must be a side effect of the apple. Sigurd realized. *I could get stabbed through the chest and still wouldn't die. Not that I'd want to try putting that to the test.*

"I'll make sure she can't touch you again," Baldur pressed his index finger against Sigurd's forehead and drew a symbol, and then he did the same for Sinfjotli. The mark momentarily glowed blue and vanished from Sinfjotli's forehead before Sigurd could get a good look at it.

"We need to get moving," Baldur warned. "I'll protect and guide you through the City of the Lost. As long as you stay near me, the legions of the dead and even Hel won't be able to harm you. However, I can only escort you as far as the Gjallerbru, the Bridge of the Damned. You'll be on your own beyond that. Now get up and get dressed. We must leave while Hel is occupied. My brother Hodr is strong, but even he can't hold the goddess of death at bay forever."

As Sigurd put on his armor and Sinfjotli dressed, Baldur brought his fingers to his lips and whistled loudly. The sleeping dragon Twilight woke up and swooped down to the deck. The dragon hissed angrily at Hel but calmed down when it heard Baldur's soothing words. Twilight stretched out flat on his belly like a horse waiting to be mounted.

Baldur vaulted onto the base of the dragon's long, scaly neck. He motioned for Sigurd and his brother to join him. Once they were all mounted, Baldur shouted a command, and the dragon leaped into the air. Sigurd grabbed the hard scales and held on for dear life as the great wings spread and flapped, ascending into the air.

As they climbed higher above the ship, a fearsome, icy gale blasted them. The snowflakes and icy wind needled against Sigurd's face. Dizzy, Sigurd closed his eyes. When he opened them again, the ship beneath him grew smaller and smaller as the dragon raced toward the thick emerald clouds.

"Onwards!" Baldur shouted.

The dragon purred as its great wings beat the air. Sigurd could feel the hard scales and the heat from inside its body between his thighs. As they soared north toward the city, Sigurd's excitement relieved his fear.

Yes. He thought. *Take me away. Take me far away from her!*

Chapter Fifteen

The Terrible Triplets

Riding a dragon through the skies of Helheim was such an exhilarating experience. The wind at this height cut like a knife and shrilled like a mother mourning her slain children. Sigurd's eyes started watering, and he felt the tears freeze upon his cheeks. Higher in the sky they went, and as Sigurd held on for dear life, the vast panorama of Helheim was in clear view. He could see the City of the Lost's towering skyscrapers and the River Gjöll's vast expanse. Sigurd could not see a shore in any direction due to the river's vastness.

The Hringhorni swayed like a toy boat in a bathtub from this height. By contrast, the dark stone city and Hel's windswept palace looked enormous even from this height. And the western and eastern horizons were tinged emerald green. Sigurd had never seen such a stunning vista. As Twilight soared north, Sigurd closed his eyes and felt the frigid wind and the heat of the dragon beneath him. He felt as free as a bird in flight.

Unfortunately, the ride didn't last long. Sigurd assumed the dragon would fly them across the City of the Lost to the Bridge of the Dead. Instead, the dragon landed where the Bridge of Judgment connected with the dark city and refused to venture further.

"What's wrong?" Sinfjotli inquired. "Why is the dragon stopping?"

"This is as far as Twilight can go," Baldur explained. "He's bound to the Hringhorni like the other spirits, and he can only maintain a tangible body so long as he remains near my ship. If we fly farther, his body will turn into mist, and we'll plummet to the earth. I'm afraid we'll have to walk the rest of the way."

Sigurd sighed, and Sinfjotli cursed. They were both peeved by this inconvenience, but not as much as Twilight. Plumes of smoke billowed from the dragon's nostrils as it gazed forlornly at the sky. Sigurd knew the dragon wanted to fly them all north, and it yearned to soar through the open sky more than anything. Twilight was like a caged bird in Helheim.

Still, Baldur's pet dragon had proved helpful. It saved them the trouble of climbing up the support columns of the Bridge of Judgment and flew them far away from Hel. Sigurd patted its scales and thanked the magnificent beast for its help as he slid off its back.

Sigurd wasn't out of danger yet. As soon as his feet touched the snowy ground, he heard a rattling sound followed by a loud CLANG before a sudden blast of cold air almost knocked him off his feet. He turned and discovered that Hel had appeared behind them. If Baldur hadn't intervened, she would have killed him and Sinfjotli with her scythe. He had moved faster than Sigurd could see and caught the scythe's crescent-shaped blade with his bare hands.

As Twilight roared and hissed angrily at the Queen of Helheim, Sigurd glanced back at the giant ship docked several miles away. He could see Hodr lying sprawled on his back on the deck three miles from their current location, and Nanna was running over to help him. Hel's stallion, Helhest, stood motionless on the deck, patiently awaiting his master's order.

Sigurd's mind reeled in terror as he realized what had happened. Hel had broken free of Hodr's grasp mere moments ago and traversed the entire distance between the ship, the bridge, and the city in the blink of an eye.

As Sigurd struggled to comprehend Hel's absurd speed, she and Baldur continued their tense standoff. They seemed locked in a stalemate until Hel unexpectedly drew her knife and hurled it at Sigurd's face before Baldur could react.

Time seemed to slow down at that moment. Sigurd had only a second to blink before the knife reached his face. He should have died at that moment. But before the point of the blade touched his forehead, an invisible force repelled the knife. The blade spun wildly through the air before landing in a nearby snowdrift. The snow surrounding the blade hissed as it rapidly melted into a sickly green vapor.

As Sigurd rubbed his forehead, questioning how he was still alive, he saw an aura of light covering his arm. He glanced at Sinfjotli and saw the same aura surrounding his body. He also saw a glowing twig-shaped symbol on Sinfjotli's forehead. It was the same symbol he'd seen on Hodr and the spirits on the ship.

Hel noticed this as well. She let go of her scythe and moved in front of Sigurd before Baldur could stop her. She tried to grasp his throat, but the aura enveloping his body repelled her.

Hel stepped back, rubbing her scorched hand. She glowered at the glowing symbol on Sigurd's forehead and sighed in frustration.

"It seems I won't even be able to touch them as long as you're near them." Hel conceded. "But you and your brand won't be able to protect them forever, Baldur."

"Oh, but it will." Baldur countered. He dropped her scythe and pointed at Hel's forehead, where another glowing symbol had appeared. After a moment, Sigurd realized it was the Åndsrostaven, a magical rune that shamans drew onto amulets to repel malevolent spirit voices and prevent intrusion into someone's consciousness and subconscious.

"I placed that mark on you when I repelled you on the ship earlier," Baldur explained. "That brand is designed to work in conjunction with the one I drew on their foreheads to protect them from you. As long as they're still alive, you won't be able to touch them."

"I see," Hel mused. "You and Nanna have created a potent protection spell. But there are many ways to kill someone. Even if *I* can't harm them directly, I'm guessing that protection won't extend to my army, will it? And based on your word choice, I'm guessing the spell won't protect them from me once they're dead?"

Baldur remained silent. He and Hel stared at each other in a tense standoff until she chuckled. "All right, Baldur, if this is how you'd like to do this, I'll play along. And I'll make sure their ordeal is entertaining. Helhest, come here!"

Seven seconds later, Hel's horse appeared behind her. Hel retrieved her scythe and knife and then mounted her dreaded black stallion. Hel veered Helhest around and looked down at Baldur.

"As a courtesy, I'll give you three hours to make it to the Bridge of the Damned," she promised. "After that, I will send my entire army after them. Do you understand, sons of Sigmund? Once you reach the Gjallerbru, the full might of Helheim will come crashing down on you. I look forward to watching you struggle."

With that, Helhest galloped down the Bridge of Judgment toward her palace. As soon as Hel vanished from sight, Sigurd and Sinfjotli collapsed to the ground, panting. Their fear had stifled their breath. The indescribable atmosphere around them changed drastically after Hel had left. It wasn't just a simple sense of relief, like the kind one feels after a fearsome storm has passed. It was felt as if they had survived a hurricane, tsunami, earthquake, and volcanic eruption all at once. They had only survived thanks to Baldur's divine intervention.

"I've never been that terrified in my entire life!" Sinfjotli panted. "I've seen the worst in men and encountered many wicked spirits from the underworld disguised as men before. But I have never seen evil so singularly personified as in that woman's face."

"She's not as bad as you think," Baldur said, pulling them back to their feet. He thanked Twilight for his temporary assistance and sent him on his way. The dragon spread its wings and flew south toward the ship, and they then began traveling north through the city.

"Hel has more reason than most to feel bitter and spiteful toward others, especially toward those who carry the blood of Odin in their veins," Baldur continued.

"Are you kidding?" Sigurd asked incredulously. "You actually feel sympathetic for her?"

"I do," Baldur affirmed proudly. "To understand why she is like this, you must consider her origins. She and her younger brothers were born to Loki and Angrboda. And they..."

"Wait, isn't Loki's wife supposed to be Sigyn, the goddess of fidelity?" Sinfjotli interrupted.

"She is," Baldur admitted. "But their marriage was more of a political union designed to further bind Loki to the Aesir after he became blood brothers with my father, Odin. From what I understand, he and Angrboda were childhood sweethearts in Jotunheim. Loki had wanted to bring her with him to Asgard after he joined the ranks of the Aesir, but Odin and Freyja objected, insisting that he take a proper Aesir bride. That isn't to say he never loved Sigyn. Loki was genuinely happy for a long time and seemed intent on making Sigyn happy. However, he still secretly visited Angrboda in the Iron Woods of Gálgviðr. They say first love never dies, and distance and time only inflamed their passion. Eventually, Angrboda became pregnant and bore Loki three triplets: Hel, Fenrir the Devourer, and Jörmungandr the World Serpent."

A chill ran up Sigurd's spine. *Fenrir and Jörmungandr.* Those were names that every warrior feared. Fenrir was a giant wolf prophesied to devour the

All-Father Odin at Ragnarök. Jörmungandr, a massive serpent who could encircle the world and bite its own tail, was prophesied to battle the god Thor at Ragnarök. They were the most powerful and feared monsters in the Nine Realms. But it seemed their sister was even more powerful and terrifying.

"Something's not adding up," Sinfjotli noted with a frown. "If they're triplets, why is Hel human in appearance while her brothers are a giant wolf and a serpent?"

"Well, that happened because during these...visits, Loki and Angrboda often shapeshifted into different creatures so as not to get caught, which resulted in their sons Fenrir and Jörmungandr taking on the forms of a wolf and serpent when they were born," Baldur explained. "But Loki was a fool to think he could hide a secret from Heimdall's all-seeing gaze through such a simple gimmick. Eventually, the scandalous truth of his affair came out. When my father learned that these children, prophesied to be harbingers of destruction at Ragnarök, were being raised by the giants, he acted quickly. He galloped to Jotunheim on Sleipnir, scooped up the children, and spirited them back to Asgard while Angrboda was hunting. My father hoped he could raise the children and teach them to love the Aesir to mitigate *some* of the destruction that shall come at Ragnarök.

"Unfortunately, it seems the Norns had other plans. As my father left Jotunheim and rode Sleipnir across the World Tree with the triplets, Angrboda unexpectedly returned early from her hunt. When she discovered her children had been abducted, she mounted the giant red soot eagle Fjalar and chased Odin across the Nine Realms, desperate to recover them. As Odin fled Angrboda, he veered south and rode Sleipnir toward Muspelheim. The immense heat of the fiery realm singed Fjalar's feathers and forced Angrboda and the giant eagle to cease their pursuit or risk getting burned out of existence. Having momentarily thrown off his pursuer, my father veered Sleipnir around and galloped up the trunk of the World Tree toward Asgard, where Angrboda couldn't follow.

"But that diversion came at a grievous cost. Sleipnir had gotten too close to Muspelheim, and the left half of Hel's body became scarred from the fiery realm's immense heat, giving her that ghastly appearance you saw. Thus, their time in Asgard began on a grievous note. Fenrir and Jörmungandr never forgave my father for causing their sister's disfigurement or abducting them from their mother.

"The children soon proved more trouble than we anticipated. The youngest sibling, Jörmungandr, was a serpent that grew every day, even when he wasn't fed. After living in Asgard for only a month, Jörmungandr had grown over nine miles long! Before he could grow large enough to encircle Asgard and threaten the realm's foundations, my father ordered Thor to cast the great serpent into the oceans of Midgard. But that did nothing to stop his growth spurt. Jörmungandr grew so large that he now encircles Midgard and bites on his tail.

"His older brother Fenrir was more trouble from the start. My father had foreseen long ago that Fenrir would be the instrument of his demise. Odin hoped that being raised by the Aesir in Asgard might change that and teach the young pup love. But it only made the wolf grow bigger and more hateful of the gods. Their relationship worsened after Odin cast Fenrir's sons, Sköll and Hati, into the heavens and chained his youngest son, Garm, in the underworld. Odin claimed he was granting the pups a great honor. Sköll and Hati would ensure that the sun and moon continued to move across the heavens, and Garm would be the guard dog of the underworld and ensure the dishonorable dead remained in the underworld. But Fenrir believed he had turned his children into hostages to ensure his good behavior and became even more indignant and spiteful toward the All-Father.

"In all his years in Asgard, Fenrir only trusted my brother Týr. The indefatigable upholder of law and honor was the only one who dared to approach Fenrir to feed him. The two formed an uneasy friendship. But like his brother, Fenrir grew so large that we realized that if he were allowed to roam free, he'd become a threat to all creation. And so, it was agreed that he must be bound.

"We brought the wolf to an island named Mörhogg and attempted to bind him with various chains. We gained the wolf's consent by telling him that each fetter we brought was meant to test his strength, and we clapped and cheered when he broke free from each new chain we presented him.

"Meanwhile, the Aesir sent a messenger down to Svartalfheim, the realm of the dwarves. The dwarves were able to forge a chain named Gleipnir, whose strength and durability cannot be equaled. It was crafted from unusual materials such as the sound of a cat's footsteps, a woman's beard, a mountains' roots, a fish's breath, and a bird's spittle. These are things that no longer exist and are thus futile to struggle against.

"We presented Fenrir with Gleipnir, which was surprisingly light and flexible. However, the wolf became suspicious and refused to be bound with it unless one of the Aesir placed their hand in his jaws as a pledge of good faith. None of us volunteered at first, knowing that this would mean the loss of a hand and breaking an oath. At last, brave Týr volunteered to fulfill the wolf's demand. And, sure enough, when Fenrir realized that he had been tricked and could not escape from Gleipnir, he chomped off and swallowed Týr's hand.

"As Fenrir struggled, we tied Gleipnir to a boulder, burying it deep underground, and drove a sword through his upper jaw, pinning it open and ensuring he could not bite anyone. We left him in that sordid state in that lonely and desolate place. Ever since then, Fenrir has been consumed by a black rage. The Aesir and even Týr, the only person he trusted, had tricked him. But it was Odin he hated most of all. The king of the Aesir had kidnapped him from his mother, mistreated his pups Sköll, Hati, and Garm, cast his brother into the ocean, and schemed to have the only person he ever trusted ensnare him in that humiliating trap. As the Aesir marched back to Asgard, Fenrir howled a terrible oath of vengeance on Odin."

"And now we come to Hel." Baldur sighed. "Among the three triplets, Hel was the eldest and the most human in appearance. In her youth, she possessed a beauty unrivaled by any Aesir or Vanir except Freyja. Out of all three siblings, she was the one who should have had the best chance at being accepted amongst the Aesir. But as I said earlier, her time in Asgard began on a grievous and tragic note. The left half of her body became scarred after Odin rode Sleipnir too close to Muspelheim. Thus, when they arrived in Asgard, the Aesir took one look at Hel, and they found her grotesque. They soon found a different reason to shun her. Hel had been born with immense power, enough to contend with Odin. Even as a child, she possessed enough power to raze and remake the realms in her image. As time passed, many in Asgard worried that someday, she'd become even more dangerous than her brothers.

"Thus, she became an outcast in Asgard, ostracized by everyone except for me, Týr, Heimdall, Odin, and her father, Loki. The five of us tried to treat her with kindness and love. But it was all in vain. A seed of hatred had been planted within her. And as the Aesir continued to ostracize her and mistreat her brothers and nephews, the seed grew. It finally sprouted the day the Aesir betrayed and bound her brother Fenrir. The next day, Hel confronted the Aesir in Valhalla and promised we would suffer for what we'd done to her brothers.

"At this, we became terrified. All of our worst fears about Hel had come to pass. In their paranoia, my family demanded that she be sent away from Asgard, where she couldn't do any harm. And so, at the insistence of my mother Frigga, Freyja, and the other Aesir, Odin reluctantly agreed to banish her to the lowest echelons of the World Tree, where she could not harm anyone.

"But before the sentence could be carried out, Hel vanished without a trace from Asgard. We frantically searched for her, but it was in vain. A month later, she appeared in Valhalla wielding a scythe forged by her great-great-grandfather Surtr in one hand and dragging a defeated Heimdall in the other. She vowed to make the Aesir pay dearly for everything they had done to her and her brothers and attacked Odin.

"The ensuing battle was on a scale you can't even imagine. For months, Odin and Hel fought each other across the realms in an epic battle that permanently scarred the landscapes. Eventually, it came to a stop in the icy realm of Niflheim. Odin knew there was no use continuing the battle since neither of them could overcome the other. And if it continued, they'd risk damaging the World Tree and disrupting the stability of the realms. So he offered a truce. Hel agreed to make peace, but only if she was given her sovereign realm to govern the dishonorable dead. My father had no choice but to agree."

"Consider for a moment what all those experiences do to a young child." Baldur entreated. "Being abducted from your mother and the only home you've ever known by a stranger you've been taught is your mortal enemy and becoming hideously scarred in the process. Watching your brothers be cast away, humiliated, and imprisoned by that same person. And worst of all, the Aesir banish you into the land of the dead because they believe you are hideous to look upon and fear what you *might* do. It's small wonder then that her moods are at one with the drizzle and darkness of Helheim."

Baldur stopped walking and gazed at the emerald sky, deep in thought. "Now that I think about it, her father, Loki, was present through it all. Seeing his children mistreated by the Aesir must have hardened Loki's heart, and it probably reminded him of his own ostracization."

"What do you mean?" Sinfjotli asked

"Loki was always a black sheep amongst the Aesir," Baldur explained. "Although he became blood brothers with Odin, married Freyja's daughter Sigyn, and his mother was the goddess Laufey, many Aesir still treated him like an outcast because his father had been the violent frost giant Fárbauti."

"Why is that so offensive?" Sinfjotli asked. "Aren't most of the Aesir the sons and daughters of Jötnar?"

"Having a giantess as your mother and a god for your father is normal for the Aesir," Baldur explained. "Some might even say it's expected. But having a goddess as your mother and a giant as your father, especially one as violent as Fárbauti, is a stigma in Asgard."

"That is nothing but baseless prejudice!" Sinfjotli growled. "No child deserves to be treated as an outcast because of who their parents were!"

Sinfjotli gnashed his teeth and clenched his fists. Sigurd understood why this resonated so strongly with his brother. Since Sinfjotli had been born of an incestuous union, he must have been spurned and ostracized by people disgusted by the nature of his birth.

"I agree," Baldur affirmed. "But the rest of my family was not as open-minded or accepting. Thus, Loki was treated like an outcast in Asgard from the start. This social isolation caused Loki to crave acknowledgment and attention, which he would gain by pulling pranks and getting up to all manner of mischief. Sometimes, his antics would lead to wild adventures, such as when he shaved Sif's beautiful hair while she slept."

"I've heard that story before." Sigurd smiled. "When her husband, Thor, found out, he threatened to break every bone in Loki's body unless he found her a wig that grew like real hair. So he went to the dwarves of Svartalfheim and commissioned the Sons of Ivaldi to make the wig along with Odin's spear Gungnir and Freyr's ship Skidbladnir to placate the other Aesir."

"Loki didn't stop there either," Baldur chuckled. "He once wagered his head with the Huldra Brothers that they could not make three treasures as valuable as the ones the Sons of Ivaldi had crafted. And when Brok and Sindri crafted Freyr's board Gullinbursti, my father's ring Draupnir, and Thor's hammer Mjolnir, Loki narrowly avoided losing his head because of a technicality. So Brok sowed his mouth shut with wires as payback. But that was typical for Loki. Most of his early pranks were harmless mischief that sometimes benefited the Aesir somehow."

"But everything changed after Jörmungandr was thrown into the sea, Fenrir was bound, and Hel was banished to the underworld," Baldur continued in a severe tone. "After that, his pranks stopped being harmless acts of mischief and became much more malicious. Sometimes it seemed like he was trying to spread outright discord, conflict, and strife amongst the Aesir. Hmm...perhaps that is the true reason he schemed to have me murdered."

Baldur stared up at the emerald sky and sighed. "Loki... everyone despised him for his role in Hodr and my deaths. But no one ever wondered why he did it. They never considered, even for a moment, what would compel him to commit such a heinous act. Moreover, they never considered how he must have felt as a father watching his beloved children endure the same ostracization he had suffered. I suppose he wanted vengeance for his children's mistreatment and to make the Aesir feel the same pain he experienced as he watched his children suffer."

As he spoke, Baldur's eyes began to tear up.

"Baldur... are you...sad?" Sigurd asked.

"That emotion doesn't exist within me," Baldur informed as he wiped his eyes clean. "I suppose... I miss my old friend. I miss the person Loki used to be. And I feel bad for the person he became. Vengeance can turn us all into monsters and villains."

Sigurd was speechless. Baldur had every right to feel angry and spiteful toward Loki for what he had done. Instead, he felt *compassionate* toward the man who had orchestrated his death. Even now, he considered Loki an old friend. Sigurd could not even begin to comprehend this act of kindness and fidelity. It proved Baldur was the kindest, noblest, and most companionate person he had ever met.

"I suppose it is all water under the bridge now." Baldur shook his head. "I can't change what happened or leave this realm. But you two can. Let's continue. We have a long road ahead of us. And I fear you'll have many obstacles to overcome along the way."

CHAPTER SIXTEEN

A GLIMPSE FROM THE PAST

So tired, Sigurd thought as he slogged one foot in front of the other. His mind felt foggy, and his eyelids drooped like a heavy blanket.

Hel's three-hour start encouraged them to continue without stopping, but they occasionally needed to stop to catch their breath. Walking north through the dark city was proving to be quite an arduous challenge, even with the power and energy of Idun's Apple coursing through their veins. Earlier, while following Baldur south to his ship, it seemed effortless, as if they were descending a hill. Now it felt as if they were trudging up a steep hill despite the flat topography. It was as if Helheim's gravity increased with every step they took north.

Baldur claimed they were currently a quarter of the way through the city near the courtyard where they had met and fought each other earlier. But a bone-tired Sigurd felt like they had been marching even farther. It was as if Helheim itself was urging his heavy feet to give up this foolish journey, join the spirits on the Path of the Dead, and travel back to the safety of Baldur's ship.

The unhelpful weather brought unceasing snow, and the wind cut like a knife against Sigurd and Sinfjotli's skin as it blew through the dark city.

Eventually, it became too much to bear. The trio stopped and sought refuge inside a six-story building near the black road. As soon as Sigurd and

Sinfjotli entered the bleak black room, they collapsed breathlessly onto the stone floor. Baldur decided they would resume their journey after a break to replenish their stamina and warm up from the cold. Thankfully, that wouldn't take long. The golden apples they had eaten earlier invigorated them. Sigurd felt like there was a raging bonfire inside him, replenishing his strength and warming his body like a furnace.

In the meantime, they gazed at the emerald sky outside, watching the snow fall on the ground and listening to the strange-sounding wind as it blew through the city's windows and doors.

"Why is it snowing so much?" Sinfjotli complained while shaking the ice and snow out of his hair. "And why is it so fucking cold?"

"I've been wondering about that myself," Sigurd said. "Growing up, I always heard that Hel's domain was in Niflheim. Is this place, Helheim, a part of Niflheim?"

"It used to be," Baldur replied. "Ah...I can tell from your confused faces I should elaborate. There were originally only eight realms: Asgard, Vanaheim, Alfheim, Svartalfheim, Midgard, Jotunheim, Niflheim, and Muspelheim. Odin banished Hel to Niflheim, leaving her in charge of the dishonorable dead. But after a while, Hel grew bored of that cold realm of eternal darkness and split the realm in half."

"She did what?!" Sinfjotli blurted out.

"You heard right," Baldur assured. "Drawing upon her immense powers, Hel split Niflheim in half and created a new realm which she named after herself: Helheim, the ninth realm."

"I see." Sigurd looked up at the emerald sky. "So it's always snowing and windy in Helheim because this realm was once part of Niflheim?"

"Well... yes, but there is more to the story. The eternal blizzards of Helheim are a permanent reminder that this realm was once part of Niflheim. However, the wind is caused by another source."

Baldur paused as another strong gale raced through the city. Far to the east, on the city's outskirts where Sigurd had met and fought Sinfjotli, the wind shrilled like a mother mourning her slain children. But here in the center of the city, the gale produced a deep, almost musical sound as it traveled through the skyscrapers. If Sigurd listened closely, it resembled the noise a flute made as air traveled through its holes. But the wind's whistling sound was far louder and more baritone than any melody a bard could play.

"What I'm about to say may sound strange, but the winds that blow throughout this realm are because of a giant eagle." Baldur began. "Three giant eagles are perched on each layer of the World Tree. At the top of the World Tree sits Gullinkambi the Golden. In Jotunheim, which resides on the hanging branches of Yggdrasil next to Midgard, the crimson eagle Fjalar nests in the Ironwood Forest. And here in the underworld sits the silver eagle Hræsvelgr the Corpse Eater. One day, all three eagles will caw synchronously, announcing the onset of Ragnarök. Until then, they wait and create the winds which flow throughout the realms. The gale force winds you are experiencing result from Hræsvelgr flapping his wings as he feasts on corpses of the dishonorable dead."

Admittedly, Baldur's explanation was outlandish. Back in Midgard, Sigurd would have burst out laughing if someone had given such an absurd explanation for why the wind blows. But he stopped questioning the nature of the universe after he woke up in Helheim, discovered and fought his long-lost brother in a vicious duel, met and shared a meal with actual gods, and survived an encounter with Hel herself. After those wild experiences, the notion that a giant eagle produced these icy gales by flapping its wings seemed rather mundane.

But it also felt somewhat comforting for Sigurd. He had a special connection with birds. He could communicate with them and often enlisted them as his special scouts. It felt reassuring knowing there was a creature here in Helheim only he could talk to, assuming they lived long enough to meet it.

Soon, Baldur decided it was time they resumed their journey. When they stepped outside, another gust of wind blew through the city, producing that deep humming sound as it traveled through the buildings. Sigurd closed his eyes and listened to the hum, wondering if he might hear Hræsvelgr's voice mixed into the wind.

"Sigurd." A voice echoed.

"Who's there?" Sigurd demanded, drawing Gram.

"Is something wrong?" Baldur asked.

"I...I heard a voice call my name just now." Sigurd replied.

"Sigurd." The voice whispered again.

Sigurd spun around, pointing his sword at nothing. He definitely heard a voice just now. But it didn't sound like a distant echo carried on the wind. It sounded like someone had whispered over his shoulder.

"What was that?" Sinfjotli demanded. "Who's there? Show yourself, coward!"

"You heard it too?" Sigurd muttered. *Then the voice couldn't be Hræsvelgr's.*

If Sinfjotli could hear the voice, it couldn't have been spoken by an eagle since only Sigurd could communicate with birds and hear their true language.

"Sigurd!" The voice whispered even louder than before. This time, Sigurd recognized it. He realized this voice didn't belong to an eagle or any bird. It belonged to someone he knew very well.

"Regin!" Sigurd gasped.

"What's that now?" Sinfjotli asked.

"My foster father," Sigurd replied. "That voice...it was Regin's."

"You mean the dwarf that mentored you?" Sinfjotli asked. "The one you said reforged your sword back on the ship?"

Before Sigurd could answer, an emerald green fog raced through the streets and alleyways of the city and enveloped all three of them.

Sigurd struggled and swung his sword uselessly at the fog. But as the fog dissipated and his vision cleared, he realized he wasn't standing in the City of the Lost. He was now standing in a desolate rocky wasteland. Large, dead trees rose like tombstones from the ground around him. This place might have once been a vast forested ridge filled with spruce, beech, and Scots pine trees. But all the trees had been reduced to pale ash-white sticks devoid of leaves. Above the desolate canopy, he saw a large, snowcapped mountain rising into the clouds. The air on this mountainous terrain was chilly but nowhere near as frigid as Helheim had been moments ago.

Sigurd wasn't sure why, but this place seemed vaguely familiar.

"What is this?" Sigurd demanded. "Sinfjotli? Baldur? Where did you go?"

"I'm here, Sigurd," Sinfjotli said while placing a hand on his shoulder. Baldur was also standing nearby with a worried expression.

"So it's started." Baldur sighed. "I had a feeling this might happen."

"Baldur, what's going on?" Sigurd asked. "Did we just get teleported to Midgard?"

"Calm down Sigurd," Baldur replied. "We're still in Helheim. This is just a vision."

"A vision?" Sigurd repeated.

"That's right." Baldur looked like he wanted to say more. But at that moment, Sinfjotli pointed behind them and shouted: "By the gods, what is that vile creature!"

Sigurd turned to where his brother was pointing, and his whole world flipped upside down.

Almost every tree on the rocky ridge behind them had been knocked down. Their bark had turned sickly green, and the land was covered in scorch marks. Lying sprawled across the ground in front of the trail of destruction was the corpse of a giant, disemboweled dragon. The dragon had four dark, scaly, reddish-black legs with two front legs shaped like hands, two enormous bat-like wings sprouting from his back, a crest of spurs and horns on his head at least six feet long, and a long snake-like tail. Spines and spikes jutted along his back and the back of his long, serpentine neck.

"That's Fafnir!" Sigurd gasped. It was the dragon he had slain long ago, which earned him the moniker 'Sigurd the Dragon Slayer.'

But what left Sigurd even more dumbfounded were the two people sitting next to the corpse roasting the dragon's heart on a spit. The figure to the left was a dwarf about four feet tall with a stout, broad body and long, shaggy red beard. The person roasting the heart was Sigurd, or rather, a younger version of himself! His eyes hadn't taken on their golden slit appearance yet, but he still had the bright amber eyes he'd inherited from his mother. He was covered head to toe in the dragon's steaming wet blood.

As Sigurd stared dumbly at the younger version of himself, he realized that he was witnessing a vision of his past. One figure spoke before he could dwell on the matter any further.

"Is it ready yet?" Regin asked impatiently.

"Let me check." The young Sigurd pressed his thumb against the meat to check if it was cooked. As he did, the juices bubbled and burned his thumb.

"Ouch!" Sigurd's past self-exclaimed, instinctively putting his thumb in his mouth to cool it. A second later, his amber eyes dilated. His pupils narrowed and became slits, while the color of his sclera changed to a golden hue. In a literal blink of an eye, Sigurd's amber eyes had taken on the appearance of a golden serpent's.

Regin didn't notice the change since he was too busy drinking a horn full of Fafnir's blood.

A moment later, the young Sigurd's eyes widened, and he glanced at a pair of chirping nuthatches perched on a nearby branch with a bewildered expression. He sat for several minutes, staring intently at the chirping nuthatches with his thumb still in his mouth.

"Would you quit sucking on your thumb already?" Regin asked after a minute had passed. "Your burn can't be that bad. You look ridiculous right now."

The young Sigurd looked back at Regin. The dwarf winced and fell out of his chair when he noticed Sigurd's eyes.

"By the gods, what's happened to your eyes?" Regin gasped as he staggered to his feet.

Sigurd didn't reply. He continued staring intently at Regin, and his face conveyed a flurry of emotions: shock, anger, hesitation, and finally, bitter resignation.

"Sigurd?" Reign asked nervously as Sigurd stood up and glared at the dwarf with his new golden snake eyes.

"I'm sorry," Sigurd replied sadly. Without further warning, he drew Gram and decapitated Regin before the dwarf could utter another word. The young Sigurd then sat down and began eating the dragon's heart. As the vision faded away with the green fog, one nuthatch flew over, perched itself on the young Sigurd's shoulder, and said something peculiar.

A moment later, the fog vanished, and Sigurd stood back in the City of the Lost outside the building they had taken refuge in.

"What...what was that?" Sinfjotli asked, bewildered.

"A vision," Baldur explained. "Helheim is infamous for them. Helheim tortures its inhabitants by conjuring illusions of memories of their past lives. It doesn't discriminate between the saints and sinners, either. They're all forced to relive the memories of their deepest regrets, their greatest sins, and the most painful memories of their past lives. But let's not waste any more time dwelling on it. Hel gave us a three-hour head start, and we must make haste to the Gjallerbru."

***

"Why did you kill Regin?" Sinfjotli asked spontaneously as they resumed trekking north. "I thought you mentioned back on Baldur's ship that the dwarf was like a father to you."

"Because the birds told me to do it," Sigurd answered sadly.

"The birds told you to kill him?" Sinfjotli repeated with a frown. "Is that supposed to be a joke?"

"No, I mean the birds *literally* told me to kill him," Sigurd reiterated. "You saw what happened. While I cooked Fafnir's heart, I pressed my thumb against the meat to check if it was ready, and the juices burned my thumb. Without thinking, I thrust my thumb into my mouth. The moment my tongue tasted those juices, I gained the ability to understand and communicate with birds and read the hearts of men. Then I heard the nuthatches speaking in the tree. They said: '*Look at Sigurd sitting there splattered with Fafnir's blood and cooking for his mentor! He'd be better off eating the heart and gaining some sense.' 'I agree. Just look at Regin sitting there plotting to betray his student. Sigurd's got no idea!' 'Sigurd should think of what's best for himself, not for that two-faced dwarf. Oh, look at the way he's staring at us! He has such a bewildered expression. It's as if he can understand what we're saying. Cut off that treacherous dwarf's head and keep Fafnir's heart and treasure for yourself, Sigurd! That's what I'd advise.'*"

"Those birds really said all that?" Sinfjotli asked.

Sigurd nodded. "I thought I was going mad when I heard those nuthatches speaking to me. But when I looked into Regin's eyes after he inquired if I was all right, I unknowingly read his heart and realized the nuthatches were telling the truth. Beneath his mask of polite concern, I could tell that Regin was plotting to kill me and take the gold for himself once he devoured his brother's heart."

Sigurd paused and looked up at the emerald sky. "For a moment, I was torn over what I should do. Regin wasn't some two-faced scoundrel. He was the man who'd raised me, taught me how to read and write, and repaired my sword. He was like a father to me. Yet there he was, plotting to kill me after *everything* I'd done for him and after I'd achieved my greatest victory. I promised myself that my story wouldn't end there in that cave. So, I drew Gram and did what needed to be done. Still... I've always felt guilty whenever I think back to that day."

Sinfjotli listened to Sigurd in stony silence. Sigurd stared at him, expecting him to judge or call him a murderer. Instead, Sinfjotli smiled.

"So, you can talk to birds, huh?" Sinfjotli remarked. "That's a curious ability."

"It comes in handy, especially for reconnaissance. Birds are much smarter than we give them credit for. Their vision is four or five times greater than any human, although I am an exception. Birds make excellent scouts and spies because nobody pays much attention to them. None of my enemies ever suspected that a swan, a blue jay, a pigeon, a raven, or an eagle perched in a tree above their camp could be a spy reporting back to me. I was rarely taken by surprise."

"Never underestimate the usefulness of birds." Baldur chuckled. "Now let's keep moving."

***

As they trudged north, Sigurd couldn't stop thinking about the vision he'd just witnessed.

"Is something the matter, Sigurd?" Baldur asked. "You seem perturbed. Are you feeling all right after reliving the murder of your mentor?"

"No, it's not that," Sigurd assured. "Something was amiss with that vision. Right before the emerald fog faded, one bird said something peculiar. They told my younger self: 'Once you finish eating Fafnir's heart and seize his treasure, head north to the mountain of Hindarfjall. There, you will find a palace surrounded by flames where a sleeping maiden lies imprisoned, waiting to bestow great wisdom.' But I don't remember them saying anything like that after I slew Regin."

"Maybe it was a trick," Sinfjotli guessed. "Maybe Helheim added that bit at the end just to mess with you?"

"That's not how it works." Baldur shook his head. "Helheim torments you by showing you visions of traumatic memories from your past. But it cannot alter those past events or show you something that never happened. It shows you the whole painful truth and nothing else. Everything you saw in that vision was *exactly* what happened on the day you slew Regin, including what the nuthatches mentioned at the end."

"Then why can't I remember it?" Sigurd questioned. "I remember every moment of the day I slew Fafnir and Regin in picturesque detail. So why don't I remember them telling me this?"

"Perhaps it's one of the memories suppressed by the magical barrier in your mind?" Baldur theorized. "Back on the ship, you mentioned that the gap in your memory starts after you took Fafnir's treasure. And you can't remember anything that happened before you returned home to attend your mother's funeral. We already established that someone went to great lengths to make you forget a specific event during that gap. Perhaps the nuthatch's final instruction was somehow related to that important event, so it was magically suppressed."

Baldur's theory seemed plausible. But it also left Sigurd with more questions. Who erased his memory, and why? What exactly did they want him to forget? And how was it related to "a sleeping maiden in a palace surrounded by flames?"

"The nuthatch mentioned Hindarfjall," Sigurd recalled. "That was the name of a famous mountain wreathed by clouds. I remember traveling there once with my brother-in-law Gunnar and helping him to..."

"Hang on!" Sinfjotli interrupted. "Sigurd, do you hear that?"

Sigurd listened intently. After a moment, he heard screaming and shouting.

"Run!" Someone screamed. "Evacuate the castle! It's Sigmund! Sigmund has returned from the grave!"

"Sigmund?" Sigurd repeated. He watched as an emerald fog rolled in through the streets, and another vision manifested.

CHAPTER SEVENTEEN

A BLOODY DEBT

When his vision cleared, Sigurd found himself inside the great hall of a burning castle. The tapestries on the walls were ablaze, and the roof was on fire. People were scrambling about, knocking over tables, choking on the smoke, and desperately trying to flee. But there was no escape. He could see a younger version of Sinfjotli guarding the exit, cutting down everyone who tried to escape. Standing next to him was a beautiful woman in a suit of crimson armor. She helped Sinfjotli butcher any fools who strayed too close.

In the middle of the burning hall was a tall, muscular man slaughtering foes left and right. After a moment, Sigurd realized that the sword he was holding was Gram!

"That's...my father?" It was the first time Sigurd had seen his father, Sigmund. Sigurd recognized many physical similarities between himself and the warrior, although he admittedly looked more like Sinfjotli.

Sigmund was a stocky bull of a man. He was six feet seven inches tall, broad-shouldered, and mighty in appearance, with piercing steel blue eyes and long and wild brown hair. In his black scales and fur armor, Sigmund looked every bit like a warrior king. He looked to be in his early forties, but his handsome features helped mask his age.

While Sinfjotli and the female warrior stood guard at the exit and slew everyone who tried to escape, Sigmund fought his way to the other end of the burning hall where a king in heavy armor stood behind a retinue of a dozen armed warriors.

The king, about fifty years old, had oily black hair and wore a vainglorious crown made from precious gemstones. He wore a heavy suit of steel armor and wielded an enormous two-handed claymore. Well-kept mutton chops connected to his mustache, but he was otherwise clean-shaven. The king's face might've been handsome once. But a permanent scowl and a fierce look in his eyes gave him a sinister expression.

"I have waited for this day for so long, Siggeir," Sigmund told the king. "Years ago, you slaughtered my father and brothers in cold blood after inviting us into your home. And to this day, you've shown no remorse for that betrayal. I fear I'll enjoy killing you so much that my heart may burst!"

Siggeir looked around anxiously. "Guards, kill him!" His guards rushed forward, but Sigmund promptly killed six of them in mere moments with Gram. The rest of the king's guards dropped their weapons and fled toward the exit, only to be slain by Sinfjotli and the woman.

Meanwhile, Siggeir attempted to sneak away toward the exit by creeping along the wall. But before he made it halfway across the room, Sigmund picked up one of the fallen guards' swords and hurled it like a javelin at the wall. The massive broadsword jammed into the stone wall an inch in front of Siggeir's chest, stopping him in his tracks.

"Not this time!" Sigmund seethed. "There is no escape."

Siggeir looked at the sword before him, then glanced back at Sigmund with ire and begrudging respect.

"You misunderstand my intentions. I'm not running away." Siggeir reached over the sword Sigmund had just thrown and removed a massive wooden shield from its mount on the stone wall. The enormous wooden shield had twelve metal spikes jutting from the sides in every direction and had a wicked ten-inch point in its center. Siggeir fastened the shield to his left arm. Then he dipped his claymore into a nearby barrel of oil and ignited the blade with one of the nearby fires.

"I should have killed you years ago when you and your brothers were at my mercy!" Siggeir growled. "I should have killed you yesterday instead of burying you alive with that traitorous son of mine! But I let my pride and anger get the better of me. I will rectify that mistake now."

"It ends now, Siggeir," Sigmund promised, pointing Gram at the Geatish King. "There are no more plots, armies, or distractions between us. Now, 'Slayer of the Volsungs,' let us see if you can live up to your reputation."

With that, the two men began their epic duel. Sigurd was mesmerized as he watched his father fight. Sigmund used Gram as if it were an extension of his arm and wasted nothing in his movements. The blade flashed like the flowing rapids of a river with every strike.

Siggeir was no pushover, either. He managed to hold his own against Sigmund and lasted far longer than his guards had. The fact that he could wield a claymore with a single hand and a large shield in the other was a testament to his strength. But he was not Sigmund's equal, and it became apparent as they fought on. His weapons were mere toys compared to Sigmund's sword. As Sigurd knew well, no weapon in Midgard could parry Gram, and the legendary blade gradually whittled Siggeir's weapons.

Eventually, Sigmund parried a thrust by Siggeir and sliced off the tip of the claymore. Gram passed through the metal blade like a hot knife through butter. Angered, Siggeir tried to swing what remained of his sword at Sigmund.

Sigmund knocked the claymore aside and slashed Siggeir from his navel to his left collarbone. Gram shredded through the king's heavy steel plate like parchment. Siggeir grimaced, but he refused to relent. He charged forward, intending to skewer Sigmund with his shield's spikes. But Sigmund effortlessly cut the shield in half with a single swing of Gram.

Siggeir staggered backward and examined his injured left arm. Gram hadn't just sliced the shield in half. The sword also shredded Siggeir's left vambrace, sliced off his thumb, and flayed an entire layer of skin from his forearm.

Siggeir cast the broken shield aside and swung his damaged claymore at Sigmund again. But in a masterful stroke, Sigmund parried the sword and pirouetted out of the way while thrusting the tip of Gram into Siggeir's left eye. Siggeir roared in pain and backed away.

"Pathetic!" Sigmund growled. "In your heyday, you might've stood a chance against me. But after almost thirty years of hiding behind your castle and armies, you've gotten weak and rusty."

"Don't speak to me... in that condescending tone... as if... you've already won," Siggeir growled, still clutching his bleeding eye socket. "Our fight... isn't over yet!"

"It just ended," Sigmund replied coldly.

Siggeir glared at Sigmund with his one remaining eye. Then he started laughing. It was a crazed laugh full of emotion and hate. He clutched his sword hilt so tightly that his right hand started bleeding.

"This is what infuriates me the most about you, Volsungs!" Siggeir exploded. "The way you speak to me and look at me with those condescending eyes sickens me! No matter what I do, somewhere deep inside, you always believe you're superior to me! I can't stand it! Anyone who looks down on me deserves to be crushed!"

Siggeir rushed forward, but Sigmund lunged and stabbed him in the torso, inflicting a mortal injury before his opponent could swing his sword. As Siggeir staggered backward, Sigmund sliced through a nearby support column, causing a large chunk of the burning roof above them to cave in and crush Siggeir.

When the dust and smoke settled, Sigmund discovered Siggeir lying on the floor and buried beneath the pile of rubble. Everything below his neck had been crushed beneath the falling debris. But somehow, Siggeir was still alive. The two mortal enemies glowered at each other. The rubble ignited as Sigmund stepped forward to deliver the coup de grâce. The flames spread across the wooden support beams and inched toward Siggeir's neck.

"Go on then," Siggeir pleaded. "Finish me! Take your revenge, Sigmund!"

Sigmund had a muted expression as he stared at the old king. He glanced at the flames creeping closer toward Siggeir's neck.

"What are you waiting for?!" Siggeir screamed. "Kill *ME*!"

"No." Sigmund refused coldly. "A swift death would be a mercy you don't deserve."

Sigmund kneeled over Siggeir and looked his mortal enemy in the eye as the flames burned closer to the king's flesh.

"You violated guest right. You butchered your guests after inviting them into your home. You stabbed my father in the back, then tore out his heart and fed it to your hounds. When my sister begged you to spare me and my brothers, you placed a log over our legs and ordered your mother to turn into a wolf and devour one of us each night. You had your men hunt me like an animal in the wild for years! And throughout all that time, you did unspeakable things to my twin sister! You committed all these atrocities against my family because I refused to give you this sword as a wedding present! I won't grant a wicked scoundrel like you the mercy of a quick death. You will die screaming!"

With that, Sigmund stood and walked away as the flames reached Siggeir's neck and consumed his flesh. As Sigmund promised, the Geatish king died screaming as he burned alive beneath the rubble of his castle.

CHAPTER EIGHTEEN

A SOUL-SHATTERING TRUTH

Sigurd watched as his father trekked through the blazing inferno. Sigmund walked past piles of corpses and waded through puddles of red blood before exiting the burning castle. A beautiful woman in crimson red battle armor and the young version of Sinfjotli waited outside.

Now that the chaotic battle was over, Sigurd could get a good look at the two of them. The young Sinfjotli looked around sixteen years old but was remarkably tall for that age. Even at such a young age, he was already muscular and broad-shouldered like an ox.

The woman standing next to him was obviously Sigmund's twin sister, Signy, since she looked identical to him in every respect save for the color of her hair. She was beautiful, with long, flowing golden hair and piercing blue eyes. However, her beauty had an edge to it. She looked fierce, stern, and unforgiving in her suit of crimson-red armor. She looked every bit like the warrior Sigmund did. Judging from her blood-stained sword and the nearby corpses, Signy had killed her fair share of Geatish alongside her son.

Sigmund nodded at Sinfjotli and then hugged Signy. "It's done, Signy." He reported while pulling away.

Signy let out a long sigh and looked up at the starry sky. "We killed him. The monster is dead."

"And I ended his bloodline," Sinfjotli announced proudly. "The rest of Siggeir's children and extended family members are dead by my hand."

Sigmund regarded Sinfjotli with a horrified and sad expression. "Sinfjotli, you shouldn't be so complacent and proud about that. They were your kin. And Hansel and Aurora were your siblings."

"They were *Siggeir's* children." Sinfjotli reminded him. "And I swore a blood oath to Mother that I would end his bloodline for his crimes."

Sigmund sighed but didn't argue the point any further. The three turned and stared at the burning castle in silence as if they were expecting a monster to come lunging at them from the flames. But there was nothing inside the castle but flames and death.

"It's finished," Signy muttered in disbelief. "We did it, Sigmund. After all these years, our father and brothers can finally rest in peace."

There was no joy in her voice nor any trace of celebration or accomplishment. Nor should there have been any. The three of them had just slaughtered hundreds of servants, aristocrats, and warriors for the crimes of their king. Even women and children hadn't been spared from their wrath. Everyone had been mercilessly slaughtered as they tried to flee the burning castle. Instead of rejoicing, the three of them stood covered in the blood of their enemies, watching the castle burn.

"What will you do now?" Signy asked, breaking the silence.

"I don't know," Sigmund admitted. "For nearly thirty years, I've strived to avenge our father and brothers. But throughout all that time, I never gave a moment's thought about what I would do when it was over."

"Sigmund, you've spent half your life serving the memory of our father and brother," Signy said. "Now that it's over, it is time you started living for yourself. Go back to our home, to Hunaland. Take Sinfjotli with you. And live your life."

"Aren't you coming with us?" Sigmund asked.

"No." Signy glanced down at her blood-soaked hands. "I forfeited that right long ago. Everything I've done these past three decades has been to bring about the death of my wretched husband. But now that he's dead… I realize that I have worked so hard to achieve vengeance and committed so many wicked deeds that I am no longer fit to live. This is where my story ends."

"I won't be leaving either," Sinfjotli announced. "This is the end for me as well."

Sigmund turned to find Sinfjotli kneeling on the ground. He had removed his chest plate and held a knife pointed at his heart.

"Sinfjotli," Sigmund shouted in alarm. "What are you doing?"

"Finishing it," Sinfjotli replied. "I swore a blood oath to end Siggeir's entire bloodline for his crimes. I already killed Hansel and Aurora and all his other relatives. Now, there is just one left that must die. Siggeir's tainted blood runs through my veins as well. For my blood oath to be fulfilled, I must die as well. Goodbye, Uncle. Thank you for everything you taught me."

"Sinfjotli, NO!" Sigmund screamed as Sinfjotli plunged the knife toward his heart. But before the blade could pierce his chest, Signy thrust out her hand, stopping the knife and getting her hand impaled.

"That's enough, Sinfjotli!" Signy shouted. "You've done enough!"

Sinfjotli looked at his mother with utter confusion and despair. Then he began weeping.

"Why are you stopping me, Mother?" He asked as tears began rolling down his cheeks. "Isn't this what you wanted? You made me swear a blood oath to end Siggeir's bloodline to avenge grandfather Völsung and my nine uncles. That is my purpose and sole reason for living. I've already killed his other children, but his demonic blood still flows in my veins. I must do this."

"You foolish boy," Signy muttered as she pulled the knife from her hand and tossed it aside. She kneeled and hugged Sinfjotli in a fierce embrace. "You misunderstand. You've already fulfilled your oath. There is no need for you to do this because...because Siggeir wasn't your real father. She turned and pointed right at Sigmund. "He is."

Sigmund smiled. "You are kind to say that, Signy. My nephew Sinfjotli is like a son to me. But I can never be his father by blood."

"You are," Signy insisted. "Sinfjotli is much more than a surrogate son to you. He *is* your biological son and heir."

"That's impossible." Sigmund insisted. "Do you even realize what you're insinuating? You're my twin sister, and I would never..."

"Seventeen years ago, a beautiful sorceress visited you in your cave in the forest." Signy interrupted.

Sigmund lost his composure and gaped in shock. He stumbled backward as if he had just been shot by an arrow. "How do you know about...?"

"You hadn't been with a woman since you were sixteen." Signy continued. "The sorceress was enchantingly beautiful, and you found you desired the company of a woman. You spent three days and nights with her before she departed and never saw her again. I know all this because...because that sorceress was me in disguise."

Sinfjotli and Sigmund gaped in shock. The entire castle became eerily quiet, aside from the crackling of the fire. The silence was broken when Sigmund dropped Gram and covered his mouth in horror.

"Signy!" Sigmund gasped horrified. "How?"

"I made a deal with a sorceress from the Scanades Mountains," Signy explained. "We agreed to trade our physical forms for three days. And..."

"I don't give a shit about *how* you did it!" Sigmund exploded. "Why did you do that to *me*? How could you *use* me like that? I'm your twin brother!"

"You think I wanted to do it?!" Signy sprang to her feet with tears in her eyes. "For years, I've wanted nothing but to see our father and brothers' deaths avenged. But I knew we couldn't achieve this alone. Years ago, the sorceress from the Scanades Mountains prophesied that 'only Sigmund and the *true* grandson of Völsung could bring about Siggeir's demise.' I sent you my first-born son, Ragr, to help in this endeavor. But you deemed him unworthy after he failed your test of courage, so I ordered you to kill him. After the same happened to my second son Rekkr, I realized what the prophecy truly meant and what needed to be done. I sought the sorceress who had given me the prophecy and made a deal to exchange shapes with her. I sought you out, did what needed to be done, then returned to this castle four days later and regained my appearance. After a time, I gave birth to our son Sinfjotli, a true grandson of Völsung on both sides."

Sigmund panted. He studied Signy's face, desperately hoping this was all nonsense. But these were not the ravings of a madwoman or grieving mother. One look at the resolve, sincerity, and shame written across her face made it clear she meant every single word.

"Signy," Sigmund gasped. "You're not the sister I remember. You've become a monster."

Signy nodded sadly. "You're right. Everything I've done these past three decades has been to bring about the death of King Siggeir. But now that he's dead... I realize just how monstrous I've become. I sacrificed everything, including my children, in the name of vengeance. I... I had you murder my sons for being weak and timid. I seduced you, my twin brother, to fulfill a prophecy. Worst of all, I... I conditioned our son to murder my other children because Siggeir was their father. I realize that I have committed so many wicked deeds for vengeance that I am not fit to live."

Signy looked down at her bleeding hand. She noticed her sword lying on the cobblestone road. She unstrapped her scabbard from her belt, sheathed the sword, and handed it to Sigmund.

"Give this to one of your future sons." She instructed. "I hope they'll be more worthy of it than I am. Goodbye, brother. When you think of me in the future... try remembering the woman I once was rather than the monster I became."

She turned to Sinfjotli and embraced him for a long while. She wiped the tears from his cheeks, leaving smears of her blood under his eyes. "Sinfjotli, my son, the path ahead of you may be difficult. People may despise your existence. But I promise you that someday, you'll meet people who will accept you for who you are. No matter what, you are a true grandson of Völsung, and I am proud to be your mother. I love you with all of myself. And I always will."

Signy kissed her son on the forehead and walked inside the burning castle. Walking toward where Siggeir lay buried beneath the burning debris, she removed her armor and clothing, stripping down to her undergarments.

She stood over the spot where Siggeir had burned to death. The flesh had already burned away from his skull, and smoke billowed from his mouth and eye sockets like a chimney. Signy looked groggy, most likely from the smoke and how much blood she had lost.

"You took everything from me!" Signy sobbed. "I swore I would make you feel the worst pain imaginable for what you did. I despised you with every fiber of my being. But even though I married reluctantly, you were still my husband. At the very least, I can die by your side."

With that, Signy threw herself onto the burning wreckage. Sigmund and Sinfjotli watched in horror as she allowed the flames to consume her body. The vision and fog faded away as the rest of the ceiling collapsed.

CHAPTER NINETEEN

NOTHING ELSE MATTERS

When the emerald fog faded away, Sinfjotli collapsed to the ground sobbing. Sigurd, meanwhile, was speechless. He finally understood what Sinfjotli meant earlier when he claimed that his mother had "*used* Sigmund." Signy had used her twin brother to create "a true grandson of Völsung," the perfect harbinger of her vengeance.

"Sinfjotli," Sigurd muttered sadly as his brother sobbed on the ground. Sigurd couldn't imagine how Sinfjotli must have felt after reliving the night he learned about the shameful circumstances of his birth and watching his mother end her life in the flames of Siggeir's castle. He struggled to think of something, anything that might comfort Sinfjotli.

Instead, Baldur stepped forth to comfort Sinfjotli. He helped Sigurd's brother to his feet and hugged him as Sinfjotli continued sobbing on his shoulder.

"Vengeance can make monsters out of all of us," Baldur remarked as he hugged Sinfjotli. "At least your mother died with her dignity intact, her greatest secret exposed, and a clear conscience."

"Baldur, why are we seeing these memories of our past?" Sinfjotli sobbed.

"Because this is what Helheim does. Hel has been torturing wicked souls for millennia. But even she can't come up with anything half so cruel as showing sinners the repressed memories and thoughts in the back of their minds. Helheim tortures the dishonorable dead with the most painful memories of their past, such as their sins, greatest regrets, or even the most traumatizing memory of their lives. This realm continues to torment them, even after they've lost all hope. And then it rebuilds them, molding them into Hel's undead minions."

"Wait, you just said these visions are supposed to torment the dishonorable dead." Sigurd frowned. "So why are we being shown these visions if we're technically alive?"

Baldur shrugged as he stepped away from Sinfjotli. "Perhaps Helheim cannot distinguish between the living and the dead and is tormenting you both indiscriminately. Regardless, you mustn't allow these visions of your past to bog you down or distract you. Hel gave us a three-hour head start. If you continue allowing these visions of your past to haunt you, you'll waste precious time, and it will be harder for you to escape from Helheim."

Nobody raised objections. They resumed their journey, walking at an even faster pace through the city. Sigurd's mind was still trying to come to terms with the visions. Being reminded of Regin's death was one thing. Seeing his father for the first time, seeing Sinfjotli try to commit suicide, and seeing the moment his brother learned he was conceived through an incestuous union between their father and his twin sister was a lot to process. But one thing bothered him more than everything else.

"Sinfjotli, in that vision, our father told Siggeir, 'You did all that because I wouldn't give you this sword as a wedding present.' Was that true?"

"Y-yes," Sinfjotli sniffled. "H-he meant every w-word. I already told you... about our family's long and bloody history on Baldur's ship. And ...well...you saw and heard how it ended in that vision."

"I...I never knew." Sigurd muttered in disbelief. He drew Gram and studied the fuller of the blade. "I never knew our family had such a long bloody history or that it started because of this sword. The only things I knew about this sword were based on what Mother told me on the day she gave me its broken fragments. She told me it had broken in my father's final battle when he needed it most."

Sinfjotli scowled and wiped his tears away. "In a way, that sword was the beginning of the end for our family. But Gram never failed him. Even when Father had lost everything and lived as an exile and outlaw in Gautland, that sword remained by his side."

Sigurd smiled at the comforting thought. Gram had never left his side either, and it had even accompanied him to the afterlife.

As they continued trekking north along the Path of the Dead, Sigurd reflected on what he'd witnessed and what Sinfjotli had recounted on the Hringhorni about Gram and the Volsungs' long and bloody history. One thing still lingered in Sigurd's mind, which he could not keep to himself because of Baldur's aura.

"I'm still shocked about what your mother confessed before she died. I can't believe she seduced her own brother and remorselessly ordered Father to kill her sons. Why did she go so far in her quest for vengeance? Couldn't she have just slit Siggeir's throat as he slept? She was his wife. Surely, she would have had plenty of opportunities to catch him off guard and kill him herself."

"That was never an option!" Sinfjotli snapped. His voice, while still despondent, now sounded defensive. "Siggeir was a cruel and paranoid tyrant. But he wasn't stupid. He knew just how much my mother despised him. That's why he kept a keen eye on her and always had his guards by his side. He always slept with at least five guards watching over him every night he... *slept* with her. Even if she wanted to slit his throat with a smuggled dagger, the guards would have killed my mother before she could unsheathe the knife."

"Besides, Mother wouldn't have taken it even if another opportunity presented itself." Sinfjotli continued. "She would never have allowed Siggeir to die such a quick and easy death. After watching Siggeir execute her brothers, my mother swore a dire oath of vengeance against him. For her, it wasn't enough to kill Siggeir. She wanted to obliterate his kingdom and bloodline and erase all traces of him from history. And more than anything, she wanted him to experience a fraction of the same pain he had inflicted on her."

"Is that why... she had you murder your siblings?" Sigurd asked hesitantly.

Sinfjotli glared at him. Sigurd realized from the look on his brother's face that he was treading into treacherous waters. Normally, he wouldn't even consider asking Sinfjotli a dangerous and audacious question like that. But because of Baldur's aura, neither could keep these risky questions or thoughts to themselves.

"Yes," Sinfjotli admitted. "It happened a day before that vision you just saw. When I turned sixteen, our father decided I was ready. And so we infiltrated Siggeir's castle and met with my mother. But as we strategized how best to assault the main hall, Hansel and Aurora chanced upon us. Since my parents were twins, they realized that Sigmund was their uncle and the man their father, Siggeir, had been hunting. Before they could expose us, my mother gave them a ring to play with. When they were gone, she turned to us and ordered Sigmund to kill them. Father protested that they had done nothing. My mother insisted they had to die to prevent our cover from being blown and to eradicate Siggeir's bloodline. But Father refused to do it. He had already killed her previous sons and refused to kill any more of her children. But I wasn't so reluctant. And so I did what needed to be done."

"Did you not feel any remorse?" Sigurd asked. "Even if they were Siggeir's progeny, they were still your younger siblings, like me."

"Even if I did, it didn't matter in the end." Sinfjotli sighed. "It didn't work."

Sigurd narrowed his eyes. "What do you mean?"

"Killing Hansel and Aurora didn't hurt Siggeir as much as my mother or I expected." Sinfjotli elaborated. "Once they were dead, we stormed into Siggeir's hall and threw their corpses at his feet. We then slew countless warriors and allowed ourselves to get captured. When Siggeir had us at his mercy and pondered how best to kill us, I looked him straight in the eyes and told him I murdered his children.

"And that's when I realized the terrible truth about Siggeir. He didn't care. Oh, he was certainly shocked and horrified by what I had done. But there was no genuine grief in his eyes over the deaths of his children, only frustration that he had lost the heirs to his throne. That's when I realized Siggeir didn't care about me, his children, his people, or anyone. He was a monster to whom the sanctity of life meant nothing. So, to answer your question, Sigurd, I do feel remorse. I regret that Hansel and Aurora were the progeny of such a heartless monster."

"Right, well on that grim thought, let's change subjects," Baldur suggested. "We're only halfway through the city, and if possible, I'd like to talk about something more pleasant."

Their continued trek north through the city became increasingly difficult. Earlier, it felt as if they were trudging uphill. Now, it felt like they were ascending a steep mountain, even though the ground was flat. Every step became more arduous, as if Helheim itself was trying to discourage them from traveling farther. Still, they trudged onwards.

Thankfully, they were making progress. Sigurd could now see the outline of a bridge just beyond the horizon, though it was still quite far away.

Sinfjotli had also recovered from experiencing that traumatizing vision of his mother's death. He wasn't as melancholic as earlier, but he had a grave expression, as if something was still bothering him. The next time they stopped for a break at a small junction in the Path of the Dead, Sinfjotli pulled Sigurd aside.

"There's something I want to ask," Sinfjotli began. "Earlier, you claimed Gram failed our father when he needed it most. What did you mean by that?"

"I can't tell you the complete story because I don't know it," Sigurd forewarned. "All I know is that Gram somehow shattered during his final battle against King Lyngvi's army. But I have no idea how it happened, and I can't begin to imagine how..."

"Wait a minute." Sinfjotli interrupted. "Do you hear that?"

"What is it?" Sigurd asked.

"That voice!" Sinfjotli exclaimed wide-eyed. "It can't be!"

Sigurd concentrated. He could now hear a garbled voice becoming louder.

"Is that all you got?!" the voice demanded. *"You're dying fast! Like roaches under my boot! Is there no one on this battlefield that can match Sigmund, son of Völsung?"*

"Father?" Sigurd gasped.

"No, Sigurd!" Baldur warned. "Don't give in! Don't let it take hold!"

His warning came too late. The emerald fog of Helheim rolled in, and another vision manifested before Sigurd's eyes.

They were standing amid a great battlefield. Bodies littered the ground around them. Before them was a familiar-looking man cutting down enemies left and right.

It was the second time Sigurd had seen his father. Sigmund's long beard had turned gray, and he wore a simple iron crown around his gray hair. He had aged since the last vision but was not feeble. Even in old age, he had a stomach as flat as oak and the strength of three men. He was unstoppable. No one could stand before him as he effortlessly sliced through armored enemies with Gram.

Suddenly, Sigurd noticed an old man with a wide-brimmed hat walking into the melee. No weapons touched him as he bore his spear through the carnage. He came to the thick of the fighting and held his spear aloft as Sigmund swung Gram at him. The instant the sword touched the spear's shaft, the famous blade shattered with an ominous crackling sound.

Everything seemed to freeze in that instant. The shrieking echo of the shattered sword drowned out the sounds of people fighting and dying. Sigurd covered his ears as the sound continued rumbling in his head. It was a cold, awful jangle that scrapped Sigurd's bones and hollowed his guts. It was similar to the unnatural sound Gram produced when he swung the sword at Baldur earlier. That noise sounded like a loud cry of anguish. But this awful jangle reverberating through his head sounded more like a bloodcurdling metallic scream.

The old man in the vision was utterly unfazed by the petrifying sound. Sigmund backed away and stared at the broken sword in his right hand and the metal fragments scattered across the ground. He had a dazed and stupefied expression, as if his mind still couldn't process what had happened.

Sigmund's surprise melted as he groaned and clutched his right side. When he removed his hand, Sigurd saw his father was bleeding. One of Gram's fragments had flung straight at Sigmund after the sword shattered. The shrapnel sliced straight through his armor and undergarment, leaving a long but shallow scratch across his skin.

Sigmund stared at the nearby shrapnel jutting from the ground and then at the broken sword in his hand. Then he glanced back at the old man casually holding his spear.

"W-who are you?" Sigmund demanded.

The old man looked up and pushed back his wide-brimmed hat, allowing Sigurd to see his face clearly. He had a long, flowing white beard and was missing his left eye. His pale blue right eye was the color of the sky on a bright winter's day with thick frost coating the ground. Sigurd didn't recognize him, but Sigmund seemed taken aback by the old man's face. "You!" Sigmund gasped. "I...I haven't seen you since Signy's wedding. Why are you...? Why did my sword...?" He paused, and a look of realization washed over him. "Oh...I see. I...I understand."

"What a shame," an unfamiliar voice called. A middle-aged man in steel armor appeared. Etched on his shield was the image of a horned bull's skull on a red field. It was the sigil of house Hunding, the same noble house Sigurd extinguished in retribution for his father's death.

"Rumor has it you wield a sword that puts all others to shame. I hoped to take it from your corpse as a spoil of war. But it seems it is worthless now. I'll have to settle for your head and *this one* as trophies instead."

The warrior held a freshly severed head that wore an elaborate golden band.

"King Eylimi," Sigmund muttered sadly as he gazed at the head.

That's my grandfather! Sigurd realized.

"Do you like it?" the stranger asked, holding the severed head. "I think I'll claim it as his daughter's dowry on my brother's behalf. Fate's a funny thing, isn't it? We were on the verge of sealing our alliance with him in matrimony a year ago. And then *you* showed up, the last remnant of an ancient disgraced line. My brother spent years courting Hjordis and her father. And yet the day you showed up, the whole plan went to shit!"

"Eylimi let Hjordis choose between her two suitors to avoid insulting either of us. '"King Sigmund is very old,"' he said, imitating a woman's voice while using the severed head's mouth like a ventriloquist puppet. '"But he is the most famous of all kings. I choose him."' And look at where that 'wise' decision got him." He tossed the severed head at Sigmund's feet in disgust.

"You have lived too long, old man." The warrior said. "Your family has taken so much from us. Years ago, your sons murdered my father and brothers and massacred our people. And then you stole my brother's beloved. Well, he'll soon have her to himself. As we speak, my brother is searching for her through your kingdom. But in the meantime, it's only fitting that I, Hávard, twin brother of King Lyngvi and general of his army, take your life and head to settle the score for all you Volsungs have wrought!"

Sigmund didn't move from the spot where Gram had shattered. He looked down at the severed head of his father-in-law near his feet, kneeled, and gently closed its eyelids.

"I'll be with you soon, old friend." He promised. He glanced at the mysterious old man with the spear and bowed his head. "Please, grant me vengeance one last time."

The old man nodded. He picked up Eylimi's severed head and retreated from the carnage, still untouched by the vicious battle unfolding around him.

Sigmund defiantly stood up and pointed his broken sword at Hávard. He seemed...oddly content. "There's something rather comforting about facing death like this, wouldn't you agree?"

"What do you mean?" Hávard asked.

"This fight between us is all that matters." Sigmund elaborated. "Now that I know this will be my last duel, nothing else seems to exist outside my instinct to kill you. Rank, personal history and birth, sex, the sins I've committed, this battle raging around us, and even the prospect of my imminent death. It's all meaningless! *This* is the only thing that's real: to fight to avenge my friend and father-in-law's death and *nothing* else. I've never felt so complete. Is this how my father and great-grandfather felt? Ha, I guess you could say I've finally arrived."

"I don't know what you're blathering about, old man, but it sounds like you're prepared to die." Hávard smiled. "In that case, I'm happy to oblige."

"Then shut your trap and fight!" Sigmund retorted.

A KING'S LAST STAND

Sometimes, fighting with a weapon you are comfortable and familiar with can be the deciding factor between life and death in a duel. Sigmund had been invincible whenever he held Gram. But in its current broken state, it was little more than a sizeable sharp dagger. And Sigmund's instincts were hindered as a result. He miscalculated blocks and parries and missed strikes, and Hávard made him pay for every mistake with a fresh wound. Yet the grizzled warrior king fought on to the bitter end.

Although, Sigurd noted that his father hardly attempted to defend himself from Hávard. The tide of battle had turned against Sigmund and his men, and he no longer sought to protect himself. He had accepted that this would be his final fight, so he fought with the cold recognition of a man with nothing left to lose. He was so drunk with battle fever that he did not even seem to feel the scores of wounds Hávard inflicted on him. Yet they took their grievous toll.

Ultimately, Hávard inflicted a mortal injury on Sigmund, forcing him to his knees. But as the cackling Hávard raised his sword to inflict the coup de grâce, Sigmund lunged forward and stabbed Hávard's forearm with Gram's jagged blade, disarming his foe. He then picked up Hávard's sword and sliced open Hávard from his groin to his throat with his own weapon. Finally,

Sigmund dislodged Gram from Hávard's sword arm and jammed the broken blade hilt deep into his foe's face.

Sigmund had won his final duel and avenged his friend and father-in-law. But it had cost him his life. Sigmund coughed up blood after dislodging Gram from Hávard's head and collapsed.

The vision and fog faded away. Sigurd was left speechless, unable to think, and unsure how to process or respond to what he had just witnessed. Meanwhile, Sinfjotli collapsed to his knees in shock and grief.

Sigurd had often heard about his father and grandfather's final battle from his mother and the few survivors of the Sack of Hunaland. But seeing Sigmund's last duel unfold before his own eyes left Sigurd dumbstruck, especially seeing how Gram had shattered.

Baldur broke the silence by placing his hands on their shoulders. "Your father died a warrior's death fighting to defend his kingdom and avenge his friend. He was one truly worthy of Valhalla."

As Sigurd processed what he had seen in the vision, only one question remained on his mind. "Who was the old man who broke Gram?"

"That was my father, Odin. He often travels the realms in disguise. That gray cloak and broad hat is one of his favorite disguises."

"But why did he appear during our father's final battle?" Sinfjotli asked.

"Because it was Sigmund's time," Baldur answered. "Normally, the valkyries are the ones who choose the slain from every battle and escort them to either Valhalla or Fólkvangr. But sometimes Odin himself appears to personally collect those he deems exceptional. You should feel honored. My father has only done this for a handful of heroes."

"*Honored*?!" Sinfjotli repeated indignantly. "He broke Gram! Father would have won that fateful battle if Odin hadn't interfered."

"Try to think about it another way," Baldur suggested. "Your father was such a skilled warrior that Odin himself had to personally ensure that it would be his final battle. And based on everything I've heard, I imagine Sigmund felt content knowing Odin deemed this would be his final fight."

Sigurd's eyes hardened and narrowed into slits as he stared daggers at Baldur. Admittedly, the notion that Sigmund had been such a skilled warrior that Odin himself had to personally ensure he would die was a flattering thought. But it did nothing to abate the rage Sigurd now felt. If his father had survived that fateful battle, he could have triumphed against Lyngvi and prevented all the pain and misery the insidious king and his psychotic nephews inflicted on Hunaland. But because of Odin...!

Sigurd clenched his fists and flared his nostrils. He considered marching over to a glacier in a nearby alley and punching it as Sinfjotli did earlier to abate his rage. But his anger vanished because of the effects of Baldur's aura, and he calmed down before he could do anything brash.

"I'd always heard he and my grandfather died fighting in that battle against the Hundings. But seeing it actually happen... and seeing how Gram broke..."

Sigurd paused as a troubling thought crossed his mind. "Baldur?"

"Yes?"

"Earlier, you theorized Helheim is tormenting us with visions of our past because it can't distinguish between the living and dead. You also said that it tortures its inhabitants with their worst memories. But neither of us was alive when our father died. So why did Helheim show us a vision of something that we've never witnessed and isn't a part of our subjective past?"

Sigurd's eyes widened as he realized what was happening. "It's not that Helheim can't distinguish between the living and dead. Hel herself must be conjuring these visions!"

Baldur nodded. "It seems that's the case."

Sinfjotli's forehead creased in worry. "Is there anything you can do to stop them?"

Baldur shook his head. "Not while you have Hel's attention. She usually maintains a hands-off approach and allows the realm to conjure visions on its own. But things will become much nastier now that she's taken the reins. The most you can do is keep your curiosity and fear in check. Otherwise, the fog will appear, and another vision will take hold of you. Once the vision starts, you'll have no choice but to see it through, wasting valuable time and giving Hel more time to prepare her army."

Baldur pulled Sinfjotli to his feet. "We have no more time to waste. If the undead army overtakes us before we reach the Gjallerbru, even I won't be able to protect you from their endless assaults forever."

Chapter Twenty-One

The Only Path Forward

They ignored the ghastly voices whispering in their ears as they marched north to prevent any more visions from conjuring. They had been trekking through the icy city for what seemed like an entire day. But at long last, Sigurd glimpsed the Gjallerbru. The giant bridge's glimmering golden towers and cables were visible just over the horizon. And with his telescopic vision, he could see the entire structure.

"We're nearly there now," Baldur announced. "But don't let down your guard yet. It's been over two hours since we parted with Hel at the Bridge of Judgment. Her army will soon be upon us. You should be ready for a fight."

"What enemies should we expect to face?" Sigurd asked.

"Draugirs mostly," Baldur answered. "I'm sure you've heard of them before. They are the souls of the restless dead trapped within decaying bodies. They are quite strong, but they shouldn't pose a threat to seasoned warriors like you. It's the draugs that have me worried, though. I'm certain she'll send some after you."

"Draugs," Sinfjotli frowned. "Aren't they the souls of restless dead doomed to wander the earth and fight?

"You're confusing them with draugirs," Baldur corrected, shaking his head. "Draugs are very different. They are arch-wraiths, the most powerful spirits in Helheim. Only those who were kings, generals, or commanders in life can become a draug. They are Helheim's elite generals whose power and authority over other souls is second only to Hel herself."

Sinfjotli smiled with anticipation. "They sound like formidable opponents."

"Indeed, they are." Baldur agreed. "In many stories that involve the underworld or the undead, a draug is usually cast as the hero's archenemy, and for a good reason. They are some of the most powerful adversaries a warrior can face. They can take on all kinds of shapes and sizes. Draugs possess tremendous strength, bloodlust, and power. They can also summon the dead, and their deathly minions blindly obey every order they give."

"So, how should we fight them all?" Sigurd asked.

"Oh, the draugirs are simple enough," Baldur promised. "They're strong and swift, but if you cut them to pieces, their souls will be sent back to this city where they will wait for their bodies to reform. However, a draug is much trickier because the mere act of challenging one is quite the ordeal. Putting aside its tremendous strength and bloodlust, one cannot defeat a draug using conventional means."

"Are you saying they're invincible?" Sigurd asked.

"In a sense, yes," Baldur nodded. "Draugs are bound to a certain 'story,' a series of traumatic events that led to their death. They are untouchable, unreachable to anyone and anything that isn't a part of that story."

Sinfjotli frowned. "I don't follow. What does that mean?"

"He's saying that you cannot harm a draug unless you were somehow involved in its death or were involved in the 'story' it is bound by," Sigurd simplified.

"Not exactly," Baldur corrected. "Being personally involved in the draug's death is the surest way for a warrior to harm the arch-wraith. But there *is* another loophole you can exploit. If a warrior possesses an item from the draug's past, they can harm it. In many stories, a hero must overcome many trials to locate an item from the draug's past before becoming worthy of facing the draug."

Baldur paused and looked up at the sky with apprehension. "Actually, it's more accurate to say that acquiring the artifact is necessary to become *capable* of facing the monstrosity. And that condition is precisely what worries me. We're already in Helheim, meaning you do not have the luxury of searching for the necessary items related to a specific draug's past, as most heroes do."

"So you're saying that if we encounter a draug now, we'll be forced to fight an invincible creature that we have no way to truly harm." Sigurd deduced.

"Precisely," Baldur nodded. His smile then faded. "However, the Guardians of Helheim concern me most."

Sinfjotli frowned. "What guardians?"

"Garm and Móðguðr," Baldur clarified. "The Hound of Hel and The Frenzied Daughter of Helheim will be your greatest obstacles. They guard Helheim's borders, ensuring no living soul trespasses and no soul damned soul escapes."

He said the last part, looking pointedly at the two of them, then gave them a moment to grasp the danger.

"How do we defeat them?" Sinfjotli ventured.

"Defeat?" Baldur repeated humorlessly. "That'd be like trying to murder a continent or drown an ocean. You are two of the greatest mortal warriors I've had the pleasure to meet. But Garm and Móðguðr are beyond you both. They're more like forces of nature."

Sigurd swallowed. Garm's ferocity and temper were legendary. Growing up, Sigurd heard stories claiming Garm could consume entire mountain ranges. They also claimed he was bound by an unbreakable chain here in Helheim, but that didn't ease Sigurd's mind. He'd never heard of Móðguðr, but she sounded just as dangerous as her co-guardian.

Sigurd tried to clear his mind of fear and doubt to plan ahead, which proved easy since Baldur's aura soon siphoned his negative thoughts.

"If fighting them isn't viable, how else can we bypass them? Could we challenge them to a game of wits? Trick them?"

Baldur shook his head. "Bartering and conversation won't get you anywhere with those two. Their only purpose is their duty, and they take great pride in it. So they won't abandon it for pride, honor, or material gain."

"Well, how are we supposed to get past them?" Sinfjotli demanded, almost pleading. "Putting aside the draugs and Hel's undead army, we'll never escape the underworld so long as those two block our path. Is there truly nothing we can do?"

Baldur stopped walking and crossed his arms in deep thought.

"I may have oversold the gravity of this situation. Bypassing Garm will be very tricky, but it *might* be possible. He is an extremely dangerous foe but remains bound by an unbreakable chain to Gnipa Cave. It keeps him chained and prevents him from leaving his post. Assuming you had some way to distract him, you could bypass him. But you'd have to move fast, for he can lunge from his cave as fast as lightning..." Baldur shook his head. "Never mind. It's too risky. He might bring down the entire mountain range while trying to chase after you. And even if you got far enough away from him, you'd soon have to deal with Móðguðr. And she would quite literally block your path and force you back to Gnipa Cave." He stared at the sky. "To be caught in a pincer between Garm and Móðguðr? That is a fate I wouldn't wish on..."

Baldur trailed off and frowned as he stared more intently at the sky.

"Is something the matter?" Sigurd ventured after an uncomfortably long silence.

"Something powerful has entered Helheim," Baldur muttered. "Actually, it entered the underworld quite some time ago."

"What is it?" Sigurd pressed.

"Not sure," Baldur admitted. "It feels familiar but also distinct. It's stuck in a state between life and death, just like you two were before you ate those apples. Whatever it is, it's powerful. And it's making a beeline through the Valley of Shadows."

"Is it friendly?" Sinfjotli ventured. "Or will it be a problem?"

"Not sure about that either," Baldur admitted. "I can tell that it's come here with a grand purpose. But its intentions may not be in your best interest. I sense great power and negative emotions flowing from this entity's heart."

"Could it be another obstacle that Hel's laid for us?" Sinfjotli conjectured.

"Unlikely," Baldur demurred. "This entity has been traveling through the Valley of Shadows for many days, but I just didn't sense it until now."

"Days?" Sigurd repeated.

Baldur nodded. "The Road to Helheim is long. And the distance is even longer for those who wish to leave this realm."

Sigurd's eyes widened as he imagined how long the road ahead must be. Helheim's gravity overwhelmed him once more, and he staggered off the Path of the Dead and sat upon the steps of a skyscraper. The frozen steps sent shivers throughout his body, but his spine already felt like a giant slab of ice as he reflected on how high the chips were stacked against them.

First, they had to contend with Helheim's gravity vexing their every step. Once they made it through the city, they'd have to dash across the Gjallerbru, which Baldur claimed was so large that someone in the center of the bridge could not see the shores or anything else beyond the horizon. Hel's undead army would surely catch up before they reached Gnipa Cave.

Then, they'd have to contend with Garm, who could not be reasoned with or fought. But if by some miracle they made it past the Hound of Hel, they'd have to deal with Móðguðr, presumably Helheim's army, and whatever obstacles Hel threw at them as they fought their way out. And they'd have to keep fighting for every inch of ground for over nine consecutive days! And to top it all off, they might also have to contend with this unknown entity blazing its way through the Valley of Shadows.

To say they were in over their heads would be a grievous understatement. Sigurd felt like he was sinking into a bottomless sea, and no matter how hard he struggled, the surface would elude him. But Baldur's aura washed away his despair as the god sat beside him.

"It's not too late to reconsider my offer," Baldur reminded. "The Hringhorni may be a far cry from the Hall of Heroes, but my family and I will protect you."

"Can you, though?" Sinfjotli asked. "Truly?"

"Sinfjotli!" Sigurd reprimanded. "How dare you—!"

"I'm asking a serious question." Sinfjotli turned to Baldur. "Can you truly protect us from Hel now that she's set her sights on us?"

"Hel cannot touch you so long as you bear my brand," Baldur reminded calmly.

"I remember," Sinfjotli nodded. "But I also remember her mentioning that this protection doesn't extend to her army. And she vowed she would throw everything in her arsenal at us. Hypothetically, let's say that Sigurd and I abandon all hope of escaping this realm and head back to your ship with our tails between our legs. What would stop Hel from appearing on the ship and keeping you, Hodr, and Nanna busy while a million undead soldiers swarm the Hringhorni and cut us both to pieces?"

"Hel would never dare," Baldur assured. "She vowed long ago never to interfere with my affairs on the Hringhorni."

"She appeared on deck after we ate the apples," Sinfjotli reminded. "What's to stop her from doing it a second time with an undead army at her back? You've done so much for us already, and I won't repay your kindness by letting your home be destroyed on our account. You built a wonderful sanctuary here in Helheim for yourself, your family, and all those virtuous souls. I refuse to let you compromise that peaceful life for our sake."

He grabbed Sigurd's arm and roughly pulled him to his feet. "I know the path ahead of us is dark and filled with terror beyond anything we can imagine. But the die has been cast. Now that we ate the Apples of Idun and royally pissed Hel off, there is no other way except forward for us."

Sinfjotli stepped onto the path. "Baldur won't be here to protect us or purge our despair. So when you feel helpless and terrified, keep walking forward. Walk until your feet bleed, fight until you've shed every last drop of your blood, and keep pushing forward!"

Baldur stood and patted both their shoulders. "Beautifully said, Sinfjotli. Let us not dally any longer."

CHAPTER TWENTY-TWO

A HEARTBREAKING REUNION

They continued north at an even faster pace. Far to the south, they could vaguely hear an army marching, like booming thunder, in the distance.

They tried to avoid any more distractions. They hoped and prayed that Helheim wouldn't conjure up another vision to impede them. Unfortunately, Hel had one last diversion to play when they were within sight of the gigantic bridge.

They had just taken refuge inside a dilapidated building. Baldur was explaining what to expect once they reached the other side of the Gjallerbru when a woman's voice cried out: "Sigurd!"

Sigurd glanced north. One spirit on the bridge broke off from the group and approached the three of them as they stepped outside the building. As it drew closer to Baldur, the spirit's body solidified until it appeared like a woman.

Sigurd felt his jaw drop and his eyes sink. She had aged since he had last seen her. Her dark brown hair had turned white, and multiple childbirths had tarnished her once muscular figure, but she still possessed the beauty of cold iron. There was no mistaking her.

"Gudrun!" Sigurd gasped. The two rushed toward each other for an embrace. But as they touched, Gudrun's body faded like mist, and Sigurd phased right through her. Gudrun turned around, confused, and attempted to touch Sigurd's face, but her hand vanished like smoke as soon as it touched his skin. Her face conveyed a flurry of emotions until she nodded sadly with acceptance.

"It was always going to be like this," Gudrun said miserably. "After everything that happened, I thought I could at least be with you in death. But it seems the Norns played one final cruel trick on me."

"What do you mean?" Sigurd inquired.

Gudrun began sobbing. "Oh, Sigurd, my whole life became one miserable living hell after you died! Every moment of my life from the night you died was a ringing echo of loss. And whenever I thought it had diminished, fate found a way to make it worse."

As soon as she spoke the final word, the ugly scar on Sigurd's chest flared in pain. It brought many traumatizing memories to the forefront of his mind. Sigurd remembered lying in a bed of his own blood, with a sword impaled through his chest. He remembered Gudrun screaming. He remembered using his last breath to throw Gram at his murderer, slicing him in half. It all came back to him in perfect clarity.

"Guttorm murdered me," Sigurd recalled. "Your youngest brother murdered me in our bed!"

"Not just you," Gudrun shrieked. "Before he entered our room and drove a sword through your chest, he snuck into the adjacent room and murdered our son Sigmund."

"He murdered Sigmund as well?!" Sigurd's mind reeled in horror, grief, and anger. His son Sigmund was only three years old. It was one thing for Guttorm to murder him, but why kill his young son?

"Why did he do that?" Sigurd demanded. "Tell me, Gudrun, why did he...?"

Sigurd trailed off as his mind grasped the reality of this situation. He was in Helheim, the Norse underworld. And Gudrun was a spirit who had just come from the other side of the Gjallerbru. Sigurd gulped as he considered the implications.

"Gudrun, why are you here in Helheim?" He asked. "Did you... Did you die a dishonorable death?"

"That's not the only reason she was sent here," Baldur warned. The god of joy looked strange and somewhat apprehensive as he examined the sobbing woman. "Your wife has committed many wicked sins, Sigurd."

Sigurd didn't know how to process that, but he needed answers. He looked back at Gudrun, still crying and staring at the ground.

"Gudrun, look at me," Sigurd ordered.

Gudrun looked up. Her intangible eyes were red and wet with nonexistent tears.

"Stop crying and tell me why you're here in Helheim," Sigurd urged. "What happened to you?"

Gudrun's face was streaked with incorporeal tears as she lifted her smoking hand to brush them away. Her gaze fell upon Sigurd, communicating the profound sadness she felt before she even uttered a word.

"After you died, I turned into a monster."

CHAPTER TWENTY-THREE

THE BLOODY WIDOW

"The night you died was when I lost everything," Gudrun explained. "On that fateful night, my brother Guttorm murdered our son and drove a sword through your chest. And with your dying breath, you slew him. In one fell swoop, I had lost my brother, my husband, and our son.

"That night was so traumatic that I can only remember glimpses of what happened before or afterward. But I clearly remember that as I lay on the bed cradling your body, Gunnar's wife, Brynhild, appeared in the doorway. She looked at me and laughed aloud. However, her laughter soon turned into tears as she became overcome with grief. She was so distraught that she pulled Gram from the wall and stabbed herself under the arm with it. I was so horrified and confused that I backed away from the bed as she limped forward. With the last of her strength, she collapsed on the bed and lay down next to you. And as the blood drained from her body, she asked to be burned together with you on the same funeral pyre.

"My family honored her last request and laid her next to you on a longship with our son Sigmund and your sword lying between you. So many flowers, bejeweled offerings, and burial gifts were left on the ship that it took thirty men to launch it to sea. As Gunnar prepared to fire a flaming arrow to set the ship alight, an old man with a long beard wearing a gray cloak and broad hat appeared next to me. He watched as the ship caught fire and then looked at me with his pale blue eye. The graybeard warned me that this was only the beginning of my suffering. 'Sigurd was worth ten thousand times more than you,' he said. 'You Gjukungs will pay *dearly* for his death.' He promised that my entire family would die violent deaths and our bloodline would be extinguished within two generations.

"After your funeral, my brothers Gunnar and Hagen inherited Andvari's cursed gold. They showered me with countless golden gifts, but nothing could ease my pain. One day, I realized I could no longer endure living with them or inhabiting the same home where you had died, and so I fled with our daughter, Svanhild. But before I left, I released Grani into the wild."

"Grani wasn't burned with me on the pyre?" Sigurd interrupted. It was customary for a great hero or king to have his horse and all he possessed burned alongside him on the ship so that they might accompany him to the afterlife. Given the grandeur of his funeral, he assumed the Gjukungs would have followed the tradition and buried his faithful horse with him.

"Gunnar and Hagen refused to sacrifice such a mighty horse to the flames," Gudrun explained. "They hoped to make him their mount and ride him into battle as you had, but Grani angrily spurned them and everyone else who tried to ride him. He even killed one fool who brazenly climbed on his back as he slept. Even though you were dead, Grani refused to accept anyone else as his master. But my brothers were determined. They tried to break his spirit by locking him in a stable and starving him. It broke my heart to see him treated like that. It was also the final straw that compelled me to leave. The day I left with Svanhild, I released Grani from his stable, and he bolted into the wilderness. I never saw him again."

"That's probably for the best," Sigurd muttered. To him, Grani was much more than a mere horse. He was Sigurd's closest companion, whom he treated like a brother. He had accompanied Sigurd on every adventure, triumph, and hardship. Knowing that Grani was roaming free in the wild put Sigurd's mind at ease. "So, what happened after you left?"

"After months of wandering aimlessly, Svanhild and I found ourselves in the kingdom of the Danes." Gudrun continued. "We sought refuge with your stepfather, King Alf. He and his new wife, Thora, welcomed me and agreed to raise Svanhild as if she were their adoptive granddaughter. I was too mad with grief by then to be the parent she needed. In the meantime, I took to weaving, and it slowly helped relieve much of my pain.

"But my peace didn't last. After seven years, my mother and brothers tracked me down. They told me things had escalated with our fearsome neighbor, King Atli of the Huns. He and Brynhild had been as close as siblings in his youth, and he blamed my family and Gunnar for failing to prevent her death. They feared he would invade our kingdom unless he was placated, so he and Gunnar came to an accord to heal enmities. They then revealed why they had come: I was to marry Atli in an arranged marriage."

"I told them outright that I wanted no part in any of this," Gudrun insisted. "I warned them that no good would come of this, and this union would only hasten their demise. I spurned all their gifts and conciliating pleas and told them flatly that I would rather live the rest of my life as a grieving widow. But my mother always found a way to get what she wanted. She tricked me into drinking a potion spiked with runes and bitter herbs that caused me to forget about my grief over your death. This made me more pliable. I consented to the marriage and left Svanhild in the care of your stepfather in Denmark.

"It was only after I married Atli that my memory returned, and I realized what a terrible mistake had been made. Still, I tried to make the most of the situation and ease tensions between Atli and my family. I even bore him two sons, Ernak and Eitel. But our marriage proved loveless from the start. I realized he was an avaricious king who had only agreed to marry me because he assumed I possessed your vast treasure as your widow. Only after our lavish wedding did he learn Gunnar and Hagen kept the mighty hoard, and they hadn't given me a single gold coin even though by right of inheritance, the entire treasure should have belonged to me, and now Atli. The only remnant I possessed from Fafnir's hoard was the golden ring Andvaranaut. It allowed me to locate rich gold mines in the mountains for Atli, which helped enrich his kingdom. But it did nothing to slate his lust for gold.

"I warned Atli that Fafnir's hoard would bring him nothing but tragedy as it had for you, but he didn't listen. When Atli closed his eyes at night, he could see the red gold of Fafnir's hoard and dreamed of the power it would bring. Eventually, his avarice became too much to bear, and he became determined to obtain the gold at whatever cost. And the price would be paid with blood and treachery.

"Together with the leaders of his war band, Atli concocted a treacherous plan. They planned to invite Gunnar and Hagen to a feast at his hall, pretend to offer them the honor due to them as his in-laws, and then force them at sword point to hand over the treasure. I tried to warn my brothers that it was a trap by sending a coded message inscribed on a gold ring wrapped in wolf's hair along with the other lavish gifts Atli sent with the delegation. But something must have gone wrong. Perhaps one of Atli's men found the ring and altered my message? Maybe Gunnar's new wife, Glaumvor, mistranslated my warning? Or maybe Gunnar and Hagen were too stubborn to ignore what they perceived as a challenge to their manhood? Regardless, my brothers soon arrived at Atli's stronghold. They had brought only a few dozen warriors, but were ready for a fight.

"Atli offered them peace if they swore to share the treasure you had taken from Fafnir with him. But my brothers brazenly refused to ransom their lives, and the battle began with a rain of arrows. When I heard the clamor of battle, I tore off my jewelry and emerged from the great hall dressed in chain mail with a sword. I pushed through Atli's men and fought alongside my brothers. I would have made you proud that day, Sigurd. I butchered everyone around me with a keen blade and me the onslaught head-on. We defended ourselves so well that the battle lasted for almost a day. The conflict spilled into Atli's great hall, and the floor became slippery from spilled blood. When the fight ended, the Huns could not rejoice because their victory had come at a heavy toll.

"But the grievous toll we took on Atli's forces couldn't prevent what followed. Gunnar was overpowered and taken prisoner. Atli personally defeated and captured me. But Hagen continued to fight in a bloody last stand, killing many men before he was finally brought to heel. Atli, exhausted and grieving for his brothers who had perished amidst the fighting, impulsively ordered Hagen's heart to be cut from his chest and presented to Gunnar on a platter. He hoped the sight would break Gunnar's will so he could threaten him to reveal where he had hidden your treasure under the imminent pain of death. But when he saw our brother's heart on the platter, Gunnar laughed and brazenly told Atli, 'Now that you've killed Hagen, I'll die happy knowing you'll never find where Sigurd's gold is hidden.'

"When he realized Gunnar would never reveal the treasure's whereabouts, Atli ordered him thrown into a pit full of snakes with his hands tied behind his back. All I could do to help him was throw a nearby harp into the pit. His hands were bound tight, but he played the instrument so well with his toes that, for a time, the serpents were enchanted by his music. But one adder couldn't be charmed and bit him near his heart. Realizing his end was nigh, Gunnar used the last of his strength to stomp on the serpents so he could at least die resisting and screaming curses at his foes."

"After their deaths, Atli sent his armies to plunder Gunnar, Hagen, and my father's kingdoms in one last hope he could recover your famous treasure. They slew my father, butchered all my people, and razed the entire landscape, searching in vain for the gold my brothers had hidden. When they were finished, all that was left of my homeland was ash and bones. But the treasure was nowhere to be found.

"Gunnar and Hagen's deaths and the destruction of their kingdoms had been treacherous, and it had come at a great and bloody cost to Atli. He was no closer to finding your famous gold, and even worse, I had turned against him and fought alongside my brothers. But against the advice of his counselors, he spared my life and restored all the rights, incomes, and privileges I was due as his wife and queen. He wasn't motivated by love or altruism. He was convinced I had an inkling of where my brothers had hidden the treasure and hoped to winkle the truth out of me in time. He also looked forward to tormenting me with the memory of the deaths of my brothers and took every liberty to mock me by reminding me I had chosen the losing side. I pretended to be chastised and cowed into submissiveness and gentleness by the victory. I remained silent and wore the mask of an obedient wife when Atli sent his armies to destroy my father's and brothers' kingdoms. But I was only going through the motions. I had a terrible vengeance planned.

"After Atli's armies finished destroying my family's kingdom and razed the entire landscape to the ground searching for the curse hoard, Atli decided to hold a sumptuous feast. He might have failed to find your famous treasure, but he had still killed Gunnar and Hagen, destroyed their kingdoms, and thus avenged the death of his adoptive sister, Brynhild. And that was still a cause for a grand celebration. He invited all his chieftains and their vassals to attend the feast and celebrate his triumphs. I was at the center of preparations for his victory feast and set my plan into motion. The feast was raucous, and wine flowed freely from the bejeweled cups. Atli became drunk and called for more meat and wine. I served him generous cuts of meat I had prepared and watched as he drained the cup I had poured. As he finished eating and gave a thunderous burp, he innocently wondered aloud where our sons were, as he hadn't seen them all evening. I told him they were already there and gestured to his empty plate and cup. I explained that during the festivities, I slipped into the room where Ernak and Eitel were playing, gathered them in my arms, slit their throats, and chopped up their bodies. I looked Atli straight in the eyes and revealed that he had been devouring the flesh of our sons, and the wine he'd been gulping was mixed with their blood.

"I'll never forget how silent the hall became as the full weight of my words sunk in. As Atli entered a state of shock, I leaned in close and whispered: 'You'll never hold our boys on your lap again or watch them grow up. Can you feel my loss now, Atli? You made me watch as your men tore out my brother's heart. You forced me to watch as Gunnar was bitten to death by snakes. You obliterated my family's kingdom and destroyed everything I loved to satiate your lust for Sigurd's gold. Do you finally understand how much I despise you?'

"Atli called me a monster and ordered me stoned to death, but no one obeyed. At first, Atli thought it was because they were still paralyzed by the horror of it all and urged them to act. But then, one by one, his servants and guards collapsed to the ground. I revealed I had already spiked their drinks with a paralytic agent that I'd received from my mother, and that same agent was also in the wine he'd gulped down. With him unable to defend himself, I drew his sword from his scabbard and buried it deep in his chest. As I drove the blade deeper into his chest, I bitterly told him I would have preferred living the rest of my life a widow than marrying him. But I promised that as his wife, I'd do him a final favor and turn the entire castle into his funerary pyre.

"I then rewarded the few servants who had been loyal to me shares of Atli's treasury, and they helped me set the castle ablaze. Atli's warriors and chieftains couldn't move, but they were still conscious enough to feel themselves being burned alive. I remember how empty I felt standing outside the burning castle and listening to their screams. I had achieved my vengeance, but I had waded so deep into killing that I didn't want to live any longer. The next morning, I walked into the sea clutching heavy rocks and waited for the waves to drag me into Rán's icy depths."

Gudrun let out a long moan. "Unfortunately, the Norns weren't finished with me yet. Instead of drowning me, the waves carried me away. I drifted across the fjord and washed up alive on the shores of Denmark. I was then found and rescued by Jonakr, the king who ruled those lands. He took me in and nursed me back to health. We eventually married and had three sons: Sorli, Hamdir, and Erp. Our daughter Svanhild came to live with me, and she became the balm for much of my pain. She had grown into a beautiful young woman by then. When I dressed her in gold, she shone like the sun, and the snake eyes she inherited from you bewitched many men. Seeing her always filled me with such joy, and she became the apple of my eye.

"But looking back, I now realize that the Norns granted me this brief happiness only to snatch it away." Gudrun wailed. "My brief respite of joy came to a devastating end when it came time for Svanhild to wed.

"One day, a delegation arrived from Jormunrek, the King of the Goths. He had heard great tales of Svanhild's beauty and had sent his son Randver to ask for her hand in marriage on his behalf. Svanhild and I disapproved of the match. King Jormunrek was three times older than Svanhild and was reputed to be a stern ruler, but nobody else supported our misgivings. Jonakr assured me the match was right, and I eventually consented."

Gudrun clenched her misty hands. "It was the worst decision I ever made! The delegation left for home with Svanhild. But the journey back to the land of the Goths was very long, and during that time, Svanhild became lovers with Randver, who was closer to her in age. When the delegation arrived home, Jormunrek's advisor, Bikki, informed him about his son's affair with Svanhild, and the old king flew into a jealous rage. His son had dared seduce his bride-to-be, and for that, Jormunrek ordered his son hanged. He then had Svanhild tied to the gates of his castle with a bag placed over her head and had her trampled to death by horses.

"When I learned about this insidious act, I summoned my sons Hamdir, Sorli, and Erp and incited them to seek vengeance on Jormunrek. I gave them enchanted chain mail and helmets so strong that iron could not pierce them. Before they rode away, my son Hamdir looked back at me and said: 'You've lost your only daughter and are now sending your remaining children to their deaths. I swear we will punish Jormunrek, but I doubt this will bring you much relief.'

"My sons then rode out, fought through Jormunrek's army, cornered him inside his hall, and hacked off the elderly king's hands, feet, and penis. They had all fought valiantly but were eventually slain. Somehow, Jormunrek figured out that their armor was specifically designed to protect them from iron. And so, with his last breath, he ordered his remaining men to throw stones at them, and they all met their end in the hall of the Goths.

"When the news of my sons' triumph and demise reached me, I decided I had lived long enough. At that point, I was now as barren and lonely as a tree in winter. I had achieved vengeance for my family and bested all my enemies. But I had also eradicated two ancestral families, murdered my children, and lost all my brothers, friends, and children, and none of it had brought me any semblance of peace. I built a funerary pyre and prayed to the Norns to finally let me die so that I could reunite in death with everyone I had lost."

CHAPTER TWENTY-FOUR

THE LONG GOODBYE

As Gudrun concluded her tale, Sigurd covered his mouth, sickened by her many wicked deeds. The woman he had married was no more. The spirit before him was just a ghost broken by tragedy, grief, and hate. He was no stranger to vengeance, but Gudrun's actions wrought more than he could stomach. By killing her own sons and carving up their bodies for a feast, she had committed the most unforgivable crime a mother could commit.

"Gudrun," he gasped. "You...you're not the woman I once knew. You've become...you've become..." He couldn't bring himself to say it.

"You're wrong." Gudrun's face contracted and contorted, her eyes filled with incorporeal tears, and her nose ran. "I have *always* been a monster, Sigurd. I've been a monster...ever since the day I stole you from *her*. I knew that I'd be sent here to Helheim for it and everything else I did. But the one hope I clung to was that, at the very least, I'd be by your side in death. But it seems the Norns played one last cruel trick on me. Here I am about to be punished for everything I've done, yet you are being escorted out of Helheim."

"Her?" Sigurd frowned. "Who and what are you talking about? You stole me from someone?"

Gudrun didn't hear the question. Sobbing and wailing, she crumpled to the ground, consumed by her misery. The Gudrun that Sigurd knew had been a stoic and determined woman with iron beauty. But now, she looked like a broken, sorrowful child wailing as the total weight of her crimes crashed upon her, and the callous hands of fate had snatched away her last hope.

Sigurd felt just as melancholy. Learning that their children, Svanhild and Sigmund, had been murdered utterly devastated him. His heart sank even further as he realized the last remnant of the Volsung bloodline had been extinguished with their deaths.

Sigurd watched silently as Gudrun continued wailing on the ground. He wanted to comfort her but couldn't embrace her because she was a spirit. What could he say to comfort someone who had suffered as much tragedy and committed so many atrocious deeds?

Thankfully, Baldur did what he could not. The most beloved god stepped forward, lifted Gudrun off the ground, and drew her into a warm embrace. For a moment, Sigurd was shocked that Baldur could physically touch her. Then he remembered Baldur was also technically dead and a de facto lord of the afterlife. The rules didn't apply to him.

"You poor, poor child," Baldur sighed sadly as Gudrun cried on his shoulder. "The Norns have not been kind to you."

"You must be Baldur." Gudrun deduced as she wiped nonexistent tears from her eyes. "What will happen to me now, my lord? Will I be tormented by my past? Will I now be punished for my many sins?"

"No," Baldur promised. "You've suffered enough. It's time for you to know peace."

He nuzzled her away. He then held out his index finger and touched her forehead. As he traced his finger across her forehead, Gudrun screamed in pain.

"What are you doing?" Sigurd demanded.

"I'm granting her sanctuary." Baldur removed his hand, and Sigurd saw a glowing blue symbol on her forehead.

"That is the Algiz rune," Baldur explained. "This rune grants protection from enemies and defense of that which one loves. It's modeled after the protection spell my parents placed on me long ago. Think of this rune as my personal brand I bestow on the souls I take pity on. Now that she has the mark, neither Hel nor any other spirit in Helheim can harm her."

"W-Why are you doing this?" Gudrun sniffled. "Why are you helping a worthless monster like me?"

"Because that is my purpose," Baldur answered proudly. "To help and protect those I take pity on. Now listen closely, my dear, because our time is short. You must follow this path through the city to the Bridge of Judgment. From there, seek my wife and brother on my ship. Once Nanna sees that rune, she'll know what it means and will provide you sanctuary."

Gudrun tearfully thanked Baldur. Then she looked at Sigurd and studied him for a long time, a range of emotions washing over her until she held up her left hand.

"Could you please remove this from my finger?"

Baldur frowned, confused but intrigued by her request. He reached out and grasped something invisible on her left ring finger. A bright light flashed as he withdrew his hand, fading as Baldur opened his palm, and Sigurd saw that a gold ring had appeared.

The ring's gold band was set with a large green emerald gemstone. The ring's outer band depicted a dragon biting its tail.

"That's the Andvaranaut!" Sigurd gasped. He knew it all too well. He had found that legendary ring among Fafnir's hoard and gave it to Gudrun after they married.

"It remained with me throughout my life and even in death," Gudrun explained. "I want you to take it back now."

Sigurd hesitated to take the ring from Baldur as an old memory resurfaced. "In his last moments, Fafnir had warned me not to take the ring. He claimed it would bring misfortune upon whoever possessed it."

"And it did," Gudrun affirmed. "But I insist you take it. It's all I have left to give. Consider it my last gift for you. Perhaps you can find some use for it."

Sigurd reluctantly took the ring from Baldur and slipped it on his finger. The ring felt mind-numbingly cold as it magically adjusted its size to fit his left ring finger. But he suppressed the urge to hurl it away as he looked back at Gudrun one last time. "Gudrun, I wish I could..."

"You don't have to say anything." She interrupted. "This is where we part ways forever. My place is here in Helheim, and yours is in Valhalla. I'll never forget what we shared. But now, you must return to *her*."

"Her?" Sigurd repeated. "Who are you...?"

"Sigurd, we need to hurry." Baldur interrupted. "Our time is almost up." He wasn't exaggerating. The sound of an encroaching army drew closer.

"But..." Sigurd protested.

"Sigurd, please go," Gudrun insisted. "Go and never look back. Just...promise me one thing. When you learn the truth about us...please don't judge me too harshly. I did what I did...because I truly love you. Goodbye."

Gudrun departed with that strange and cryptic farewell, joining the other spirits as they made their way to the City of the Lost. Sigurd watched silently as his wife mingled with the other souls, soon becoming indiscernible in the crowd. Sigurd turned to Baldur.

"Thank you," he said as he bowed in gratitude. "Please...keep her safe for me."

"Of course," Baldur promised. "We will treat her well on my ship and try to help her find peace. Not a single haunting vision or ghost will torment her while she is under my protection. Furthermore, I promise to find your daughter, your son, and all Gudrun's family members who died dishonorably and grant them sanctuary. You have my solemn word on this."

Sigurd smiled and turned south, but Gudrun's spirit had already vanished in the crowd of souls. He searched for her until someone grasped his shoulder.

"So, did you have a pleasant reunion with your sweetheart?"

"Sinfjotli," Sigurd exclaimed. "I didn't even notice you had vanished. Where did you run off to?"

"Oh, I ran into an old friend while you were chatting with your wife," Sinfjotli admitted. "We had a nice long chat. But that's unimportant. The army of the dead is approaching us!"

"What?!" Sigurd glanced south, and terror gripped his heart. In the distance, a giant snow cloud was billowing off the road and racing toward them. He peered through that cloud of snow and almost screamed in terror.

"I can see them all from here!" He gasped. "Gods, there's so many! And Gudrun is headed straight into them!"

"She'll be fine," Baldur promised. "That rune will protect her in the same way that I'm protected from all harm. Regardless, we're out of time, and we must hurry!"

They ran the rest of the way toward the bridge, stopping where the bridge anchored to the city and connected to the Path of the Dead.

"This is where we must part ways," Baldur announced worriedly. "I'm afraid this is as far as I can go. But I hope we meet again someday. I look forward to the stories you'll tell."

Sigurd smiled. "In that case, we won't say goodbye."

Suddenly, a rain of spears and arrows blanketed the sky. Baldur loomed over them and shielded them with his body as arrows and spears ricocheted off his back. Hel's massive army had finally arrived in force.

The undead army looked exactly how Sigurd had envisioned them. Walking corpses in armor brandishing countless weapons composed their ranks. Besides the draugirs, there were massive trolls, hellhounds, ogres, and even the rotting skeleton of an undead dragon amongst their ranks!

Their sheer numbers terrified Sigurd. There were so many enemies; the army ranged as far as the eye could see and stretched beyond the southern horizon like an endless ocean of death.

"You'll be dead before you make it a tenth of the way across that bridge," Baldur observed. "I'll give you a head start and hold them off for as long as possible."

He scooped up Sigurd and Sinfjotli in his arms and lifted them off the ground.

"Wait, what are you planning to do?" Sinfjotli demanded.

"I'm sorry in advance for these desperate measures, but we're out of time. Once you cross the bridge and reach Gnipa Cave, you must find a way to bypass Garm. Good luck! I know that you'll succeed."

With that final encouragement, Baldur hurled them both through the air like javelins, sending them soaring over the bridge.

***

Baldur watched as Sigurd and Sinfjotli sailed through the air like spears in flight, their figures growing smaller until they became tiny dots on the horizon. Turning his attention back to the battlefield, he peered over his shoulder at the undead army loping toward the bridge through the shadowed highway.

Packs of hellhounds comprised the first wave of the front lines. Though resembling large dogs, their eyes brimmed with infernal rage, and flames seeped from their maws instead of drool. Behind them stood an ocean of skeletal draugirs, wraiths in armor, and demons that looked like human beings that had been skinned and whose exposed musculature glistened with some kind of slimy black liquid. Beside them stood twisted chimeric creatures that looked like crosses between men and beasts.

Farther behind the army's lines were massive golems, some half as tall as the skyscrapers they stood between. The most enormous creature among their ranks was the skeletal dragon now perched atop a building. But it was far from the most powerful. Baldur could sense multiple archliches, giant skeletal warriors with war scythes whose bodies overflowed with shadowy black energy, and even several draugs deeper behind enemy lines.

"Hel wasn't exaggerating," Baldur whistled. "She isn't showing any restraint against Sigurd and Sinfjotli."

By his estimate, at least two hundred thousand undead creatures were amassing toward the Gjallerbru. And he was the only one standing in their way.

Baldur wondered if this was reminiscent of what his brother Sigi saw during his last stand against his scheming brothers-in-law's enormous army. The sight of the massive army was enough to make even the most battle-hardened warrior lose heart. But Baldur smiled excitedly. The hellhounds approaching him paused, unsure what to make of his reaction. A shadow enveloped him, and he looked up to see the undead dragon spreading its massive wingspan wide as it prepared to take flight. With a deafening roar, the dragon launched off the towering skyscraper, chasing after Sigurd and Sinfjotli, whose figures were growing smaller in the distance.

"Come on! Do you think I'll let you approach that easily?" Baldur crouched his legs and jumped high in the air, racing toward the dragon as it flew over his head. The creature saw him coming, and its lidless eyes dilated in shock.

"I wish Twilight could fly as freely as you can," Baldur admitted as he landed a powerful punch on its side, knocking the beast out of the air and sending it crashing into the nearest skyscraper. The powerful impact shook the building, sending debris everywhere. The disoriented dragon tried to right itself and gain altitude. But before it could do so, it slammed against the Path of the Dead, crushing many of the army's ranks beneath its massive bulk. The ground shook violently as the dragon's weight caused a wave of devastation, leaving a trail of destruction in its wake as it rolled over the undead army.

All four hundred thousand eyes stared at Baldur as he landed gracefully on the ground and cracked his knuckles with a fat grin.

"Contrary to what most mortals think of me, I'm not at all averse to violence so long as it's for sport. It must be the Aesir blood in my veins, but I love a good scrap! Back in Asgard, I always enjoyed fighting with the Einherjar in Valhalla. Even before my mother made me invulnerable, they complained that facing me was no fun, as I usually won. After she made all of creation swear not to harm me, no one wanted to train with me since I was guaranteed to win. Even Sigi and Thor stopped wanting to fight me after a while."

Baldur's smile widened as he thought more about Sigi. "My little brother once told me, 'You feel most alive when faced with death.' It's an ironic thing to say, given that we're all dead. But I haven't felt this excited in ages! I can't follow Sigurd and Sinfjotli any further. But I can ensure you all can't follow them, either!"

The dragon rose from the rubble of a building with a deafening roar, shaking the ground beneath Baldur's feet. The undead army brandished their weapons and charged, in the greatest attack on a single being in the history of the Nine Realms. Baldur never flinched, dodged, or even thought about retreating as the might of the underworld surged toward him. He trembled excitedly as he stood against these impossible odds to support his friends.

"This will be my first battle in ages! An army that cannot die versus an Aesir that cannot be harmed by any physical or magical threats. Let's find out who will capitulate first!"

CHAPTER TWENTY-FIVE

A HARD LANDING

Ten minutes. Sinfjotli and his brother soared through the frigid air like a pair of javelins for almost ten *agonizing* minutes. The Bridge of the Dead passed like a golden blur beneath them. Sinfjotli squeezed his eyes shut to avoid being blinded by the falling snowflakes whipping against his face. The wind and cold air stabbed his face like a thousand sharp needles until it went numb. But after ten excruciating minutes of soaring through the freezing air, they lost altitude and plummeted toward the bridge deck.

Everything faded into black when Sinfjotli's body touched the bridge. When he next opened his eyes, he found himself lying on his back in a deep snowdrift. He quickly discovered that his whole body had been paralyzed from the impact.

But not for long. After a moment, Sinfjotli's body began recovering. He could move his neck, and then his arms, and finally his legs. But as tactile sense returned to his feet, the magnitude of his injuries registered in his mind, and he nearly blacked out from the pain.

The snow covering the bridge's surface had somewhat cushioned his impact, but he was still severely injured. Brush burns and frostbite covered his limbs. Bones protruded through the skin of his arms at an ugly angle.

Sinfjotli's extreme pain prevented him from screaming in agony. But soon, a warm sensation spread throughout his body. Sinfjotli could feel the color returning to his face. The bones in his arms reset themselves, and his skin closed over the wounds.

All my injuries are healing, Sinfjotli realized as he flexed his fingers. This rapid healing must be a side effect of the Apple of Idun he ate earlier. Its healing properties hadn't worn off yet.

As his body healed, Sinfjotli heard Sigurd groan in pain nearby. His brother leaned against one of the bridge's pylons, his face covered in frostbite, presumably because of traveling through the cold air so blindingly fast. His armor must have cushioned his impact somewhat, because he wasn't as injured as Sinfjotli was. But he had clearly broken some bones when he struck the bridge. Fortunately, Sigurd's body was recovering quickly, and his injuries were healing even faster than Sinfjotli's.

After ten agonizing minutes, their bodies healed enough for them to stand on the bridge's surface, which was buried beneath five feet of snow. All around them, the intangible dead spirits continued marching across the bridge, leaving no footprints in the deep snow. The only indentations in the snow were the ones Sinfjotli and Sigurd had created when they crash-landed.

"Desperate times call for desperate measures," Sigurd groaned. "But that was ludicrous!"

"As painful as that was, he did give us a head start as promised," Sinfjotli pointed out. "I can't even see the other side of the bridge or the city. Just how far did Baldur throw us?"

"Baldur mentioned this bridge is over nine hundred miles long." Sigurd glanced south, and his golden snake eyes seemed to dilate and flicker momentarily.

"I can see him fending off the undead army from here. Judging from the distance, I reckon he threw us six hundred seventy-five miles or about three-quarters of the way across the bridge."

"Wait, you can *see* that far away?!" Sinfjotli gasped.

"Of course," Sigurd sighed, rolling his eyes. "Weren't you paying attention on the ship when I told Baldur my life story?"

"I...only listened to bits and pieces of it. My mind was still trying to come to terms with the fact that I had died. And that my stepmother had murdered me."

"That's...fair. Let me put it to you this way. My eyesight is so sharp that I can spot a field mouse scouring in a field from nine hundred miles away."

"Impressive." Sinfjotli glanced at the spirits making their way across the bridge and then turned north. "So...can you determine how far we are from the other side of the Gjallerbru?"

Sigurd nodded. His serpentine pupils became more distinct, and the veins near his temples bulged from increased blood flow to his eyes. He looked around, trying to get their bearings. But as he gazed west, his eyes widened.

"By the gods," he exclaimed. "Is that who I think it is?"

Sigurd pointed west, where an enormous silver eagle perched on a mountain of corpses on an islet in the River Gjöll about a mile from the bridge. The eagle was five hundred feet tall. Its silver feathers reflected the emerald light of the sky, giving it a green tinge.

"That must be Hræsvelgr the Corpse Eater." Sinfjotli faintly recalled Baldur's earlier explanation that the cold winds that blew throughout Helheim originated from a giant eagle. It was easy to infer why it was called the 'Corpse Eater' from the mountain of human corpses it perched on.

"So that's the eagle responsible for the cold wind here?" Sinfjotli wondered aloud. As if on cue, the eagle ruffled its feathers ever so slightly, and a mighty icy gale slammed into them, blowing two feet of snow off the bridge deck.

"I'll take that as a yes," Sinfjotli shivered. He cocked his head to the side, deep in thought. "Sigurd, you mentioned earlier that you can talk to birds. Is he...saying anything right now?"

Sigurd stared intently at the eagle. "He's not saying anything," he reported after a few moments. "I think he's just refusing to speak to us."

Sinfjotli watched warily as the eagle reached down and gobbled up some corpses from its perch into its beak. "Will that eagle be a threat to us?"

"I wouldn't worry about him. He seems indifferent to everything happening here other than his meal. He shouldn't bother us as long as we don't provoke him."

"I see." Sinfjotli sighed. "So...how far are we from the other end of the Gjallerbru?"

Sigurd resumed looking around with his telescopic vision and to get their bearings. "Baldur gave us an excellent head start, but we still have another quarter of the bridge to cross. By my estimate, that's over two hundred twenty-five miles. We'd better start walking."

They didn't get very far. They both became winded after trudging a few paltry steps forward. The snowdrifts covering the surface of the bridge were very deep, but that wasn't what slowed them down. Every laborious step planted through the deep snow felt like traveling up a steep incline. It was the same heavy feeling they'd experienced as they traveled north through the City of the Lost, which compelled everyone to head south to Hel's palace. Baldur's presence had somehow nullified that sensation and allowed them to travel north through the City of the Lost relatively unimpeded, barring the few times they needed to stop and rest. But without him here, that heavy feeling had returned and was now compelling them to head back south toward the city. Sinfjotli's legs felt like heavy boulders. It took every ounce of stamina he had to take a single step forward. They traveled at a snail's pace, barely moving thirty yards before Sinfjotli decided he'd had enough and gestured for Sigurd to stop.

"We'll get nowhere if we both try walking two hundred miles on foot through all this snow," Sinfjotli concluded. "But I might have a way around that. Give me a moment."

He closed his eyes and concentrated. Sinfjotli's clothes magically vanished as he transformed into a ten-foot-tall wolf. He noticed he could shapeshift much faster than usual, and the transfiguration didn't feel as painful as it ordinarily did. Perhaps this was another benefit of Idun's Apple?

"Hop on," Sinfjotli ordered when the transformation finished. "We'll get there faster this way. You should conserve your energy for whatever awaits us on the other side."

Sigurd complied and climbed onto Sinfjotli's back, gripping his fur as the wolf reared up and sprinted across the snow-covered bridge.

"That transformation looked painful," Sigurd noted as they raced north. "Does it hurt?"

"Every time," Sinfjotli admitted as he sprinted north.

CHAPTER TWENTY-SIX

THE HOUND OF HELL

Sinfjotli, powered by the magic apple inside his stomach, kept running through the deep snow and against the heavy gravity without needing any rest. But he was even more impressed with the absurd size of the Bridge of the Damned and how far it stretched beyond the horizon. The giant eagle Hræsvelgr soon became a blurry dot and vanished behind them.

As they raced closer to the underworld's entrance, he noticed it was becoming easier to travel north. Most of the snowdrifts were concentrated in the center of the bridge, and fewer snowdrifts covered the northernmost section of the bridge. But more importantly, that heavy feeling that impeded them every step of their journey was beginning to subside. After running nearly a hundred miles from where they had crash-landed, the snowdrifts disappeared altogether, and the heavy feeling vanished along with them. A grateful Sinfjotli relished the solid ground of the bridge beneath his paws. Now, he could really cut loose. Sigurd complained of frostbite, but Sinfjotli told him to suck it up and kept moving.

After running north for what felt like half a day at top speed, Sinfjotli reached the end of the bridge and beheld the entrance to the underworld. The Bride of the Damned was connected to a massive continent of ice-covered black mountains. A gigantic ravine sat in between two of the ridges.

A giant curved stone archway stretched across either side of the ravine about a mile away from the bridge. The formation was carved from the same oily black stone found throughout the City of the Lost. Thirty feet long icicles dangled like long white teeth from the arch. From this distance, the stone arch and the icicles looked like the gaping mouth of a beast waiting to swallow them.

Beneath that stone arch, a long-paved road connected to the Gjallerbru and traversed through the dark gully. The spirits arriving in Helheim slowly traveled south along that paved road toward the Gjallerbru.

The canyon's interior was too dark and distant for Sinfjotli to discern much. But Sinfjotli could see a giant tree root rising from the ground into the sky. The primary root was incomprehensibly enormous. Its rough bark resembled flaking gray clay, and the secondary roots sprouting from it and burying into the ice-covered continent were the size of mountains. A giant green waterfall flowed from the root into the mountain range, which he assumed was the source of the River Gjöll.

"That must be the root of Yggdrasil, the World Tree." Sinfjotli guessed.

"No doubt about that," Sigurd agreed. "There's only one tree in existence with roots that big."

"It's enormous!" Sinfjotli exclaimed. "I'm not sure how far away it is."

"If you can see it clearly from this distance with your non-telescopic vision, then that root must be truly titanic in scale."

"Well, what can *you* see with your telescopic vision? Is that giant stone arch supposed to be the entrance of Helheim?"

"I think so," Sigurd replied, squinting. "I think I can see runes engraved along that archway. The road beneath it travels north through the vale toward the tree root. I'm guessing the entire canyon was carved naturally when the root of the World Tree burrowed deep into the ground. I can see glaciers and statues lining the path. And there's something else. It's hard to discern from this distance, but souls are materializing from the exact spot where the root connects with the ground."

"That's all I needed to hear." Sinfjotli smiled as he resumed running.

"Hey!" Sigurd shouted. "What the hell are you doing? Slow down!"

"No," Sinfjotli refused as he sprinted even faster. "I'm eager to leave this place. All we have to do is make it to that tree root, and we can leave this ghastly place."

"But we still don't know what's waiting for us in that canyon. Hel's probably laid a trap there for us."

"All the more reason to hurry. If I keep running at this speed, we could catch whatever's waiting to ambush us off guard and escape!"

"But…"

"Did you forget we're on a time limit here? I don't know how long the effects of those golden apples will last. But I'm not going to wait to find out."

Sigurd kept arguing, but Sinfjotli ignored him. He was dead set on reaching that tree root. After a couple of minutes, they reached the bridge's end. As he sprinted across the paved road, the stone arch and the tree root beyond it became more extensive.

"Brother, you need to stop!" Sigurd warned as they neared the archway.

"No!" Sinfjotli refused. "Our salvation is just beyond the horizon, Sigurd."

"I said *STOP*!" Sigurd grabbed Sinfjotli's head and shoved him to the ground with surprising strength. Sinfjotli rolled across the icy stone ground until Sigurd leaped in front of him and stopped him with one hand before he passed beneath the arch's shadow. Before Sinfjotli could ask Sigurd why he did that, he saw what his brother was trying to warn him about.

Next to the archway was a massive cave carved into the side of the canyon. A bloodcurdling howl erupted from the grotto, echoing throughout the canyon like a mountain cracking in half. Half a heartbeat later, a giant, shackled wolf, ten times larger than Sinfjotli, lunged from the cave and barreled toward them.

At the last second, its chain went taunt, stopping it right before the stone arch's shadow. As Sinfjotli picked himself off the ground and stared at the beast, he realized that if Sigurd hadn't stopped him and allowed him to pass beyond that shadow, they would now be this monster's dinner.

The giant wolf was about ten times larger than Sinfjotli's wolf form. He possessed five bright yellow, fiery eyes that appeared to lack pupils. The black fur of his chest, neck, and back was covered in dried, crusted blood. Sinfjotli couldn't tell whether the blood on his coat came from his victims or his own wounds. Around his neck was an oversized spiked collar with a chain connected to the inside of the cave.

"You must be Garm." Sigurd guessed.

The guard dog of Helheim reared on his hind legs and howled so loudly it made Sinfjotli's ears ring. He began snapping his jaws and swiping his paws at them, desperately trying to reach them. But then he seemed to notice something and stopped struggling against the chain that bound him. He sniffed the air and glared at them with his five baleful, yellow eyes.

"You must be the escapees that Mistress Hel warned me about." Garm curled his lips back, baring his enormous fangs. "But...she didn't mention that you have Odin's blood coursing through your veins! So you're descendants of that trickster? That makes you kin to that traitor, Týr! Come closer! I'll RIP you to SHREDS!"

"In that case, we'll keep our distance," Sinfjotli retorted as he transformed back into a human. He and Sigurd backed away from the snarling monster.

They watched as Garm reared on his hind legs, struggling against the chain that bound him. His howls echoed throughout the canyon like rolling thunder as he cursed and called down maledictions upon them and "that traitor Týr." His five yellow eyes were full of hatred as he continued snapping his jaws and swiping his paws at them, desperately trying to reach them.

After a moment, Sigurd bravely stepped forward and locked eyes with the snarling hellhound.

"Let us pass, beast," He demanded. "We do not have any quarrel with you."

"Oh, but you do," Garm countered. "All who carry the blood of Odin and are kin to Týr are my sworn enemy!"

"Why?" Sigurd inquired. "Why do you hate Týr and Odin so much?"

"Surely, you jest?!" Garm growled indignantly. "They are the ones who put me here! Odin abducted me and my brothers Sköll and Hati from our father Fenrir when I was just a pup. He used ancient magic to chain me here in the underworld and cast my older brothers into the heavens to chase the sun and moon. Odin assured our father that he was granting us great honors, ensuring that the restless dead remained in the underworld and that the sun and moon would never stand still. But we were just hostages to ensure his good behavior."

"That alone was enough to earn my enmity," Garm growled, tugging at the chain that bound him. "But what Týr did next to my father forever cemented my hatred of Odin and his kin!

"Unlike my Uncle Jörmungandr, my father Fenrir was kept in the kennels of Asgard, but he inspired such fear in the gods that only Týr was brave enough to approach the wolf and give him food. The two formed an uneasy friendship, and the war god became the only person my father trusted. In time, the Aesir noticed that Fenrir was rapidly growing bigger with every passing day, making them more fearful of him due to the ridiculous prophecy that the wolf would bring them great harm. Thus, they decided to try to imprison Fenrir even though he had done nothing to threaten them.

"But my father was so large and powerful that no ordinary chain could bind him. So the Aesir commissioned Ivaldi and the dwarves of Svartalfheim to create a silken chain forged from rare mythical ingredients. They brought him to the island of Lyngvi, showed him the silken chain Gleipnir, and challenged him to break it.

"But my father was suspicious of the chain's deceptive appearance and the Aesir's traitorous nature. He refused to let himself be bound, believing that the ribbon was made with art and trickery. But the Aesir slighted him, claiming that if Fenrir could not break the silken binds, it would be apparent to them that he was no threat to be feared.

"Fenrir, offended but still wary, responded that he would only allow himself to be bound if one of the Aesir put their hand in his mouth as a show of good faith. No one took up the offer except Týr, who placed his right hand in my father's mouth, after which Fenrir allowed the Aesir to bind him again. He kicked and thrashed to free himself, but Gleipnir grew stronger and tighter. When Fenrir realized he'd been tricked, he bit off Týr's traitorous hand. Then the Aesir took a singular cord that hung from Gleipnir, threaded it through a giant stone, and fastened it underground. After that, they put another great rock as large as a mountain on top of it to act as an anchoring peg. And to add injury to insult, Odin thrust a sword into the roof of my father's mouth. The hilt jammed against his lower jaw, ensuring he could never close his mouth."

"My father has remained bound in that humiliating and painful position ever since!" Garm howled. "And it's all because of that traitorous Týr! People claim that the loss of Týr's hand was a noble sacrifice for the greater good. But to me, it was nothing short of betrayal! My father opened his heart to Týr, but the traitor inevitably deceived and betrayed him as the Aesir always do. One day, I'll finish what Father started and devour that traitor alive!"

"You have a right to feel angry," Sinfjotli conceded. "But you've got the wrong sow by the ear. We weren't there and had nothing to do with the binding of Fenrir, and we hadn't even been born yet. Besides, our ancestor is Sigi, not Týr."

"That doesn't matter!" Garm snarled. "To me, *anyone* who carries the blood of Odin in their veins is a relative of Týr and thus my sworn enemy."

"Well, it's good to know where things stand between us," Sigurd joked. He gestured to the canyon and the stone arch above them. "You obviously won't let us pass by, so why don't you tell us a bit about this place instead? What does that message carved into the arch above us say? I don't recognize those symbols."

"There's no reason you would, cretin," Garm growled. "The language predates your own by millennia. But the message is simple and clear: 'None may leave without permission.' The stone arch above us represents the boundary of Mistress Hel's domain. Once someone passes beneath this arch, they become permanent denizens of Helheim."

"There is only one iron rule here in Helheim," Garm warned. "All are welcome in Helheim, but no soul may leave this realm or pass beyond this arch unless Mistress Hel allows it. It is my duty as the guard dog of Helheim to enforce that law and punish anyone stupid or brash enough to break it."

Garm bared his fangs and glared at them with five eyes. "If you take one step past that arch, you are **REALLY** not going to like what happens next."

Sinfjotli turned to Sigurd. "Think we could fight him?"

"No, it's too risky," Sigurd replied.

"I don't see any other way to get past him," Sinfjotli demurred. "We may have to slay him."

"And that would be disastrous!" Sigurd countered. "There's more at stake here than our lives. You know he's the guardian of Helheim who keeps its inhabitants from leaving, right?"

"Yes," Sinfjotli nodded. "But why does that…?"

"Then you know that slaying him would have grave consequences," Sigurd interrupted. "Think about it. Millions of restless and violent spirits reside here in Helheim. You saw how many were marching toward us in the city earlier. I could tell they all wished to return to Midgard and exact vengeance on the people who wronged them. Garm is the only thing stopping them.

What would stop those restless dead from invading and overrunning Midgard and the other realms if he died?"

There was wisdom in his brother's words. "All right," Sinfjotli conceded. "I understand that slaying Garm would have dire consequences, assuming it's even possible to kill him. But that doesn't change the fact that he's preventing us from leaving this accursed realm. What should we do?"

"*YOU DIE!*" a booming metallic voice roared. Before Sinfjotli could register where the voice had come from, a high-pitched whine pierced his ears like an incoming projectile. Half a heartbeat later, something exploded in front of him, rocking the hillside and sending Sinfjotli and Sigurd flying backward.

CHAPTER TWENTY-SEVEN

ARMY OF DEATH

It took a full minute for Sinfjotli to fully recover from the explosion. The shockwave had sent him and Sigurd flying backward to the Gjallerbru, and it had happened so fast that he hadn't had time to protect himself. Painful first-degree burns simmered his arms, face, and torso. But after a minute, the healing properties of the golden apple kicked in, and all his burns vanished.

As Sinfjotli stood up, he heard the sounds of incoherent, ghastly whisperings all around them. As he turned to locate the source, he witnessed great green lights glowing from nearby mounds like foxfire. As the will-o'-the-wisps shone brighter, dozens of rotting skeletal hands burst from the ground as the dead began dragging themselves from the earth.

"Draugirs," Sigurd exclaimed, drawing Gram.

Sinfjotli instinctively reached to his side but remembered that he was currently weaponless. He could only watch as the dead roused themselves from the icy ground.

The draugirs looked more or less how Sinfjotli had envisioned based on Baldur's earlier description and their brief encounter with the army in the city to the south. Most of them looked like rotting reanimated corpses wearing suits of armor. A dim aura of blue light surrounded their bodies. Some draugirs were in better condition than others. Their skin and muscles were intact, although their flesh mostly had rotted away. Others were maimed, missing limbs, or had damaged skulls, indicating violent deaths. Almost all of them showed signs of lengthy decomposition, suggesting they had been buried in the ground for a long time. Many of them were skeletal, with exposed bones held together by sinews and shreds of muscle. However, a few looked lifelike, as if they had died recently.

Their armor wasn't in much better condition. Many wore rusted chain mail, dented and rusted iron plates, or ragged leather armor. But their weapons, while in poor condition, still looked sharp.

For a moment, the draugirs locked eyes with Sinfjotli and Sigurd. Then, with an unearthly ear-piercing screech, the restless dead surged forth.

Sigurd rushed forward with Gram in hand. Sinfjotli still didn't have a weapon, but that quickly changed. As the first draugir charged at him, Sinfjotli maneuvered out of the way and grabbed the shaft of its two-handed pole axe. Sinfjotli then tore the weapon from the draugir with enough force to rip off its skeletal arm. Sinfjotli then shattered the draugir's skull into dust with the axe's spike.

But it wasn't the end. Despite having its head destroyed and its arm torn off, the draugir's headless body rushed at Sinfjotli. Even after he cut it in half, its dismembered body continued moving on the ground, albeit robbed of its sensory organs.

Sinfjotli cast aside his horror at this macabre sight as another draugir with a rusty sword approached. Sinfjotli instinctively blocked the incoming strike.

Or at least he tried to. As soon as their weapons clashed, Sinfjotli's pole axe flew from his hand. The absurdly powerful force behind the draugir's blow disarmed Sinfjotli, leaving him no choice but to back away as the draugir attacked him with a whirlwind of strikes.

Sinfjotli continued dodging attacks in an attempt to escape the perilous situation. Despite their corpse-like and skeletal appearance, the surprisingly nimble and incredibly strong draugirs were in no way inhibited by the decayed state of their bodies. Even this skeletal draugir attacking him, whose exposed bones were held together by sinews and thin shreds of muscle, possessed enough strength to shatter iron.

Sinfjotli continued dodging the draugir's attacks until his back pressed against a two-ton glacier. Sinfjotli dive-rolled to safety as the draugir swung its sword at him. The powerful force behind the blow shattered the sword as it struck the ice and caused an entire section of the glacier to crumble apart.

If an ordinary man tried to parry such a mighty blow from a draugir, his shield would have shattered, and his arm would have broken from the immense pressure.

But Sinfjotli was no ordinary man. As a skinchanger, he possessed the strength of twenty men, even in his human form. Seizing the opportunity, Sinfjotli rushed forward, grabbed the draugir's arms, and began slowly overpowering it with brute strength.

He was on the cusp of overpowering it when something barreled into him and threw him to the ground. He started to wrestle with the thing that had jumped him... another draugir.

Sinfjotli landed an elbow in the draugir's face and squirmed onto his back to face the undead warrior as it straddled him.

But before Sinfjotli could force the undead creature off him, seven more draugirs swarmed him and pinned him to the ground. They scratched and bit his torso and legs with rotten teeth as Sinfjotli struggled to break free. Sinfjotli could overpower a single draugir, but he couldn't free himself through brute strength with eight piled on top of him at once.

When that failed, he resorted to keeping the hands of the draugir straddling him off of his neck...and somehow, he succeeded. The head stared at him with rage in its shining blue eyes. It opened its mouth and screamed at him, its rank breath adding to the nightmare Sinfjotli found himself in. It started chomping at him, trying to bite his face off.

The teeth came closer and closer to his face, the stench of its breath growing stronger and stronger as the face inched closer and closer. Sinfjotli held it at bay for the moment, but he couldn't keep this up forever. Meanwhile, the other draugirs continued biting and scratching at his legs, torso, and arms.

Was this it? Had he been saved from Hel by Baldur and given a second chance at Valhalla, only to die at the hands of mere foot soldiers?

A scream of rage echoed in Sinfjotli's ears as gray-rippled metal ripped through the draugir's head. The draugir straddling him spasmed once and then went limp atop him. He saw that its skull was sliced in half. Another white blur passed over Sinfjotli, and a moment later, the other draugirs pinning him to the ground collapsed lifelessly on top of him.

Sinfjotli saw Sigurd standing over him, holding Gram in one hand and the pole axe Sinfjotli had been using earlier in the other. Sigurd's face was grimmer than Sinfjotli had seen before. And there was a hint of disappointment in his eyes.

Sinfjotli threw the corpses of the draugirs off him and clawed to his feet in a frenzy. He looked down to find that all the draugirs were dead or at least immobilized. Sigurd had sliced through the skulls of the other seven draugirs in a single swing. Behind him, Sinfjotli saw fifteen more lifeless corpses strewn across the ground.

Sinfjotli looked back to congratulate his brother but paused when he saw his glowing snake eyes. Sigurd had that creepy look in his eyes. It was the same cold, calculating look Sinfjotli had seen earlier when they'd fought in the plaza. His eyes looked emotionless, calculating, and steadfast, like a falcon scanning the ground for prey.

Sigurd looked askance at Sinfjotli's sizzling wounds and sneered.

"That was careless," Sigurd chastised as he tossed Sinfjotli his pole axe. "Never underestimate your opponent solely on their appearance."

"I'll remember that," Sinfjotli promised.

They didn't have time to talk further. The other draugirs had regrouped and swarmed them. Sigurd wasted no time lunging back into the fray. Sinfjotli waited until his wounds finished healing before joining him.

As he fought, Sinfjotli realized why the draugirs were so dangerous. Since they were already dead, they felt no pain and would continue to fight regardless of injury dismemberment. Their limbs continued moving even after being detached from their bodies. The only guaranteed way to incapacitate them was total dismemberment, but going so far to dispatch a single one would leave him open to attack from the others.

Despite their corpse-like and skeletal appearance, the draugirs surprising speed and incredible strength posed an additional threat. Every draugir was strong enough to shatter iron and crush bone with a single blow.

Sinfjotli was impressed. However, their strength paled in comparison to his. As a skinchanger, Sinfjotli's enhanced strength could overwhelm their strikes with brute force alone if he wished. But he had taken a liking to his new weapon, which he continued using to fend off the draugirs.

As Sinfjotli fought, he noticed Sigurd fighting out of the corner of his eye and felt a pang of jealousy toward his brother. Although Sinfjotli was putting up a good fight, Sigurd had already killed twice as many foes as him. Gram effortlessly sliced through the draugirs and their armor.

Curiously, the draugirs cut down by Gram remained dead, or at least as close to death as an undead warrior could be. The light faded from their eye sockets, and their bodies remained motionless on the ground after Sigurd cut them down. Sinfjotli suspected it was because Gram was an enchanted weapon, and he continued fighting with a pang of envy.

Sinfjotli and Sigurd fought until one last draugir remained. But as Sigurd raised Gram for the coup de grâce, the undead warrior unexpectedly dropped its weapons and kneeled in submission.

"Mercy, my lords," the spirit pleaded with a mix of respect and fear. "I yield. I refuse to fight another descendant of Völsung."

"Another descendant of Völsung?" Sinfjotli repeated, unsure if he heard it right. He looked closer at the spirit's armor and noticed the sigil of a black wolf on a white field howling at the moon on its breastplate. After a moment, he remembered this was the sigil of an ancient Geatish clan from Gautland.

"Who are you?" Sinfjotli demanded.

Before the spirit could answer, Sinfjotli felt the ground tremor beneath his feet. A moment later, he heard giant thumping sounds so loud that a chunk of ice accumulating on the Gjallerbru's suspension cable broke off and splashed into the river below. Sinfjotli and Sigurd turned east to observe something big and bright advancing toward them on the icy shore of this dark continent. Its aura was more radiant and far more malevolent than the other draugirs.

"That must be a draug," Sigurd muttered. "This won't be easy. Remember, Baldur warned us that those creatures are Helheim's elite generals whose authority over the dead will be second only to Hel herself. Don't let your guard down."

"Same goes for you," Sinfjotli replied while twirling his pole axe.

The draug was now close enough for Sinfjotli to make out its features. After facing the draugirs, Sinfjotli expected their leader to look something akin to a giant, armored skeleton. But the draug looked nothing like the other restless dead. It stood as big as a barn and possessed a humanoid shape. But instead of flesh and bones, its body was composed of wood, scraps of armor, faded standards, twisted weapons, charred rubble, and faded burned shields, all lashed together by rope and chains into a humanoid form. Its head was largely absent of facial features, apart from a large gaping mouth-like hole at the center. Flames erupted from another hole in the back of its head. It looked like someone had collected pieces of burning rubble and weapons from a castle and shaped it into a humanoid form. The creature carried a giant shield in its left hand with burning spikes jutting from each side like points on a clock.

Sinfjotli decided to take the initiative. He rushed forward with his two-handed pole axe and swung it at the creature's torso. The axe passed harmlessly through the draug's body like smoke and embedded itself in a nearby glacier. Alarmed, Sinfjotli dislodged the axe from the ice and spun around, prepared to block an incoming strike.

But to his surprise, the draug didn't attack. It hadn't even turned its head. It ignored him and even walked right past Sigurd. Its attention was fixated on the draugir that had surrendered and was now prostrating itself in fear.

"You have failed me!" the draug announced in a booming, metallic voice. It was the same voice they had heard minutes earlier before the explosion.

Before the spirit could plead for mercy, the draug bashed it with its fist, sending the draugir flying through the air and past the boundary of the arch. That draugir must have weighed at least three hundred pounds with all its heavy armor. But the draug had swatted it through the air like a pebble.

The draugir crashed into the icy road a hundred feet beyond the boundary of Gnipa Cave. Before the restless spirit could pick itself off the ground, Garm lunged out of his cave and gobbled the poor screaming soul up in seconds. Garm looked back and growled at Sinfjotli, Sigurd, and the draug before retreating inside his cave. His unspoken message was clear: if anyone passed beyond the arch and in front of Gnipa Cave, Garm would instantly devour them, regardless of whether they were alive or one of Helheim's restless spirits.

Sinfjotli glanced up at the draug towering over them as he felt a wave of power wash over him from the undead lord. The scars on Sinfjotli's wrists throbbed and burned with every word the draug spoke. *This monster's bloodlust is overwhelming. It almost feels like a sword thrust right at my heart. It feels so familiar, but where have I felt it before?*

"You should be honored that Mistress Hel sent me," the draug boasted as it turned around to face them. He drew his gargantuan two-handed great sword, which was the size of a row boat with a large guard with side rings and integral parrying hooks, and held it aloft. "We draugs normally never stoop to doing anything with our own hands. But when she told me who the escapees were, I couldn't resist. Now rejoice! You'll have the honor of dying at the hands of one of Helheim's best generals."

"That voice," Sinfjotli gasped. "I know that voice!"

The draug spoke in a rough, unnatural, but vaguely familiar tone. Sinfjotli's surprise soon turned into horror and disgust as he recognized the shield it carried. It was a giant wooden shield with twelve burning prongs jutting from the rim in every direction and a long spike in its center. There was only one person Sinfjotli knew of who wielded a spiked shield like that.

"It's you, isn't it?" Sinfjotli demanded. "King Siggeir!"

CHAPTER TWENTY-EIGHT

A HELLISH FAMILY REUNION

As Sinfjotli glared at the ghost of Siggeir, the draug's unorthodox body structure started to make sense. The wood, armor, the Geatish standards, weapons, shields, lashed ropes, rubble, and fire were all parts of the debris of the castle Siggeir had been buried under when he died. In a sense, his body was composed of the same burning wreckage of the palace he'd been buried under after Sigmund cut him down.

The draug loomed over them. It had no discernible eyes, but Sinfjotli knew it was looking at them. He could tell that it was relishing in his growing fear and horror as he gazed upon the specter of his malevolent stepfather.

"Hello, *fratricide!*" Siggeir hissed venomously.

"Don't you *dare* call me that, you vile hypocrite!" Sinfjotli exploded. "You're the traitorous monster who broke guest right! You murdered your father and brothers-in-law after inviting them into your home. You, of all people, have no right to judge me or call me a kinslayer!"

"Perhaps," Siggeir conceded. "But only one of us is a genuine kinslayer who slew his blood relatives. And watch your tone, boy! Is that any way to speak to your *stepfather?*"

It took several moments for Sinfjotli's already strained mind to realize the full import of that last word. When he did, he felt his whole world turn upside down.

"You...you know?" He stammered. "You *know* I'm not your son?"

"That's right," Siggeir laughed. "Hel told me all about your salacious origins, *bastard*! It shed light on so many things. I cursed you as a traitorous son at the moment of my death. I couldn't fathom how my own child could so viciously murder his siblings without exhibiting a shred of remorse. I despaired at how thoroughly Sigmund had brainwashed you and turned my own blood against me. But it turns out you were never my child but a bastard born of vile incest all along!" He chortled. "I never imagined that Völsung's detestable slut of a daughter would sink so low for vengeance!"

As the draug cackled, Sigurd stepped forward and drew Gram. "I've heard enough of this prattle. I'll not stand hearing my father, aunt, or the Volsung name besmirched. Be gone, wraith! Or suffer our wrath!"

Siggeir turned toward Sigurd. The draug had no discernible eyes, but Sinfjotli could tell the arch-wraith was looking at his brother. Or, more specifically, at Gram.

"That sword," Siggeir remarked. "I remember that blade! That is the very same sword Sigmund used to cut me down! I recognize your horrid blood. You are another son of that despicable Sigmund!"

"And damn proud of it," Sigurd proclaimed. "So you're the monster who brought our family's bloodline to the brink of extinction? I saw you in a vision earlier, and I must say, you look far less grotesque now than when you were alive."

Siggeir tightened his grip on his claymore. The blade's tip glowed red hot as the draug stared daggers at Sigurd and then glanced back at Gram.

"You know, that sword you wield is what started the blood feud between me and you Volsungs," Siggeir informed.

Sigurd blinked. "What?"

"Ah, this takes me back," Siggeir reminisced. "I clearly remember the first time I saw that sword on my wedding day. A man wearing a gray hat and robe came into the hall and stabbed that sword into the Volsungs' ancestral tree, announcing that only the best warrior among us may draw it. We all tried, but only Sigmund could dislodge the blade. Sigmund then refused to give me that sword even when I offered to pay three times its weight in gold for it. He refused *ME* a gift on my wedding day and dared to claim I was unworthy! I slaughtered Völsung and his sons to acquire that sword. But in the end, Sigmund cut down me and my entire line with it."

"So it's true? You... you *butchered* our grandfather and uncles over a sword?" Sigurd growled. "You really are a monster!" He looked like he was on the verge of lunging at Siggeir. But Sinfjotli grabbed his shoulder, stopping him.

"Don't let him get to you. Siggeir is a manipulative, heartless monster always looking to expose a moment of weakness. His favorite tactic is manipulating his opponents' emotions and getting them to lose focus during combat. He's a monster who will do whatever it takes to win a fight. Siggeir once executed a hundred men, women, and children in a village our father happened to pass through in a desperate attempt to flush him out of hiding." Sinfjotli looked up at the draug and gnashed his teeth. "If you lose your composure, he gets exactly what he wants. No matter what he says or does, you must control your anger, or he wins."

"How dare you think so little of me," Siggeir chortled, sarcastically feigning offense. "I may be spiteful and a king who shows no mercy to his foes. But heartless? Give me a bit more consideration. Think about how gravely your family wronged me. Sigmund refused me a gift on my wedding day and demeaned me in front of everyone. He and his father and brothers butchered some of my best men when they came into my castle! Then, he brutally murdered my mother and plagued my kingdom for years. As for your whore of a mother, she remorselessly ordered the deaths of our sons, then cuckolded me with her own twin brother and my bitterest foe. As for you, *fratricide,* you massacred hundreds of my citizens, murdered your own siblings just to hurt me, and then set my castle ablaze and cut down my entire court. And you stood by and watched with glee as Sigmund left me to burn! Is it any wonder why I swallowed my pride as a draug and came to face you personally?"

Sinfjotli tightened his grip on his atgeir. He wanted to refute Siggeir's false angst and remind his wicked stepfather that he had broken guest right and massacred ten times more of his own citizens than Sinfjotli and his father ever. But he held his tongue, knowing Siggeir was attempting to get under his skin. He inhaled the frigid air, then exhaled the fire of anger growing within him.

"Speaking with you is a waste of time and words," Sinfjotli declared calmly. "I've tolerated your presence long enough."

"Likewise," Siggeir agreed coldly. "It's past time I settled the score."

Siggeir turned his sword upside down and jammed it into the ground. The ghastly chattering returned, and an entire legion of skeletal armored draugirs crawled out of the ice and rock. Many bore the sigil of Geatish tribes on their shields, and the rest had sigils Sinfjotli wasn't familiar with.

"As I said before, we draugs seldom stoop to doing anything with our own hands," Siggeir reiterated as he withdrew the gargantuan sword from the ground. "We have our lackeys for that. But I'll make an exception if it means getting revenge on the bastard that ended my bloodline and finally claiming Sigmund's sword!"

"Father and I already killed you once, Siggeir," Sinfjotli warned. "I will gladly do it again in his stead!"

"Come and try it then," Siggeir challenged. "I'll bring you both to the point of death and then feed you to Garm! It'll be just like the time I had my mother turn into a wolf and devour each of your nine uncles. Oh, I look forward to feeding another descendant of Völsung to a wolf!"

Siggeir's legion of undead warriors surged forward. There were at least two hundred skeletal warriors, but they were no match for Sigurd and Sinfjotli. With Gram in hand, Sigurd shredded through their weapons and armor as if they were made of straw.

Sinfjotli effortlessly cut his way through twenty draugirs and lunged at the ghost of his stepfather. He swung his pole axe in a downward strike, but Siggeir blocked the strike with his spiked shield. Siggeir swung his shield arm in a backhand strike, sending Sinfjotli flying backward. Sinfjotli somersaulted midair and landed gracefully on the ground. He then lunged back into the fray again and cut down draugirs left and right.

But everything changed after he cut off one draugir's arm, and he heard a voice cry out: "Stop! Don't hurt me, brother!"

"What the... Sigurd, did you say something?" As soon as he asked, Sinfjotli realized that voice couldn't have been Sigurd's. Sigurd was on the other side of the battlefield fighting twenty draugirs. Moreover, the voice sounded like it belonged to a little girl.

Sinfjotli glanced at the now one-armed skeletal draugir cowering on the ground before him. He realized this wretched creature had been the one speaking to him. But why did it call him 'brother?'

"Not quite," Siggeir laughed. "You're addressing the wrong sibling." The one-armed draugir Sinfjotli had hesitated to kill lunged forward and wrapped its remaining arm around his waist. Three more draugirs burst from the ground around his feet, and they all grabbed Sinfjotli from each direction and held him in place.

"Look closely at the one whose arm you hacked off and the other whose skull you just cracked with your elbow," Siggeir advised.

Sinfjotli glanced down at the draugir clutching his chest. Emerald mist swirled around the draugir's body. Its form became clearer until Sinfjotli could see skin and hair. After a moment, Sinfjotli could clearly see the draugir exactly how it looked when it was alive. It was a little girl with blond pigtails and blue eyes.

No... Sinfjotli thought. *It can't be.*

"Please don't hurt me again, big brother!" The girl pleaded.

"Aurora," Sinfjotli muttered. There was no mistaking it. This was his maternal half-sister.

"It's a bit late for that, dear sister." The draugir to his right spoke. "We're both dead. He killed us with his own hands."

Just like Aurora, emerald mist swirled around this draugir's body. Its form became clearer until it appeared like a plump, bookish ten-year-old boy with curly blond hair.

"Hansel," Sinfjotli whispered as he recognized his younger maternal half-brother.

"Why?" Aurora pleaded. "Why did you do it, big brother? Why did you kill us? What did we do to hurt you?"

"We didn't do a damn thing," the draugir to Sinfjotli's left answered. "But what did you expect? He's as cruel as his wretched father."

"Of course," the draugir holding Sinfjotli from behind agreed. "Uncle Sigmund didn't hesitate when he cut us down even though we were his nephews. So why would his own son hesitate to murder his siblings?"

Like before, the draugirs holding Sinfjotli from the left and behind took on human appearances. They both had black hair and blue eyes and looked about twelve or thirteen years old. Sinfjotli didn't recognize these boys. But based on what they just said, he figured they were most likely his eldest maternal half-brothers whom Sigmund had murdered at Signy's behest when they failed to pass his test of courage.

"You two must be Ragr and Rekkr," Sinfjotli deduced.

"That's right," Siggeir laughed. "Now, all five children of Signy are here together. Oh, what's wrong, *fratricide*? I thought you'd enjoy this little family reunion with your siblings."

The rest of the draugirs Siggeir had summoned surged forth. When Sinfjotli tried to push his siblings away, Aurora clutched him tighter. Despite having only one arm, she was surprisingly strong. Then he remembered that she was still a draugir.

"Please don't go, big brother!" she pleaded, burying her head in his chest. "Please don't leave us alone! It's scary here!"

"Yes, brother," Rekkr urged. "Stay with us, and we'll be a family again."

Sinfjotli looked back at the draug. He imagined that Siggeir would be smirking right now if he had a face. Sinfjotli figured Siggeir was trying to corner him by using his own children as obstacles. If Sinfjotli wished to defend himself from the encroaching wave of draugirs, he'd have to eliminate his half-siblings first. This was a truly despicable act, even for a black-hearted monster like Siggeir. The draug cackled as his draugirs marched closer, believing Sinfjotli wouldn't do it.

He could not have been more wrong. Sinfjotli broke free of his siblings' grasp, brandished his pole axe, and slew all four of them without a single shred of remorse or emotion.

"You're just as heartless as ever, Siggeir," Sinfjotli said calmly as he lunged at the approaching draugirs. "Using your own children as an obstacle is despicable even for you. But did you really think summoning my maternal half-siblings would make me hesitate and allow you to overwhelm me? I didn't hesitate when I killed them the first time. Why would I show the slightest compunction now in Helheim?"

"We'll see about that," Siggeir promised. "Since you value your *father's* side of the family so much, let's try this instead."

Siggeir jammed his sword into the ground. Fissures spread across the earth, and nine skeletal figures crawled to the surface. These draugirs, distinct from the rest of Siggeir's minions, stood at least seven feet tall in full suits of steel plate armor. Their armor was in better condition than the rest of Siggeir's minions, and their aura was more powerful than an ordinary draugir's. They looked powerful and challenging. But Sinfjotli was unimpressed.

"You can summon nine or nine hundred," Sinfjotli shouted at Siggeir. "They won't stop me." Sinfjotli brandished his pole axe and charged at the newcomers.

"Is that Sigmund?" One of the draugirs asked. "He looks just like our older brother."

Sinfjotli stopped dead in his tracks. He felt his blood turn to ice in his veins as his mind processed what he had just heard.

"What...what did you say?" He demanded.

"What's wrong, *fratricide*," Siggeir asked. "You look so confused. Perhaps this will help."

Siggeir snapped his fingers, and emerald mist swirled around the nine draugirs. Their forms shimmered as they took on human appearances. They all possessed piercing steel blue eyes, wild brown hair, muscular builds, and comely features. Bite marks and open wounds covered their bodies as if they had been recently mauled to death by a savage beast.

Sinfjotli was speechless. They each looked so much like his father in his younger years.

"A-Are you really Sigmund's brothers," Sinfjotli demanded.

"Indeed," Siggeir laughed. "Oh, that's right. You've never met them before, have you? Well then, allow me to introduce you. These are Sigmund and Signy's younger brothers: Arne the Swift, Colborn Blood Axe, Frode the Wise, Gerald the Devote, Halvard Squint-Eye, Jerrik the Undying, Orwig the Protector, Thurmond the Mighty, and Ulf the Bloodletter."

As Siggeir spoke, emerald mist swirled around Sinfjotli's uncles. When it faded, Sinfjotli noticed that their weapons had changed. Jerrik the Undying now held two heavy shields in each hand. Gerald the Devote had an axe and hammer in each hand and several throwing axes holstered in his belt. Halvard Squint-Eye held a massive double bow capable of firing two arrows simultaneously. Colberd Blood-Axe unsurprisingly wielded a large and wicked-looking double-bladed battle axe. Orwig the Protector possessed a large shield and halberd. Thurmond the Mighty held a massive war hammer. Frode the Wise had a giant great sword. Ulf the Bloodletter held two short swords in each hand. And Arne the Swift wielded two large spears in each hand.

Sinfjotli instinctively stepped backward. These nine warriors looked tough. And the way they held their weapons indicated they were very skilled combatants.

"Feeling intimidated, fratricide?" Siggeir asked. "You should be. They were some of the greatest warriors of their time, and their fighting prowess was unmatched by anyone except for Sigmund and their father, Völsung. And now, they're my loyal slaves!"

Siggeir turned to the nine sons of Völsung and pointed at Sinfjotli. "Take a good look at the vile creature in front of you. That unholy abomination is your nephew, the bastard son of Sigmund and Signy."

"What," Arne gasped. "He's their son? But then that means..."

"Did I give you permission to speak?!" Siggeir roared. He backhanded the spirit, knocking Arne to the ground, and then ordered him to stand up.

"Now that we're finished with formalities, go slaughter your nephew!" Siggeir ordered.

Siggeir pointed his claymore at Sinfjotli. Sinfjotli braced himself, but nothing happened. The ghosts of his uncles hadn't budged.

"What are you doing," Siggeir demanded angrily. "I told you to kill him."

"I...I refuse," Gerald proclaimed. "I won't raise a hand against Sigmund's son."

"Nor will I," Halvard agreed.

"He's our flesh and blood," Orwig proclaimed. "We cannot fight him."

"Didn't you hear me?" Siggeir seethed. "I gave you a clear and straightforward order. I told you to *kill* the little bastard!"

He clenched his right fist, and the nine sons of Völsung screamed in pain. Their bodies began moving on their own accord, and they attacked Sinfjotli.

Völsung's nine sons pleaded for forgiveness with every strike. Although they couldn't disobey Siggeir, they tried to assist Sinfjotli by warning him when and how they would attack. But their efforts were in vain because Sinfjotli could not bring himself to harm them. They looked too much like his father. To him, slaying his uncles was the same as cutting down his father, a line Sinfjotli outright refused to cross.

"I'm sure Sigmund and Signy told you about what I did to their nine brothers many times," Siggeir taunted as he watched Sinfjotli desperately defend himself. "After I ambushed them and killed Völsung, Sigmund and his brothers were at my mercy. Your mother pleaded with me to spare her brothers. So I left them in the woods chained to the trees with a log placed over their legs. Then, I arranged for my mother to turn into a wolf and devour them alive each night. She devoured them one by one until only Sigmund was left. In life, they were amongst the bravest of you accursed Volsungs, and all were denied death in battle by my decree. Now, in death, they're my slaves, forced to fight against their kin."

Sinfjotli screamed in rage. He wanted to cut his way to Siggeir and tear the wicked king to pieces. But his body and mind just wouldn't let him harm his uncles. They might be draugirs now, but they had once been his father's brothers. And the one thing Sinfjotli could never bring himself to do was to attack his forebears.

But Sigurd showed no such compunction. As Sinfjotli was about to be overwhelmed by his uncles, Sigurd lunged forward and cut down Colborn and Orwig with a single stroke of Gram.

"Wait, are you also...?" Halvard started. But Sigurd cut off his head before his uncle could finish his question.

"I hate archery," Sigurd remarked as the spirit and its double bow faded into ash and mist.

"What are you doing," Sinfjotli shouted. "They're our uncles!"

"What of it," Sigurd asked coldly as he sliced Ulf the Bloodletter in half. "These wraiths may have been our father's brothers in life. They might also mean something to you, Sinfjotli. But I have no emotional connection to any of them. They're just another hoard of restless spirits in my way. If you can't bring yourself to fight them, just keep moving and deal with the others. I'll handle them. Siggeir denied them the chance to die fighting in life. I'll give them that chance in death."

Inspired by his brother's words, Sinfjotli retrieved his pole axe and pointed it at the draug, challenging his stepfather to face him. Siggeir gladly accepted the challenge but also summoned a hundred more draugirs as he made his way toward Sinfjotli, indicating this wouldn't be a one-on-one duel.

"Can you deal with the other draugirs as well, brother?" Sinfjotli requested. "Siggeir is mine! I'll cut off that vile snake's head and end this nightmare."

CHAPTER TWENTY-NINE

BLIND RAGE

While Sigurd faced off against the spirits of their uncles and the rest of the draugirs Siggeir had summoned, Sinfjotli and the draug clashed against each other. But as they fought, Sinfjotli encountered a predicament: he couldn't harm Siggeir. No matter how he attacked, his pole axe passed harmlessly through the draug's body.

On the other hand, Siggeir had no such handicap. He swung his sword and bashed Sinfjotli with his spiked shield in devastatingly powerful attacks. Sinfjotli could only resort to defense as the draug bombarded him with powerful blows.

Siggeir charged at Sinfjotli, intending to skewer him with his shield's prongs. Sinfjotli dodged left, got to his feet, and thrust the spike of his pole axe at Siggeir's undefended right side. However, his axe passed through the draug's body like smoke. Siggeir turned and swung his sword at Sinfjotli. Sinfjotli managed to parry the slash, stopping the claymore with his axe head. But the blow was so powerful that the ice beneath his feet cracked.

"Why can't I harm him?" Sinfjotli growled as he pushed aside the claymore. *My pole axe keeps passing through him, no matter how much I attack.*

Suddenly, Sinfjotli faintly recalled something Baldur had mentioned: *"Draugs are bound to a certain 'story,' the series of traumatic events leading* *up to their death. They are untouchable, unreachable to anyone and **anything** that isn't a part of that story."*

Are you kidding me?! Sinfjotli thought in disbelief. *That means Siggeir is invincible! No weapon can even scratch him!*

Sinfjotli's heart raced, but he was determined to find a way to defeat Siggeir and refused to believe that winning was impossible.

"Is something wrong, fratricide?" Siggeir asked as he swung his sword. "You're wavering. Have you realized just how outmatched you are? Or perhaps the guilt over killing your siblings a second time caught up to you."

"I have no feelings whatsoever toward Rekkr, Ragr, Hansel, or Aurora," Sinfjotli answered emotionlessly as he parried the incoming strike. "I never harbored any hatred toward Hansel and Aurora. They just had the terrible misfortune of being your children. I swore I would end your bloodline, and the fact that they also happened to be my maternal half-siblings was just an unfortunate coincidence."

Siggeir momentarily faltered as if taken aback by Sinfjotli's words. Sinfjotli capitalized on that moment and rushed forward. He channeled all his strength into a single punch. Siggeir blocked it with his shield, but the mighty blow sent him skidding backward twenty feet.

Although it made Sinfjotli feel a bit better, the impressive show of strength was pointless. All Sinfjotli did was shove the ten-foot draug a couple of yards backward. Siggeir hadn't even lost his balance or fallen to one knee.

"Signy brainwashed you well," Siggeir tittered as he recomposed himself. "You were always her greatest sin."

"A monster like you has no right to lecture me about sin," Sinfjotli growled.

"No need to get agitated," Siggeir taunted. "You *know* I'm speaking the truth. Your mother was a truly spiteful woman. I always knew how much Signy hated me for what I did to her father and brothers. In hindsight, I probably should have killed her and taken another wife when she pleaded with me to spare her brothers. Would you like to know why I didn't? The truth is I enjoyed keeping her in that position! She was forced into a marriage that she didn't want and forced to bear the children of her greatest enemy, who had butchered her entire family. What greater humiliation is there for a woman than that?"

"You rotten bastard!" Sinfjotli rushed forward and swung his pole axe, which passed harmlessly through the draug's body. Siggeir swung his claymore in response, and it took all of Sinfjotli's strength to parry the blow.

"I knew she'd hatch some plan to get vengeance on me somehow," Siggeir continued. "But even *I* was shocked that she went so far as deceiving and seducing her twin brother for revenge. And then she groomed you, the child born of that incestuous union, into a heartless harbinger of her vengeance. Now, she resides here in Helheim, suffering agonizing torment for her many crimes. Tell me, *fratricide*, would you like to see her?"

"What?" Sinfjotli blinked. Before fully comprehending what the draug had said, Siggeir rammed his shield into Sinfjotli while momentarily distracted. The blow sent Sinfjotli tumbling about thirty feet backward. When he stood up, he noticed that the force of the impact had also snapped his pole axe in half. As he tossed the broken weapon aside, he looked back at Siggeir and discovered that the distance between him and the draug had already been filled by dozens of other draugirs the arch-wraith had summoned.

"Watch closely," Siggeir commanded. He jammed his sword into the ground. A fissure opened, and a geyser of green flames erupted from the icy ground. Green will-o'-the-wisp began swirling through the air. A screaming skeletal figure grabbed the fissure's edge and started crawling out. However, the spirit appeared in immense pain and struggled to pull itself out of the burning crevice. Siggeir impatiently grabbed the ghost's neck and lifted it out of the fissure in full view of Sinfjotli. As the spectral form hung there, dangling by its neck, its body began to rematerialize, becoming opaque and solid as it took on the form of a beautiful but mutilated woman. Her hair was a matted and tangled mess, and her piercing blue eyes were bloody. But Sinfjotli instantly recognized her.

"Mother!" Sinfjotli gasped.

"Yes," Siggeir replied with venomous glee. "This is indeed Signy, daughter of Völsung, twin sister of Sigmund, and the mother of his bastard son! You'd be sickened by all the things they do to her here in Helheim, *fratricide*. And with good reason, too."

He squeezed Signy's throat tighter, causing her to gasp in pain. Her eyes bulged in their sockets, and her arms went limp at her sides. Sinfjotli tried to come to her aid, but the draugirs blocked his path.

"Let's see," Siggeir pondered. "How many sins did you commit against me in your mad quest for vengeance, my dear treacherous wife? Oh, that's right, you helped Sigmund murder my mother and escape that fateful night! You coated his face in honey and instructed him to keep his mouth open so that he could rip out her tongue when she came to devour him that night! Then you made Sigmund murder our two eldest sons when they proved useless to your quest for vengeance. You ordered your twin brother to murder *your own children* because *I* was their father! Ah, and let's not forget your infidelity. With your twin brother, no less! You traded forms with a sorceress so that he'd unknowingly put a babe in your belly to fulfill a prophecy. Then you groomed that boy into a hardened killer! When he was only ten years old, you sowed the cuffs of his shirt into his wrists and tore off entire ribbons of his flesh as a test of manhood! From there, you slowly groomed him into a monstrous agent of your vengeance who wanted nothing beyond slaughtering my entire family and his younger siblings to avenge the deaths of a grandfather and nine uncles he never knew! As a parent, you conditioned your son to murder your own *children* just to hurt me! And I have not forgotten how you smuggled Sigmund and your bastard into my castle and helped them murder me! You set fire to my castle and helped them cut down everyone who tried to escape the inferno. My entire bloodline and kingdom perished because of that final betrayal!"

Siggeir impaled Signy's torso with one of the sharp prongs of his shield and proceeded to torment Signy further in full view of Sinfjotli. First, he chucked her to the ground and stomped on her legs, making her shriek in agony. He picked her up only to slam her into the ground again four times. Then he picked her up and squeezed her chest with both hands until her rib cage broke. The entire time, Signy wailed in agony.

As he watched the sadistic sight unfold, Sinfjotli went berserk, and he howled in rage. He transformed into a giant wolf and charged at Siggeir. Sinfjotli laid waste to every draugir in his path. But when he lunged at Siggeir, the arch-wraith unexpectedly blocked with his shield, piercing Sinfjotli's underbelly with the shield's central spike. The draug then used Sinfjotli's inertia to vault the giant wolf over his body and slammed him against the ground behind him.

When Sinfjotli recovered some sense of himself, he tried to stand up, but Siggeir pinned him against the ground with his spiked shield. The shield's sharp prongs pierced Sinfjotli's hide in several places, keeping him pinned. Siggeir then tossed Signy at a glacier. Sinfjotli watched helplessly as his mother's spirit sailed through the air and slammed into the ice with a sickening crack.

"You caught me by surprise just now," Siggeir sincerely admitted while retrieving his claymore. "I never knew you were a skinchanger. Even Hel didn't divulge that detail to me. But this explains so many things. Namely, how you escaped the grave mound where I buried you and Sigmund alive. You must have turned into a wolf and dug your way to freedom. Afterward, you, Sigmund, and Signy stormed and set fire to my castle while I was celebrating being rid of you Volsungs, and caught me when I was most vulnerable."

Siggeir glanced toward the glacier where Signy's spirit lay crumbled on the ground. "So, you forced your son to undergo the Trial of Svarblood just like my mother?" He snickered. "That's yet another dark deed to add to your many sins, Signy. Regardless, this is the end. Thank you for losing control of yourself, *fratricide*. Now I can savor killing you! Afterward, I'll drag your screaming soul back to Eljudnir. Signy's suffering will be like a drop in a pond compared to what I intend to put you through!"

Siggeir raised the claymore above his head and aimed at Sinfjotli's neck. Sinfjotli struggled to escape, but the draug's shield and its sharp prongs kept him pinned to the ground at an awkward angle. Sinfjotli could only watch as Siggeir swung his sword.

Forgive me, Father, Sinfjotli despaired. *I failed you*. He closed his eyes as Siggeir delivered the death blow.

CHAPTER THIRTY

TWO CONDITIONS

C LANG

Something sharp sliced Sinfjotli's right ear and nicked the back of his neck. Then he heard the ground crumble just above his head. For a moment, Sinfjotli thought he was dead. Then he realized that he was still breathing.

"Damn it, Sinfjotli," a familiar voice scolded. "You can't let him provoke you like that!"

Sinfjotli opened his eyes and saw Sigurd standing before him and holding Gram above his head. Sigurd had intercepted the blow at the last second and effortlessly sliced Siggeir's blade in half. The lower half of the claymore, which Siggeir was still holding, had struck into the ground in front of Sigurd's feet. The other half of the blade lay embedded in the earth an inch above Sinfjotli's head. Miraculously, the blade's tip had spun in the air and merely scratched the back of Sinfjotli's neck.

"You?!" Siggeir staggered backward. "But what happened to my soldiers?"

Sinfjotli and Siggeir glanced south toward the Gjallerbru, where Sigurd had been fighting. Littered across the ground were numerous piles of corpses, severed limbs, shredded armor, and broken weapons. Everything and everyone around the bridge had been sliced to ribbons by Gram.

"There were at least a hundred draugirs there," Siggeir recalled with a hint of begrudging admiration. "And you killed them all *this* quickly?! Impressive! But don't assume you've accomplished anything, boy! The dead are endless here in Helheim! Those warriors you cut down were nothing more than a few water droplets in the ocean of souls that is Helheim!"

Siggeir thrust out his left hand. His spiked shield withdrew itself from Sinfjotli's body and magically returned to his hand. Siggeir raised it over his head and chanted: "Dreadful darkness, hear my cry! Bring forth those who cannot die. Oh restless dead, who know no fear, come forth now and reappear! Destroy it all, leave nothing behind. Give me your strength so I can take what is mine!"

As he spoke, his left hand and shield glowed green. The wispy light traveled from his hand to the icy ground and danced over the mounds around the Gjallerbru like foxfire. As the green lights brightened, hundreds of skeletal hands burst forth from the pack ice around the bridge and clawed their way to the surface.

When it was over, Sinfjotli stared at a massive army of draugirs. They were better equipped than the undead warriors he and Sigurd had fought earlier, and many wielded strange weapons and bore unfamiliar sigils on their armor and shields.

"Here are a thousand more warriors for you to fight until I finish dealing with this traitorous kinslayer," Siggeir announced. "Until then, wait your turn, oath breaker!"

Siggeir tried to bash Sigurd with his spiked shield. Rather than dodge, Sigurd swung his sword. Gram cut straight through the shield and sliced straight through Siggeir's left arm up to his elbow.

As Siggeir reeled in shock, Sigurd rushed forward and swung again. But before Gram could connect, Siggeir's torso disassembled itself into floating pieces of debris and armor, causing Gram to pass through his chest. His entire body flew away in a spinning tornado of wood, armor, weapons, and rope.

Sigurd watched the pieces of Siggeir's body float away farther downriver along the shore west of the Gjallerbru. Then he glanced back at Sinfjotli with a look of utter disappointment.

"That was reckless. You lunged straight at him in a fit of uncontrollable rage without regard for strategy and fell into his trap. You'd be dead if I hadn't finished annihilating the other draugirs and rushed back here. I cannot believe you let him play you like a fiddle. Despite all the warnings you gave me to keep my emotions in check, you lost your temper and would have lost your head if I hadn't intervened."

"You're right," Sinfjotli admitted without protest. "Thank you for saving me."

As Sinfjotli rose from the ground, something whizzed past his ear. The top half of Siggeir's blade had dislodged itself from the ground and was now speeding after the tornado. After a moment, the metal and wooden fragments of Siggeir's shield and left arm levitated off the ground and floated away. As he watched the pieces chase after the tornado, Sinfjotli struggled to comprehend what just happened. Until now, Siggeir had seemed invincible. Nothing Sinfjotli attempted earlier could harm the draug. And yet, with a single swing of Gram, Sigurd cleaved through the shield, wood, and armor.

I don't understand. Sigurd broke Siggeir's sword in half and sliced his shield arm. He actually hurt a draug! How is that possible? Unless...?

Sinfjotli faintly recalled what Baldur mentioned earlier: "*Draugs are arch-wraiths that are bound to a 'story,' the series of traumatic events leading up to their death. They are untouchable, unreachable to anyone and **anything** that isn't a part of that story.*"

Sinfjotli glanced at the floating tornado of wood, armor, weapons, and rope heading west along the shore of the River Gjöll. Upon closer inspection, he noticed that the individual wooden sections of Siggeir's body looked like ceiling-support beams. Moreover, his neck and head looked like parts of a giant support column used in a great hall.

Siggeir's body is composed of the rubble of his castle that he was buried under, Sinfjotli realized. *That must mean that the 'story' he is bound by is the events from the night he died.*

Sinfjotli glanced at Gram and remembered that his father had used that same sword to slay Siggeir. He thought about all the draugirs Sigurd had cut down with it. Every draugir Sigurd effortlessly dispatched with Gram had been Geatish warriors their father Sigmund had slain. All the pieces came together, and Sinfjotli realized what he needed to do to defeat Siggeir.

"Sigurd, give me your sword," Sinfjotli requested, though it sounded more like an order.

"Are you serious," Sigurd asked incredulously. He pointed at the massive undead army sweeping toward them. "You want to fight over this sword *again* while all these draugirs attack us?"

"I only need to borrow it for a bit," Sinfjotli insisted as he transformed back into his human form. "Do you remember what Baldur told us about draugs? He said: 'In many stories, a hero must acquire an item from the draug's past before facing it.' Gram can harm Siggeir and his army because our father used it to defeat them. Gram may be the only weapon capable of harming Siggeir."

Sigurd narrowed his eyes. Deep in thought, he glanced west at the swirling tornado traveling along the banks of the River Gjöll.

"I don't think you'll need my sword to harm him. You can manage just fine on your own."

"Sigurd, this is no time to..."

"Siggeir sees you as a threat," Sigurd interrupted. "Didn't you notice that while you were battling him? Whenever you swung your pole axe, it passed through his body. But he blocked with his shield when you attacked him with your fists or body. Think about it. Moments ago, Siggeir used his shield to defend himself when you lunged at him as a wolf. He'd only bother defending himself because he sees your physical attacks as a threat, which means *you* can also harm him."

Sigurd wasn't wrong. The only times Siggeir *had* blocked Sinfjotli's attacks throughout their battle was when he tried to physically touch the draug, such as when he'd punched him earlier or charged straight at the undead king in his wolf form.

"I don't understand," Sinfjotli said. "How could I harm a draug with just my body?"

"Isn't it obvious? It's because you've fulfilled the *other* condition required to face a draug. Remember, Baldur specifically told us that a draug can only be harmed by an object or *person* from its past. You were with our father on the night he killed Siggeir. That means you're as much a part of Siggeir's 'story' as Gram is. Right now, you're like his natural enemy. You can harm him yourself, albeit without using a weapon."

Sinfjotli let his brother's words sink in as he finished reverting to his human form. Sigurd's theory made sense. But even if he could harm Siggeir with his body, he felt that wouldn't be enough. Siggeir was too powerful to be defeated by physical blows alone. And Sinfjotli wasn't ready to wager his life over a supernatural condition he didn't fully understand.

"Please, brother, just lend me the sword," Sinfjotli insisted. "I can't fight him properly without a weapon. And Gram is the only one capable of harming him."

"Let me ask a different question," Sigurd replied. "Why do *you* need to be the one to defeat him? I can harm him just as easily you can, if not easier. Why don't I fight him while you handle the draugirs he's summoned?"

"It has to be me! I swore a blood oath to my parents that I would punish Siggeir for what he did to our family. I owe it to my mother, father, grandfather, and entire family to vanquish him. I won't be able to live with myself if I'm not the one who defeats him."

Sigurd studied him with his sharp, murderous snake eyes, which Sinfjotli found slightly unnerving. Even when happy or calm, Sigurd's gaze was like that of an angry serpent that could lash out and strike at any moment. It was impossible to discern precisely what Sigurd was thinking right now.

"All right," Sigurd decided. He handed Gram to Sinfjotli. "But this is only a loan, understand? I'll want my sword back once it's over."

"You have my word," Sinfjotli vowed. He glanced west, where the swirling whirlwind of debris began reassembling into a humanoid form. Sinfjotli glanced back at his mother's spirit lying by the glacier Siggeir had slammed her into. He silently vowed to make Siggeir pay a hundredfold for what he had just done to her.

But before he could do anything rash, Sigurd grabbed his shoulder.

"Just a moment, Sinfjotli. Before you go, you must know something about Siggeir. He's jealous."

"Jealous?" Sinfjotli frowned. Of all the adjectives he could use to describe Siggeir, jealous seemed inaccurate. "What makes you say that?"

"It's another gift of mine." Sigurd pointed at his snake eyes. "In addition to my telescopic vision and ability to communicate with birds, I can also peer right into a person's soul and read their heart. It allows me to instantly determine their character, intentions, and emotions, predict their attack forms, and then use what I learn against them in battle. I can also tell a person's inner thoughts by the fluctuations in their voice, expressions, and partialities."

Sigurd pointed downriver at the now reforming draug with a sour expression. "When I look at Siggeir, all I see is a soul filled with envy and hatred."

"But why are you telling me this now?" Sinfjotli asked.

Sigurd looked at him and grinned. "You mentioned Siggeir is an expert at psychological warfare. He made you lose control of your emotions earlier. Maybe you can do the same thing to him."

"I'll try." Sinfjotli glanced back at the encroaching army of undead warriors crowding around the Bridge of the Damned. They were marching slowly, waiting for Sigurd to come to them. Sinfjotli looked down at Gram and suddenly felt guilty about the disadvantageous position he had put his brother in.

"Will you be able to take on the draugirs without a weapon," Sinfjotli asked worriedly.

"Don't worry about me," Sigurd assured while excitedly cracking his knuckles. "I prefer to use Gram, but I'm skilled with just about any weapon on the battlefield. This should be interesting."

"Have at it then," Sinfjotli nodded. "I have my own battle to fight and many old debts to settle."

CHAPTER THIRTY-ONE

A HAIL OF STEEL

As Sinfjotli headed west, he turned back and watched as Sigurd clashed against the army of undead warriors with nothing but his bare hands. Sigurd proved that even without Gram, he was a force to be reckoned with.

As Sigurd stormed the front lines, he disarmed a draugir of its axe and sliced its head off with its own weapon before it could react. Another five draugirs advanced, and Sigurd chopped off the first attacker's limbs, sliced the next three in half in a single swing, and buried the axe into the final draugir's skull.

He picked up that last draugir's spiky club and bashed several more draugirs' skulls before discarding it for a sword and spear. Sigurd fought with both hands independently as he dual-wielded both weapons in an impressive display of ambidexterity and skill.

Sinfjotli watched in utter amazement as his brother continued using a variety of weapons to slay the undead army, proving that he was indeed proficient with just about every weapon on the battlefield as he boasted. Sinfjotli hadn't seen a seasoned warrior this proficient since their other half-brother, Helgi.

Sinfjotli shook his head. This wasn't the time to get nostalgic or mesmerized by his brother's battle. He had his own battle to fight and *many* old debts to settle with Siggeir.

As Sigurd continued his one-man onslaught against the army of the dead, Sinfjotli ran farther down the shore to the spot west of the Bridge of the Dead where Siggeir had finished reassembling himself. Before Sinfjotli could do anything, Siggeir pivoted and swung his sword in a downward strike. Instinctually, Sinfjotli rolled out of the way and felt grateful to have done so. He hadn't realized until the last moment that Siggeir's sword was once again whole.

Before Sinfjotli could even stand up, Siggeir rushed at him with his spiked shield, which had also repaired itself. Sinfjotli had only seconds to slice off the shield's central spike and pierce through the shield's disk with Gram before the draug rammed into him. Siggeir kept charging forward, causing Sinfjotli to skid backward across the icy ground. But he held his ground until he could safely roll to the side.

His sword repaired itself, Sinfjotli observed after getting back on his feet. *And it looks like the damage Sigurd inflicted earlier on his shield and left arm has been mended. Tsk! How cumbersome.*

Siggeir didn't relent, and the two resumed their titanic clash. Although Sinfjotli now had a weapon capable of hurting Siggeir, the draug was still a formidable foe. Whatever parts of his body or weapons Sinfjotli damaged regenerated. But Sinfjotli persisted.

Siggeir charged Sinfjotli with his shield again. Sinfjotli didn't dodge. He waited until the draug was close enough, then jumped up, vaulted off the shield's disk, and splintered Siggeir's hollow head with a mighty kick.

Sinfjotli grinned as he landed on the ground and watched Siggeir stagger backward. "Sigurd was right! Right now, I am your natural enemy."

"So, you figured out a draug's weakness," Siggeir deduced as his hollow head regenerated. "But that doesn't change a thing! Even if you are wielding Sigmund's sword and were there the day I died, you still won't be able to defeat me!"

Siggeir reared his arm back and swung his sword in a powerful downward strike that rent the ground asunder. Sinfjotli dive-rolled out of the way and landed in the space between Siggeir's feet. Before the draug could react, Sinfjotli swung Gram with all his might, chopping off Siggeir's legs. Siggeir roared in pain and shock as his body crashed to the ground.

This is my chance! Sinfjotli realized. He jumped high and swung Gram down at the draug's exposed back. But before Gram could make contact, Siggeir's body disassembled itself. Gram passed through the draug's body and struck the ground as the dismantled pieces floated away.

Sinfjotli withdrew Gram from the cleft in the ground as the wind began strengthening. He glanced up and discovered he was now standing in the center of a tornado. The pieces of Siggeir's disassembled body swirled around him in a whirlwind of weapons, armor, and debris. High above him, a fiery ball of energy materialized in the center of the tornado. The tornado and the pieces of Siggeir's body orbited around that flaming sphere like satellites around a planet.

That flaming ball must be his true essence, Sinfjotli realized. *If I destroy it, this fight should end.* He brandished Gram and waited for the draug to reform.

However, instead of reassembling into a humanoid form, the pieces of Siggeir's body began raining down on Sinfjotli from all directions. Sinfjotli defended himself to the best of his ability, slicing and batting Gram at the oncoming debris. But there were too many strikes coming at him from every direction. Pieces of serrated armor slashed his back. A sharp prong from Siggeir's shield impaled his shoulder. Some rope cords strangled Sinfjotli's throat like serpents and would have pulled him to the ground if he hadn't cut them in time.

I underestimated him, Sinfjotli panicked. *His arsenal isn't limited to his claymore and spiked shield. Every part of his body is a weapon!*

As Sinfjotli desperately defended himself from the onslaught of raining debris, he noticed Siggeir's severed legs levitate off the ground out of the corner of his eye. One leg flung itself at Sinfjotli, who sliced it in half. As the two bifurcated halves of the leg zipped past Sinfjotli, he felt something grasp the back of his head. He had a measly second to realize Siggeir's left arm had reassembled itself and grabbed him from behind before the draug slammed him face-first into the ground.

"Pathetic," Siggeir mocked as the rest of his body reassembled into its humanoid form. He let go of Sinfjotli's head but kept one foot planted on his back, pinning him to the ground. "Did you think having a weapon that can harm me would guarantee victory? Did you honestly believe that was all you needed to defeat a draug?"

Sinfjotli didn't respond to his stepfather's provocations. He needed to escape from this compromising position. When wiggling free proved unviable, Sinfjotli forced the draug off his back with brute strength. He planted his hands on the ground and pushed with all his might. Despite having a giant foot planted on his back, Sinfjotli lifted himself a couple of inches off the ground before Siggeir stomped on him again.

"It seems you still do not appreciate nor comprehend the power I've attained since Sigmund killed me," Siggeir seethed. "Let me show you exactly why we draugs are considered Hel's elite generals and the power that comes with that honor."

As Sinfjotli struggled to remove the draug from his back, Siggeir thrust his spiked shield down at Sinfjotli's neck. Sinfjotli felt pain flare up along the back and sides of his neck.

For a second, Sinfjotli feared the worst. But he realized he was still alive when the draug lifted its foot off his back. The prongs of the shield hadn't impaled him through his neck or damaged his spinal cord as he feared. But when Sinfjotli tried to stand up, he discovered he was stuck. Two of the shield's prongs had burrowed deep into the ground on either side of Sinfjotli's neck like a pillory, keeping him pinned to the icy ground.

"Don't worry. I won't kill you just yet, *fratricide*." Siggeir promised. "There's something I want you to see first."

Siggeir stood before Sinfjotli and thrust his sword into the ground. Fissures spread across the icy ground, and green smoke billowed from the crevices as four skeletons crawled to the surface. After a moment, their bodies rematerialized amidst green fog, and Sinfjotli could see what the skeletons looked like when they were alive.

It looked like a family of four. The boy and the girl looked about ten and twelve years old, respectively. The woman was gorgeous, with green eyes and an athletic physique. Her hair was white, but the woman's face showed no signs of aging. She looked like she was in her forties. Her husband looked to be in his late fifties. Despite his advanced age, he looked as tall, muscular, and handsome as a man half his age. He had sad blue eyes, long white hair that touched his shoulders, and a full white beard that touched his neck.

Sinfjotli recognized them as a family that had once given him food and shelter. And the old man was Selkirk, the former general of Siggeir's army and the most skilled and righteous warrior in all of Gautland.

Seeing the old warrior and his family brought back many memories. Growing up with his father in the wilderness, Sinfjotli often had to change hideouts since Siggeir's hunters were constantly scouring his kingdom for any trace of Sigmund. And the man at the head of that hunting corps was always Selkirk.

Sigmund and Selkirk had clashed many times, yet neither bore the other ill will. Despite being enemies, Sigmund often praised Selkirk as the most skilled, gallant, and righteous warrior in Gautland.

And with good reason. During Siggeir's ambush of the Volsungs, Selkirk had fought an epic duel with Völsung, one of the greatest warriors alive at that time. They fought each other to a standstill for almost an hour until Siggeir dishonorably stabbed Völsung in the back. Selkirk and Sigmund had fought each other many times. According to Sigmund, he and Selkirk were evenly matched with regular swords. However, if Sigmund wielded Gram, he would beat Selkirk. Yet whenever they clashed, he chose not to do so, claiming, "It wouldn't be a fair fight."

But Selkirk was much more than a seasoned warrior. He was the only person in Gautland Sigmund respected and admired because he was genuinely honorable. He had sworn an oath toward Siggeir's father and dutifully served the royal family.

However, that oath occasionally put him at odds with his sense of morality. A drengr bound to his king does not question or go against his king's wishes, no matter what the king does or will do. And so, after Siggeir returned from his wedding, Selkirk was forced to participate in the treacherous ambush of the Volsungs. Afterward, he could only watch as Siggeir tore out Völsung's heart and sentenced Sigmund and his brothers to be eaten alive by a wolf. And when Siggeir ordered him to hunt down Sigmund, Selkirk had to begrudgingly obey.

Despite his loyalty to his king, Selkirk never compromised his integrity. While the other marauders in Siggeir's army burned down forests and massacred entire villages to find Sigmund, Selkirk treated the inhabitants with honor and earned their trust during his search. Furthermore, Selkirk always paid the serfs for what he and his forces took and addressed their grievances before Siggeir, unlike later generals who stole and extorted from them. Despite being admired by women from every village, Selkirk remained faithful to his wife.

Sinfjotli had witnessed Selkirk prove his honor when he was thirteen. He and his father unknowingly stumbled across Selkirk's family while foraging for food. His wife noticed how gaunt they looked and invited them into her home for dinner, not realizing who they were. That night, Selkirk returned home after a fruitless day of searching for Sigmund to discover the very man he was sworn to capture sitting at his table. However, his wife had already offered Sigmund and Sinfjotli bread and salt, meaning they were now his guests, and honor stipulated they not be harmed. Instead of fighting them or reporting their location to Siggeir, Selkirk honored the ancient law of guest right. He let them stay in his home, shared a succulent meal with them, and promised them a day's head start before he gathered his men.

A few weeks later, Sigmund and Sinfjotli revisited that village and discovered that Selkirk and his family had been brutally murdered. According to the villagers' testimony, Siggeir arrived in the town two days after Sigmund left upon hearing reports that he was spotted there. While there, Siggeir brutally murdered Selkirk and his entire family. The villagers could not fathom why Siggeir had committed such a barbarous act against his best general. But Sigmund and Sinfjotli suspected it was because Selkirk kept failing to capture Sigmund and even let him slip through his fingers because of ancient law.

When Sigmund heard about Selkirk's death, he wept, lamenting: "The only ray of light in Gautland is gone. And the world seems darker for it."

But the situation Sinfjotli now found himself in was even darker than *anything* his father could have imagined.

Helheim had taken its toll on the old warrior. His once handsome and chiseled face now looked gaunt, and his skin had turned pasty. His hair was white and brittle, and his olive-brown eyes were bloodshot. And his family looked as aged and weathered as he did.

Seeing the pitiful state of Selkirk and his family made Sinfjotli boil over in anger. Selkirk was a warrior who deserved to be in Valhalla. Instead, he was trapped in Helheim because Siggeir had brutally murdered him outside of combat, as he had done to Sinfjotli's uncles.

"Come here," Siggeir ordered. Selkirk's ghost obeyed and looked up at the draug, anxiously awaiting the following order. Without warning, Siggeir punched him into the ground.

"Lick the ground," Siggeir ordered.

"Yes...yes, my lord," Selkirk stammered. He stuck his tongue out and pressed it to the ground.

"You sick bastard!" Sinfjotli cursed. In life, Selkirk had been one of the most righteous warriors Sinfjotli had ever known. He was the only person in Gautland his father had considered an honorable man. He obeyed Siggeir because honor demanded that he follow his king. Now Siggeir was forcing him to follow his every command and lick the ground like a dog. Sinfjotli struggled to remove Siggeir's shield from his neck and stop this insidious show, but the shield wouldn't budge.

"Now look up," Siggeir commanded. "You too, *fratricide*. I don't want you to miss this." He pointed at Selkirk's wife and children. "These are your wife and children, right? Woman, I order you to kill your children. Children, I order you to kill your mother."

"No," Selkirk wailed.

"YES!" Siggeir bellowed. He clenched his burning fist, and Selkirk's family shuddered in pain.

"As... you wish, my lord," Selkirk's wife stammered.

Sinfjotli watched, horrified, as Selkirk's wife and children began attacking each other for Siggeir's entertainment.

"Stop!" Sinfjotli pleaded. "You don't have to do this. Don't obey him!"

"You're wasting your breath, fratricide," Siggeir informed. "Their will to resist dried up long ago! You'll suffer along with them shortly. But for now, watch!"

"Please, stop this," Selkirk wailed. "In the name of all that is good and holy, please stop this."

"Shut up," Siggeir bellowed. He impaled Selkirk with his sword. The old warrior's spirit and skeleton dissolved and faded away. Siggeir turned back to Selkirk's family and ordered them to keep fighting. His family did as they were commanded and continued killing each other until only the little girl was left crying over the slain bodies of her mother and brother.

"Well done, child," Siggeir commended. "Here's your reward." He stabbed the little girl with his claymore just like he had done to her father. He lifted her high into the air and cackled as her body and the rest of her family's spirits faded away.

"AAAA HAHAHAHAHAHAHAHAHA!" Siggeir cackled. "You see, *fratricide*? *This* is the power and authority of a draug! Hel is the Queen of Helheim. Her will is absolute, and we all respect that. However, to the average spirits of this realm, we draugs command the same authority and fear as she does. The dead obey my every whim and follow every order I give out of fear. Should I demand it, a mighty warrior like Selkirk would lick the ground beneath my boot. Should I demand it, a mother and her children would slaughter each other for my amusement. *This* is the authority of a draug!"

Sinfjotli decided he had endured enough. He slid his hand across the ground until he felt Gram's hilt. He grasped it and used the blade to saw through the shield's prongs, freeing himself. Siggeir was unimpressed. He summoned the fragments of his shield back to his left hand, and the weapon repaired itself.

Sinfjotli got to one knee and glanced up at the ghost of his wicked stepfather. As he stared into the flames burning inside the draug's hollow head, Sinfjotli recalled something Siggeir said during his final battle against Sigmund: "*The way you speak to me and look at me with those condescending eyes! It makes me sick! No matter what I do, somewhere deep inside, you always believe you're superior to me! I can't stand it! Anyone who looks down on me deserves to be crushed!*"

Sinfjotli then remembered something else. When he learned of Selkirk's sad fate, he assumed Siggeir had executed Selkirk for repeatedly failing to capture Sigmund and letting him escape when they were within his own home because of ancient custom. But after witnessing how sadistically

Siggeir tormented Selkirk and his family, Sinfjotli realized that wasn't why he murdered his most skilled and loyal general. He had murdered Selkirk and his family for a far more wicked and despicable reason.

"Sigurd was right about you," Sinfjotli said while staggering to his feet. "You are so full of envy and hate. Is that truly all you could offer me and your children as a parent?"

"Envy? What are you blathering about now, *fratricide*?" Siggeir asked.

"There it is," Sinfjotli scoffed. "You keep calling me a 'fratricide.' I can almost taste the venom in your voice whenever you speak that word. You say the word 'fratricide' as if it means something to you. As if you were a victim. You make it sound like I took something precious away from you when I killed Aurora and Hansel. But I know it's an act. As I recall, you never cared or paid much attention to me or any of your children when you were alive."

"What," Siggeir demanded.

"Think about it. My father killed your first and second-born sons at mother's behest when they failed his test of courage. And you didn't even seem to care that they had died. You accepted the lie that wild animals had devoured them and never investigated the matter further. You didn't even attend their funerals out of fear that Sigmund would use the opportunity to assassinate you. And later, when I ran away to train with Father for six years, you never once searched for me. You didn't even bother to offer a reward for information about my location. It was as if you didn't even notice that I had vanished or forgotten that I existed. Admit it, Siggeir. You have never cared one wit about me or any of your children. We were all just a means to prolong your bloodline, nothing more."

"Be quiet, *bastard*," Siggeir warned.

Sinfjotli had struck a nerve. So, he plunged the knife even deeper.

"If I'm being honest, I haven't thought about Aurora and Hansel in a long time. Their deaths never left much of an impact on me. I never bore them any personal ill will. I was only fulfilling a blood oath I had made to my mother long ago when I slew them. But now, after seeing what you became after you died... or rather... seeing what you *truly* are, I pity them. I feel bad that Hansel and Aurora had such a jealous, spiteful monster like you as their father!"

"YOU LITTLE SHIT STAIN!" Siggeir bellowed. He barreled forward and savagely attacked in a blind rage. But Sinfjotli effortlessly countered the blow, and they resumed their deadly clash.

Chapter Thirty-Two

Jealous

Earlier, Sinfjotli wouldn't have stood a chance against his stepfather, even with Gram. Siggeir was now attacking him in a blind rage, but Sinfjotli held his ground and slowly gained the upper hand. Sinfjotli continued mocking Siggeir as they clashed, and his words cut just as profoundly as his blade.

"Don't deny it, Siggeir," Sinfjotli said as he chopped Siggeir's spiked shield in half. "We both know you never cared for your children. I realized it when I saw the way you reacted after I dragged Hansel and Aurora's disjointed bodies in front of you and announced that I had killed them. You were shocked that I had killed my siblings and visibly upset I had taken away your heirs. But you did not exhibit *any* of the emotions of a grieving father. That's when I was certain that Hansel and Aurora meant nothing to you at all. They were nothing but a means to prolong your bloodline."

"Shut up!" Siggeir roared. "Shut up!" He swung his sword in a powerful downward strike that split the ground. But Sinfjotli rolled out of the way, lunged forward, thrust Gram at Siggeir's chest, and punched a hole straight through the draug's torso.

"I can see straight through you," Sinfjotli quipped as he passed through the gaping hole in Siggeir's chest. "I know exactly why you wanted this sword and the real reason you murdered my grandfather and uncles. It wasn't because

Sigmund had disrespected you and refused to give you this sword on your wedding day. It was because you were jealous of my family, weren't you?"

"Be silent!" Siggeir spun around, but Sinfjotli bisected his body at the waist before the arch-wraith could do anything. Wood and armor splintered as the draug's body collapsed.

"You were jealous of Sigmund," Sinfjotli continued. "You knew the old man who appeared at your wedding feast was Odin, right? You realized that the All-Father had intended for Sigmund to have this sword and deemed you unworthy of it. And that filled you with jealousy and hate toward him."

"Just shut up and DIE already!" Siggeir bellowed. He tried to swing his sword, but Sinfjotli chopped off his right arm.

"You were jealous of my grandfather as well, weren't you?" Sinfjotli continued. "Völsung married a valkyrie and created a magnificent kingdom by himself. He earned his right to be called a king. But you had your entire kingdom and everything else handed to you because you were born into royalty!"

"SHUT UP!" Siggeir bellowed. His entire body finished reforming. He tried to stand up, but Sinfjotli chopped off his legs before he could move. Then he sliced off the draug's arms for good measure.

"You were even jealous of poor Selkirk," Sinfjotli continued while standing over the draug's limbless torso. "That's why you murdered your best general, isn't it? It wasn't because he failed too many times to capture us or because he allowed me and my father to walk away that day because of the ancient laws of hospitality. It was because you were jealous! He was a shining ray of light, the only honest and virtuous warrior in Gautland. Selkirk treated his enemies and the poor honorably. He had a loving wife and beautiful children and was well-loved by the people. And you *killed* him on a jealous whim before his fame eclipsed your own. You were jealous of how popular he became with the people of Gautland. You were jealous of his strength, battle prowess, and his loving family! You envied *everything* he represented!"

"SHUT UP!!!" Siggeir wailed as his limbs began regenerating.

"You were jealous of my family's strength and skill at arms. You were jealous of my nine uncles and even my mother! All of Völsung's children distinguished themselves through mighty deeds and brought Hunaland even greater wealth and glory. You were jealous of everything our family represented!

"That's all you have ever been, Siggeir," Sinfjotli continued. "You're nothing but a jealous, angry little tyrant who hates being reminded of how weak, miserable, and irrelevant you are by the achievements of greater men. And you feel compelled to murder those heroes to prove your worth and escape their shadows."

"WHY WON'T YOU DIE?!" Siggeir bellowed in frustration as his body finished repairing itself. He stood up and tried to pick up his sword. But Sinfjotli stomped his foot down on the fuller of the blade, preventing the draug from lifting the claymore off the ground.

"Because I will never lose to someone like you," Sinfjotli proclaimed. "I will never lose to a jealous tyrant who rules through fear and relies on others to fight his battles for him."

Sinfjotli thrust Gram at the burning hollow hole in the center of Siggeir's head. "You wanted this sword so badly? Then you can have it. My father left you to burn alive beneath that pile of rubble instead of killing you with it. I'll do what he refused to do that day!"

Sinfjotli jumped high into the air and swung Gram with all his might. Alarmed, Siggeir raised his sword and shield to defend himself. But Gram sliced straight through both weapons and vertically bisected Siggeir's body from his head to his groin. His hollowed head split in half, and his torso separated.

But Sinfjotli wasn't finished. When his feet touched the ground, he continued slicing and hacking the draug in a vicious whirlwind of strikes. When he stopped swinging, Siggeir's body exploded into hundreds of pieces of shattered wood and armor. Even the glowing sphere of flame within the armor dispersed into sizzling embers. For a while, Sinfjotli stood gazing over the smoldering remains of his family's arch-enemy.

"You enjoyed that a bit too much," a familiar voice remarked.

Sinfjotli turned to find Sigurd leaning against a nearby glacier with a black sword in his hand. His golden armor had taken dozens of notches and slash marks, but he looked utterly unharmed otherwise. Behind him on the Bridge of the Dead, the entire army of undead warriors Siggeir had summoned earlier lay scattered in piles of corpses, severed limbs, shattered weapons, and broken armor.

Sinfjotli whistled in admiration. "You vanquished Siggeir's entire army by yourself!"

"You sound surprised," Sigurd quipped.

"Of course not," Sinfjotli laughed. "I always had faith. Still, I'm amazed you killed a thousand draugirs without your trusty sword. You're a true son of Sigmund, after all. Speaking of which, you can have Gram back now. This sword is yours by right and deed. I must say, you handled yourself just fine against the draugirs without it."

"I told you earlier, I'm proficient with any weapon on the battlefield," Sigurd reminded as he seized Gram's hilt. "But I feel most comfortable when I'm wielding Gram. I feel naked without this sword in my hand. Still, brandishing various weapons and adjusting my fighting style on the fly was quite interesting. I haven't faced a challenge like that in a long time. It gave me a chance to cut loose."

"Indeed," Sinfjotli laughed. He glanced at the other sword in Sigurd's left hand. "I see you have two swords now. Is that black one a spoil of war?"

Sigurd looked away. "Yes."

Sinfjotli arched an eyebrow. He noticed his brother seemed wary of his new dark sword. Sigurd consciously held the sword away from his body as if he feared the blade might cut him. His trepidation seemed well-founded.

Sinfjotli didn't recognize the ebony blade's metal, and the fuller was engraved with runes he couldn't read. And an eerie layer of shadowy miasma covered the blade. There was something ominous about the sword that made Sinfjotli's skin crawl.

"That's no ordinary sword," Sinfjotli remarked. "How did you get it?"

"It's a long story," Sigurd dismissed. "I'll tell you about it another..."

A burning prong from Siggeir's shield zipped past Sinfjotli's ear and impaled Sigurd in the chest. Three more prongs followed, piercing him in his shoulders and chest. Sigurd coughed up blood and fell to his knees.

"Sigurd!" Sinfjotli turned to find a barely humanoid form rising from the smoldering remains of the draug. The ball of flame had reformed, and parts of Siggeir's body began amassing around that sphere. Pieces of armor, wood, and debris rolled toward it, levitated off the ground, and assumed their appropriate places on his body.

"Now... you've...done it," Siggeir wheezed. "Just...look at the *state* I'm in!"

At that moment, rage gripped Sinfjotli's mind. Once again, Siggeir had attacked Sinfjotli's family member while their guard was down, just like he had done to their grandfather, Völsung.

"You monster," Sinfjotli roared. "That was the LAST time you **EVER** hurt a member of my family!"

Sinfjotli picked up Gram from where Sigurd had dropped it and rushed forward. Siggeir flung pieces of his body at Sinfjotli, but he dodged them all and hacked and slashed Siggeir's half-formed body to pieces once more.

Sinfjotli knew that wouldn't be enough to vanquish his foe. The pieces of Siggeir's body had already begun reassembling themselves. So Sinfjotli opted for a different approach. He stabbed Gram into the ground and turned into a wolf. The transformation occurred faster than usual, and his rage helped dull whatever pain he felt. He then lunged at Siggeir as a giant wolf before the draug was halfway finished repairing its body.

Sinfjotli mauled his foe, tearing off barely formed limbs, slashing away at armor, splintering wood, and shredding through metal like paper. He ripped off Siggeir's half-formed arms and legs, gathered the draug's limbless torso in his mouth, and chewed on it like a chunk of meat. His teeth tore through wood and crushed metal plate-like twigs.

Unfortunately, Siggeir didn't die. Pieces of his body began floating around Sinfjotli's snout and head like satellites around a planet. A few sharper fragments began piercing and slashing his body, but this did little but annoy the wolf.

Why isn't he dead yet? Sinfjotli wondered as he continued gnawing on Siggeir's torso. *Baldur told us a draug could only be harmed by a person or object from its past. I was there when Father killed him, and I've been using the same sword he used to slay Siggeir. I've fulfilled both conditions. So why the hell isn't Siggeir dead yet? How does he keep coming back?*

Suddenly, Sinfjotli felt an immense burning sensation within his mouth. A second later, one of the burning prongs from Siggeir's shield stabbed the roof of his mouth and pierced his snout. Sinfjotli reeled in pain and spat out the crushed pieces of Siggeir's torso.

Sinfjotli backed away and assessed his injuries as he licked the bloody hole in the roof of his mouth. His tongue felt charbroiled, and his gums felt like they were melting. Serrated pieces of Siggeir's body had sliced his back and shoulders up. And the gaping hole in his snout made a strange whistling noise when he breathed.

After a few painful moments, the regenerative properties of the Apple of Idun he ate earlier began healing his damaged mouth. He could feel the burns on his tongue and gums vanish. However, the apple didn't eliminate the flood of pain from the deep wound. It took all his willpower to remain standing as the hole in the roof of his mouth began to slowly but painfully seal itself with new flesh and bone.

When Sinfjotli's vision cleared, he noticed the giant flaming ball hovering nearby. The scattered fragments of his body began converging and rebuilding around the fiery sphere.

"I suppose you deserve some credit, ***Sinfjotli***!" Siggeir begrudgingly praised. It was the first time in this battle that Siggeir referred to Sinfjotli by his name. And Siggeir pronounced each syllable slowly, as if speaking the name made him feel like he was drinking bile.

"You've done well against me," Siggeir conceded. "However, there are two things you have failed to comprehend. First, you can never kill me. A wraith cannot be killed or destroyed, only driven away or sealed. Normally, if we were fighting in Midgard or the other seven realms, you would have triumphed by now. You would have vanquished me, and my soul would get banished back to Helheim. But that leads me to my second point. Since we're currently fighting in Helheim, I cannot be defeated! The undead are at their strongest in the underworld. You already witnessed what a couple of skeletal draugirs were capable of earlier. And as a draug, one of the most powerful spirits in Helheim, I am practically invincible! No matter what you do to me, my soul will remain on the battlefield."

"You...!" Sinfjotli gurgled.

"Do you understand now?" Siggeir laughed as his torso began regenerating around the flaming sphere. "Even if you have Sigmund's sword and were present the night I died, that's not enough to defeat me. Helheim will restore my body no matter how badly you damage it. You won't slay me even if you hack my body into ribbons. Even if you grind my body to dust with your teeth, I will not be vanquished." Siggeir cackled. "You're doomed! No matter what you do, my soul will remain on the battlefield. You don't have the power to defeat a draug in Helheim!"

For once, Siggeir couldn't back up his boasts with an attack. At the moment, he was just a floating, half-formed, and limbless torso. Sinfjotli had inflicted so much damage and broken his body into such tiny particles that it took far longer for Siggeir to regenerate himself than usual.

If Sinfjotli could speak, he would have told Siggeir that he was also stuck in the same frustrating deadlock. Since he ate an Apple of Idun earlier, any damage Siggeir inflicted on Sinfjotli's body would rapidly heal. But Sinfjotli knew the effects of the apple were temporary. All Siggeir had to do was fight until the apple's effects wore off. It could take days, weeks, or even months. But eventually, Siggeir would win.

Sinfjotli noticed something as he waited for his mouth to heal and tried formulating a new strategy. Without Siggeir's massive bulk obscuring his field of vision, Sinfjotli saw Garm lying outside his cave further north. The giant chained hellhound had been watching their battle unfold with mute appeal.

Sinfjotli faintly recalled something Garm mentioned earlier as he gazed at the four-eyed hellhound. "*There is only one iron rule here in Helheim. All are welcome in Helheim, but no soul may leave this realm or go past my cave unless Mistress Hel allows it.*"

Sinfjotli curled his lips in a literal wolfish grin as an idea formed.

"You're right, Siggeir," Sinfjotli conceded as his mouth healed, and the draug finished reassembling its body. "*I* don't have the power to kill a draug in Helheim. But *he* might."

Sinfjotli stormed straight at the draug. Siggeir reached for his weapons, but Sinfjotli slammed his paws on Siggeir's sword and shield before he could lift them off the ground. He closed his jaws around Siggeir's head and torso, chewed him a bit, and then flung him through the air like a rag doll toward Gnipa Cave.

The draug sailed through the air, passed beneath the Arch of Helheim, and crash-landed beyond the boundary of Gnipa Cave. The instant Siggeir hit the ground, Garm lunged forward and seized the arch-wraith in his mouth.

"What are you doing?!" Siggeir screamed as Garm sank his teeth deep into his body. "Release me at once! Obey me, beast! I am a king. I am a draug! I...!"

"You are nothing but a trespasser now," Garm snarled. "You broke Helheim's only iron rule. Now suffer the consequences!"

Sinfjotli watched gleefully as the giant chained hellhound dragged the screaming draug inside Gnipa Cave. Even if Siggeir was a draug and one of Hel's best generals, as he boasted, he had involuntarily broken Helheim's only iron rule by crossing the boundary of Gnipa Cave. And Garm was now duty-bound to punish him for it.

"Now you'll know how it feels to be devoured by a wolf," Sinfjotli snarled as the guard dog of Helheim began tearing the ghost of his wicked stepfather to pieces.

"You say that as if... you're speaking from personal experience," a familiar voice remarked. Sinfjotli turned to find Sigurd standing beside him, holding Gram and his new black sword in each hand.

"Sigurd," Sinfjotli exclaimed. "You're all right?!"

"Yes, I'm fine," Sigurd grunted. But he certainly didn't *look* all right. His armor was severely damaged, and his chest bled like a raw steak.

"Don't worry, it looks worse than it is," Sigurd assured. "My armor absorbed most of the damage. Besides, the Apple of Idun I ate earlier is healing my injuries. So, I was never in any real danger of dying."

"Still, he had the temerity to attack you while your guard was down," Sinfjotli growled as he began morphing back into his human form. "Siggeir never was a man of honor. Are you sure you're all right?"

"Don't worry about it." Sigurd tapped the scar in the center of his chest. "That wasn't the first time I've been impaled, and with our luck, it probably won't be the last."

"Probably," Sinfjotli chuckled as he finished reverting into a human. He and Sigurd then watched Garm devour the ghost of their family's greatest enemy. Garm didn't kill Siggeir right away. Instead, the hellhound sadistically toyed with the draug like a chew toy. He would dismember Siggeir, wait for his limbs and torso to reassemble, and then dismember him again.

As they silently watched the macabre sight unfold, Sinfjotli noticed that the spirits of the dead arriving in Helheim were walking right by Gnipa Cave, utterly indifferent to the horrific scene occurring next to them. They passed right by Sigurd and Sinfjotli, oblivious to the fact that there were two humans in Helheim. They continued walking toward the Gjallerbru, utterly apathetic to the mountains of corpses and armaments Sigurd had single-handedly vanquished in his epic battle. Sinfjotli recalled earlier that as he fought Siggeir, the spirits had continued walking right by them, utterly indifferent to the epic fight around them. Nothing seemed to matter to these spirits, and they just carelessly continued walking along the Gjallerbru and the Road to Hel toward whatever fate awaited them at Hel's palace.

Kings rise and fall, warriors fight and die, and the dead don't even notice or care, Sinfjotli realized.

"We should leave now while Garm is preoccupied with his new chew toy," Sigurd suggested, breaking the silence. "If we're quick, we may bypass him."

Sinfjotli was about to agree until he remembered that his mother's ghost was still there. He turned and saw her lying in a fetal position next to the glacier Siggeir had contemptuously tossed her into earlier. In her youth, she had been a proud and beautiful shield-maiden. But now she looked like a broken melancholic creature. Sinfjotli's heard withered seeing her like this.

"Not yet," Sinfjotli refused. "I have to help my mother."

"I understand how you feel," Sigurd said. "I saw what he did to her earlier. But she's dead, Sinfjotli. Unlike us, she can't leave this place. We can do nothing to change that. This may be our one chance to get past Garm unmolested, and we can't afford to squander..."

"I don't care!" Sinfjotli shouted so loudly Sigurd took a step backward. "She's my mother, Sigurd! I... I know it's selfish, but I can't leave her like this. And I can't leave without saying goodbye. Father wouldn't have abandoned her like this, and neither will I."

Sigurd studied him with his golden snake eyes and then glanced at the four-eyed hellhound tormenting Siggeir.

"So be it," Sigurd sighed. "We're in this together, brother. Besides, this will be the first time meeting my aunt, and I ought to make a good first impression."

CHAPTER THIRTY-THREE

THE TROUBLEMAKER

"Aren't you going to sheathe your new sword," Sinfjotli asked as they approached Signy.

Sigurd glanced down at the ebony sword in his left hand. He had already sheathed Gram but kept his new sword drawn.

"Not yet," Sigurd replied. "We haven't escaped Helheim yet. There may be more enemies to fight, and I can't risk sheathing it until then."

Sinfjotli arched an eyebrow. He glanced at the smoky miasma enveloping the blade.

"That's no ordinary sword," Sinfjotli remarked. "How did you get it?"

"I told you it's a long story," Sigurd reminded. "Assuming we escape, I'll tell you another time... and why I can't sheathe it yet."

Sinfjotli didn't press the matter any further. As they walked toward the glacier Siggeir had contemptuously slammed Signy into, Sigurd stared at the ebony sword in his left hand. He thought about how he acquired it and why he couldn't sheathe it yet.

Earlier, Sigurd dispatched their remaining uncles and the draugirs summoned by the draug while Sinfjotli battled Siggeir. Sinfjotli later remarked that Sigurd had easily cut them to pieces. That had been true... for the most part. One draugir managed to stand up to Sigurd and give him quite a challenge.

After Sigurd dispatched the rest of his uncles, he turned his wrath on the other draugirs Siggeir had summoned and effortlessly cut down fifty of them in rapid succession. He was unstoppable as he carved through the dead with Gram like a scythe through wheat...until one draugir abruptly halted him.

It happened while Sigurd was facing five of the remaining twenty-five draugirs. All five lunged at him at once, and he effortlessly bisected four of them with a single swing of Gram. But as he swung his sword at the fifth draugir, his arm stopped, and he heard a loud, unearthly sound. To his amazement, the fifth draugir had done the impossible. It blocked Gram with its black sword!

As Sigurd registered what had happened, the draugir took advantage of his momentary confusion and swung its sword. Sigurd cast aside his bewilderment and instinctively parried the strike with Gram. The moment their blades clashed, Sigurd heard another high-pitched, unearthly sound. It sounded like a mix between a song and a scream, as if both swords cried in pain and ecstasy.

Sigurd pushed aside the black blade and instinctively backed away. This was the second time in his life Gram had failed to cut something, and it was the first time anyone had parried Gram in actual combat. He had to be careful.

Sigurd glanced at the draugir's unnatural and otherworldly sword. He didn't recognize the blade's black metal or the ancient dwarven runes engraved into the fuller. An eerie layer of shadowy black miasma enveloped the sword, and a red eye glowed ominously on its hilt.

The sword's owner stood out from the other draugirs, possessing a noticeable amount of flesh and hair. Compared to the other skeletal draugirs, this one looked very lifelike, as if he died recently. However, his flesh was soft and wrinkly, hanging over his bones. His skin was the color of curdled milk, with gray-green mottling and brown blooms of decay.

He wore an iron ring mail shirt over what looked like leather armor made from deerskin. He wore what appeared to be lamellar armor. He was tall and athletic, and his long, collar-length blond hair flowed loosely beneath his lamellar helmet. But his eyes were unnerving. His pupils and sclerae were black as a moonless, starless sky.

Sigurd could see through a gash in the center of his armor and a gaping sword wound in his chest. The skin around that wound was dry and shriveled, and the greenish-black color indicated signs of gangrene. This warrior appeared to have died when someone thrust a sword straight through his chest. Staring at it made the scar on Sigurd's chest flare with phantom pains.

"You're different from the other draugirs," Sigurd observed. "Who are you?"

Before the mysterious undead warrior could respond, the remaining draugirs surged at Sigurd.

"You small fry never learn." Sigurd brandished Gram, preparing to slay them all.

But before Sigurd could do anything, the mysterious warrior with the black sword stepped forward and cut down ten of its comrades. The undead spirit then pointed its dark sword at the remaining eleven draugirs, sending a clear message. He wanted the glory of defeating Sigurd for himself. And he would kill anyone else who got in his way. The restless dead realized this and respectfully formed a large U-shaped perimeter around Sigurd and the rogue draugir.

"That's quite the sword you've got there," Sigurd commended. "This is the second time Gram has failed to cut through something."

"I'm just as impressed by your weapon," the maverick draugir replied. "As far as I'm aware, this is the first time *anyone* has parried a strike from Tyrfing without their sword shattering."

Sigurd felt a sudden chill in his blood, and his eyes widened. "Did you say…Tyrfing?"

Tyrfing. Every Viking and Norse warrior feared the name, and rightly so. According to legend, Tyrfing was a cursed sword so deadly that it could not be sheathed until it had killed a man. The blade had a long and storied history, but it vanished without a trace two centuries before Sigurd was born. Sigurd assumed the sword was just a myth designed to frighten children. But the ebony sword in his opponent's hand was definitely cursed. It oozed darkness and an unnatural aura. Sigurd's instincts warned him to avoid that sword at all costs.

"That's right," the undead warrior confirmed with a smile. "This is indeed Tyrfing. And to answer your earlier query, my name is King Heidrek the Wise. But my enemies often called me Heidrek the Troublemaker. Call me whichever you prefer, but do remember the name of your killer."

"You're different from the other undead," Sigurd noted. "Are you a draug like Siggeir?"

"Not yet," Heidrek answered vaguely. "But I will be. Mistress Hel has promised to turn me into a draug and promote me to one of her elite generals after I kill you."

"I see." Sigurd glanced at the other eleven draugirs, forming a wide U-shaped perimeter around them. "Still, you're different from the rest. You have more muscle and flesh on your bones than the other draugirs... Hang on, you're casting a shadow! But that's impossible! Unless... Are you... alive?"

"I wouldn't say that," Heidrek replied. "Like you, I'm caught in a state between life and death. It's a necessary condition for me. My sword, Tyrfing, is the deadliest sword ever wielded by man, but it can *only* be wielded by the living. Therefore, Hel had to make certain... arrangements for me to fight you."

"So, Hel sent a half-dead warrior with a cursed sword to face me? Did she finally realize these mooks pose no real threat to me?" Sigurd jerked his head toward the remaining draugirs, who now cautiously kept their distance.

"Don't lump me together with this hoard of weaklings!" Heidrek glared contemptuously at the other draugirs. "I may not be a draug yet, but I am just as dangerous as one. Once I kill you, Hel's promised to promote me to the ranks of her draugs. And afterward, she'll permit me to travel to Midgard with an army of undead warriors to punish the thralls who rebelled and murdered me and their descendants."

Heidrek smiled. "But I'm getting ahead of myself. Hel talked a great deal about you, Sigurd. She spoke about you and your battle prowess as if you were a demigod. I am looking forward to an excellent, fulfilling fight from you."

Sigurd brandished Gram. "You said your name is Heidrek the Troublemaker? My name is Sigurd the Dragon Slayer."

"I'll remember that name," Heidrek vowed as he brandished Tyrfing. "Let whoever triumphs in this fight sing praises of the other!"

CHAPTER THIRTY-FOUR

TOUGH LOVE

Heidrek proved to be a worthy adversary. As he and Sigurd clashed, their swords canceled each other out. But they also sliced through any draugir stupid or careless enough to get too close to their duel.

They clashed for over five minutes without either gaining the upper hand. But in the heat of battle, Sigurd performed a counter riposte and landed a light blow on Heidrek's chest with Gram. While Heidrek was momentarily distracted, Sigurd kicked up a fallen draugir's sword with his left foot, grabbed the hilt in his left hand, and jammed the weapon into Heidrek's right shoulder. Sigurd and Heidrek disengaged and backed away to catch their breath.

Heidrek laughed as he examined the gash in his breastplate and the sword sticking from his right shoulder.

"That was both a masterful move and a dirty trick!" Heidrek commended.

"There's nothing special or dirty about it," Sigurd replied humbly. "This is just the way I fight. What kind of warrior wields his sword in one hand but does nothing whatsoever with the other or leaves weapons lying about the battlefield without utilizing them? Or takes full advantage of his surroundings? When I fight, I use every fiber of my being and weapon at my disposal to dispatch my opponents. In my view, there is no such thing as a 'dirty trick' in the heat of battle. I'll even use my teeth if I have to. So don't be surprised if this fight ends with me feasting on your throat!"

Heidrek narrowed his eyes. He glanced at the sword sticking from his shoulder and the slash on his chest and then stared at the piles of corpses behind Sigurd that he had left earlier in his wake.

"Hel was right about you," Heidrek laughed as he grasped the sword jutting from his shoulder. "You are dangerous! It's rare to come across seasoned warriors like you."

"Oh, don't give me that," Sigurd scoffed dismissively. "What could you possibly gain from praising your enemy?"

Heidrek acted like he hadn't heard the question. He grunted as he pulled the rusty sword from his shoulder and studied it momentarily. "To think you wounded me twice without getting hit. I'm amazed you managed to wound me, pick up this sword in the heat of battle, and stab me without getting hit. I commend your battle prowess, Sigurd. I've never seen a sword handled more gently or with more grace. However, I ought to warn you that scoring lucky hits like these is pointless against me."

"What do you mean?"

Heidrek cast aside the rusty sword and stared intently at Sigurd. "When I fight someone, I can learn their attack pattern. I still haven't inferred the full extent of your repertoire, but I can tell that your fighting style is precise and surgical. You specifically target your opponent's pressure points and the other vital areas required for movement. You disable them hit by hit before inflicting the coup de grâce. It's an extremely disciplined fighting style. However, that strategy won't work on me."

As he spoke, Heidrek loosened the straps of his breastplate. The gaping hole in his bare chest made Sigurd queasy.

"There are three things you haven't realized yet," Heidrek continued. "First, armor is useless in this duel since our swords are too sharp. Second, I'm already dead and a draugir, so I can afford to take a hit from you and continue fighting unimpeded. Third, unlike your sword, any wound inflicted by Tyrfing is permanent and will remain unhealed even in the afterlife."

He gestured to the hideous hole in his chest to prove his point. Staring at the rotting hole made Sigurd feel phantom pains from when Guttorm stabbed him.

"You're looking a bit green," Hedrick observed. "What's wrong? Does this wound remind you of anything in particular? Are you, perhaps, feeling the phantom pains of a sword being driven through your chest?"

"That's not your concern!" Sigurd snarled dismissively.

Heidrek chuckled. "No need to act shy, Sigurd. I already know how you died. Hel told me all about you before I arrived, and she even mentioned the grisly circumstances of your death. Incidentally, I also got murdered in my sleep. Perhaps that's one of the many reasons Hel picked me to face you. I'm like a shadowy reflection of you in so many ways.

"I lived quite an eventful life. People called me Heidrek the Troublemaker, and I was hailed as the wonder and terror of my day. It's an apt name, I'll admit. I'm still ashamed of some of the things I did. I lived as an undefeated warrior, mercenary, marauder, murderer, and often a fugitive fleeing the noose. As a young drengr, I sought out the most powerful jarls, chieftains, and kings to serve as their mercenary. I'd work my way into their inner circle by performing impossible tasks and then enrich myself with lavish rewards. I'd slay monstrous beasts plaguing their kingdoms and wipe out their enemies. I'd lull my employers into a false sense of security while gathering my allies and power structure within their realm. And when I felt the time was right, I'd stage a coup d'état and take their leader's head.

"But I never laid a finger on their wives, children, commanders, or drengr. I wasn't interested in my former master's position or territory. Instead, I'd plunder their valuables and enjoy watching the surviving heirs and emerging factions eat themselves alive in the bloody power struggles that followed my assassinations."

"You are one demented, honorless scoundrel," Sigurd growled.

Heidrek grinned. "My enemies said much the same. I soon became a target of sweet vengeance. I made a last stand in a formidable castle and fought them all off while mocking their efforts. Once all my foes were dead, I decided I needed a fresh start and traveled to the ends of the world. I helped an old king in the land of the Goths dispatch two rebellious jarls and married his daughter. I later led a rebellion against him, after which his daughter hanged herself.

"But this time, I decided to settle down for good. I extended my new kingdom by warring with the Huns and remarried the daughter of a Saxon king. She ended up cuckolding me with a servant whenever she returned home to visit her father. I brought the adultery to light and left the whore where she belonged. I later remarried the daughter of Gardariki, one of my more sordid actions. He let me foster his son to stave off an invasion, but denied me his daughter's hand. So, I hatched a scheme in which I had the boy wait in the woods and told my mistress Sifka I'd accidentally killed the boy after I'd drawn Tyrfing to cut some apples. The gossiping whore ratted me out as I envisioned, and I was seized, chained up, and sentenced to death. But the boy turned up alive and well before anyone could execute me. Ashamed by his treatment, Gardariki let me marry his daughter, and I killed that gossiping, jealous slut Sifka by breaking her back in a river and allowing her body to float away.

"By then, I had grown weary of battle and settled in my kingdom. I ruled sensibly, and bards soon claimed that there had never been a wiser king than I. Truer words have never been spoken. And to prove it was true, I made it a policy that any criminal summoned before me for judgment could be pardoned of their crime by besting me in a riddle contest. Those that failed faced my sentence and were executed.

"One day, I summoned a powerful but insubordinate jarl named Gestumblindi, who had displeased me. The next day, he appeared in my court with a wide-brimmed hat pulled low over one eye. I gave him the usual offer: 'Face my judgment or save your neck by besting me with a riddle I cannot solve.' He agreed to riddles, but first asked me for some ale. I had a servant bring him some ale, and the contest began.

"The riddles started simple enough but became harder and stranger with each question. But I was a match for every riddle and was never long in finding the solution. But eventually, he asked that one unanswerable question: 'What did Odin whisper to Baldur on his funerary pyre?' I realized I had been testing my wits against the All-Father himself, as he was the only one who could know the answer to that unfathomable question. I was livid that he had deceived me, and I pulled Tyrfing from its sheath and attacked.

"Odin transformed into a hawk and flew away before the blow connected. He flew to the door, transformed back into the guise of a man, and bid me farewell, saying, 'For this grave insult, you will die at the hands of your servants tonight.' I killed the nearest thrall to sheathe Tyrfing and remind them of their place. But that very night, the family of the thrall I'd killed broke into my bedchamber and stabbed me with Tyrfing as I slept. Damn ingrates! I'll make sure to torment them all for murdering me."

"They had every right to kill you," Sigurd scowled. "They ought to call you 'Heidrek the Foolish.' Do you even realize the gravity of your crime? You broke the guest right and attacked a guest after inviting him into your home and letting him partake of your mead. And you attacked *Odin*, no less. I can't decide if you're bold, stubborn, crazy, or just plain foolish. The parallels between us aren't parallel after all. 'Shadowy reflection of me?' You're more like the shadowy *inverse* of me. We may have had similar beginnings and deaths. But we lived very different lives. You lived a life of butchery, deceit, rape, and treachery. I lived my life with honor, dignity, and humility."

Heidrek snorted. "Humility? Coming from the warrior dressed in golden armor?" He sighed. "I suppose it's irrelevant. But do you finally understand the stakes? I can afford to take hits from your sword. But all I need to do is cut you once with Tyrfing, and you'll receive a mortal injury that'll remain unhealed even in the afterlife. Just like this one." He gestured to the gaping hole in his chest to emphasize his point.

When Heidrek finished prattling, Sigurd did something unexpected. He laughed! Sigurd burst into crazed laughter that scared him as much as it did the remaining draugirs, who backed away in fear.

"What's so damn funny," Heidrek demanded angrily. "Are you looking down on me?!"

"Not at all," Sigurd chuckled. "I'm laughing because I'm happy! This is the first time I've faced a worthy opponent I can call my equal!"

Heidrek arched an eyebrow and gave a perplexed look. "How so?"

"My sword, Gram, can effortlessly cut through anything—be it weapons, armor, flesh, or bone—like fruit. But such a powerful weapon often makes combat boring for me. Most opponents I fight die within eight seconds, even when I hold back. It feels like I'm living in a world of glass or swinging around my sword alone in the dark. But you're the first to last this long against Gram and me. I can't remember how long it's been since I fought someone who could challenge me on that level! I'm laughing because I finally found an opponent I can battle using my entire body and soul!"

"I see." Heidrek smiled, baring his rotten teeth. "Now that you mention it, the same applies to me! But don't assume you're my equal because you have a blade that can oppose mine!"

"Why waste time debating and trading insults? Let's have our swords speak for us and decide who the superior warrior is!"

"Beautifully said, Sigurd! Now come! Let us bludgeon each other to our heart's content!"

Sigurd and Heidrek lunged at each other and viciously clashed. They slashed at each other quickly enough to stop snowflakes from hitting the ground around them, even though they were caught in a heavy blizzard. To the draugirs watching nearby, their violent clash must have seemed more like a fierce whirlwind of death than an epic duel between warriors.

They continued hacking and slashing at each other for over ten minutes. Whenever they clashed or parried, their swords sang out in that unearthly metallic chorus as they canceled each other out. Throughout the fight, Sigurd felt like he was melting away. His body bristled with goosebumps. When was the last time he'd felt this exhilarated?

His mind wandered to a distant memory where he and his mother clashed in his stepfather's castle courtyard. She was armed with a sword while he was using a battle axe. It was not a weapon he was accustomed to. But he would make do.

He took three steps and performed a half-pirouette. When his mother ignored the ruse and attacked, he did a back flip, avoiding her blade and letting himself fall into a squatting position. He lunged forward, dodging under her sword and twisting his wrists to deliver a decisive blow. Euphoria seized him, and he could taste victory.

Instead, there was a hard, piercing clang of metal on metal and a sudden flash in his eyes, followed by shock and pain. Sigurd collapsed to the ground and tasted dirt and blood.

She parried back! He realized. *It's over. She's won.*

Hjordis kicked him in the stomach, and then she knocked the battle axe away from his hand with a second kick aimed at Sigurd's elbow. Sigurd clutched his throbbing head, fearing the worst, but he could feel no cut or blood against his fingers.

She parried with her hilt and then punched me with her free left hand! He opened his eyes to find his mother standing over him with her sword pointed at his throat. She sighed and then offered him a hand to stand up.

"Not good enough, Sigurd," Hjordis scolded. "Flashy tricks like that won't do you any good against an opponent who knows what they're doing. Keep your guard up. Don't assume your opponent can't recompose themselves or that they won't use their free hand."

"I was trying to hit you with my axe!" Sigurd groaned.

"And that mentality is precisely what's holding you back," Hjordis chided. "You can't afford to focus only on your weapon alone. That'll get you killed in battle. A weapon is just one means of attacking. Try incorporating your hands, feet, knees, elbows, and whole body into your method. Fight with your teeth if you must."

"I..." Sigurd groaned.

"Moreover, you must always remain calm and collected," Hjordis cut him off. "Your combat skills cannot improve unless you have control over your mind. And don't let go of your weapon that easily. This isn't a game. Your head would be on the ground if this were an actual battle. Now straighten up, pick up that axe, and we'll try again. I vow to teach you everything I know until you are proficient with the weapon."

Hjordis walked back to the center of the training yard. Sigurd glanced at the battle axe lying in the sand by his feet and sighed.

"Why do we have to train this hard, Mother? Today, we're training with battle axes. Yesterday, you made me use a spear. The day before, you had me use a measly knife. And three days ago, you made me use only my bare hands."

"Do you have a point?" Hjordis pressed.

"Why can't you just give me the pieces of Gram? You already know I'm a protégé when it comes to swords. With that sword in my hand, I'd be invincible."

"Invincible?" Hjordis criticized. "I used to think your father was invincible. And for a long time, that seemed true. As long as he possessed Gram, Sigmund never lost a fight. But somehow, Gram broke during his final battle. Sigmund was so accustomed to using that sword that he was near helpless when it broke. I won't let the same thing happen to you. I need to ensure that you won't fall in battle the way your father did. Since he's no longer here, I must teach you everything I know. I must teach you every skill I possess, drill you in every form of combat, and have you train with every type of weapon before I consider giving you that sword. Now, pick up your weapon. We'll start over."

That had been Sigurd's childhood. Every day at the crack of dawn, he'd meet his mother in the training yard and endure her brutal training regimen. She warned that she wouldn't give him Gram's broken shards until he managed to best her in battle, and she spent years drilling him to achieve that unattainable height.

When he was sixteen, Sigurd felt ready and challenged his mother to a fateful duel. That day, he felt more excited than he had ever been. He had trained his whole life for that moment.

Their duel lasted only twelve seconds. Afterward, Hjordis was speechless. Sigurd had surpassed both her and Sigmund. Overjoyed, she embraced him, proclaiming how proud she was. But all Sigurd felt at that moment was immense disappointment. With every battle that followed, that disappointment grew. His mother had been the greatest warrior he had ever known. But she and every other worthy opponent didn't last long whenever Sigurd wielded Gram.

But not Heidrek. Even though Sigurd was holding nothing back, Heidrek was still standing. Sigurd's excitement grew as he clashed with a worthy opponent capable of killing him. His heart pounded inside his chest. His lips were thick with the taste of his blood. He had forgotten what this sensation felt like. This was indeed a battle between equals!

But like any battle, it eventually came to an end. After ten minutes of savage fighting, Sigurd slashed Heidrek across his chest a second time. The two warriors disengaged and backed away from each other to catch their breath.

Heidrek examined the slash in his armor. Gram had shredded through his armor and inflicted a gash from his navel to his left collarbone.

"Who needs armor in a battle like ours, anyway?" Heidrek chortled.

"Your boasting is unseemly." Sigurd chided.

Heidrek had a point, however. Gram and Tyrfing shred through any armor. Even Sigurd's enchanted golden hauberk wouldn't protect him from Tyrfing if he got careless. One false step, and he could lose his life.

Heidrek grinned as he unfastened his damaged chest plate and cast it aside.

Sigurd silently wished he had kept it on because now he could see even more of Heidrek's grotesque wound. The flesh around the hole was putrid black. And the wrinkly flesh of his chest was a sickly green color. Sigurd could even see parts of Heidrek's spine and ribcage in the cavernous hole in his body.

As Sigurd steadied his breath, he vaguely noticed that every other draugir aside from Heidrek was now dead. Apparently, during their epic clash, the draugirs had either bravely or stupidly gotten too close, and they were all hacked to pieces by their swords.

"Worthless creatures," Heidrek scoffed as he kicked a nearby draugir's leg away. "Nothing I hate more than outside meddling during a worthwhile duel. Now then, shall we continue where we left off?"

Sigurd brandished his sword, preparing for the next clash. Suddenly, he heard the howling roar of an angry beast, and he turned around in time to see Sinfjotli transform into a giant wolf and charge at the army of draugirs Siggeir had summoned.

"Shit!" Sigurd cursed. "Sinfjotli, what are you doing?"

"You let your guard down," Heidrek warned.

Sigurd whirled around in alarm. He instinctively swung Gram to deflect an incoming strike. But to his surprise, Heidrek hadn't moved an inch.

"Y-You didn't attack?" Sigurd realized. "You could have easily struck me from behind. Why didn't you?"

"That would have been a coward's attack." Heidrek growled. "I wield the deadliest sword in the world. Why would I need to resort shameful tactic to win a fight? Defeating you at the apex of your power is the only victory worthy of my sword."

Sigurd blinked. Heidrek may have been an arrogant braggart. But beneath all the vainglory, there was a strict, albeit twisted, code of honor and chivalry.

But Sigurd had no time to contemplate this as he heard another bloodcurdling roar. He turned around in time to see Sinfjotli lunge at Siggeir. He watched as the draug vaulted the giant wolf over its head and then pinned Sinfjotli to the ground with its pronged shield.

"Shit!" Sigurd turned back to Heidrek. "Would you mind putting our duel on hold for the moment? I must save my idiot brother. I give you my word that I'll be right back."

Heidrek sneered but nodded in a sign of honor and chivalry. He had already refrained from attacking Sigurd twice while he was distracted. And for that, Sigurd respected his opponent even more.

CHAPTER THIRTY-FIVE

WORTHY OPPONENT

After saving Sinfjotli and reluctantly lending him Gram, Sigurd returned to the bridge to finish his duel. He fought his way back to Heidrek through the army of one thousand undead warriors Siggeir had summoned as the warrior king waited patiently for him.

After cutting down eight hundred fifty draugirs, Sigurd returned to the Gjallerbru. After seeing so many comrades fall, the remaining one hundred fifty draugirs retreated from the bridge and kept their distance. They knew better than to interfere with the duel about to resume.

Sigurd found Heidrek leaning against one of the Bridge of the Dead's pylons. Heidrek lazily looked at Sigurd. Sigurd saw a twinkle of admiration and respect in Heidrek's eyes as the undead king gazed at the sea of corpses and weapons Sigurd had left behind in his wake.

"Where's your sword?" Heidrek asked, pointing at the empty scabbard hanging from Sigurd's waist. "The sword you're holding isn't the same one you used earlier."

"I had to loan Gram to my brother. He needs it more than I do right now."

"You're a fool!" Heidrek laughed. "You might have had some chance against me before with that magic sword. But now your doom is certain."

"I won't need Gram to defeat you." Sigurd picked up a fallen draugir's atgeir in his left hand. "Gram is just a weapon, a tool to be used in battle like any other. And I have plenty of weapons at my disposal." He gestured behind him to the mountains of corpses and piles of weapons he'd left behind in his wake.

"You seem rather confident that you can beat me," Heidrek observed. "You can attack me with every type of weapon imaginable, but the outcome of this battle won't change. No weapon, save the one you had before, can match Tyrfing."

"You may wield the deadliest sword ever wielded by man, but that alone won't guarantee victory." Sigurd countered. "A weapon is only as good as the hand that wields it. Ultimately, the warrior, not his weapon, decides the battle's outcome."

"That is a bold and interesting claim." Heidrek grinned, stepping away from the bridge's pylon. "Let's put those words to the test, shall we?"

Heidrek wasn't wrong. Without Gram, Sigurd was in a difficult position. Tyrfing shattered every sword, axe, spear, mace, pole axe, and every other weapon Sigurd picked up from the ground. Despite this disadvantage, Sigurd persevered and kept fighting. Whenever his current weapon shattered, he grabbed another one and use it until it also broke.

But he wasn't fighting like this out of desperation. Whenever Sigurd attacked Heidrek with a new weapon, he analyzed his opponent's attack pattern and reaction time.

After fighting like this for over ten minutes, Sigurd finished analyzing his opponent. He disengaged and retreated several yards.

He glanced down at the broken battle axe he'd been using. None of the fallen draugirs' weapons stood a chance against Tyrfing's sharp edge.

"I'm impressed, Sigurd." Heidrek twirled his sword. "Who taught you to fight like this?"

"Why do you want to know? I don't see how that information would benefit you now."

"You piqued my interest. You must have had many teachers from all over the world. You've incorporated countless martial arts and swordsmanship into your repertoire. But even so, the way you fight still isn't natural. Earlier, when you used that enchanted sword, it felt like your entire fighting style changed after every attack. It was so unpredictable I couldn't get a read on it. That's why you were able to injure me twice. I've never faced an opponent this proficient and unpredictable before. I can only imagine how much training you took to achieve this astounding skill level. So, let me circle back to my original question: Who taught you to fight like this? How many teachers and pioneers did you need to pave your path to become this proficient at fighting?"

"Just one. My mother, Hjordis, taught me everything she knew about fighting."

"You don't say?" Heidrek laughed. "What a coincidence! My mother, Hervor, taught me how to fight as well. Ha, it seems we have more in common than I thought."

"The similarities end there," Sigurd declared. "We might have similar pasts, but our personalities are as different as night and day."

"True enough," Heidrek conceded. "Nevertheless, you've earned my respect. In the past ten minutes, you've demonstrated that you're proficient with almost every weapon and form of combat there is. The number of methods, weapons, and attacks you've tried to defeat me so far prove your imagination and strength of will as a warrior. But they also represent your desperation as you try to overcome Tyrfing."

"I can't tell if you're praising me or belittling me. What are you trying to say?"

"It doesn't matter how skilled you are. As all these broken weapons scattered across the battlefield demonstrate, the result will be the same against me. No matter how skilled you are, you will never overcome Tyrfing."

"That remains to be seen." Sigurd discarded the broken battle axe and seized a double-edged longsword from a vanquished draugir. The sword was in far finer condition compared to its predecessors. It had a soft leather grip and a marble pommel fashioned into the likeness of a snarling wolf's head with chips of rubies set into the eyes. When Sigurd turned it sideways, he saw ripples in the dark steel where the metal had been folded back on itself repeatedly, a testament to its sharpness. Although not as good as Gram, Sigurd knew it could handle the task ahead. He brandished the sword and mentally prepared himself for what was to come.

"What's wrong?" Heidrek asked. "There are still plenty of weapons lying on the ground. You've got another free hand. I'll wait for you to pick up another."

"I don't need them," Sigurd declined as he brandished the sword. "This sword is sufficient. Although the blade is longer than what I'm used to, it will work."

"Oh, I see," Heidrek realized after a moment. "You intend to gamble your life on a single swing of your sword. Interesting. But your logic is flawed. No weapon, save the one you had earlier, can parry Tyrfing. My sword will slice you in half before yours ever reaches my body. ...Nevertheless, I admire your courage. When I was alive, most men fled in terror as soon as they heard my sword's name. But you refuse to back down."

"I don't have a choice. I intend to escape this accursed realm no matter what it takes. You and that cursed sword are nothing more than an annoying obstacle in my path."

"You've got gusto, boy!" Heidrek growled, holding up Tyrfing. "Very well. I accept your challenge. Come at me when you're ready."

The two warriors faced each other, swords in hand, as snowflakes fell around them. They glared at each other in silence, both bracing for the impending clash.

I've analyzed all my attacks so far and grasped the full implication of their outcomes, Sigurd reflected. *Heidrek can swing his sword in less than one-hundredth of a second. However, he's too overconfident in his sword's inability to be blocked. He believes his sword makes him invincible, so he rarely bothers defending himself. This fight will ultimately be decided by whoever manages to strike first. All I have to do is strike him faster than he can hit me.*

The two warriors glared at each other, mentally preparing for the final strike. Time seemed to slow down. The falling snowflakes appeared almost motionless in the air. Then, a cold gust of wind picked up a cloud of snow dust off the ground. In that instant, the two warriors lunged forward and swung their swords faster than the eye could see. They skidded to a stop with their backs turned to each other.

The tip of Sigurd's sword had been sliced off. It made a whistling nose as it spun through the air and landed in a nearby snowdrift. A trail of blood painted the snow red.

But Sigurd wasn't the one who had been cut. As the snowflakes settled on the ground, Heidrek bellowed in pain as he discovered that Sigurd sliced off his left arm and a large section of his torso.

"How?!" Heidrek collapsed on the ground, gasping in disbelief. Blood gushed from his wound, staining the snow red. He picked up Sigurd's sword from the nearby snowdrift and stared at it in amazement, wondering how it could have inflicted such damage.

"It's not even enchanted," Heidrek muttered. "This is just an ordinary steel sword! How could such a mundane weapon like this defeat me and Tyrfing?"

"I already told you it's the warrior, not his sword, which decides a battle's outcome," Sigurd reminded as he turned to face Heidrek. "A sword is only as good as the hand that wields it."

"Quit spouting that nonsense!" Heidrek growled.

"It's not nonsense," Sigurd insisted. "You're the most skilled warrior I've faced since my mother. But you were overconfident in your sword's inability to be blocked. You assumed that Tyrfing made you invincible and that not having Gram disadvantaged me. Thus, you didn't defend yourself and focused only on attacking me."

Heidrek wasn't listening. The old king stared at the broken sword in Sigurd's hand.

Sigurd let out a sigh. "You still don't understand what just happened, do you? Then, allow me to explain. As I predicted, you swung your sword within one-hundredth of a second. But I swung my sword much faster and struck you within four-thousandth of a second! I had already cut you and maneuvered to safety before Tyrfing could get near me."

Heidrek reeled at that revelation, his mouth drooping in surprise as he clutched his bleeding torso. "Y-you deduced my attack speed down to the nearest millisecond? How? How long have you been analyzing me?"

"From the very beginning," Sigurd replied calmly. "From the moment we started fighting, I've studied our attacks and analyzed your movements. As we clashed, I continued to observe and measure everything about you: your movements, experience, and tactics. Since our swords and skills were evenly matched, I realized the outcome of our battle would be decided by whoever landed the killing blow first. I would have preferred to use Gram for the final strike, but after loaning it to my brother, I had to adjust my strategy somewhat."

"You...anticipated that far ahead?" Heidrek gasped. "You were analyzing me...from the start?"

"Of course," Sigurd nodded. "This is how I naturally fight. My greatest strength in battle is not my magic sword or my vast plethora of fighting styles. It's in my ability to read and analyze my opponent. You treat battle as if it's a game. But I view it like a puzzle. Whenever I face an opponent, I analyze my attacks and grasp the full implications of their outcomes. I never waste a move. Every strike, block, and parry will bring me one step closer to victory. You probably assumed I was picking up random weapons from the ground and attacking you out of sheer desperation. In truth, with every weapon I picked up, I analyzed your movements, attack patterns, respiration rate, reaction times, muscle strength, and flexibility to determine exactly how long it takes to swing your sword and from what direction you'd most likely swing it. As I already mentioned, I knew the outcome of our battle would be decided by whoever landed the killing blow first. It was just a matter of figuring out your attack speed down to the nearest microsecond and then overcoming it."

"That's...way too...extreme," Heidrek wheezed.

"What makes you say that?" Sigurd leaned closer, glaring at Heidrek with his golden snake eyes. "We're talking about battle. It's not a game. There are no rules, niceties, or do-overs. Make one misstep, and you're dead. It's that simple. That's why I was trained to never underestimate an opponent and to always be able to improvise. All the power and weapons in the Nine Realms are useless unless they are directed by proper tactical thinking. Over-preparing, over-analyzing, and pushing myself to the brink is just the way I naturally fight. It gives me the best odds of survival in any situation."

"I see..." Heidrek wheezed while gripping his bleeding torso. "You've got quite the frightening drive."

"And that's why I told you we're as different as night and day. You treated our battle as a mere game while I remained focused on the end goal. You placed undue faith in your sword and assumed that not having Gram disadvantaged me. Thus, you rarely bothered to defend yourself or strategized and focused only on attacking me. In short, you restricted your abilities and gave me too much time to prepare for the final strike. The outcome may have been different if you had placed more trust in your skills and less in your sword. I might be the one lying there with a severed arm and bifurcated torso."

"You're right," Heidrek lamented. "My conceit was my undoing. Throughout my life, I've been nothing but a damn fool who never listened to anyone." He stared at the sky. "The day I was banished, my father, Höfund, warned me never to assist murderers, allow my wife to visit her family too frequently, or foster the son of an important king. But I decided to do the exact opposite. I gave gold to murderers I met on the road, allowed my Saxon wife to visit her family to the point that she cuckolded me, and spread nothing but misery everywhere I went. I was clever, but not wise. If I had listened to my father, I might not be here in Helheim now."

Heidrek glanced down at Tyrfing lying next to him in the snow. "My mother was the only person who ever tamed this blade. The day she passed it on to me, she warned me that it must kill a man every time it's drawn, and I learned that lesson the hard way when I accidentally killed my brother with it. But she also warned me that although it grants victory in battle, it doesn't guarantee its owner victory. King Svafrlami of Gardariki, the original owner of this sword, died from that hubris. And it seems I was just as conceited as he was."

"You may have been arrogant," Sigurd agreed. "But you conducted yourself with true honor and chivalry. You refused to attack me while I was distracted by my brother's battle with Siggeir. And you waited until I fetched a new weapon every time my current one broke. That was truly admirable. It's rare to come across a warrior with such a strict code of honor."

Heidrek stared at him, then smiled. "I guess you really did see right through me. Earlier, I told you Hel promised to make me a draug should I defeat you. That wasn't a lie, but it wasn't why I agreed to fight you. Becoming an arch-wraith was something utterly unimportant and trivial. To me, only the strong truly matter. I lived my whole life slaying warrior after warrior until battle itself lost all meaning to me. I dreamed of facing a worthy foe who could challenge me and give my life meaning. I was robbed of that chance by my treacherous servants. But in you, I finally fulfilled my dream."

Heidrek stared at Tyrfing. "It seems the Norns no longer want me to wield this sword." He looked back at Sigurd, an idea forming in his mind. "Sigurd, you mentioned you intend to escape Helheim. I know you can do it. If anyone can escape Helheim and earn their way to Valhalla, it's you."

"Why is that important to you all of a sudden?"

"My mother Hervor is in Valhalla. She was the only person in history to master this sword. It should return to her side. Could you please bequeath it to her when you reach Valhalla?"

"Of course. You have my word."

"Good. In the meantime, if you were to become its master, I'm certain Tyrfing would be pleased. I'm sure it'll be of some use to you."

Heidrek slid the cursed sword across the icy ground toward Sigurd. Sigurd stamped his foot on the hilt to ensure the blade couldn't scratch him before picking up the sword.

Holding the infamous, cursed sword felt different than what Sigurd expected. He thought a chill would race up his arm, or he'd start hearing voices in his head. But it felt comfortable even, despite the unnerving, gaping eye in the hilt.

"I have one last request." Heidrek fidgeted with his belt with his right hand, removed the scabbard, and placed it on the ground. Then he kneeled up, his back arched straight, proudly awaiting the end.

"Please, kill me with Tyrfing. Since I'm still technically alive, I'm certain you'll be able to sheathe it once it tastes my blood."

"All right..." Sigurd agreed, although he did not understand the full implications of Heidrek's words. "I'll gladly carry out your last request."

As he stepped forward and prepared the coup de grâce, Heidrek raised his hand. "One second. I have one final bit of advice for you. The day my mother passed Tyrfing on to me, she warned me that it must kill a man every time it's drawn. I learned that lesson the hard way when I drew it in a forest and accidentally killed my brother, Angantyr, with it. Don't make the same mistakes I did. If you value your brother's life, never draw this sword unless an unprecedented threat appears. And as a precaution, don't sheathe it until you leave Helheim."

"I'll remember that," Sigurd promised as he swung the cursed sword. He watched Heidrek's bifurcated body crumble to ash that scattered in the wind and then gave his opponent one final salute.

"You might have been cocky, but your talent as a fighter was real. You had many opportunities to slay me, but you gave me a fighting chance for the sake of honor. You have my deep respect as a fellow warrior. I will gladly take your sword and hold you and the last moments we spent together forever in my memory. Farewell, Heidrek the Wise."

When the last remnants of Heidrek's body became one with the wind, Sigurd picked up the bloody scabbard. The red eye on Tyrfing's hilt had turned blue, presumably indicating it could now be sheathed. But Sigurd shelved that thought as he turned to face the remaining one hundred fifty draugirs who had hitherto kept their distance away from the bridge.

"Anyone else?" Sigurd pointed the cursed sword at them. "What's the matter? Whoever wants to die next can come forward."

The draugirs all trembled. One of them took a single step backward.

"No," Sigurd snarled. "You don't get to run away."

It took Sigurd less than five minutes to cut down the remaining one hundred fifty draugirs with Tyrfing. When it was over, he returned to Sinfjotli just as his brother sliced Siggeir to pieces with Gram.

As they made their way to Signy's ghost, Sigurd stared at the ebony sword in his hands. He looked at Sinfjotli, and Heidrek's final warning echoed in his mind. *If you value your brother's life, never draw this sword unless absolutely necessary.*

I can't sheathe Tyrfing yet, Sigurd decided. *For Sinfjotli's sake, I shouldn't sheathe it until we leave this accursed realm.*

CHAPTER THIRTY-SIX

GOODBYE, MY SON

They reached the glacier Siggeir had contemptuously tossed Signy into and found her lying in a fetal position.

Sinfjotli kneeled near her. "Mother, are you all right?"

"Hansel, is that you?" Signy croaked weakly.

"What?" Sinfjotli asked. "No, Mother, it's me, Sinfjotli!"

"Sinfjotli," Signy repeated slowly. She looked up, and Sigurd felt his heart sink. In the vision of Sigmund's final battle against Siggeir, Signy seemed like a valiant and beautiful shield-maiden. Her skill and courage in that final battle against Siggeir had been matched only by her beauty. But now, she looked utterly broken. The melancholic and miserable look in her eyes reflected so much torture and abuse in Helheim. Seeing her reduced to such a pitiful state filled Sigurd with immense pity. He couldn't fathom how Sinfjotli must feel seeing his mother like this.

"Mother," Sinfjotli gasped. He reached out to touch her shoulder.

"Stay away!" Signy scrambled back against the glacier.

"Mother," Sinfjotli said, sounding hurt. "What's wrong? It's me."

"No! This isn't real!" Signy screamed, cowering in fear. "You're not real! None of this is real!"

"Mother... please just look at me." Sinfjotli turned to Sigurd. "What's wrong with her?"

"She thinks we're a hallucination," Sigurd explained. "She's convinced we're a part of one of Helheim's hellish visions meant to torture her."

"Damn you, Hel!" Signy wailed, covering her face with her hands. "Damn you, Siggeir! Why won't you leave me be? Haven't you done enough?"

"Mother, it's me!" Sinfjotli insisted. "Look." He rolled up his tattered sleeves and pointed at his scarred wrists. "I still have the scars from my tenth birthday. Do you remember? You sewed the cuffs of my shirt into my wrists and tore off entire ribbons of my flesh as a test of manhood! But I didn't flinch. I told you, 'Grandfather Völsung wouldn't have complained, and neither will I.' You were so proud of me. Don't you remember?"

Sigurd covered his mouth, feeling queasy. He knew Signy had committed many wicked deeds to bring about her depraved husband's demise, including seducing her twin brother to fulfill a prophecy and conditioning her son to murder his younger siblings and Siggeir's entire family. But tearing the flesh off her son's arms as a test of courage went far beyond the pall of vengeance and into the realm of madness and sadism. Just how desperate had Signy *been* for revenge?

But Sigurd was more baffled by how Sinfjotli dearly cherished that memory. How could anyone in their right mind recall such a traumatic and painful experience from such a young age and beam with pride?

Signy inspected the scars on Sinfjotli's wrists and gasped. Tears filled her eyes. "It can't be...Sinfjotli? It's... it's you? It's really you! This isn't...one of Hel's tricks?"

"I'm really here," Sinfjotli assured.

Sobbing, Signy lunged forward and hugged her son. To Sigurd's surprise, Signy's spirit made physical contact with Sinfjotli's body. Since she was a ghost, he assumed her body would have faded into smoke when they tried making contact, like when he and Gudrun tried to embrace each other earlier. Then Sigurd remembered that Signy was a draugir whom Siggeir had summoned and given a corporeal form. Also, the fact that Sinfjotli had been present in Signy's final moments might have been a factor.

"Look at you." Signy sobbed as she cupped her son's face in her hands. "You're a man now. I...I..."

A wave of guilt and shame washed over her face. Signy collapsed to the ground, crying tears of sorrow. "I'm so sorry, my son. I forced you to do unspeakable things for the sake of my vengeance. But I see now how wrong I was. I was your mother, yet I groomed you into a monster."

"Nonsense," Sigurd chimed in. "You raised a fine son. He is a capable warrior. Trust me, I know from experience."

Signy looked up at him as if finally noticing his presence. She eyed him up and paused upon seeing Gram hanging at his waist.

"Who are you, stranger? And why do you wield my brother's sword?"

"It's a family heirloom. I am Sigurd, son of Sigmund and Hjordis. I suppose... that makes you my aunt."

"So Sigmund married and had another son?" Signy sighed in relief. "That's good. At least our family's bloodline has endured."

"Well...I can't confirm if it has or not." Sigurd admitted. "You see... I died before either of my children reached adulthood." Sigurd chose his words carefully. He decided he shouldn't mention that both his children had been murdered, according to Gudrun. Signy had been through so much here in Helheim, and he didn't want to ruin such a joyful reunion with the news that the Völsung bloodline, which she cherished and sacrificed so much for, might have gone extinct.

"You died?" Signy repeated, confused. Then her eyes widened as the reality of the situation dawned on her. "Wait a minute! Why are you both here in Helheim?"

"It's a long story, and we don't have time to tell it," Sigurd snapped. "Sinfjotli and I must go before Garm finishes playing with his chew toy. Say your goodbyes, brother, and let's hurry."

"Did you just say *Garm*?" Signy gasped. She glanced behind them toward Gnipa Cave, where Garm was still gobbling Siggeir. As she watched Helheim's guard dog devour her wicked husband's ghost, a series of expressions flashed across Signy's face: surprise, horror, joy, revelry, realization, and then fear.

"Why haven't you left?" Signy admonished. "You shouldn't squander your chance at escaping Helheim to speak with a ghost like me."

"I had to make sure you were all right," Sinfjotli insisted. "It's what Father would have done."

"But why," Signy demanded. "I'm already in Helheim. I...I committed too many wicked deeds for the sake of vengeance. Unlike you, I belong here and can never leave."

"I know that," Sinfjotli acknowledged. "But I just couldn't stand seeing you like this. I... I had to say goodbye."

Signy stared at him and began crying tears of joy again. "Oh, my son, despite everything that happened, you still have a noble heart." She embraced him again.

"Sinfjotli, we should go," Sigurd reminded urgently.

"But..." Sinfjotli protested.

"He's right." Signy pulled away. She wiped the tears from her eyes and recomposed herself. For a moment, Sigurd saw a hint of his aunt's former, strong-willed self. "You must go now! I'm sure Hel will torment me further over the loss of one of her best generals. She might even punish me for your sins as well. But if you make it out of here, then I'll be at peace."

"Actually, there *is* a way to end your torment," Sigurd realized. "Let me try something." He jammed his new black sword into the ground, unsheathed Gram, and pressed its point against Signy's forehead. As he suspected, the blade made physical contact with Signy's spirit just like it had with Siggeir's. He proceeded to carve a runic symbol into his aunt's forehead.

"It's done," Sigurd announced, sheathing the blade. Signy now had a blue branch-shaped rune on her forehead. It was the same runic symbol Baldur had carved into Gudrun's forehead earlier.

"That is the Algiz rune," Sigurd explained. "This will protect you from Helheim's monsters and visions. Head across the Gjallerbru and seek Baldur. Once he sees this symbol, he'll know what it means, and he will grant you sanctuary. You'll finally be free from Helheim's torment."

"Thank you." Signy smiled while rubbing her bleeding forehead. "Since arriving in Helheim, I've known naught but despair and agony. But now... you've both given me a reason to hold on to hope. I wish I could speak with you further, but you're running out of time."

Signy looked at Sigurd. For a moment, Sigurd saw a glimpse of the old Signy, the one who had fought valiantly alongside her twin brother and son in that haunting vision he'd seen earlier.

"Please look after my son," she pleaded.

"I will," Sigurd vowed. "Whatever happens, Sinfjotli is still my brother."

Signy looked taken aback. Then her eyes welled with tears, her lips forming a smile. "You have no idea how much those words mean to me."

Sigurd was a bit confused by her mirthful reaction to his words. But then he remembered the last thing Signy told Sinfjotli before she died: "*I promise you that someday, you'll meet people who will accept you for who you are.*"

"You're just like your father, you know." Signy smiled. "Before our blood feud with Siggeir, Sigmund always had a kind and noble heart. He did not discriminate or judge people for their race, gender, social status, or the circumstances of their birth. He saw past that and appreciated people for who they were. You are truly worthy of wielding his sword. I am so glad I got to meet you, Sigurd."

"That... means a lot to me." Sigurd smiled. "Thank you."

Signy nodded and turned to face Sinfjotli. Many emotions danced across her face, and tears still streamed down her cheeks. But she maintained a brave, stoic composure as she grasped his shoulders.

"Sinfjotli, my son, I'm sorry for everything that happened. I—I guided you down the wrong path, and it led you here to Helheim. I realize that might be a slight comfort now, and it's all right if you never forgive me. But let me impart this truth to you. No matter what you do from here on out, know I will always love you."

"I know, Mother."

Smiling, Signy hugged Sinfjotli a final time. Then she joined the other spirits making their way toward the Gjallerbru. Sigurd and Sinfjotli stood idly watching her walk away when Sinfjotli suddenly ran after her.

"Mother, wait!" Sinfjotli called. "There's... There's a message I'd like you to pass on to Baldur when you see him."

"What is it?" Signy requested, turning around to face him.

"When you meet Baldur, tell him I'd like him to find a certain soul," Sinfjotli instructed. "Selkirk. He was the most honorable man in Gautland and the only warrior who could match Grandfather Völsung in combat. He carried out Siggeir's orders because honor demanded that he obey his king. Siggeir butchered him and his family. He does not deserve to be here. And he certainly did not deserve the horrid things Siggeir did to him here. When you meet Baldur, please ask him to find Selkirk and his family and offer them sanctuary on his ship as well."

"I will," Signy promised. "I'll make sure he finds the souls of my other children as well. Goodbye, my son."

With that, Signy joined the spirits making their way across the Bridge of the Damned. Sigurd and Sinfjotli watched until it became impossible to identify her in the crowd of souls.

Then a dark shadow loomed over them. A wave of hot air lapped Sigurd's back, making his hair dance like a flag in the wind. Sigurd turned around to find Garm standing behind them near the Arch of Helheim, blocking the path to the canyon.

"You humans are such fascinating creatures," Garm bemused. "After everything that woman did, you still harbor affection for her. I can see why Mistress Hel is so captivated by you."

"It looks like we missed our chance to escape while Garm was distracted by his new toy," Sigurd sighed. He wasn't upset or angry. Instead, he felt surprisingly grateful. In his heart, he knew trying to bypass Garm was a vain hope. As it was, only the heavy chain connected to his cave prevented Garm from mauling them.

"Looks that way," Sinfjotli murmured with a hint of guilt. "I'm sorry that my selfishness cost us our one chance at leaving this realm unhindered."

"You needn't be," Sigurd assured him. "If that were my mother, I would have done the same thing. Besides, it was a feeble plan, and I doubt Garm would have stood idly by as we passed by his cave."

Garm licked his lips. "If you had taken even one step beyond that arch, I would have devoured you along with Siggeir. But if you're feeling brave, go ahead and try."

Sinfjotli glowered at Garm but did not respond to the hellhound's challenge. Instead, he anxiously looked around, expecting that Siggeir would reappear at any moment and attack them. But the only remnants of the draug were its broken claymore and fragments of its shield scattered across the ground.

"Will Siggeir stay dead this time?" Sinfjotli asked the hellhound.

Garm curled his lips back. "What a foolish question! A wraith cannot be killed, only driven away. Even if you had vanquished Siggeir, his soul would have returned to Hel's palace. From there, it would reform, and he would have marched back here to face you. In short, you would have accomplished nothing! ...Having said that, this is the last you will ever see of your archenemy. Now that I've devoured him, his soul will remain trapped inside my stomach along with the other malefactors who tried to escape Helheim. It's the end of his tenure as a draug. But not to his suffering, for the souls I devour become twined together by a tempest of hatred, locked in ceaseless agony inside my stomach for all time. He shall be in pain as I feast on his life for all eternity. Siggeir's mind will erode like sand into nothing but ceaseless agony."

Sinfjotli stared at the hellhound for a moment before throwing his head back and releasing a peal of wild and maniacal laughter that echoed throughout the canyon. Sigurd felt a shiver run down his spine and flinched at the loud, unnerving laughter, but didn't say anything.

"You find that amusing?" Garm asked.

"I do," Sinfjotli verified mirthfully. "Siggeir had our nine uncles eaten alive by a wolf. And now he has been devoured by the guard dog of Helheim! I could not imagine a more fitting and ironic fate for a monster like Siggeir."

Recognizing the irony, Sigurd cracked a smile but didn't join Sinfjotli in his revelry. Now was not the time to celebrate. They still had to escape this accursed realm somehow. Sigurd gazed south with his telescopic vision and saw that Baldur, against all odds, was keeping the entire army at bay on the other end of the bridge. Sigurd then glanced at the mountains of corpses he'd created in his earlier onslaught. Aside from the enormous hellhound and the ethereal spirits silently making their way south, there was no one else here at Gnipa Cave.

"Now that Siggeir is gone, I think we'll have a brief moment of respite," Sigurd sighed.

"Wouldn't you like to think so?" Garm scoffed. "This isn't the end of your struggle. Siggeir was a raindrop before the storm."

Before Sigurd could ask Garm what he meant, he heard the booming sound of marching footsteps to his left and right.

Sigurd whirled around and saw two massive armies of undead warriors marching toward them from either side of the bridge along the shore of the River Gjöll.

"How did they catch up with us?" Sinfjotli demanded as he picked up two of the fallen draugirs' weapons. "I thought Baldur was keeping them at bay!"

"He is," Sigurd confirmed as he checked beyond the southern horizon with his telescopic vision. "I can see him from here. He's still fending off Hel's entire army on the other side of the bridge."

"Then how the fuck did they catch up to us?" Sinfjotli demanded.

"Hel must have sent part of her army to an alternative route across the River Gjöll to circumnavigate Baldur and flank us while we were distracted fighting Siggeir," Sigurd theorized.

Garm snarled behind them, which was probably the closest sound the hellhound could come to laughter.

"That is an interesting theory," he admitted. "But the truth is far simpler. The dead don't need to circumnavigate Baldur. As a matter of fact..."

Something grabbed Sigurd's ankle. He looked down and saw it was a draugir that had partially dug itself out of the ground. Sigurd slashed Gram at the decayed bony and kicked the corpse in the face.

At that moment, a mighty icy gale blew in from the south, lapped at Sigurd's back, and blew away all the excess snow covering the ground, revealing the horrors beneath their feet. Twisting around, Sigurd could see hundreds of decayed corpses buried beneath the ice. Some were moving, pressing against the ice, struggling to escape.

"...they've been under your feet this whole time!" Garm finished.

Dozens of skeletal hands burst through the icy ground. Sigurd and Sinfjotli retreated from Gnipa Cave and the stone archway as the dead crawled to the surface.

"The ground you're standing on is part of Náströnd, the Shore of Corpses," Garm explained. "It's a continent composed of corpses. Siggeir could have raised them all at any time he wanted. In fact, that is precisely what Mistress Hel instructed him to do when he arrived. But he wanted to fight you alone. But I am not so haughty."

Garm reared his head back and howled. The terrible and baneful sound was like a blast of thunder that made Sigurd's bones thrum within his body and burned his ears as it echoed throughout the canyon.

Thousands of skeletal hands burst from the icy ground around them. Sigurd noticed that this army wasn't composed entirely of human draugirs as the dead clawed to the surface. There were massive trolls, hellhounds, ogres, monstrous undead beasts, and even the reanimated skeleton of a dragon among their ranks!

"Now go!" Garm howled. "Eliminate them for the glory of Mistress Hel!"

The armies of death surged forward, and Sigurd and Sinfjotli braced themselves for the biggest fight of their lives.

CHAPTER THIRTY-SEVEN

A FINAL DEFIANCE

Sigurd and Sinfjotli were in such deep shit they were treading water. With two armies advancing upon them from their flanks, a third army of undead warriors emerging from the ground beneath their feet, and Garm blocking the only path out of Helheim, Sigurd realized that he and Sinfjotli had only one option left.

"Fall back to the Bridge of the Dead!" Sigurd shouted. "We'll use their superior numbers against them. They can't envelop us if we force them to fight us in a narrow space."

They withdrew to the Gjallerbru and watched the three armies descend into chaos as they tried to funnel onto the bridge. Retreating to the narrow bridge seemed like a good idea and it prevented them from getting encircled by the sea of undead. This slowed their pace and forced them to attack in waves of only a dozen warriors at a time, making it easier for Sigurd and Sinfjotli to dispatch them.

However, Sigurd soon regretted this desperate tactic. The undead army continued funneling onto the bridge in five single-file shoulder-to-shoulder lines, which forced Sigurd and Sinfjotli to retreat farther south and away from the Náströnd. Although they slew countless undead soldiers, the dead kept coming in endless tidal waves of death. With every wave of enemies they defeated, another wave crashed down upon them, forcing them to retreat even farther down the bridge. By the time Sigurd realized his mistake, they had already lost so much ground that Garm had become a blurry black dot on the horizon.

Sigurd realized their only hope of salvation was to fight back to Gnipa Cave. With a renewed singular purpose, he and Sinfjotli charged straight into the endless waves of undead warriors.

Sinfjotli fought like a mad demon, swinging his arms faster than the eye could see. He had already taken dozens of injuries but was so drunk with battle that he seemed impervious to pain. He continued picking up new weapons, and whenever his current ones broke or lost their edge, he would toss them aside, disarm another draugir (quite literally), and continue using its weapon instead.

Sigurd saw all this out of the corner of his eye, but paid no attention. He was focused entirely on defending himself from the endless swells of undead warriors. That was all that mattered. He didn't feel his wounds, aching muscles, or the sweat running into his eyes. Nothing else even seemed to exist outside of his pure instinct to survive and return to Gnipa Cave. His mind and body had become like an automaton, whose only purpose was to cut down the foe in front of him, then the next, and every other foe that followed. He'd lost count of how many undead monsters he'd killed already. It didn't matter. Aside from Sinfjotli, every single creature on this bridge was his enemy.

The army of formidable draugirs Garm had summoned seemed endless. Besides the souls of undead warriors, they also fought massive trolls, hellhounds, ogres, monstrous undead beasts, and even the reanimated skeleton of a dragon!

Worst of all, another draug was leading the vanguard of the undead army. This one looked different from Siggeir. Siggeir's unorthodox body had been composed of the rubble and fire he'd been buried under when he died. By contrast, this draug had a very humanoid, almost mundane-looking form.

It was a thirty-foot-tall knight clad head-to-toe in heavy metal armor and a distinctive pitch-black helmet that obscured its face. It wielded a long lance and a heavy metal scutum shield the size of a two-story building.

This draug also differed from Siggeir in temperament. Siggeir had defied Hel's orders and belligerently attacked Sigurd and his brother because of his bloody history with their family. But this draug was more focused and reserved. It seemed reluctant to fight them, preferring to let its lackeys do all the fighting instead. The draug hadn't issued an order to its minions or even uttered a single word throughout this battle. It mostly stood on the bridge like a giant sentinel while its underlings attacked them in endless surges. But if Sigurd and Sinfjotli got too close, the draug would bestir itself, repel them, and force them to retreat farther south down the bridge.

Based on its inaction and jaded eyes, Sigurd concluded this draug was utterly disinterested in fighting them. If Garm himself hadn't summoned it, this draug would never have appeared before them. Whomever this draug might have been in life, it obviously had no personal history or grievance with either Sigurd or Sinfjotli.

But that was precisely the problem. To slay... or rather to *challenge* a draug, a warrior needed to have a personal connection to the draug's past life or possess an item from the final events of the draug's life. The only reason why they stood a chance against Siggeir was because they had unknowingly fulfilled both conditions. Sinfjotli had a personal connection to Siggeir's past since he had helped Sigmund slay him. And by sheer luck, Sigurd possessed the same sword Sigmund used to kill him.

But whomever this draug might have been in life, it had no personal history or strife with either Sigurd or Sinfjotli. And without a personal connection to the draug or an artifact from its past, Sigurd and Sinfjotli had no way to even harm it. Under the circumstances, it was utterly invincible.

With no way to harm or bypass the draug, all Sigurd and Sinfjotli could do was fight and defend themselves from the unending sea of draugirs and other undead monsters. For one brief moment, Sigurd and Sinfjotli seemed like they were on the verge of breaking through after they slew the skeleton dragon...until the draug once again repelled them. It slammed its gigantic scutum shield down on the bridge's deck, and the shock wave sent them tumbling farther south.

As Sigurd scrambled to his feet, he glanced past the southern horizon with his telescopic vision to check how much ground they'd lost. And what he saw made blood run cold.

"Sinfjotli, we have a serious problem!" Sigurd warned.

"What is it?" Sinfjotli asked in between fending off draugirs with an atgeir he'd picked up.

"The undead in the city have started advancing toward us from the other side of the bridge!"

"What?!" Sinfjotli balked. "But I thought Baldur was...?"

"He held them off for as long as he could," Sigurd replied between strikes. "He kept his word and bought us valuable time...which we squandered fighting Siggeir and his lackeys!"

"Shit!" Sinfjotli cursed. "How long do we have?"

"We still have time before they reach us," Sigurd assured. "This bridge is absurdly long. There are still another seven hundred miles between them and us. But based on their current pace, we've got maybe two hours before they reach us. We need to hurry and fight our way back to Náströnd. If they reach us, both armies will catch us in a pincer maneuver, and that will be the end. We can't afford to fight them on two fronts."

THOOM!

THOOM!

THOOM!

"I think we have more pressing matters," Sinfjotli remarked while looking back at their invincible foe.

The draug advanced toward them, causing the ground to quake. The general had grown impatient waiting for Sigurd and Sinfjotli to perish, and decided to fight seriously to expedite their deaths. But this wouldn't be a fair duel. Even though the draug had bestirred itself, its lackeys continued to attack Sigurd and Sinfjotli in endless droves.

CHAPTER THIRTY-EIGHT

THE INVULNERABLE AESIR VS. THE INVINCIBLE GHOSTS

"*An army that cannot die versus an Aesir who cannot be harmed by any physical or magical threats. Let's find out who will capitulate first!*"

As Baldur lay buried beneath tons of rubble from the demolished skyscraper that had collapsed on top of him, he couldn't help but recall that brazen challenge he'd issued to Helheim's undead army hours ago. He'd given it his all, dispatching foe after foe. Yet for every undead being he eliminated, another thirty took its place and continued the onslaught. Moreover, the souls he'd crushed to dust soon revived inside Hel's palace farther south and marched north to resume the fight. He estimated he'd slain the undead dragon twelve times in a row already.

For many hours, the battle became an exhausting yet exhilarating cycle. Dispatch a foe, fight its comrades, wait for them to respawn inside Eljudnir and march north, then dispatch them again. Baldur was having the time of his life making sure the undead army couldn't make it one inch past him.

But the fun came to a crushing end when the undead army's generals shifted tactics and bestirred themselves. The draugirs, hellhounds, and wraiths parted ranks, letting the draugs, who'd stood by and watched the battle from deeper behind enemy lines, march to the front lines. Although

Baldur was incapable of feeling either fear or sadness, his smile faded as he faced the mightiest foes in Helheim.

Who wins in a fight between an undead army and an invulnerable Aesir? The side that had more invincible foes.

Sighing, Baldur pushed against the rubble and tunneled a path through the debris. It took a solid minute before he emerged atop the ruins covered in stone and dust.

Gazing to the northwest, Baldur spotted the undead army advancing unimpeded across the Path of the Dead and onto the Gjallerbru. However, he could do little to stop them as ten draugs blocked his path.

Draugs were the pinnacle of power for the undead, second only to Hel in authority and power. Even elder liches and other arch-wraiths couldn't hold a candle to them because of their stubborn invulnerability. Only a person or object related to a draug's past could harm them. And Baldur was no exception to that rule. Despite his storied invulnerability, strength, and being an Aesir, he could do little against another invincible foe.

He could hold his own against one of them. But he couldn't fend off ten invincible foes attacking him at once. Attacking him simultaneously, the draugs swept Baldur aside, pushing him farther into the city's eastern section and freeing the way for their army to advance onto the bridge.

Baldur turned west, sensing the unimpeded army advancing north through the city like an evil flood. Hundreds of undead foes stepped on the Gjallerbru every second. It was only a matter of time before that army reached Sigurd and Sinfjotli. He hoped they had found a way to bypass...

Baldur's eyes widened as he gazed north, sensing that Sigurd and Sinfjotli had just retreated onto the Gjallerbru. They were getting pushed back to the bridge by an overwhelming army surging around Gnipa Cave.

"I must buy them more time." Baldur channeled energy to his feet and leaped over the rubble, hurtling toward a nearby skyscraper. He propelled himself from the sixtieth floor with a powerful kick and soared through the air like a frog leaping off a lily pad.

Suddenly, a humanoid figure brandishing a war hammer appeared in the air before him. This draug bore an antlered helm and was muscled like a bull. In life, King Durran must have looked like a maiden's fantasy with his clean-shaven face and coarse black hair. But in death, he'd become a haunting sight with glowing blue eyes and an atrophied face.

"You shall not pass!" The draug declared as he swung its mighty war hammer upon Baldur's head. The blow couldn't harm him because of his invulnerability. But the strike's tremendous force sent him rocketing downward toward the street below, where another draug stood waiting.

This warrior was fatter and more menacing than Durran, wore thick iron plates adorned with intricate engravings, and had sharp spikes protruding from various parts. Pieces of his fat flesh protruded through gashes in the armor. Yet his corpulent, rotting flesh masked his powerful muscles. As Baldur sailed toward him, the draug assumed a wrestler's stance, ignoring the large battle axe holstered on his back. Baldur's head vanished inside his enormous palm as he delivered a mighty open-hand strike that sent Baldur sailing backward.

Baldur slammed against the ground several times with tremendous force, each impact sending him skidding a dozen feet farther before finally stopping. He struggled to rise to his feet, but before he could catch his breath, another draug launched itself at him. This one was a towering skeleton, wreathed in eerie blue flames that cast an otherworldly glow. The fearsome draug was adorned with crimson feathered shoulder pads and sprouted actual deer antlers from its skull. It swung a massive sword, measuring an impressive seventy-two inches long, at Baldur's neck.

Anyone else might have dodged or ducked. But Baldur stood his ground and let the blade strike his invulnerable skin. He then lunged forward, dealing a mighty blow to the draug's chest, followed by a powerful uppercut that sent him soaring high into the air. With his opponent airborne, Baldur leaped upward, intending to deliver a third blow.

Suddenly, something seized Baldur's torso, lifting him higher into the sky. The next thing Baldur knew, he was sailing over the city. Looking up, he saw a massive eagle had grabbed him. Worse, he recognized it from a misadventure long ago in Asgard.

"Release me at once, Thiazi!" Baldur ordered.

"You sure about that?" The eagle warned.

The city below them vanished, replaced by the vast expanse of the River Gjöll. Baldur thought Thiazi was about to drop him into the river. Instead, the eagle executed a perfect somersault, releasing Baldur at the apex of the flip.

With the added momentum of the flip, Baldur hurtled back toward the city at an incredible speed. He crashed through at least five skyscrapers before plummeting back to the earth.

As Baldur pulled himself free of the snowdrift he'd crash-landed in, the eagle landed in the street. The bird shapeshifted into a humanoid form, revealing a giant figure that towered over him. The giant grinned a wicked smile as if daring Baldur to try getting past them again.

"My daughter yearned to make you her husband once upon a time," Thiazi recalled. "It disgusts me to think of it, but perhaps you should have taken her to wife instead of Nanna. Skadi would have protected you from that mistletoe spear."

Baldur refrained from taking the bait, knowing it was a feeble attempt by Thiazi to provoke him. But as he rose to his feet, the ground trembled beneath him. Glancing left, Baldur glimpsed the twenty-foot-tall draug that had dropped the building on him earlier swing a massive pillar against his head, sending him flying into a nearby building. Baldur's body careened off the stone wall, bouncing like a ball against several more ice-covered buildings before skidding to a stop.

As Baldur stood, he noticed a distinctive mist surrounding him and several nearby alleys and buildings. It seemed different from Helheim's fog, which forces those it encompassed to relive their pasts. Baldur sensed that this mist was alive with a will of its own, and he could feel it probing his defenses, searching for a weakness to exploit.

Glancing up at the top of the nearby skyscraper, he saw a towering cumulonimbus cloud hovering about twenty feet above the roof. The misty cloud had a fanged humanoid face in its center with glowing eyes looking down on him. Baldur could feel the mist's malevolent gaze upon him, and he knew it was another draug.

As Durran approached with his war hammer, the cloud crackled with electricity.

Moments later, twenty-nine lightning bolts rained down upon him in quick succession, striking the street with incredible force. The bolts blasted the road and vaporized all the ice in their path, leaving behind a trail of smoldering debris. Yet, both Baldur and the stone buildings surrounding him remained unharmed. The lightning seemed to part around him like a river flowing around a rock. The air around him crackled with energy, and the blue glow of the lightning reflected off his clothes.

King Durran stumbled backward in shock. Baldur took advantage of the moment and lunged forward, striking the draug with a powerful blow that sent it flying into a nearby building. The impact shattered the wall, sending chunks of stone flying everywhere. Glancing up at the humanoid thundercloud hovering above, Baldur weighed his options, knowing he could not fight the mist directly. He tried to sense the mist's weakness.

He felt a faint pulse of energy coming from between the face's brow and knew he had found his opening. He took a deep breath and channeled his power into a beam of pure energy that shot toward the mist.

The draug howled in surprise. A humanoid shape fell out of the cloud, and the mist dissipated as the draug crashed against the ground.

To an ordinary person, this spirit would appear like an otherworldly human-like form surrounded by a harsh, glowing aura that emanated from its body and shimmered in a fluid motion like a flag tossed about by the wind. But Baldur could see the draug exactly how it looked when it was alive. He was an overweight, bearded, turban-wearing ruler whose mustache concealed an unusually wide mouth full of fangs. Baldur racked his memory, recalling that this draug was once a mighty king who ruled a land called Paurava, though his name eluded him. The arch-wraith's eyes were full of murder and rage as he gazed up at Baldur.

"Stand down," Baldur commanded, although he realized it was futile. "Don't obstruct me."

"You're wasting your words, darling," a seductive voice warned.

Baldur turned toward the approaching draug. This one stood out from the others because she was a woman with leathery black wings and vine-like hair. Baldur only knew of this queen by her chilling reputation. If memory served, she had once been the queen of an island nation that decimated the population she ruled over the course of thirty-three years. She'd killed rivals, sold her subjects into slavery, executed foreigners, and boiled devout worshipers alive while claiming the gods wanted her to rule.

The harpy-like draug smiled, revealing sharpened teeth like a shark's. "Our orders were clear: 'Go play with Baldur and keep him busy.' As frustrating as it may be to bestir ourselves, we cannot disobey Mistress Hel's commands."

"Speak for yourself, Tamara, you lazy, hateful hag." The giant draug with the pillar scoffed as he approached. "I relish the chance to fight an Aesir."

Baldur studied the draug. He wore a bronze helmet obscuring his atrophied face, a coat of scale armor, and bronze greaves to protect his legs. Upon closer inspection, the pillar was a large spear tipped with an iron point. Yet, given his immense size, one couldn't help but mistake the goliath object for a giant column.

"That's bold talk coming from the general who got killed by a shepherd with a slingshot," the corpulent draug mocked.

"Goliath makes a valid point, Zhuo," countered the skeletal warrior with the great sword and antlers sprouting from his skull. As he brandished his sword, Baldur vaguely recalled him introducing himself as Atli of the Huns, Gudrun's former husband whom she'd brutally murdered.

"To be able to clash against an Aesir is such a tantalizing prospect. Given a choice between fighting my bloodthirsty wife's ex-husband and a god, it's an easy choice to make."

Thiazi snorted. "I've clashed with the Aesir before, Atli. It loses its appeal after a while. They talk a big game, but when push comes to shove, they're afraid of death and aging just like any other mortal."

As the draugs surrounded him, Baldur smiled defiantly. "I'm never afraid, Thiazi. That emotion doesn't exist in me, nor despair."

Baldur gritted his teeth as he faced off against the seven draugs at once. Despite possessing invulnerability comparable to his own, his quick reflexes allowed him to avoid the draugs' initial onslaught. He darted around, striking them with precision and skill. Even against eight invincible foes, Baldur held his own.

He managed to gain an edge, and just as he was about to land a devastating punch on Thiazi's face, a sudden impact rocked his body. Before Baldur could register what had happened, his feet lost contact with the ground, and he rocketed backward.

After blinking away his surprise, Baldur looked at the nine objects pressing against his body. Nine arrows had simultaneously struck him. The arrow tips pressed harmlessly against his invulnerable skin, but each projectile's absurd power and momentum kept him flying parallel to the ground.

As he rocketed through the cold air, propelled by the force of the arrows, Baldur glanced past the draugs he was fighting and saw an archer crouched on the roof of a three-story building far away, holding a vibrating bow with a giant eye on the grip. The archer was a draug, just like the others, and his arrows had been magically infused and launched with absurd power.

Before he could think to break the arrows pushing against his body, gravity finally caught up with him, and he crashed headlong against the pavement, tumbling and spinning uncontrollably until he crashed into the side of a building.

However, when the wall shifted slightly beneath him, Baldur realized it wasn't a building he'd slammed into, but an enormous shield! He was then shoved against the ground with enough force to crack the pavement. Turning, Baldur saw a tall figure holding a scutum, two pilums strapped to his back, and wielding an oversized flaming gladius. He wore armor made of silver hands and fingers that were grafted to his skin. His eyes were pure gold, lacking both pupils and sclera.

"General Antony," Baldur muttered, "that wasn't very sporting."

"Neither is this!" Antony swung his sword against Baldur's side before he could even stand. The burning sword pressed harmlessly against Baldur's invulnerable skin, but the force of the blow sent him crashing into the side of a nearby building. The impact caused a shower of rubble and debris to rain down upon the Aesir, burying him beneath the wreckage.

As Baldur rose unharmed from the rubble, he overlooked Antony and the other draugs closing in on him, focusing on the far-away archer. The archer let loose another volley, launching nine arrows at once. Baldur readied himself and met the force of the arrows head-on, letting them shatter against his body. But as he grabbed the last arrow before it slammed against his face, a surge of magic run up his arm and he sensed something was awry.

Baldur looked down at the arrow he had just caught, his eyes drawn to the glowing rune on the shaft. Before he could even process its meaning, its archer appeared in front of him in a burst of light. Baldur overcame his surprise and threw a punch.

But before he could connect, the archer somersaulted over him with graceful ease, drawing his bow in midair as he sailed over Baldur's head. In one smooth motion, he fired an arrow at point-blank range against Baldur's skull with enough force to make him sink through the solid rock beneath him, burying Baldur up to his waist in asphalt.

Baldur struggled to free himself, his invincibility and strength useless against the arrow's magical properties. As he strained against his bindings, the archer approached him with a smirk, twirling his bow in one hand. His white eyes lacked corneas and irises, making Baldur wonder if he'd fired those arrows based on sound or if the giant eye on his bow served as his source of vision. Either way, he somersaulted to safety as Baldur's hand burst from the asphalt, failing to grab the archer's ankle.

"Nice try, Aesir," the archer laughed. "But you're not the only one with tricks up your sleeve."

"You've yet to see any of mine, Yue Fei," Baldur retorted as he freed himself from the ground. But the second he took a step, someone grabbed him from behind and suplexed him onto a pile of rubble.

Blinking in surprise, Baldur saw a tall, imposing figure in a suit of armor with a red cape fluttering from his broad shoulders. As Baldur sat up, the draug drew his sword and shield, both of which were adorned with intricate designs and symbols.

Baldur recognized this one from his distinctive armor and cadence, though his name eluded him. He did remember how he'd been a king who ruled a martial kingdom far to the south in Midgard, led tens of thousands of warriors into a war on his brother's behalf after a lustful prince abducted his sister-in-law, slighted his best warrior, sacked a grand city, and was murdered by his wife and her lover, his own cousin when he returned home.

"Grabbing me from behind while I get up? That's not a very intricate strategy."

"Who needs strategy when you've got numbers?" The old warrior king retorted as the other draugs converged. All ten draugs circled or hovered above him like an eagle and humanoid cloud. Baldur eyed them individually, then bent down and jumped. He pretended to be aiming at Thiazi, then kicked off the side of the building, which changed his course and allowed him to land on the roof of a building on the opposite street. He wasted no time and made a mad dash across the rooftops, hoping to reach the Gjallerbru again. But other draugs were on him in a heartbeat.

"You're too honest for your own good, Baldur," Tamara warned as she flew beside him. "Your intentions are so transparent you might as well have announced them yourself!"

She cracked a whip, wrapped it around Baldur's waist, and sent him flying backward. The humanoid cloud draug then brought down a lightning bolt upon Baldur, which sent him crashing into the ground below at a quarter of the speed of light.

As Baldur struggled to regain his footing, the other draugs pounced on him, attacking from every direction. Although their attacks were futile against his invulnerability, Baldur found it impossible to defend himself against their relentless onslaught. He searched desperately for an opening, but their simultaneous attacks left him with no breathing space.

A shadow washed over Baldur as Goliath appeared behind him, bringing his spear crashing down on his back. The force drove Baldur deep into the ground, burying him up to his neck in concrete.

Yet he felt no pain—only frustration at being unable to stem the tide.

He was strong. He was invincible. He was Aesir. Yet he couldn't fend off this many draugs attacking him simultaneously.

"Your little rebellion ends here, Lord Baldur," Thiazi declared as he and the other nine draugs loomed over Baldur. "It's only a matter of time before those two mortals are dealt with."

"You chose the wrong souls to bet on." Mocked Durran as he slung his war hammer over one shoulder. "Mistress Hel refuses to let you leave her realm. Why would she be lenient to these mortals?"

"Our brother-in-arms, Allant, has bestirred himself and faces them even as we speak," the corpulent Dong Zhou informed.

"He wouldn't have needed to if Siggeir hadn't gone rogue and stuck to the plan," Goliath added. "That jealous oaf got what he deserved."

"At any rate, Siggeir did his duty and kept them occupied long enough for us to deal with you," Goliath intoned. "We draugs consider it an honor to battle an Aesir like you. But your efforts are in vain. Surely you've realized that by now."

"Oh? And what *have* you accomplished exactly?" Baldur challenged. "You all knocked me around and wrecked your master's city. But you've failed to leave a scratch on me or break my spirits. And you never will!"

"Be that as it may, your efforts are still for naught," Thiazi countered.

Baldur burst out laughing. "I see you've finally gained a sense of humor in death and picked up the bad habit of condescending, Thiazi. All my efforts have been in vain? What makes you say that?"

Baldur wrenched his arms free of the stone ground and leaped from the earth, landing gracefully on his toes. He stared down at the ten draugs before him and grinned defiantly.

"I'm keeping the most dangerous pieces off the board while Sigurd and Sinfjotli deal with the pawns. I'd hardly call that a wasted effort. I'd argue you're the ones who have failed to accomplish anything."

"You overestimate those mortals," warned the draug who'd suplexed Baldur earlier. "I fought alongside a warrior descended from the gods who thought he was invincible. An arrow to the heel proved him wrong, just as a mistletoe arrow proved you weren't invulnerable. Those mortals won't make it a tenth of the way. You can't hold back a flood through sheer willpower alone."

"You'll find you're gravely mistaken, Agamemnon." Baldur warned resolutely. "Sigurd and Sinfjotli are certainly warriors of many qualities. However, their strengths don't come from being descended from my little brother. Those two were neither born almighty heroes nor strong, indomitable warriors upon birth. Rather, they each grew into their strength through perseverance, hard work, and unwavering determination. They've more than earned their places among the pantheon of storied heroes. They're not as strong as Sigi and aren't invincible like me. Yet, the will of the Volsungs still burns strong within them, even in death. They won't back down even in the face of insurmountable defeat. And neither will I!"

Baldur began casting a spell, his hands glowing with an ethereal light. Before any draugs could stop him, he unleashed the attack, and a titanic amount of wind erupted from his hands. The hurricane-like vortex disassembled the cloud body of the draug floating overhead, forcing him back into a corporeal form. The winds then caught the draug, sending him hurtling away toward the River Gjöll.

The other draugs watched in amazement as their fellow arch-wraith sailed out of the city, carried away by the powerful winds. As the vortex dissipated, everyone heard a faint splash in the distance, indicating that the draug had fallen into the River Gjöll. The other draugs nervously stepped back. But as they looked at Baldur, they saw a fiery look in his eyes and took another step back. They could feel the intensity of his gaze, and fear crept into their undead hearts. For the first time since their souls had evolved, they felt afraid of someone other than Hel.

Baldur's voice was a dangerous mixture of excitement and playfulness as he spoke in a low tone. "Hel ordered you to play with me, so let's keep the game going. But be warned, I like to play rough!"

CHAPTER THIRTY-NINE

WINGS OF SALVATION

Now that it was fighting them seriously, the draug proved to be a terrifyingly formidable foe. Within thirty minutes, it had single-handedly pushed Sigurd and his brother back another hundred miles down the bridge, bringing them even closer to the encroaching army from the south. In addition to the impatient arch-wraith, they still had to contend with the rest of the army, who were attacking them in endless droves.

Out of sheer desperation, Sigurd and Sinfjotli took turns fighting the draug and its lackeys, switching places every five minutes. But their efforts were in vain. Unlike Siggeir, they had no way to harm this draug. All they could do was fight until their last breath. Fight until every drop of their blood was spilled. Fight until the absolute bitter end. The only comforting fact about this dire situation was that if they died now, at least this time, they got to die fighting with weapons in hand and screaming curses at their foes.

As they took turns fighting the draug, they heard a sharp whistling sound from behind the endless enemy lines to the north.

"Brother, I hear something in the distance," Sinfjotli warned as he battled the draug. "Could you check it out?"

"I'm a little busy here," Sigurd replied while fending off ten draugirs simultaneously. "Give me a moment."

A ten-foot-tall undead troll attacked Sigurd as he finished dispatching the draugirs. It tried to crush Sigurd beneath its fist, but he dodged its attack and climbed up its arm to its shoulders. He drove Gram deep into the back of the troll's head and then jumped into the air as its body collapsed. Sigurd twisted around in the air, trying to get a good look at what was happening north with his telescopic vision for about three seconds before landing on the ground.

"Well? What did you see?" Sinfjotli inquired as he stunned a draugir who had snuck up on him by delivering an elbow to its skull. He then grabbed one of its legs to make it fall and crushed its head with his feet before dodging another of the draug's attacks.

"I'm not entirely sure," Sigurd admitted as he resumed fighting the rest of the swarm. "Something is making its way toward us."

"Maybe it's that unknown entity Baldur sensed earlier?" Sinfjotli guessed.

"Whatever that thing is, it is swift and strong," Sigurd exclaimed. "And it's no friend of the dead. It's mowing straight through them like a speeding arrow through cloth! It'll be here any minute now. Ready yourself!"

"We have a more pressing enemy at the moment," Sinfjotli reminded as he dodged another strike from the draug. "Let's switch!"

Sigurd and Sinfjotli traded places. Sigurd did his best against the draug even though he knew it was pointless. He could defend himself from the draug's attacks, but he had no way to truly harm the invincible arch-wraith even with Gram and Tyrfing in hand.

But that didn't stop him from trying. He tried swinging both his swords at the draug, and it blocked the attack with its shield, more out of instinct than necessity. But Sigurd had planned for this. While its shield was near the ground, Sigurd leaped up, sprinted across its surface, and vaulted off the shield toward its head. Sigurd then swung his swords at its neck before the draug could react.

It was a brilliant move and perfectly executed. But it was still futile. Gram and Tyrfing passed through the draug's body like smoke. As the draug's form flickered and momentarily became translucent, Sigurd noticed how close the unknown entity making a beeline toward them was. He let his guard down at that moment, and paid a painful price as the draug swatted him like a fly with its lance, sending him crashing into the ground. Thankfully, Sigurd had been struck with the shaft of the weapon rather than the pointy tip.

But the draug wasn't finished. Before Sigurd could pick himself off the ground, the draug raised its massive scutum shield above its shoulder and slammed it down on Sigurd's chest.

Sigurd felt his ribs and sternum crack under the immense pressure as the ground beneath him caved. He coughed up blood, unable to breathe.

"Sigurd!" Sinfjotli cried. He struggled to cut his way through the undead army as the draug lifted its shield from the ground. But Sinfjotli wouldn't make it in time. And Sigurd couldn't escape on his own after receiving such a devastating attack. He lay helpless at the bottom of the ten-foot-deep crater the draug had created, unable to breathe due to the immense pain in his chest. Sigurd watched as the draug raised its lance for coup de grâce.

Suddenly, it stopped moving. The draug glanced over its shoulder, and something about its demeanor changed. It almost looked afraid. Sigurd could vaguely hear something in the distance as he struggled to breathe. It sounded like ...the draugirs to the north were screaming in terror.

Meanwhile, Sinfjotli managed to cut his way to Sigurd just as the draug turned north to face the oncoming threat. He didn't bother to ask why the draug had hesitated and wasted no time dragging Sigurd out of the crater to safety.

They stopped retreating when they were about fifty yards away from the draug. Sinfjotli helped Sigurd sit up, which made Sigurd cough up more blood. The pain in his chest was unbearable. It felt like he was being stabbed by a thousand daggers from the inside. But what felt worse was how weak and helpless he felt right now. Gram had been knocked out of his hand when the draug swatted him. He still held Tyrfing in his left hand but was too weak and injured to use it or even lift his arm off the ground. All he could do was watch through blurred vision as droves of draugirs made their way around the draug and marched toward them.

Sinfjotli seemed to notice Sigurd's gloomy mood. He retrieved Gram from where it had landed and pressed its hilt into Sigurd's right hand. Holding his trusty sword helped his fingers remember their strength and provided him some comfort. As he struggled to breathe and waited for the healing properties of Idun's Apple to kick in, he could vaguely hear Sinfjotli warn him: "Whatever that thing is, it's about to appear before us. Brace yourself!"

The draug had turned its back on them and held its shield to defend against whatever was coming. The other nearby restless dead had also ceased attacking and were now gazing north in fear. Through the gap between the draug's legs, Sigurd could see a mysterious humanoid figure with golden metal wings rapidly approaching, slicing through the ranks of the undead army like a speeding missile.

The draug braced itself and thrust its lance at the oncoming figure. The mysterious winged figure twisted its body in midair, avoiding the attack. They then rocketed forward and blasted a hole straight through the draug's shield and torso like a speeding arrow through an apple.

As the draug collapsed on its back, the mysterious figure landed gracefully on the ground right before Sigurd. Sinfjotli brandished the atgeir he had been using but stopped when he got a good look at the mysterious arrival. His eyes widened, and his jaw dropped in shock. Sigurd looked up and couldn't believe his eyes.

It was a valkyrie, a chooser of the slain. The magnificent shield-maiden stood up with her golden wings fully outstretched from her back. Her wingspan was enormous, spanning around sixteen feet, and her golden wings appeared both organic and metallic. The feathers were coated with a layer of golden metal. The middle and greater coverts were dark red, while the remaining ones were bright gold. She wore a suit of steel scale armor that helped emphasize her already haunting and regal beauty. The green light of the sky above them cast an unusual color as it reflected off her gold wings and armor, making it look like a green aura enveloped her.

She also wore a golden helmet that didn't match the color of her steel armor. It looked vaguely familiar to Sigurd. Through his blurry vision, the helmet flickered, and for a moment, Sigurd thought he was staring at a dragon's head. When the valkyrie glanced over her shoulder to look at the undead warriors amassing behind her, they all stopped moving and cowered in fear. The helmet continued to change its form, shifting from a circle of black flames to a wreath of human bones, a wolf's head, an iron helm with living serpents attached, and an iron war-like crown resembling the one Hel wore. The helmet appeared to be taking the shape of everyone's worst fears.

But what was truly horrifying was how the helmet extracted all their worst fears. As Sigurd stared at it, he could feel the helmet delving into the darkest recesses of his mind, pulling out all the things he feared most, even though its power wasn't directed at him. He couldn't even fathom the ineffable terror the draugirs must feel.

As he stared at the shapeshifting helmet, Sigurd realized that his body had healed enough to stand up. When the valkyrie looked back at him, Sigurd recognized her face.

"Br...Brynhild?" Sigurd gasped. There was no mistaking it. This was his brother-in-law's wife, Brynhild. And she was a valkyrie now! He was so stunned that he dropped both of his swords. "What are you...?"

Before he could finish his question, Brynhild lunged forward. She threw her arms around his neck and embraced him fiercely. Her angelic wings wrapped around his body like a cocoon, drawing them closer together. Her lips found his lips and stuck together. A tingling sensation ran along Sigurd's body, filling him with such rapture he would have cried out if his lips weren't muffled by the passionate kiss. Sigurd surrendered to it, and for a while, they just stood there lost in a state of rapture. Nothing seemed to exist outside of the kiss. For a moment, Sigurd forgot about the threat of the dead fighting around them, the pain of his cracked ribs, and the whole world. But he knew it couldn't last. He gently pushed her away and gazed deep into her sharp, amber eyes.

"I finally caught up to you, Sigurd." Brynhild smiled. She was even more beautiful up close. Her beautiful face could bewitch an entire nation. Her long, bright scarlet hair flowed majestically from beneath her fearsome golden helmet down to her waist and occasionally rippled in the wind. Her amber eyes sparkled with fiery determination and passion. Her eyes were so sharp that they reminded Sigurd of sunlight. She looked so regal and beautiful in her steel plate armor. And the gilded wings protruding from her back gave her an angelic appearance.

"Brynhild," Sigurd muttered, still in disbelief. "Why are you...?

"I'm glad you're not an enemy," Sinfjotli interrupted. "Now, could you stop sucking each other's faces and help me!"

His brother's words snapped Sigurd back to reality. He peered over Brynhild's shoulder and saw Sinfjotli fighting the draug. And he was losing. Badly. The draug was furious now. Brynhild's attack had punched a hole straight through its shield and created a gaping hole in its torso that seemed to cause it great pain. Its helmet had also been damaged, and Sigurd could now see its disfigured face through the cracked visor. Most of the flesh from its skull had peeled away, and its lips, ears, and eyelids had been removed, making it hideous to look at. Its lidless red eyes were filled with malice and rage as it assaulted Sinfjotli.

Meanwhile, the undead army continued amassing around Sigurd and Brynhild's position. Oddly, the draugirs on the front lines kept their distance, standing in a U-shaped perimeter around Sigurd and Brynhild. Although their comrades impatiently pushed and shoved behind them, the ones on the front lines refused to budge an inch closer to Brynhild.

When she turned around to face the undead warriors, they all stopped moving and cowered in fear. One warrior dropped his weapons and prostrated himself on the ground. Another covered its face and turned away, shrieking. One fell to its knees, clasped its bony hands, and begged for mercy in their strange guttural language. One draugir even pushed its way to the edge of the bridge and jumped over the parapet into the River Gjöll below.

As the draugirs continued cowering in fear, Sigurd realized they weren't scared of Brynhild's helmet. It was her. Brynhild's very presence was anathema to them. The fear in the draugirs' eyes reminded Sigurd of the ineffable terror he had felt from standing in Hel's presence back on Baldur's ship. The draugirs must have felt the same way about Brynhild.

"Brynhild, why are you here in Helheim?" Sigurd asked as he retrieved Gram and Tyrfing. "And why are you a valkyrie?"

"Now's not the time for explanations," Brynhild replied as she drew her weapons. She held her two double-edged swords aloft in both hands. Bright runes glowed in various colors along the blades, making them radiate with power. The quills of her wings calcified into sharp metallic objects that looked more like daggers than organic feathers.

"I'll explain everything later," she promised. "For now, just know that I'm on your side. I will *always* be on your side!"

She spread her metallic angelic wings and soared forward, mowing straight through the nearest draugirs like a missile. She then turned around and flew straight toward Sinfjotli, who had just been disarmed by the draug and knocked to the ground. As the draug thrust its lance at him, Brynhild intercepted it, snapping the weapon in half like a twig with her swords. She twisted her body midair and slashed through the draug's torso with one of her metallic wings, splitting the arch-wraith in half. The draug's bifurcated body burst into blue flames and then exploded. The seemingly invincible mighty draug fell before the might of a valkyrie and vanished into a pile of smoldering ashes.

From there, Brynhild mercilessly mowed through the draug's subordinates. She swung her swords and used her metallic wings like an extra pair of arms, sweeping them left and right and shredding through the draugirs like a scythe through wheat.

Through blurred vision, Sigurd noticed that her weapons also changed form in her hands as she carved through the undead army. Sometimes, she used swords, other times scythes, then maces, and sometimes a double-bladed spear. She even employed her wings in the savage onslaught like scythes, cleaving draugirs in two with a single sweep. Whenever she cut one of their undead foes down with her wings, its body caught fire and fell into ash before Sigurd's eyes.

"Amazing," Sigurd whistled while helping Sinfjotli to his feet. "She killed the draug in a single blow!"

"And she's quite strong against the draugirs," Sinfjotli agreed. "Look at her go! It's like she's their natural enemy."

"What an apt way to put it," Brynhild remarked as she flew back toward them. "As a valkyrie, I am a psychopomp tasked with guiding souls to the afterlife. But I'm also responsible for dispatching any restless souls in Midgard that refuse to move on and turn into draugirs. That makes me the bane of draugirs and the other restless dead of Helheim."

Indeed, she was. Within just forty-nine seconds, Brynhild had eliminated at least four thousand draugirs! Sigurd glanced at the smoldering remains of the draug. Despite a full minute having passed since Brynhild effortlessly bested their deadliest foe, its ashes were still smoldering, hissing and popping on the ice. Many other blazing ash piles and lifeless bodies lay strewn about the Gjallerbru, a haunting testament to Brynhild's power and a symbol of hope for Sigurd. Until now, their situation had seemed hopeless. But now that the draug had been vanquished and they had an ally who could effortlessly dispatch the undead, perhaps Sigurd and Sinfjotli had a slim chance of making it back to Náströnd.

With so many enemies dispatched, Sigurd and Sinfjotli were able to catch their breath and allow their bodies to finish healing. But their brief respite soon ended as the rest of the undead army overcame their fear of Brynhild and surged forth. The three joined forces and charged to meet their deathly foes with fiery courage in their hearts.

CHAPTER FORTY

THE DREADED OFFER

With a valkyrie fighting on their side, Sigurd and Sinfjotli managed to recover some lost ground. The three of them laid waste to everything in their path. Draugirs, hellhounds, ogres, and massive trolls all fell before their combined might. Sigurd had lost count of how many draugirs he and Sinfjotli had killed so far. But he was certain Brynhild had already killed ten times more undead warriors than the two combined.

Unfortunately, the dead still outnumbered them, so they made little progress. For every undead warrior they cut down, another ten took its place. And worst of all, the encroaching army from the south continued marching closer to their position. Even if they had a valkyrie fighting alongside them, Sigurd knew they would be doomed if they got caught in a pincer maneuver from both sides. Their only chance was to fight their way back to Náströnd.

After an hour and a half of intense fighting, the trio managed to fight a quarter of the way north. They were within two hundred miles of Gnipa Cave when something unexpected happened. Sigurd had just slain an ogre and turned his attention to a nearby draugir. But the undead creature did not attempt to defend itself. Instead, it looked right at him and spoke:

"Let's try the diplomatic approach, shall we?"

Sigurd felt a chill in his blood as he decapitated the draugir. The draugir was clearly male, yet it had just spoken in a shrill feminine voice. Moreover, he recognized it. That was Hel's voice!

Suddenly, the entire army halted its advance. The undead soldiers stood motionless as statutes, even as Brynhild and Sinfjotli continued cutting them down.

"You can stop butchering my soldiers now." Another nearby draugir with a decayed mouth and rotting teeth announced in Hel's voice. *"I'd like to have a civil conversation."*

Sinfjotli and Brynhild finally realized the draugirs were speaking in one collective voice and ceased fighting.

"Now that I have your attention, I have an offer I'd like to discuss with you." Another draugir announced in the same collective voice.

"Speaking to us through a bunch of undead corpses, Hel?" Sigurd inferred. "You are a gloomy little thing, aren't you?"

He checked behind him and saw that the encroaching army advancing from the other side of the bridge had also halted its advance. They were standing as still as statues just beyond the southern horizon. Sigurd breathed a sigh of relief but recomposed himself, knowing he couldn't afford to lower his guard yet.

"Why don't you show yourself in person, Hel?" Sigurd suggested.

"Show myself?" Hel's maniacal laughter echoed like thunder from the mouth of every draugir standing on the Bridge of the Damned as the wind picked up.

"By the gods," Sinfjotli exclaimed. "Sigurd, what's happening to the sky?"

High above them, the dark emerald clouds of Helheim whirled in an unnatural dance of madness. When the dance stopped, the clouds resembled an image: an exact imitation of Hel's split face looking down on them from above. The entire undead army kneeled in fealty before the beautiful and grotesque face in the sky.

"You insignificant flea." Hel's voice echoed through the draugirs. *"Look around. I am everywhere. Helheim is my realm. I am the River Gjöll flowing below you. I am the draugirs you're fighting so valiantly against. I am the snowflakes falling upon your face. I am the very air you breathe. I am everything you see."*

Sigurd spent a few moments steeling his nerves. "You mentioned that you wanted to discuss something. Talk then."

"There's no need to feign bravery, Sigurd. You already know this struggle is pointless. Even with a valkyrie on your side, you are just delaying the inevitable. As mighty as you are, there are only three of you. No matter how hard you try, you'll never be able to keep up with my endless droves of draugirs. You'll collapse long before my soldiers stop pouring onto the bridge."

"If you're so certain of victory, explain why they are still alive?" Brynhild challenged, defiantly stepping forward. Her voice was stern and steady, and Sigurd silently envied her courage. "You speak of these draugirs as if they are a threat. But we have faced far more powerful foes than these walking corpses."

The clouds forming the eyes of Hel's deformed face narrowed. The face grinned, clearly intrigued by Brynhild's presence and courage.

"Well, well, this is an interesting development. I sensed a valkyrie enter Helheim earlier and battle Móðguðr. But it didn't realize it was you, Brynhild. Why are you even fighting alongside these two? Did the All-Father send you to rescue them?"

"Odin and the Aesir had nothing to do with this," Brynhild answered proudly. "I am here of my own volition."

"Interesting," Hel mused. *"Well, to answer your previous question, they are still alive because I've been holding back. I found their journey and struggles through my realm quite entertaining, and I didn't want to spoil the show by ending things too quickly."*

"You think this journey through Helheim was entertaining?!" Sinfjotli growled.

"*Of course,*" Hel affirmed. "*The emotions and despair you experienced through those visions were* delicious *to watch. And your battles against Siggeir and Heidrek were quite fascinating as well. And your valiant struggle on this bridge, while pointless, has been quite admirable. But now, this desperate struggle against* my *army has become tedious and meaningless. Surely you've realized that by now? Even if you somehow fight your way back to Gnipa Cave, what then? My nephew Garm will never let you pass. You'd have more luck convincing his older brothers Sköll and Hatti to stop chasing the sun and moon than bypassing him without my permission.*"

"If our situation is as hopeless as you say, then why did you stop your army's advance?" Sigurd demanded.

"*Because I want to talk,*" Hel reiterated. "*As I said before, I'm willing to resolve this diplomatically. I need your full attention for what I'm about to offer.*"

Sigurd glanced at the undead army. They were all kneeling in fealty with their heads bowed low. They were as motionless as statues except for their mouths from which Hel's collective voice emanated. Sigurd knew they could all spring to life and resume the onslaught any second. But for now, it seemed Hel truly had no intention of harming them. So, for the nonce, they were safe.

"I'm listening," Sigurd humored. He decided to play along to buy them more time to recover their strength and allow their wounds to finish healing.

"*Listen closely because I will only make this offer once.*" Hel forewarned. "*If you surrender now and submit, I will grant you amnesty. I won't even kill you. I will treat you as my honored guests and grant you both places of honor within my palace. I will allow you to take Siggeir's place and become generals of my army. You will be given command of the largest army in all the nine realms to conquer and be able to fulfill whatever you desire. As a bonus, Sigurd, I'll even bring your wife, Gudrun, back to life. Or you can keep that valkyrie Brynhild as your paramour. Or you could keep them both if you'd prefer. As for you, Sinfjotli, I have a special offer for you. You both have many old enemies here in Helheim besides Siggeir, who's no longer with us. King Lyngvi, King Hunding, King Högne of Östergötland, King Granmar and King Hothbrodd of Södermanland, and so many others who are all here in no small part thanks to you and your family. If you surrender and swear to serve me, you'll be free to torment them and the rest of your family's many enemies to your heart's content."*

"Are you serious?" Sigurd asked in disbelief. "You're trying to tempt us with the prospect of tormenting our past enemies?"

"*Of course,*" Hel replied. "*That* is *your heart's greatest desire, after all.*"

"What?!" Sigurd exclaimed incredulously. "Why would I **ever** want such a thing? I'm not a sadist."

"*Oh, but you are!*" Hel cackled. "*You just haven't realized it yet. Let me prove it to you.*"

A thick emerald fog rose from the River Gjöll below the bridge and enveloped them. Another vision conjured up within the mist.

CHAPTER FORTY-ONE

BLOOD EAGLE

In the vision, Sigurd saw a younger version of himself sitting on a tree stump, carefully cleaning Gram. Sigurd stared in disbelief as he saw his younger self in his vision. The image was so vivid it was as if he was looking into a mirror. He couldn't help but feel nostalgic as memories flooded his mind. The twenty-year-old version of himself was splattered head to toe in blood, and all around him were piles of corpses. Instead of golden chain mail, he was dressed in dark steel plate armor. Sigurd vaguely recalled this was the armor he used to wear before he discovered his golden hauberk in Fafnir's cave. His eyes weren't snake-eyed yet, but they still had the sharp amber pupils he'd been born with.

As the young Sigurd carefully cleaned Gram, a young man in chain mail armor approached him. He was accompanied by twelve other warriors. As he carefully made his way to Sigurd through the corpses, his subordinates began clearing them from the muddy battlefield.

"That was one mighty battle, Sigurd!" The man exclaimed as he handed a wineskin to Sigurd.

"Indeed, Folan." Sigurd smiled. He took a long, greedy sip from the wineskin. "How many men did we lose?"

"We are still doing a headcount. But it looks like we lost about two thousand," Folan reported.

"I see," Sigurd sighed sadly. "May the valkyries guide them to Valhalla."

"But compared to Lyngvi's losses, it's an overwhelming victory!" Folan smiled. "Lyngvi's army outnumbered us four to one, and we *still* triumphed. I wager you yourself killed more men than any of us combined! I saw how fiercely you fought alone against the Sons of Hunding and Lyngvi's sons. That was the finest fight and swordplay I have ever seen. Grandfathers will sing stories about this battle and your bravery to their grandchildren for generations to come."

"We're not finished," Sigurd replied grimly. "Not until Lyngvi is dead!"

"Aye," Folan nodded. "The men are still looking for him. It was a massive battlefield, so there was a chance that he might have escaped. But he couldn't have gotten far... Oh, look there! Is that Vafi?"

A burly man with a dented bear-shaped helmet approached them as Folan's men finished clearing the corpses. Like Sigurd remembered, he had a crazed look in his green eyes and four jagged scars running down his face.

Sigurd grinned while gazing at Vafi's scars, remembering the notorious encounter with the bear where he had showcased his audacious and reckless bravery and earned his nickname. Later, when Sigurd and his army made landfall in the Lands of Hunding, Vafi the Loon was the second person to set foot on the beach after Sigurd and charged alone into a band of thirty warriors, which resulted in Sigurd having to come and reinforce him before he got himself killed. To Vafi's credit, he always fought bravely and effectively against any foe, proving he had the making of a mighty warrior behind his recklessness.

"Lord Sigurd," Vafi bowed respectfully.

"Stand up, Vafi," Sigurd commanded, rolling his eyes. "We've been friends since we were children. You don't have to bow or shower me with honorific titles because my mother is a queen."

Vafi removed his dented helmet. "I call you 'lord' out of respect and awe, not etiquette or tradition. You fought like a god of war today. Some of our comrades believed you were Týr himself and come to aid us in victory."

"I examined the bodies of some warriors you cut down," Folan added. "Their wounds... I've never seen anything like it. They looked as if someone had killed them using a scythe blade mounted upright."

"All right, you two, that's enough flattery," Sigurd chuckled. He tossed Vafi the wineskin and waited as his friend took a long, greedy sip. When he finished, Vafi wiped his mouth clean and gave a crazed smile.

"I've just received a report from Birna. They found Lyngvi."

Sigurd stood up with anticipation. "Is he still alive?"

"The coward surrendered without a fight," Vafi reported, dissatisfied. "He threw down his sword and surrendered to Birna's band as soon as he heard that you'd slain all his sons and nephews."

"Good! I was worried someone might've done him in and denied me the chance to kill him myself. Tell Birna to bring him here!"

Vafi nodded and left to retrieve the vanquished king. Sigurd turned to the warriors amassing around him. "You all fought well. I am proud of all of you. And I know our fathers, brothers, and forefathers who fell at the hands of this insidious tyrant are smiling in Valhalla. In appreciation for your exemplary service and valor, I will grant you all my share of the plunder from this day to be divided equally amongst you. Moreover, I shall send compensation to our fallen comrades' widows, children, and families."

"Yyyyrrrraaaaahhhhh!" the soldiers cheered.

Sigurd raised his hands to silence the rowdy fighters. "And should any of you wish to remain behind and become lords of this land we have conquered, know that you shall have the full backing of myself and House Yngling to carve out your own domains."

"Hhhhhhhaaaaaa!" Everyone cheered louder than before.

"But we're not finished yet," Sigurd continued. "There is one last foe who must perish. The mastermind behind that insidious invasion that claimed the lives of so many. Birna captured him alive and is bringing him to me. This is the moment I've dreamed of! Today is the day I avenge my father, grandfather, and their kingdoms!"

As the troops cheered thunderously, Sigurd turned to Folan. "The time for justice is fast approaching, my friend. Are you ready?"

Folan studied Sigurd with trepidation. His fear most likely came from the disturbing smile etched across Sigurd's face. "What do you intend to do to him?"

"I haven't decided yet," Sigurd admitted. "I want to look him in the eyes before I make that decision."

"Whatever you decide... remember that he's only a man," Folan advised.

Sigurd stared incredulously at Folan. "Only a man? Have you forgotten what he and his army did to our families and kingdom? Both of our fathers lost their lives during Lyngvi's invasion, and our mothers were forced to flee in exile. When Lyngvi couldn't locate my mother, he returned and brutally sacked Hunaland. He murdered countless men, including my brother Hámundr. Your older sister was raped to death by his nephews, along with countless other women. After everything he did, you still think Lyngvi is *only* a man"

"I despise him just as much as you do, Sigurd," Folan admitted. "But I also realize that Lyngvi is still a man, just like every other warrior we slew today. Don't forget that. Don't sink to his level of cruelty."

Sigurd didn't respond. He turned away and watched anxiously as Vafi returned, escorting Birna and her war party. But his smile vanished when he saw the person his friends were dragging through the muck.

As Sigurd watched the vision unfold, he recalled how he'd grown up hearing about how King Lyngvi lusted after his mother Hjordis, started an unprovoked war against his father, and brutally sacked both Hunaland and his grandfather's kingdom when he couldn't find her. Since he was young, Sigurd had imagined Lyngvi as a colossal warrior king with shoulders as broad as mountains and arms thick as tree trunks. He had dreamed of facing the wicked king in glorious combat and avenging his father's death.

But the king whom Birna's band hauled before him that day was not the mighty warlord he'd envisioned. Instead, the king being dragged by his arms through the muck toward Sigurd was a dirty, fat old man with a long, muddy white beard that reached past his waist.

Even now, Sigurd felt disgusted by the pitiful sight of Lyngvi. But seeing Birna put Sigurd in a better mood.

She was never the most attractive woman. Birna was at least six feet three inches and looked ungainly when she wasn't wearing armor due to her muscular physique. Many men and noblewomen in Denmark mocked her for her muscular appearance, height, flat chest, and boyish appearance. Admittedly, her large, beautiful blue eyes and shoulder-length brown hair did little to compensate for her coarse features. Her face was broad and rough, her cheeks were covered in dozens of freckles, her teeth were prominent and crooked, and her nose had been broken more than once.

But Sigurd never cared about Birna's appearance or what anyone else said about her. Her courageous heart and determination always made Sigurd smile. She was a better and stronger warrior than most men and raiders. And she was an excellent strategist, which was why Sigurd had made her his right-hand woman over dozens of other seasoned warriors. In fact, it was thanks to Birna's strategy that Sigurd triumphed over Lyngvi's much larger army.

Birna nodded respectfully to Sigurd and then ordered her men to present their prized captive. They threw the defeated and broken king to the muddy ground at Sigurd's feet.

As soon as he saw Sigurd, Lyngvi shat his breeches. Sigurd could still remember the foul smell emanating from his pants that day.

"It's you," Lyngvi gasped. "Those eyes... it really is you! You're Sigmund's son. Please have mercy, my lord!"

"Is this him?" Sigurd whispered. "Is this really King Lyngvi of the Hundings?"

"Aye," Birna affirmed, dissatisfied, as she removed her boar-shaped helmet.

"Is *this* the man who lusted after my mother, invaded my father's kingdom unprovoked, and sacked both Hunaland and my grandfather's kingdom?!" Sigurd yelled. "Is *this* the man who raped so many women he earned the moniker 'Lyngvi the Lusty?' **This** is the king who defeated my father in battle?! He's nothing but an old craven with one foot in the grave!"

"I'm as disappointed as you are, Sigurd." Birna scowled. "But he's definitely the king. Look at his fancy robes. He's even got this crown to prove it."

So saying, Birna reached into her satchel and produced an elaborate golden circlet engraved with multicolored jewels. She tossed the crown to the muddy ground at Sigurd's feet.

Sigurd studied the crown momentarily until a scowl appeared on his face. "That crown! You forged that crown from the riches you plundered from my father's kingdom, didn't you? And those princes I slew were your bastard sons born from the many women of Hunaland you raped, weren't they? Answer me!"

Sigurd stomped on the crown, crushing it and smearing its precious gems into the mud.

Lyngvi squealed like a frightened pig. Birna's men laughed and let go of his arms to collect the precious gemstones. As soon as they released him, the old king collapsed face-first onto the muddy ground. He looked up at Sigurd, then pressed his face back into the mud. He seemed to be trying to bury his face in the muck just to avoid looking at Sigurd. Or perhaps he was trying to asphyxiate himself to avoid torture.

"I ordered you to speak!" Sigurd yelled, kicking the old man in the ribs. Lyngvi cried out in pain and vomited on the ground.

Then, the old king did something unexpected. Without looking up, he kneeled and pressed his forehead against the muddy ground and in prostration.

"Mercy, my lord," Lyngvi pleaded. "Please! Grant me mercy, and I will give you anything you ask."

The young Sigurd had a bewildered expression on his face. "Mercy? You dare beg for mercy? I just informed you I killed your sons and massacred your entire army, and the first words out of your mouth are, 'Mercy, my lord?' You, of all people, have the cheek to beg *me* for mercy after **everything** you did to *my* family?!"

"You misunderstand!" Lyngvi said. "You've destroyed my army. You've butchered my sons and ended my line. I know I won't live to see the sunset this day. But please...I humbly ask that you give me a sword. Allow me to die on my feet in combat, and I will give you anything you ask. Take my kingdom, my riches, my women, or my gold. But please allow me to die in combat like my brother, father, nephews, and sons before me!"

Sigurd's eyes narrowed. "You already had that chance, and you threw it away. Vafi told me you threw down your sword and surrendered to Birna as soon as you learned I'd killed your sons and nephews."

"That's because I refuse to be killed by ordinary soldiers!" Lyngvi glanced at the warriors picking up gemstones and scowled with disgust. "I am a king! I refuse to be slain by the hands of ordinary vagabonds like these. Especially at the hands of a woman!"

"You hear that, Birna?" Vafi teased. "He thinks you're a woman."

Their comrades chuckled. Birna shot Vafi an angry look and then redirected her ire at Lyngvi. "Is that why you surrendered without a fight? Were you troubled to see a woman on the battlefield and in command of the army that encircled you? Do my prowess and courage not speak for themselves? I haven't achieved this level of strength only to suffer your misogynistic bullshit!"

"Don't get the wrong impression, *woman*." Lyngvi spat. "You savages butchered my sons and nephews and ended my line. When I die, the noble blood of Hunding will be extinguished. I won't let it perish in disgrace. If I am going to die, it's only fitting that I am slain by Sigmund's son and a fellow king in combat."

"That would be more interesting," Vafi mused as he studied an azure sapphire retrieved from the muck. "Two kings fighting each other to the death would make for a much better song for future singers."

"The duel would last no longer than a verse of the song," Folan pointed out. "Even if we gave him a sword, Gram would shear through it and Lyngvi's armor much like a bird's wing through the air."

"It would still be remarkable," Vafi insisted. "It's not every day you get to see a noble prince personally slay an evil monarch in battle. That usually only happens in songs or stories."

"This is your victory, Sigurd," Birna reminded. "This is your decision to make. How shall we deal with this craven?"

The young Sigurd glanced at the old man kneeling in the muck. "Before I make up my mind, there's a question I'm going to ask you. Think carefully before you answer."

Sigurd leaned forward and looked Lyngvi dead in the eyes. The old man shivered from his gaze. "Where do you think we are right now?"

Lyngvi furrowed his brow. "I—Is this some cruel jest? I thought..."

"I won't ask again," Sigurd warned. "*Where* do you think we are?"

Lyngvi curled his lips back into a sneer. "Where else? At the backwater borders of my kingdom. It's..."

"Wrong!" Sigurd exploded. "These are not your lands! They never were! You haven't built an inch of this land! All you did was desecrate it, rape it, and raze it to the ground!"

He thrust out a finger, pointing at a barren patch of scorched earth visible beyond the tree line. "That razed earth is where my grandfather's castle once stood. These lands were once his kingdom! This land was beautiful. It was the pride and joy of so many, for it was created by generations of hard work by the Volsungs and the people who supported them. But then you and your insidious army came and ruined it all! The fields, villages, castles, people, and all their splendor were razed by your greed! Not a single flower can even grow in that place because you and your vicious nephews salted it out of spite!"

Sigurd clenched his fists so hard his palms started bleeding. "The same is true for Völsung City. I can't even say, 'I visited the ruins before I embarked on this campaign,' because there's nothing left! You and your vicious marauders brutally sacked it until not even a single stone remained!"

Sigurd picked up the crushed crown from the muck. "You prance around wearing crown jewels you didn't earn. You dare claim lordship over lands that existed long before you came, which you conquered through deceit, treachery, and atrocities. You murder people who look at you the wrong way and justify it by claiming they're rebels. You're a plague, Lyngvi! A raging wildfire who destroys everything that falls within your sight!"

Sigurd contemptuously tossed the dented crown aside. He glared silently at the shivering old king for some time and then closed his eyes. "Want to know something funny, Lyngvi? Ever since I was a boy, I dreamed of doing precisely what you're begging for. I dreamed of facing you in mortal combat and avenging my family. But now that I see what a sniveling coward you are, I've changed my mind."

The color drained from Lyngvi's face. He lowered his head so much that it made an audible impact against the ground. "No, please don't...!"

"You think pressing your head against the ground will change my mind?" Sigurd growled. "Pathetic. Our fathers, brothers, and countrymen died with dignity. Look at you, prostrating yourself in the muck and begging for your life."

"Please!" Lyngvi rubbed his forehead against the muddy ground as if trying to lower his head even further. "I will give you anything you ask. Take my kingdom, my riches, my women, or my gold. But please allow me to die in combat like my brother, father, and sons before me!"

"My father was worth far more than any amount of wealth," Sigurd said in a chilling tone. "And you took him from me along with my brother and kingdom. The debt you owe can never be repaid through gold or silver."

"Please!" Lyngvi pleaded. "I'll give you anything you wish! Name it! I'll do whatever it takes to appease you!"

"NO!" Sigurd snarled. He grabbed the old man by his long white hair, lifted him off the ground with one hand, and stared into his dirty, mud-smeared face.

"You had no mercy for my father, my grandfather, my brother, their kingdoms, or their people, you monster! So you'll have none from me! I won't allow you to die a dignified death. You will die screaming like the sniveling craven you are!"

Sigurd contemptuously tossed the old man on the muddy ground and ordered his men to hold him in place. Then Sigurd walked away toward a towering white oak tree that had miraculously survived the great battle. He drew Gram and sliced through the trunk with a single swing. The giant ashen tree tumbled to the ground.

Sigurd inspected the stump, which had a two to three feet diameter. He counted the rings and determined that the tree was approximately one hundred twenty years old.

"This'll do," Sigurd decided. "Bring him here. Tear off his robes and shirt and tie him down on his stomach to this stump."

Lyngvi went pale as he realized Sigurd's intention. The old king rose to his feet and struggled with a sudden surge of strength and adrenaline that gave the men who seized him great difficulty.

"No, please!" Lyngvi screamed. "Not the blood eagle! Anything but that!"

"You forfeited your right to a quick and painless death when you sacked my father's kingdom unprovoked," Sigurd replied in a calm and unsettlingly cold voice. "You threw away the chance to die bravely in combat when you surrendered to my men out of fear and arrogance."

Lyngvi scanned the crowd of warriors amassing around him. "Help! Help, please!"

"There's no use begging for mercy now, old man," Birna warned. "Who would come to your rescue? The slaves you tortured, violated, starved, raped, forced to live in squalor, and sent to the front lines to be slaughtered in this battle? Your army, who lies dead and scattered in pieces in the muck? Your vicious nephews and sons whom Sigurd slew? There's no escaping your fate now, Lyngvi. The least you can do is die with some small measure of dignity."

Lyngvi didn't heed her warning. Sigurd watched as the men dragged the thrashing and screaming king to the stump. They tore off his muddy garments, laid him on his stomach over the tree stump with his back facing the sky, and tied his hands and feet around the stump's base.

When Lyngvi was restrained, Sigurd stooped down to get one last look at the terrified king. "Take a good look at my face, old man, because it's the last one you'll ever see. The last thing you'll see is the son of Sigmund and Hjordis and a grandson of Völsung and Eylimi, smiling as you die!"

"Please don't do this!" Lyngvi pleaded. "I beg you...!"

"Folan, I'm sick of hearing him squeal," Sigurd said. "Stuff a rag in his mouth and make sure he doesn't say anything else. And if he spits it out, cut off his cock and balls and stuff them in his mouth instead."

After Folan reluctantly did as he was told, Sigurd stood over the decrepit king and unsheathed Gram. Behind him, two ravens perched themselves on the branches of the fallen oak tree, watching intently.

"This is for you, Father," Sigurd muttered as he glanced at the red sky. He stabbed Lyngvi near his tailbone and slowly sliced Gram upwards across the bound king's back. The old king shrieked like a stuck pig as Sigurd pried open his back and severed all his ribs from his spinal cord, leaving his internal organs on full display.

Sigurd ordered his men to pour a saline stimulant into the gaping wound as he began pulling out Lyngvi's ribs one at a time and spreading them out like giant fingers, making it appear as if Lyngvi had a pair of bony wings jutting from his back. Lyngvi remained alive throughout the entire procedure, squealing and crying like a stuck pig. He wouldn't die until Sigurd decided it was time for the coup de grâce.

As Sigurd watched his younger self pour salt into Lyngvi's wounds and pull his ribs from his spinal cord, he felt queasy and disgusted. He never regretted carving the blood eagle on Lyngvi's back and never would. But seeing it happen now before his eyes in the third person...was quite disturbing. Vafi and many of his comrades were smiling with glee as they watched the pitiful king suffer. But both Birna and Folan looked horrified. Not by the bloody execution but by the unsettling smile plastered across the young Sigurd's face and the crazed look in his amber eyes as he made the wicked old man suffer.

The vision faded as the young Sigurd reached into Lyngvi's flesh, tore out his lungs, and spread them over the ribs.

CHAPTER FORTY-TWO

THE TRUTH ABOUT YOURSELF

"*N*ow, *do you understand what I've been trying to demonstrate?*" Hel asked as the fog faded away, and Sigurd found himself standing back on the Gjallerbru. "*You and your brother thrive on punishing your enemies. You, grandsons of Völsung, are vengeance* **incarnate**! *You would enjoy punishing your family's countless enemies in my realm just like you enjoyed killing that defenseless old man, Sigurd.*"

"You're wrong!" Sigurd shouted at the deformed face in the clouds. "Lyngvi wasn't helpless or innocent. He had gathered an army of over sixty thousand warriors to face us! He was a coward who relied on others to fight his battles. But that didn't make him any less bestial. He and his army plundered, violated women, and butchered even the old and children wherever they went. I did what honor demanded and punished him accordingly."

"*Lyngvi deserved to die for his cowardice and his many sins. That much is true.*" Hel conceded. "*But did you have to execute him so savagely? Did his many crimes grant you the right to deny him a quick death and torment him instead? You could have beheaded him, stabbed him in the heart, let him drink hemlock, or allowed him to die fighting you as he wished. Instead, you chose to carve the blood eagle on his back. You chose to end his life through the most terrible and painful form of execution among the Norse. What does that say about you, Sigurd? From my view, it seems you are just as cruel as he was.*"

"Don't you *dare* compare me to that monster!" Sigurd snarled adamantly. "I am *nothing* like Lyngvi! His crimes were innumerable, and the atrocities he committed against Hunaland and its people were unspeakable. And he justified it all by claiming he'd been unable to marry my mother!"

Hel cackled. The sound echoed like a blast of thunder as the laughter emitted from the draugirs on the Gjallerbru.

"I must admit it never ceases to amaze me how short-sighted you humans can be. Even with your telescopic vision and clairvoyance, you're still incapable of seeing reality or truly understanding your enemy, Sigurd."

"What's that supposed to mean?" Sigurd demanded.

"You've never tried to see things from your enemy's perspective," Hel elaborated. *"Your mother told you that Lyngvi invaded and sacked Hunaland because Sigmund denied him the chance to marry her. But doesn't that explanation seem odd? Do you truly believe a whole army would obliterate an entire kingdom so savagely because their king was denied the right to marry a woman he lusted after? The truth is far more nuanced than that."*

Another cloud of emerald fog rolled from the river below and conjured a vision.

When the vision began, Sigurd found himself standing in the middle of an enormous field of corpses. It was the aftermath of a great battle. The bodies spread out in all directions. Some were stacked in huge piles over two stories tall. There were even some corpses with their heads plunged into the earth. It appeared they had made pits for themselves and suffocated themselves to escape the carnage.

Sigurd covered his mouth. He could practically taste the iron of the blood spilled around him. He was a battle-hardened veteran of many battlefields. But the horrifying scene before him made his stomach churn. The bodies all around them had been murdered in every cruel way imaginable.

"What is this?" Sigurd demanded.

"I—I know this place!" Sinfjotli gasped. "This is where Helgi and I fought King Högne of Östergötland, King Granmar, and Prince Hothbrodd of Södermanland!"

"Correct, Sinfjotli," Hel's disembodied voice confirmed. *"This is the aftermath of the bloody Battle of Frekastein. I'm certain you still have nightmares from this battle. On that fateful day,* over one hundred thousand men participated in a savage battle over a petty spat between Helgi and Prince Hothbrodd over who could marry King Högne's daughter, Sigrún. At its conclusion, only you, Helgi, Sigrún, and her younger brother Dagr survived. That's the story you told your father and countrymen when you returned to Hunaland. But it's not true. There were not four survivors of that battle. Not four, but six.*"

As Hel spoke, one of the mountains of corpses stirred. Two dead bodies rolled away as a small boy, barely twelve years old, crawled his way through the bodies to the surface. He was wearing a mail shirt with the image of a horned bull's skull on a red field. Another identical-looking boy in the same outfit joined him, and they stared at the field of corpses in collective horror. One brother wept. But the other boy's eyes were full of burning hatred as he gazed upon the vast field of corpses. The pure hatred in his eyes could have burned the world to ashes.

The vision changed, and Sigurd saw the two boys traveling through a market town and returning to a castle. Cheering crowds of women and children praised the lads as they made their way through the streets shouting: "Miracle Children."

Then Sigurd saw one of the boys seated on a large iron throne with a spiky iron crown on his head. His brother, several jarls, and many other boys wearing noble garments bent their knees and swore fealty to him.

"By sheer chance, Lyngvi and his twin brother Hávard survived that battle as well," Hel explained. *"You see, Lyngvi, his twin brother Hávard, their other brothers Álfr, Eyiólf, Hjörvard, and their father Hunding had also*

participated in the battle as allies of King Granmar. Both Lyngvi and Hávard were knocked unconscious early on and survived the carnage by unknowingly being buried beneath a pile of corpses. They lost their father, brothers, and all of their comrades in that savage battle. When the two boys returned to their homeland, they were proclaimed heroes, miracle children who had survived the war. The widows and orphans of all the men who had died in the battle flocked to his kingdom, declared him their king, and urged him to one day avenge the carnage Helgi had inflicted upon their people tenfold. It was a goal he passionately accepted.

"So you see, Lyngvi's motives for obliterating Hunaland weren't as simple as him being denied a woman he lusted after." Hel continued. "He had lost his father and all but one of his brothers in a savage battle that spawned from a petty squabble between Helgi and Hothbrodd over who could marry a princess. From his view, and the perspectives of the men who served him, the carnage he inflicted against Hunaland and the Volsungs was justified retribution for the carnage Helgi and his warriors had inflicted upon him and his people years earlier."

"What are you trying to say, Hel? Sigurd demanded. "Why show us this?"

"I'm trying to make a point," Hel answered. *"To you, the carnage you inflicted on Lyngvi and his army was justice for the sack of Hunaland. But the same could be said about Lyngvi and his army. To Lyngvi and his forces, the sack of Hunaland was vengeance for all their fathers, uncles, sons, and brothers who died in Helgi's stupid war. The flag, the clan, and the kingdom may differ, but the motivation is always the same. You mortals always seek retribution for some perceived wrong and think of yourselves as the victims.*

"I've watched you humans slaughter each other in your endless wars for millennia." Hel continued. *"There's rarely a clear-cut determination of a good and bad side in a war. But in my view, it doesn't matter who draws first blood. And it's pointless to try pinpointing who caused what exactly. Once war breaks*

out and blood gets spilled, both sides become evil. And the wicked all end up here in my realm."

"Enough!" Sinfjotli bellowed angrily as the vision and fog faded. "Why are you doing this, Hel? Why do you keep conjuring these visions?"

"To show you the truth about yourselves," Hel replied calmly. *"From the moment we parted ways at my palace, every spirit you encountered along the way and every vision you've experienced has been arranged by me to demonstrate one irrefutable fact: You are both monsters! Through your past actions, I've demonstrated that there is no difference between you, Siggeir, Lyngvi, or any of your family's enemies. You are just as monstrous as they were, if not worse. The punishment you wrought upon your enemies went far beyond the pale of vengeance and into the realm of sadism. And it's not just your enemies you destroy. You bring death, calamity, tragedy, ruin, and despair wherever you go, especially to those you love most. Look at what happened to your poor wife and her family, Sigurd. Would Gudrun even be here in* my realm *if it wasn't for you, Sigurd? Would her family's bloodline have been extinguished if it hadn't been for you and your cursed gold? Would she have lived such a tragic life and committed such unforgivable sins if she had never met you?"*

"I...I..." Sigurd stammered.

"And it's not just you two, Every descendant of Völsung harms those they love even long after they're dead. Think about it. Your brother Helgi's actions set the downfall of the Volsungs into motion and continued to affect you long after he died. If Helgi hadn't gone to war over the right to marry Sigrún and killed so many men, Lyngvi and his army wouldn't have had any reason to sack Hunaland so savagely. Because of Helgi's actions, you inevitably lost your father and grandfather. And your brother Hámundr then closed the curtain on Hunaland and its people when he made a final stand at Völsung City rather than fleeing with your mother."

Sigurd was at a loss for words. Hel was right. Helgi and Hámundr *had* set the downfall of the Volsungs into motion. And *he* set the destruction of the Gjukungs into motion by bringing them Andvari's cursed gold.

"Just accept the truth, Sigurd," Hel urged. *"You and Sinfjotli are in my realm because you belong here. That is why your struggle until now, while admirable, has been in vain. You cannot escape your true nature. You cannot escape my army. You cannot bypass my nephew Garm. And you cannot escape me! And even if by some miracle you escaped, what then? Do you believe the Aesir would ever welcome monsters like you into Valhalla with open arms? No! Those halls are reserved for the righteous dead! They'd reject you just as they rejected me and my brothers long ago. In their eyes, you and I are both monsters."*

A cloud of emerald fog rolled up from the River Gjöll. But rather than conjure a vision, it washed over and enveloped the draugirs kneeling on the front lines. Their skeletal bodies vanished beneath a veil of smoke as they all took on human appearances.

A gasp escaped Sigurd's lips as he stared at them. Some were warriors he fought long ago. But most looked like simple tillers, farmers, traders, fishermen, and other simple folks who had probably never held a weapon in their lives.

"Would these men and women be here in this state if you hadn't corrupted them?" Hel challenged.

"Corrupted them?" Sinfjotli questioned. "How?"

"Some of these draugirs were warriors who perished by your blades," Hel explained. *"But many were men, women, and children who died because of your actions in Hunaland and Gautland. You left those kingdoms in ashes and bones when you departed. Many here perished from starvation, banditry, rape, cannibalism, or got murdered by the men you led. They died blaming you for their fate, and their anger and resentment only grew after death and turned them into these creatures. You two are like a plague, spreading death and misery wherever you go. And you corrupt everyone you come into contact with. Would*

these people have become draugirs if you hadn't instilled so much hate and anger within them?"

Sigurd staggered backward as he stared at the draugirs' bitter faces and contemplated everything Hel had said and shown them. His whole life, his comrades and countrymen had hailed him as the greatest of heroes. But until this very moment, he had never considered his enemies' perspectives. As he thought about it more, and all of the people he had killed in his quest for what he perceived as 'justice,' a sickening feeling grew in his stomach. Was he truly as monstrous as Hel claimed? Could a hero like him also be the blackest of villains?

"You're the true monster here!" Sigurd shouted. "You find joy in the suffering of others. You treat people as if they're toys for your amusement and turn them into these wretched creatures!"

"Calling out someone for being more evil than you doesn't make you a good person, Sigurd," Hel countered. *"It just makes you a hypocrite and further proves my point."*

Sigurd had no retort for that. He looked back at the draugirs and felt their angry gazes. Some had a welcoming look in their eyes as if they were thinking, "Join us. You belong here."

"Even if what you say about us is true, I could never serve someone as wicked as you!" Sinfjotli declared.

As soon as he finished his bold declaration, every draugir on the bridge raised their arms and slammed the butts of their weapons against the ground. The sound echoed across the bridge like rolling thunder and caused the deck of the Gjallerbru to vibrate beneath their feet. It was a chilling reminder of just how outnumbered the three of them were.

"Tread carefully," Hel cautioned cooly. *"I made a* very *generous offer. Don't throw away your only chance at clemency for your crimes over your pride and misplaced loyalty to the gods who forsook you."*

"But even if we wanted the things you've offered, how could we trust you to keep such grand promises?" Sigurd challenged.

"Because unlike you, Sigurd, I always fulfill my promises." Hel sneered. *"Didn't Baldur tell you about the time I almost freed him? I promised Hermod and the Aesir that I would release him if all creation wept for Baldur, proving that he was as universally beloved as they claimed. And I almost did if one giantess hadn't stubbornly refused to weep. Regardless, I always honor my promises, no matter how grand or small they may be. Accept my offer, and I will give you everything you want. Refuse, and you'll die and be subjected to unimaginable torment. I'll give you a moment to consider."*

As Sigurd weighed their options, he used his superhuman vision to gaze past the army of the undead to the shores of Náströnd and Gnipa Cave beyond the northern horizon. Thousands of draugirs were standing on the shores of Náströnd, waiting to make their way onto the bridge. And Garm was still standing guard outside his cave.

Hel was right about one thing. Even if they made it back to Gnipa Cave, there was no way they could get past all those draugirs and bypass Garm, even with Brynhild's assistance. And the army advancing from the south would soon be upon them. They could keep fighting for a week, a month, or an entire year. But in the end, they would be defeated by Hel's undead army. Their situation seemed utterly hopeless.

Sigurd glanced south and thought about Baldur's ship. Even if he accepted Hel's offer, he'd rather stay with Baldur and his family on the Hringhorni. It was a far cry compared to the Hall of Heroes, but it was a pleasant place. Staying there with Gudrun and their children didn't sound too bad.

Suddenly, horrific images from the night her brother Guttorm murdered him flashed through his mind. As Sigurd struggled to suppress the traumatic memory, he recalled something Hel had mentioned when they first met on Baldur's ship and the name she called him.

"Before I make a decision, Hel, I want you to answer a question," Sigurd announced. "Consider it a token of good faith."

"Very well, speak," Hel acquiesced.

"Why did Guttorm murder me?" Sigurd demanded. "When we first met on Baldur's ship, you claimed I broke a promise, and it led to my demise. And from the moment I met you on Baldur's ship, you, Siggeir, Garm, and everyone here in Helheim have called me an oath breaker. Was that the reason he murdered me? If so, what oath did I break? I don't remember ever reneging on a single promise to him or anyone else in my life."

"Even now, you still *don't remember?!"* Hel's laughter echoed from the entire undead army, making the bridge beneath them shake. *"I have to give Grimhild credit. It seems the potion she tricked you into drinking was so powerful that it still affects you even in death."*

Sigurd blinked. "Grimhild? Are you referring to Gudrun's mother? What does she have to do with it?"

"Everything, my dear," Hel replied dryly, as if she were being asked to explain the punchline of an obvious joke. *"In a way, that woman was the author of all your pain. But she alone isn't the sole reason you died. And in the grand scheme, her son Guttorm was nothing but a cat's paw used as a tool for another's vengeance. If you want to know the architect of your demise and the true reason you were cast into Helheim, just look to your left."*

"What are you talking about? There's no one else here on this bridge aside... from...Brynhild?" Sigurd looked back and forth between the valkyrie and Hel's cloud face. Fear and suspicion swelled inside him as he realized what Hel was insinuating.

"Brynhild, w-what is she saying?" He demanded nervously.

"Must I spell it out for you?" Hel ridiculed. *"Brynhild conspired to have you killed. You swore an oath to her and inevitably broke it after your mother-in-law wiped your memory. Honor demanded your death, so she urged your brothers-in-law to kill you* after *convincing them that the honor of the*

Gjukungs was at stake. Although her husband Gunnar and his brother Hagen agreed to betray you a second time, they refused to do the deed themselves. They had both sworn oaths preventing them from harming you. But their younger brother, Guttorm, was not bound by any oath. They built up the boy's courage by feeding him morsels of wolf meat and snake, filling his heart with malice toward you, and pressing him to carry out the deed for their family's honor. And one fateful night, Guttorm murdered your son, Sigmund, covered his face in the child's blood, then snuck into your room and drove his sword through your chest as you slept."

Sigurd stared at the valkyrie, feeling confused and conflicted. Brynhild had saved them from the draug leading Helheim's army. She had spent the past hour and a half bravely fighting alongside them against the endless army of death in an unwinnable battle. And yet, according to Hel, she had conspired to have him murdered? None of it made any sense.

"Brynhild, is she telling the truth?" Sigurd demanded. "You urged Guttorm to murder me in my sleep?"

"I deny nothing," Brynhild admitted in an emotionless voice. "But I had nothing to do with your son's death. Guttorm did that out of envy and spite toward you."

"But then, why are you helping us?" Sigurd paused as an old memory resurfaced in his mind.

In the weeks leading up to his death, Brynhild was very reclusive and hostile toward him. It all started after she went bathing with Gudrun and several other women in the Rhine one day. When she returned, her skin was pale as a corpse, and her eyes were rage-filled. That night, she barricaded herself in her bedroom and refused to leave, eat, or drink anything. Her weeping and shouts of pain echoed throughout the halls of the Gjukungs like a howling beast. Her husband Gunnar feared she had caught an illness or gone mad and asked Sigurd to check on her. But when he entered her room, she screamed and raged at him, calling him a liar, and then forced him to leave. From there, her terrible mood worsened and darkened the hall of King Gjuki. Whenever Sigurd saw her, she would glare at him with eyes like a viper's, fiercer than his own snake eyes. And the few angry words she spoke to him were full of venom and hate.

"In the days leading up to my death, you told me: 'I want nothing more than to drive a sword through your heart,'" Sigurd recalled. "But if you despise me so much, why are you helping me now? I... None of this makes sense!"

Brynhild studied him with an unreadable expression. Then she did something unexpected. She stepped forward and kissed Sigurd on the lips. At that moment, all of Sigurd's doubts disappeared. It felt like he was once again under the effects of Baldur's aura. All of his feelings of confusion, shame, guilt, betrayal, suspicion, and fear vanished. Their kiss was the only thing that was real.

"I told you before that I'm on your side," Brynhild reminded as she pulled away. "I will *always* be by your side. Should you choose to accept Hel's offer and remain in Helheim, then I shall join you. If you wish to continue fighting and escape this realm, then I shall fight alongside you until my last breath. And if you die fighting and suffer under Hel's torment, then I shall remain by your side and suffer along with you. No matter what you decide, I will be with you, Sigurd. Nothing will stand between us anymore."

"How touching," Hel taunted. *"Well, Sigurd, I've answered your question. Now, what is your answer? Will you serve the Aesir who sent you here? Or rule like kings in Helheim?"*

For a moment, Sigurd seriously considered accepting. He gazed at the vast undead army. It seemed this was their one and only chance at staying alive. And truthfully, the prospect of bringing Gudrun back to life was tempting.

As he contemplated his options, he looked back at Brynhild and felt a twinge of guilt. If he accepted Hel's offer, he'd also damn Brynhild to this hellish realm. By her own proclamation, her fate was in his hands. He glanced at Sinfjotli and thought about their brothers, his parents, grandparents, and other family members who were probably in Valhalla. What would they do in this situation?

And then it dawned on him. Hel's offer had been sincere. But there was one thing Hel hadn't mentioned. As he thought about his father and forefathers, Sigurd realized what Hel's unspoken demand in exchange for all this would be. And the terrible price he would pay one day.

"Your offer is generous," Sigurd admitted. "But there is one thing you're not mentioning. If we agree to these terms, we will become generals of your army, but also your subordinates bound to obey your every command. That means we'd have to fight for the forces of chaos against the Einherjar at Ragnarök."

"And what's wrong with that?" Hel asked. *"You'd oversee the largest army in all the Nine Realms and partake in the greatest battle of all time. The dead would obey your every whim."*

"Our father, brothers, and the rest of our family are amongst the ranks of the Einherjar in Valhalla!" Sigurd hollered angrily. "If we accept this offer, you'll force us to fight against them at Ragnarök. If that is the price we must pay, then I refuse!"

"I refuse as well!" Sinfjotli proclaimed adamantly. "I've done many things I'm not proud of. But I will **never** raise my sword against my father or forefathers."

"Then you will DIE *here!"* Hel screamed through the draugirs. *"And all your courage and suffering will have been for* NOTHING!"

A loud explosion detonated in the distance. Sigurd gazed past the northern horizon with his superhuman vision and watched as the enormous grave mounds and mountains near Garm's cave cracked open and exploded in columns of green flame. Nine pairs of giant skeletal arms clawed their way out of the flaming fissures. When they stood up, Sigurd felt his heart freeze over in terror.

"No," Sigurd gasped in disbelief. "It can't be! Those are Jötnar, the frost giants!"

"Indeed," Hel spoke through the draugirs. *"You'd be astonished how many Jötnar the Aesir have killed over the years. They all wind up here and become the strongest soldiers in my army."*

Hel wasn't exaggerating. Every giant's body was severely damaged, indicating it had died violently. Some even had parts of their skull caved in, presumably from Thor's hammer, Mjolnir. Others were nothing but towering, skinless bodies of exposed muscles and bone. But they all looked like formidable, seasoned warriors.

The largest giant, easily over two hundred feet tall, raised its war hammer and bellowed a dreadful roar. The entire army of draugirs stood up and surged forward as the giants began advancing along the Gjallerbru.

CHAPTER FORTY-THREE

THE WRATH OF THE UNDEAD JÖTNAR

As the army of the dead surged forward with renewed zeal, Sigurd, Sinfjotli, and Brynhild rushed forward to counter them. But this time, the draugirs were fighting more viciously, attacking without any care for their own safety. They weren't even afraid of Brynhild anymore. They charged at her in overwhelming numbers even as she effortlessly cut them down by the dozens. Perhaps they feared punishment from Hel far more than getting cut down by a valkyrie.

Even worse, they had become more orderly and disciplined. It was as though an enormous swarm of insects...or rather an entire colony, was rushing toward them in a coordinated assault with the sole purpose of slaughtering them. No living army could ever hope to match these undead foes' zeal and renewed resolve.

Before long, the Jötnar Hel had summoned arrived at their position and wrought devastating havoc. Against one giant alone, the three of them might have stood a chance. But they could do nothing against nine of them *and* the entire army of the undead attacking simultaneously. With these mighty giants bolstering their ranks, the undead ferociously beat them backward, forcing them to retreat farther south and destroying chunks of the bridge in the process.

Although the army washed away everything in their path like an evil flood, there was one silver lining to this dire situation. Because of their immense size, the undead giants had to travel along the bridge in a single file, attacking only one at a time. But that proved to be a small mercy. The bridge buckled beneath their feet every time one of them stepped forward. Each time a giant attacked, its club snapped the arches and towers of the Gjallerbru like twigs and caused the bridge deck to buckle like a rippling flag in the winds. The quaking always knocked Sigurd and Sinfjotli off their feet, after which they got dogpiled by hordes of draugirs and were forced to either claw and slash their way to freedom or wait until Brynhild had a chance to rescue them before resuming battle with the undead elsewhere.

Sigurd knew that to have any chance at survival, they had to take out the Jötnar. But slaying them proved to be quite an arduous task. Even Brynhild struggled against these titanic foes. She managed to kill one on her own after a vicious assault, but the others proved harder nuts to crack. She changed tactics and tried attacking their pressure points and other vital areas needed for movement. But that proved useless.

"That method won't work!" Sigurd called out as she jammed her weapons into a pressure point beneath one giant's armpit. "Both the draugirs and giants can't feel pain and will continue attacking no matter what we do to them."

"You have any better ideas?!" Brynhild shouted back."

Sigurd ground his teeth. He had no answer to that. He had no solution to any of this. He'd been fighting for hours. While the Apple of Idun he'd eaten earlier prevented physical exhaustion, it couldn't help his mental state. Battle fatigue, despair, and guilt bogged him down like heavy anchors. He couldn't think clearly or for very long in between defending himself from countless undead foes. He could only attack, hack, stab, and then take a quick, inadequate breath before fending off the next attacker.

They were trapped on a giant bridge suspended hundreds of feet over a green river with an army of undead and giants bearing down on them from the north and a second larger army advancing upon them further south. What could they possibly do?

A shadow rippled across Sigurd's face. He had only seconds to duck as something swooped over him and racked his back.

"Argh!" Sigurd fell flat on his face as pain surged through his body. He glanced up and saw a flying undead dragon gliding overhead around the bridge. Its wings stretched out wide, and its bony, scaley frame seemed to shimmer in the green-tinted sunlight, reflecting an iridescent array of colors.

The reanimated dragon was a terrifying sight to behold. Its bones were massive and appeared to be made of blackened steel. Its bat-like wings attached to its shoulders were tattered and torn, with sharp talons at the end of each bone. It had four other fleshy legs, which looked thick and powerful despite their rotten appearance, ending in razor-sharp claws that glinted in the light. Its bony, fleshless skull was elongated and adorned with curved horns, while its empty eye sockets glowed with an eerie red light. The dragon's spine curved, giving it a hunched appearance. Its long, sharp teeth seemed to be perpetually borne in a menacing snarl, and it also had a long, spiky tail made from innumerable bones.

"Shit," Sigurd cursed as he watched it circle around the bridge. The skeletal dragon that he and Sinfjotli had faced earlier had been purely bone, with no muscle mass or flesh at all, leaving it grounded due to a lack of usable wings. However, this beast had just enough skin, muscle, membrane, and flesh to allow it to take to the air. It couldn't breathe fire, but that didn't make it any less dangerous.

It took longer than he would have liked to stand up again. The wound to his back was deep. Brynhild was busy fending off the giants, so Sinfjotli was forced to cover Sigurd from the undead army for a full minute as his body repaired itself.

When he finally managed to stand and retrieve his swords, he saw Sinfjotli on his knees, covered with a dozen different stab wounds. Then, it became Sigurd's turn to defend his brother from the undead army's wrath.

As Sigurd fended off the relentless onslaught of draugirs that attacked him from every direction, another shadow enveloped him. He realized the skeletal dragon was making another strafing run at him, and he knew he had to act fast to avoid being taken down. Sigurd dodged to the side with lightning-fast reflexes, avoiding the dragon's deadly talons.

The draugirs weren't as lucky. The dragon's talons eviscerated them, shredding through rotten flesh, bones, and armor like silk. It flapped its wings, gaining altitude and letting dozens of draugirs it had impaled fall onto their undead comrades below.

"We need to take that flying lizard out!" Sinfjotli shouted as he resumed fighting off the draugirs. "Can't you do anything?"

"It's staying out of my range," Sigurd informed. "My swords won't reach it from this distance, and Brynhild's busy dealing with the giants. I could probably reach it if I had something to jump off..."

He trailed off as a roar made the bones in his chest thrum as it echoed across the bridge. A hulking sixteen-foot-tall troll was pushing and hacking its way through the undead ranks toward them.

Sigurd smiled. "That'll do nicely."

He stood his ground, letting the troll approach while also fending off the undead surrounding him. The troll swung its club, smashing through its undead comrades. Sigurd dodged only as much as was necessary without attacking. He held back, waiting for the right moment to strike. He had to bide his time and wait for the perfect opportunity.

When the skeletal dragon made another strafing run, Sigurd seized the moment and attacked the troll. He swung his sword with deadly precision, striking the troll's weak spots and dealing heavy blows.

Predictably, it swung its club down in a sweeping motion. Sigurd sidestepped out of danger, then sprinted up the troll's arm like a surefooted goat. As the troll instinctively stood, Sigurd swung his swords across its rotten neck, lopping its head clean off its body.

As the head fell to the earth, Sigurd stood on its shoulders and turned to face the incoming dragon. The troll's headless body remained upright long enough for Sigurd to use it like a springboard, launching himself higher into the air. He brandished his swords, carefully aiming as he zipped safely past the dragon's head. With lightning-fast reflexes, Sigurd sliced off the dragon's right wing, sending it spiraling out of control. The dragon let out a fierce roar as Sigurd landed gracefully on the ground. The troll's headless body toppled behind him as the dragon soared over it, careening out of control.

Sigurd expected it to crash headlong into the ranks of the undead army. But the flying lizard managed to stay aloft far longer than he expected, likely because of how fast it had been flying. As it veered left over the side of the bridge, its bony tail slammed against the leg of the first undead giant currently fighting Brynhild. The impact caused the giant to lose his balance and topple over the side of the Gjallerbru, plummeting into the River Gjöll.

Sigurd's heart surged with pride at the fortuitous results. But he ignored the falling giant and focused on his prey. With a screech of agony that mingled the giant's bellows, the helpless dragon crashed into the River Gjöll and sank into the jade water. Half a heartbeat later, the dragon burst from the green water, struggling and writhing in agony. The beast's screams sounded almost human. The skin, muscles, and flesh sloughed off its bones and dissolved. Soon, even the bones began to sizzle and dissolve as if they were in acid. The dragon stopped struggling and sank back beneath the emerald water.

As Sigurd watched it dissolve, a realization dawned on him. Asking Sinfjotli to cover him, he fought his way to the side of the Gjallerbru and peered down where the giant had fallen. As he suspected, the Jötnar was also dissolving in the green river, thrashing and uselessly swinging its sizzling limbs, struggling to escape the acidic water until it succumbed and sank beneath the surface.

That gave Sigurd a fantastic idea as Brynhild appeared beside him and slashed the draugirs amassing around him to dust with her wings.

"Good job eliminating the big one," she praised. "He was giving me fits."

"Save the praise for after we make it out of Helheim," Sigurd urged as he stabbed an incoming draugir in the forehead. He withdrew Tyrfing and pointed the sword at the eight remaining giants advancing toward them. "Don't bother trying to cut the giants down. Just knock them over the side of the bridge. The River Gjöll will take care of the rest."

"Good plan," Brynhild muttered. "Maybe now you and Sinfjotli can topple them as well."

"That's the idea," Sigurd muttered as he reentered the fray.

***

Slaying a giant was no easy task. But toppling a giant was quite simple. Take out its feet or sever its Achilles tendons, and even the tallest titan would fall.

Sigurd watched as Brynhild swiftly approached the giant from the side, her wings and weapons at the ready. With quick and precise movements, she managed to hamstring the giant, causing it to lose balance and topple over the side of the bridge. The giant fell into the vast river below, disappearing into the murky green waters.

"Three down, six to go," Sigurd sighed as he hacked off a draugir's legs and thrust Tyrfing into its sternum.

She wouldn't be the only one to slay a giant. Sigurd and Sinfjotli managed to topple one of them, too. After Brynhild took a break from fending off the giants and performed several strafing on the front lines, thinning the undead army's numbers, Sigurd saw an opportunity to take out the nearest giant.

He and Sinfjotli fought their way through the undead army with renewed purpose, vigor, and unparalleled bravery. The clanging of swords and the screams of the undead filled the air as the two warriors pushed forward, their eyes fixed on their goal. Despite being outnumbered, they never wavered and continued to slash and hack their way through the undead horde. They both received horrific injuries for every step they took, but they pushed through the pain.

Thankfully, the giant didn't even see them approaching as it was busy trying to swat Brynhild out of the sky. It didn't even notice when Sigurd and Sinfjotli took positions on either side of its feet. Sigurd then mutilated its right foot with his swords while Sinfjotli shoved his shoulder against the side of its other foot.

The original plan had been for Sinfjotli to transform into a wolf and tear out its Achilles Tendon with his teeth. Regrettably, that wasn't an option. Sinfjotli had already transformed three times today and couldn't shapeshift again without his body tearing itself apart at the seams. But that proved a minor inconvenience. Although he couldn't risk transforming a fourth time, Sinfjotli could still topple this mighty foe. Using his increased weight, momentum, and the thick layer of ice coating the bridge's deck, he managed to sweep the giant's remaining leg out from under it, causing it to trip on its side.

They watched, wounded and on their knees from scores of injuries, as the giant slid off the bridge, desperately trying to grasp something before he splashed into the River Gjöll. The undead began to dogpile the two of them until Brynhild swooped down and hacked them to pieces, giving them time to heal and recover.

They continued targeting their legs and picking off the giants one by one in hit-and-run attacks until only two were left. Unfortunately, they were the tallest, most powerful, and smartest giants Hel had summoned. After seeing so many of their brethren cut down, the last two Jötnar worked out their strategy and put a stop to it. They stopped advancing and kept their distance, sweeping their clubs across the bridge's deck to prevent them from getting any closer while letting the other undead advance toward the three of them. They also guarded their flanks, making it far too risky for Brynhild to try crippling their legs by attacking midair from the sides. The whole debacle soon transformed into a frustrating stalemate.

"We're wasting time and energy fighting those last two giants!" Sinfjotli seethed. "The army from the south will be upon us soon. And those titans keep pushing us back closer to them. Hey, Miss Valkyrie, can't you use those pretty wings and fly us *around* those undead giants?"

"Not possible," Brynhild informed as she landed between Sigurd and Sinfjotli, slashed an ogre in half with her weapons, then spread her wings and unleashed a volley of serrated metal feathers that tore through the ranks of the undead like hot shrapnel. Many draugirs and undead monsters were caught in the crossfire and collapsed onto the bridge. More soldiers soon reinforced their front line. But for the moment, she'd bought them some time.

"I can certainly carry Sigurd," Brynhild admitted. "But not you, Sinfjotli. Since you're a skinchanger, you're a lot heavier than you look. I cannot carry you both together."

Sigurd narrowed his eyes, sensing a veiled offer. She could carry Sigurd to safety, but Sinfjotli would be left on his own. For a moment, Sigurd wondered if Brynhild might snatch up Sigurd and fly away, leaving Sinfjotli to his doom. But he reassured himself that wasn't the case. By her own admission, Brynhild was here for him. Sinfjotli was secondary to her, but she didn't seem like the type to abandon a comrade in the middle of battle. Or, at the very least, she knew Sigurd would never forsake his brother.

"Also, we're too far from the Náströnd," Brynhild added. "Even if I could carry you both, we'd have to fly two hundred fifty *miles* over an army of angry draugirs and giants. We'd be easy targets. They'd swat us into the River Gjöll before we got anywhere *close* to the Shore of Corpses."

Sigurd ground his teeth. She was right. The risk of getting swatted out of the sky was too significant. While they slew the giants and toppled them into the green river, Sigurd had realized that their greatest danger fighting in the middle of the Gjallerbru was not the giants, the draugirs attacking them with renewed vigor, or the encroaching army from the south. It was the River Gjöll beneath them. If they fell into the river, it would result in instant death. As it was, the only thing preventing them from falling into the green river was the Gjallerbru. But the giants had wrought such destruction with every attack that Sigurd feared the bridge would soon collapse.

But falling into the river wasn't the only danger. Sigurd glanced at Hel's cloudy face, observing their desperate struggle from above. Baldur claimed Hel couldn't personally harm Sigurd or Sinfjotli at the Bridge of Judgment because of his protection brand. But that protection didn't extend to Brynhild. Hel had been relying on her army to deal with Sigurd, Sinfjotli, and Brynhild while she observed. But if Brynhild took to the air with both of them and tried to circumvent her army and flee north, there was a genuine possibility that Hel could unleash her wrath on Brynhild, whereupon Sigurd and Sinfjotli would either fall to their deaths or into the clutches of her waiting army.

"Escape isn't an option," Sigurd surmised. "Retreat isn't an option. Negotiation is no longer an option. Our only path to salvation is to fight!"

"We won't get anywhere with those two colossi blocking our path," Sinfjotli reminded as he cut down an incoming draugir.

"They certainly are a nuisance," Sigurd concurred as he shoved Gram hilt-deep into another draugir's skull. He pulled his blade free and glanced up at the hulking giant standing about a hundred yards away from them.

The last two giants had ceased approaching and took up an excellent defensive position. They now kept their distance and opted to let their undead comrades advance and deal with Sigurd, Sinfjotli, and Brynhild while they kept the three of them from approaching their vulnerable feet by sweeping their clubs across the bridge's deck. They also guarded each other's flanks, making it far too risky for Brynhild to try crippling their legs by attacking midair from the sides.

She'd already tried to flank them, only for one of the giants to swing his club and score a direct hit, sending Brynhild crashing into the deck below. She'd hit the icy deck hard and coughed up blood but worked through the pain and kept fighting.

"Can't attack them from the sides, can't attack them from above, can't approach them on foot, and we can't attack their feet anymore..." Sigurd surmised. "So our only option is to hit those sons of bitches head-on at eye level."

"How?" Sinfjotli questioned. "They've already gotten used to Miss Valkyrie's attacks. They'll see her coming and swat her down before she can..."

"Brynhild won't need to," Sigurd interrupted. "I'll handle this."

Sinfjotli and Brynhild stopped fighting and looked at him as if he'd gone mad.

"How exactly do you intend to pull that off?" Sinfjotli questioned. "I don't see a pair of wings on your back."

"I've got a plan," Sigurd explained. "It's the stupidest, most outrageous thing I've ever thought of, but it's all we have left to try."

Sinfjotli and Brynhild shared a look. She shrugged and muttered, "It's worth a shot. What else do we have to lose besides some more ground?"

"Our lives," Sinfjotli replied. "But that's a small price to pay. You seem fully prepared to stake your life on this solution, Sigurd. So let's hear this idea."

***

"That is a terrible plan!" Sinfjotli shouted as Brynhild carried Sigurd high into the sky.

Sigurd felt his heart race with exhilaration as Brynhild flew higher and higher above the Gjallerbru. He couldn't help but look down and watch as Sinfjotli became smaller and smaller, bravely holding off the draugirs below. With each beat of Brynhild's mighty wings, they were getting closer and closer to their destination—the nearest giant.

They were already a hundred feet away and at eye level with the giant when it finally noticed them approaching. The giant tried swatting them out of the sky, but Brynhild dodged the strike as she swooped toward it.

"Here goes nothing!" She cried as she hurled Sigurd through the air straight toward the giant's face. Sigurd rocketed through the air with both his swords drawn and bifurcated the giant's head.

The decapitated giant toppled over the bridge into the River Gjöll below. Sigurd hadn't lost an ounce of momentum from splitting its head in half as he continued rocketing through the air toward the last remaining giant.

Unfortunately, the final Jötnar had seen him coming and was already swinging its giant club at him. The club was the size of a three-story building, and Sigurd had no way to dodge it while he was speeding toward the titan in midair.

So Sigurd didn't bother dodging. Instead, he tried something crazy. He reversed his grip on Gram so the blade pointed down along his right arm while holding Tyrfing properly in his left hand. He then twisted his body midair in a spinning motion as the club was about to hit him.

Gram and Tyrfing sliced through the club, splitting it in half. Sigurd kept spinning and zooming forward and, with astounding speed, sliced up nearly the entire length of the giant's arm. He then ran up the giant's shoulder and stabbed it in both of its eyes. The giant roared in anger as Sigurd clambered to the top of its head.

As he stood on top of the giant's skull, Sigurd glanced north and noticed something beyond the vast undead army that made his heart sink. But he didn't have time to despair. He had to take out this giant before it caused any more chaos.

Then Sigurd did something absurd. Something that only he and his light, razor-sharp swords could do. He reversed his grip on his blades, jumped off the top of the giant's head, and jammed his swords deep into the giant's skull. With nothing but empty air beneath his feet and two sharp swords as his anchors, Sigurd started sliding down the giant's head and neck. The increased gravity helped Gram and Tyrfing effortlessly shred through the giant's rotten flesh as Sigurd slid down its head, neck, and back. Seeing an opportunity, Sigurd readjusted his grips so that his swords severed every single one of the giant's vertebrae as he slid down its back.

Sigurd began free-falling after slicing through its waist and plummeting toward the undead sea. Draugirs and trolls broke their orderly formation and reached up at him with grasping hands, hoping to tear him to pieces as he fell. But they wouldn't get the chance. Brynhild swooped in and caught him before he could fall victim to the grasping hands below. Meanwhile, the blind and now crippled giant fell to its knees and then toppled over the side of the bridge. Even if it was undead, with its spinal cord and nerves shredded, it could only bellow uselessly as its paralyzed body plummeted toward the River Gjöll.

As it splashed into the green waters, sending up a gout of water that was as tall as the Gjallerbru's towers, Brynhild flew Sigurd over the angry undead army and landed next to Sinfjotli, who had hitherto held the line against the draugirs, but at a grievous price. His shoulder was gashed, several holes were bored into his abdomen, a spear protruded from his leg, and one arm was twisted in the wrong direction.

Anyone who gazed upon Sinfjotli's gory state would have mistaken him for an actual corpse even though he was standing and fighting. And indeed, Sinfjotli would have been doomed without the Apple of Idun's healing properties. Slowly, the bleeding stopped, and the wounds sizzled as Sigurd and Brynhild held off the army, giving Sinfjotli a chance to recover.

"That was spectacular, Sigurd!" Sinfjotli congratulated as he pulled the spear from his leg, surged forward, and blocked an incoming strike from a draugir. "I've never seen anything like that before!"

Usually, Sigurd would have agreed and beamed with pride. But Sigurd found no joy or fulfillment in what he'd done, not after what he'd seen atop the giant's head.

"We've got a serious problem," Sigurd warned as Brynhild swooped by and eradicated an entire troop of draugirs, shredding through their bodies like a scythe through wheat. "Those giants Hel summoned destroyed a huge section of the bridge farther north!"

"What?!" Sinfjotli screamed wide-eyed.

"The Gjallerbru isn't even connected to the Road to Hel anymore!" Sigurd elaborated. "They've cornered us and cut off our only path of escape. Even if we broke through this sea of the undead warriors by some miracle, we'd still be trapped."

Sigurd turned north and used his superhuman vision, gazing past the undead army. With the towering giants no longer blocking his view, he could now make out the distant land of Náströnd. Thousands of menacing draugirs, trolls, hellhounds, and several giants stood on the mainland, their advance halted by the broken Gjallerbru. A considerable portion of the deck that was supposed to connect the bridge with the continent had been obliterated, leaving nothing but a cavernous gap between the amassed army and their undead comrades already on the bridge. Sigurd couldn't help but imagine the frustration of the draugirs gathered around Gnipa Cave as they peered southward, catching only a blurry glimpse of the bridge's towering support columns three miles away, with the now impassable River Gjöll standing between them and their targets.

"Why would Hel go this far?" Sinfjotli wondered aloud in between strikes. "If the bridge is destroyed, then the souls of the dead can never cross over to the city."

"Actually, they will," Brynhild corrected as she fought. "The Gjallerbru exists on both a physical and astral plain. The dead spirits exist on this astral plane, so even if the physical bridge is destroyed, souls can still cross to the city unimpeded."

"But this still doesn't make sense," Sinfjotli insisted. "The draugirs and her army need the bridge intact. If it's destroyed, then the reinforcements for Hel's army coming from Náströnd can't reach us."

"At this point, they no longer need any reinforcements," Sigurd interjected. "There are over two hundred *miles* of undead warriors between us and the gap in the bridge. That's enough to keep us busy until the army from the south comes upon our rear. And that army is fresh and strong."

"This has been Hel's strategy all along!" Sinfjotli realized. "We'll be trapped between both armies and cut to pieces in a pincer maneuver, crushed like insects between a hammer and anvil!"

"And even if by some miracle we eradicate this army advancing from the north, the bridge is still destroyed," Brynhild added. "I can't fly you both across such a vast distance on my own strength, so we'll have nowhere to go. Once the southern army reaches us, they'll cut us down or push us off the bridge into the River Gjöll. It seems we're doomed no matter what we try."

"There must be something we can do!" Sinfjotli despaired. "But what?"

"We keep fighting," Sigurd vowed. "We keep fighting until our last breath!"

CHAPTER FORTY-FOUR

WINDS OF SALVATION

After thirty more minutes of fruitless fighting passed, Sigurd accepted that the tide had turned against them. They had fought the dead to a standstill. The southern army was rapidly approaching. And the bridge had been partially destroyed. Making it back to Gnipa Cave was no longer an option. Their only goal now was ensuring they lost no more ground to the northern army.

Desperate to stem the tide, Sigurd and Sinfjotli took defensive positions along the bridge's parapets. Brynhild zipped back and forth between them, desperately mowing down the draugirs whenever they were about to be overwhelmed. But it was futile. The encroaching army from the south had already reached the bridge's center and would soon be visible over the horizon. It was only a matter of time before they reached them.

Then something unexpected happened. As Sigurd finished dispatching a pack of snarling hellhounds, he heard a booming voice in his head. *"How pitiful."*

Sigurd ceased fighting and blinked in surprise. "What? Who said that?"

There was no response. Sigurd didn't hear anything else over the clamor of battle all around him. Hel was still watching their struggle in the clouds above, but this voice sounded far too loud and masculine to be hers.

Did I hear a voice? Sigurd wondered. *Or did I just think I did?*

"Damn it, Sigurd, pay attention!" Sinfjotli shouted, snapping Sigurd back to reality. Sigurd realized he was on the verge of being overwhelmed by a hoard of fifteen draugirs. Thankfully, Brynhild glided over and fought on his behalf, giving him enough time to regain his composure.

"Sinfjotli, did you hear that voice just now?" Sigurd asked as he resumed fighting.

"What are you talking about?" Sinfjotli shouted back. "I can't hear much over the clamor of this battle. Did Hel speak privately to you?"

"No, it wasn't her," Sigurd affirmed between strikes. "The voice was too masculine."

Sigurd heard the voice again. *"Look at them floundering. A bastard born from incest and an oath breaker who died in his bed are both struggling to escape Helheim? How foolish and arrogant! What makes them think they alone can escape this realm when so many others before them have failed to do so?"*

"Whose voice is that?!" Sigurd demanded. "Why am I the only one hearing this voice? Show yourself!"

"Interesting," the voice mused. *"The oath breaker waving his swords is screaming like a madman now. He must have finally realized this struggle is hopeless and gone mad with despair."*

Sigurd felt an intense, icy gale bluster against his left side. He turned west and saw an enormous silver eagle perched on a mountain of corpses on an islet in the River Gjöll about a mile from the bridge. It was the same eagle they'd spotted earlier after Baldur had tossed them like javelins across the Gjallerbru.

"Honestly, what are they hoping to accomplish?" The voice mused. *"The dead giants have already destroyed part of the bridge and severed their only path back to Náströnd. And the southern army is closing in on them. They have no means of escape or hope of winning, but they still fight on. Why? What is driving them? I suppose I'll never understand humans."*

The eagle ruffled his feathers, and another mighty, icy gale slammed into the bridge. The gust was so powerful that several draugirs on the army's left flank were sent flying over the parapets and into the river below.

Hræsvelgr the Corpse Eater must be the one who's speaking. Sigurd realized as he resumed fighting. He faintly recalled Baldur's explaining that there were three eagles perched in Asgard, Jotunheim, and Helheim that could produce powerful gales that blew throughout Midgard and the other Nine Realms.

Baldur mentioned Hræsvelgr is the source of all the chilly winds here in Helheim, Sigurd recalled as he fought. *And I'm the only one who can hear him speak because I can communicate with birds.*

Just then, an insane idea clicked in Sigurd's head.

"Sinfjotli, Brynhild!" He shouted. "I have one last idea. Brynhild, I need you to fly me over to that eagle. I know you can't fly us both, so could you please hold off the army until we return, Sinfjotli?"

"Oh sure," Sinfjotli replied sardonically while cutting down an ogre. "I'll just hold off the entire army of the dead while you and your sweetheart waste time chatting with a fucking eagle!"

"Quit complaining and do it! Here, you can use this." Sigurd tossed Gram to Sinfjotli and ran over to Brynhild. As he sprinted toward her position, he sheathed Tyrfing. He wouldn't be drawing that cursed sword again. He was about to gamble his life on one insane plan.

Meanwhile, Brynhild was busy casting what appeared to be a powerful runic spell. She had drawn floating runic symbols into the air with her swords. Now, she was holding her weapons toward the sky and fully extended her gilded wings as she chanted an incantation:

"Let the heavenly bodies shine now: The sun that shines down upon a brilliant world, the stars that keep watch while the world sleeps, the moon that guides us through the darkest night. Gather into a river of light, converge where I point, and shine forth to perish the fangs of evil! Guð Mölbrotna Stjarna!"

As Brynhild chanted, the floating runic symbols in the air glowed brightly. Her swords and metallic wings vibrated and hummed with power. High above them, the emerald clouds of Helheim tore apart and engulfed the Gjallerbru in a mastodontic, circular pillar of light. The radiant light was so intense Sigurd had to cover his face or risk being blinded.

When the pillar of light faded away, Sigurd discovered that Brynhild had eliminated over a mile of draugirs with that single mastodontic attack and obliterated a massive section of the Gjallerbru. There was now a gaping hole in the center of the bridge almost three hundred feet in diameter where the pillar of light had struck.

As Sigurd admired the destruction Brynhild had wrought, the valkyrie dropped her swords and doubled over, wheezing. She insisted she was fine, but the attack had taken a lot out of her.

"Why the hell didn't you use that attack earlier?!" Sinfjotli demanded.

"I was saving it as a last resort," Brynhild panted. "Honestly, I wasn't sure I *could* cast that spell here. Helheim is Hel's territory. She'll ensure I can't use that spell again. Regardless, this will give you some breathing room, Sinfjotli."

Their reprieve wouldn't last for very long, however. The undead army had already recovered and was skirting around the hole's perimeter.

Brynhild cast a doubtful look at the giant eagle. "Sigurd, are you sure about this?"

"It's a desperate and insane plan, but it's all I can come up with," he admitted. "Besides, we're out of time. Look there! The other army is already appearing over the southern horizon. We've got about five minutes before they reach us."

"I understand." Brynhild sheathed her weapons, wrapped her arms around Sigurd's shoulders, spread her wings, and took off. As Sinfjotli fought for his life against the northern army, Brynhild and Sigurd sailed west over the River Gjöll toward the giant silver eagle.

Hræsvelgr narrowed his eyes. <What's this? The oath breaker and valkyrie have abandoned the kinslayer and are flying straight toward me. Are they trying to save their skins? Or are they planning to use me somehow? Perhaps they intend to subjugate and force me to fly them out of Helheim? I think not! Be gone, vile sinners!>

Hræsvelgr flapped his still-furled wings ever so slightly. With that slight minimalistic movement of his wings, the giant eagle blasted them with a hurricane-force gale. Sigurd felt his skin go numb from the freezing air as layers of ice formed on his armor. Brynhild flapped her wings furiously, struggling to stay aloft in the gale-force winds. Back on the bridge, the wind sent a legion of draugirs flying off their feet and hurled them into the River Gjöll below. Sinfjotli was too heavy to be whisked away by the intense winds, and he quickly resumed his last stand against the dead.

"Are you all right?" Sigurd asked worriedly when the winds subsided.

"For now," Brynhild wheezed as she flapped her wings.

"Can you get me closer? I need to look him in the eyes."

"I'll try, but I don't think I'll be able to withstand another blast of wind like that. Whatever you're planning, you'd better do it quickly before he can swat us down."

Brynhild continued flying closer to the eagle's head. In response, Hræsvelgr unfurled one of his gigantic wings, intending to send them spiraling to the River Gjöll below with another blast of wind.

<You are an oath breaker who died in his bed!> Hræsvelgr reprimanded while extending his wing. <And the other one on the bridge is a bastard kinslayer born of incest! Monsters like you belong here in Helheim. Accept that truth and perish!>

Hræsvelgr was about to flap his wing to send them spiraling into the River Gjöll when Sigurd raised his hands and shouted: "Wait! You're right! I am an oath breaker who died in his bed. And my brother Sinfjotli is indeed a bastard born from incest. But we are both so much more than our sins."

Hræsvelgr's gigantic eyes dilated in shock. His wing stopped moving mid-flap, but Brynhild and Sigurd were nevertheless blasted by another powerful gust of air. This one was even more powerful than before. As Brynhild struggled to stay aloft, she clutched Sigurd's waist so tightly that his legs became numb. Yet the valkyrie remained in the air.

When the mighty gale subsided, Sigurd saw Hræsvelgr staring at them. His eyes were dilated, and he looked stupefied.

<You can...understand me?> Hræsvelgr asked, astonished.

"Yes," Sigurd smiled. "I've always had a special connection with birds."

<No being...even Hel herself has never conversed with me before. Who *are* you?">

"I am Sigurd the Dragon Slayer, the son of Sigmund and Hjordis. And it's like you just said. I am a murderer and an oath breaker who died in his bed. I am a vengeful killer who tied an old man to a tree and tore out his lungs like it was the most righteous thing in the world. I killed my teacher and took his brother's hoard of cursed treasure, bringing misery to me and everyone I loved. And I did many other things I'm not proud of. But I am so much more than that. I fought for the weak, fed those who were starving, and liberated those who had been enslaved. I fought for the downtrodden and in causes that I deemed just. I fought for justice and defended the fatherless and oppressed."

<Why?> Hræsvelgr pondered. <Of all the souls in Helheim, why have the Aesir helped you to get this far?>

"I have no idea why scoundrels like me and my brother have been given a second chance over all the other souls in Helheim. I don't know why we have been revived. And I don't know *why* we have been given this chance to escape Helheim. All I am certain of... is that whoever did this believes in us. They believe we can escape and are worthy of this second chance. And so does Baldur, Nanna, Hodr, Gudrun, aunt Signy, and Heidrek. They all believe that we can escape Helheim. That is why we will never stop fighting.

We *will* escape Helheim. We owe it to whoever revived us and everyone who put their faith in us to escape Helheim."

Hræsvelgr's eyes dilated. He seemed taken aback by Sigurd's response.

"Earlier, you wondered aloud why my brother and I keep struggling against such unwinnable odds," Sigurd reminded. "I'll give you an answer now. We fight for glory. We fight for our freedom. We fight for our family, our friends, and for all those who put their faith in us."

Hræsvelgr narrowed his eyes. <Why are you telling *me* all this?>

<Because we need your help,> Sigurd replied, speaking in the bird's language.

Brynhild raised her eyebrows and stared at him as if he had gone mad, likely wondering why he was chirping like a bird. But Sigurd couldn't afford to explain the situation to her. He knew he had to be careful. Hel's face had begun to reform in the clouds above them, and he couldn't risk her overhearing his plan.

<My help?> Hræsvelgr repeated, confused. <How do you expect *me* to help you?>

<You're one of the three eagles whose cawing will announce the beginning of Ragnarök,> Sigurd continued, still speaking in the bird's language. <But, you're also responsible for creating the cold winds here in Helheim. All you'd have to do is flap your wings, creating a gust of wind powerful enough to scatter Hel's army and send us rocketing out of here. That'll give Brynhild the boost she needs to carry my brother and me out of this realm.>

"Hurry up, Sigurd," Brynhild warned. "We don't have time."

She wasn't exaggerating. The southern army was already within a mile of Sinfjotli, who was currently fighting for his life against the northern brigade. The second army was a spine-chilling sight. There were at least fifteen draugs on the front lines, including the one Brynhild had dispatched earlier. If Sinfjotli got caught in a pincer maneuver between those monsters, they wouldn't be able to save him.

But they were in more pressing danger. Hel's face had fully reformed in the clouds above them. Giant bolts of green and black lighting crackled from the dark clouds.

"I don't know what you and Hræsvelgr are discussing," Hel admitted. *"But whatever it is, I'm putting a stop to it. Hræsvelgr, I order you to swat them from the sky!"*

Sigurd almost wept tears of joy. In her hubris and self-assurance, Hel had unknowingly ordered Hræsvelgr to do the very thing Sigurd was asking of the giant eagle.

Hræsvelgr glanced toward the bridge and silently watched as the second army approached Sinfjotli's position. <You humans are such fascinating creatures. You've piqued my interest, Sigurd, son of Sigmund. As I recall, no soul that died a dishonorable death has ever escaped this realm. Your struggle up until now has been spectacular to watch. If you manage to escape Helheim, I imagine your journey will become even more interesting. So be it. I'll help you.>

Hræsvelgr stood from his perch of corpses and fully extended his wings, which were so large that they blocked out the entire western horizon. Hel's army on the Gjallerbru momentarily paused to see the source of the shadow that had just blanketed them in darkness.

"Hræsvelgr, what are you doing?" Hel demanded. *"I told you to swat them out of the sky. I didn't order you to go all out like this! You'll destroy the whole Gjallerbru at this rate!"*

<You're the first person to ever speak to me, Sigurd, son of Sigmund,> Hræsvelgr said, ignoring Hel's desperate inquiries. <And this is the first real conversation I've ever had with another being. Although Hel will probably punish me for doing this, I'll help you out of gratitude and curiosity. I'm eager to see what kind of journey you'll have if you escape.>

<Thank you,> Sigurd said. <I hope we'll live up to your expectations.>

<Just so you know, I won't restrain myself,> Hræsvelgr warned. <And if you die from this...well, I'll still get to feed on your corpses. We'll most likely never meet again, Sigurd the Dragon Slayer. But if you survive this and escape, I look forward to hearing more stories about you from the dead souls who gather here. Farewell. And good luck.>

With that, Hræsvelgr cawed loudly and flapped his gigantic wings together, creating massive hurricane-force winds and tornadoes powerful enough to level a city. The wind dispersed the clouds composing Hel's grotesque face across the emerald sky. The Bridge of the Damned shattered, sending the undead legions flying into the air. Sigurd and Brynhild had only seconds to swoop down and pick up Sinfjotli before they were also blown away in the massive gale-force winds that sent them hurdling north.

"Sigurd, what the fuck did you do?!" Sinfjotli demanded amidst the howling wind.

"Hopefully, I saved our lives," Sigurd answered.

With Hræsvelgr's intense winds aiding them, Brynhild now had the momentum she needed to carry both Sigurd and Sinfjotli through the air. They continued rocketing over the dilapidated remains of the bridge and soared right over the Gate of Hel and Gnipa Cave. Garm jumped uselessly at them as they flew overhead, his chain preventing him from reaching them. He howled in frustration as the trio flew past the boundary of Gnipa Cave, over the Road to Hel, and toward the underworld's entrance.

Sigurd saw all these things but had no time to consider them. It had become difficult to breathe amidst the insane winds. His vision was beginning to blur. Sinfjotli was already unconscious due to a lack of oxygen and overexertion. Even Brynhild was starting to lose her strength as she struggled to stay aloft and conscious amidst the absurdly powerful winds.

Before Sigurd blacked out, he noticed a single draugir desperately clutching his leg. Before he kicked it away, he heard Hel scream at him through its decayed mouth: *"You think you've accomplished anything? This is merely the beginning! Even if you escape from my draugirs and my realm, you will never escape* me! *I am death. I am inevitable. I am the universal fear that fills the hearts of every being in the nine realms with terror. I will* have your souls!

CHAPTER FORTY-FIVE

A GLIMPSE OF PARADISE

Sigurd had no idea when he blacked out. He had no idea what caused the throbbing pain in his head. All he knew was that he was afraid. The battle against the draugirs on the Gjallerbru had been harrowing. But the nightmare he was having now was even more terrifying.

Sigurd found himself inside a burning great hall. The floor was littered with the bloody corpses of children, women, and warriors. In the center of the room was a mound of burning rubble shaped like a throne. A beautiful woman with blond hair emerged from behind the debris. Flames licked up her dress and spread across the floor with every step as she approached him. Sigurd saw her face and vaguely recognized her as his aunt Signy.

"Fight, Sigurd!" Signy urged as flames engulfed her. But the voice wasn't hers. It sounded masculine, like the voice of an old grizzled warrior.

Next, Sigurd found himself outside the cave of Gnitaheath, reliving the moment he killed Regin. He drew his sword and cut off the dwarf's head in a single strike. He watched the decapitated head roll over to Fafnir's corpse, feeling angry, betrayed, and guilty.

Suddenly, the dwarf's eyes snapped open, and he looked at Sigurd. "You are not fated to die here," the head spoke. But the voice wasn't Regin's. Sigurd had known Regin since he was a boy, and this voice didn't have his distinct accent. It sounded older and much more authoritative.

Out of the corner of his eye, Sigurd noticed Fafnir's corpse twitch. As Sigurd looked up, the dead dragon lunged at him, engulfing him in the darkness of its gullet.

The dream changed. Sigurd found himself lying in his old room in the hall of the Gjukungs, staring up at the ceiling. He tried to sit up, but found himself pinned to the bed. He looked up and realized with horror that a sword was piercing through his chest. He could feel blood pooling in his throat, cutting off his breathing.

Sigurd coughed up blood and fought to stay awake. He glanced left and saw Gram sticking from the wall. Beneath the sword, his youngest brother-in-law, Guttorm, lay severed in half in a pool of blood.

Standing near the sword he vaguely recalled throwing, he saw his wife, Gudrun, looking horrified and clutching their daughter, Svanhild. His daughter looked up from her mother's skirt and stared at him with the same golden snake eyes she had inherited from him. Unlike her mother, Svanhild looked calm and stoic.

"This is not the end," she said in the voice of an old man, the same voice Sigurd had already heard multiple times. But this time, Sigurd recognized it. The voice belonged to an old man who had helped Sigurd many times and given him sage advice during his adventures in Midgard.

Before Sigurd realized it, the dream changed, and the world turned to darkness as he stared at his daughter Svanhild. And then everything became still. The warm blood pooling in his throat was replaced by the cold taste of...water?

Sigurd snapped open his eyes and discovered he was submerged in a pool of knee-deep water. He rose to the surface, gasping for air. He was inside a magnificent hall next to a roaring bonfire. Nearby, he saw an old man in elegant battle armor sitting on an enormous golden throne. His face was hidden by shadows.

"Who...are you?" Sigurd slurred.

The old man rose from his throne and stepped out of the shadows. He was fully clad in battle armor with a mighty spear in hand. He had a long, wavy white beard and an eye patch covering his left eye.

"I am the All-Father Odin," he announced boomingly. "Ruler of Asgard, King of the Aesir, Lord of the Hanged, and Protector of Midgard. I have watched you become a powerful warrior, Sigurd. And I have been there to help you and your brother at the most crucial moments of your lives."

"I remember," Sigurd recalled, thinking back on the events of his life. "You were the one who helped me to pick out Grani as my mount. Then, later, when I set out to avenge my father's death, I encountered a fierce storm that turned the water the color of fresh gore. You appeared on a rock, and the storm ceased when you stepped on board. And before I slew Fafnir, you appeared and advised me the best way to slay him. After I killed him, you reappeared and instructed me to bathe in his blood to become invulnerable."

Sigurd looked around at the dark, cavernous hall around him. "Wait, where are we?"

Odin snapped his fingers, and the room lit up. Sigurd realized he was inside a cavernous hall, standing in one of the pools next to Odin's elevated throne. The rafters were made from spears, and the ceiling thatched with polished golden shields that reflected light from the braziers. The hall had five hundred and forty doors. At the end of the hall, there was a massive entry that was bigger than the rest, with two large bone-white wooden doors. Beyond the enormous entrance, he saw a beautiful tree with golden red leaves growing outside with ripe golden apples hanging from its branches.

"This is Valhalla." Sigurd gasped. The legendary Hall of Heroes was even more beautiful than he'd envisioned. It contained fourteen long rows of trestle tables with seven to each side of the central aisle. Seated at each table were many famous past warriors.

He noticed his childhood friends Folan, Vafi, Birna Bloodtusk, and their subordinates sat around one such table. He saw his father, Sigmund, his grandfather Völsung, his mother, Hjordis, his half-brothers Helgi and Hámundr, and other members of his family line seated around a table closest to Odin's throne.

"Is this the future?" Sigurd wondered. "Is this my destiny?"

"It can be," Odin replied. "But only if you and your brother make it so. Your deaths were a mistake. You are a warrior destined for greatness. A warrior meant to lead entire armies at Ragnarök. Not a craven. Only a craven accepts death and dies in his bed."

"I am no coward," Sigurd spat defiantly. "I am Sigurd the Dragon Slayer, son of Sigmund, grandson of Völsung, and the greatest hero in the north!"

"Then you must fight," Odin announced. "Seek out the Norns and receive their guidance. Travel the realms and face all that lies before you. Only then will you and your brother attain your rightful place amongst the Einherjar and be allowed inside these halls."

The warriors of Valhalla stood up, raised their drinking horns, and chanted, "Sigurd, Sigurd!" But their cheers slowly changed into a single feminine voice full of concern.

Sigurd opened his eyes and saw Brynhild clutching him in her arms, desperately screaming his name.

"Sigurd," Brynhild screamed. "Sigurd!"

"Br...Brynhild?" Sigurd slurred. "Ow! My head hurts!"

His head was throbbing in pain. His vision was blurred, and a large lump had formed above his head. It felt like he'd slammed headfirst into something solid and unmovable.

"Oh, thank Freyja!" Brynhild sighed, relieved. "I thought you'd died...again."

"It takes more than a blow to the head to kill me," Sigurd groaned. He tried to put on a mask of confidence. But the pain was more than he could bear. His vision blurred, and his brain felt like it was banging against the walls of his skull like a drum. Brynhild noticed his agony and drew a healing rune on his forehead to quiet the throbbing pain in his head. After a moment, the pain subsided enough for Sigurd to think clearly again. He opened his eyes, and as his vision cleared, he got a good look at Brynhild and became awestruck by her beauty.

In the heat of the battle, Sigurd hadn't had a chance to study Brynhild's appearance. Moreover, Sigurd realized this was the first time he had studied Brynhild in her true form as a valkyrie. And he had never seen a figure so beautiful and foreboding. She looked so regal in her steel armor. She was slender and full-breasted, and the golden wings jutting from her back gave her an angelic appearance. She had removed her helmet, allowing Sigurd to see her face, which was so beautiful it could bewitch an entire nation. Her long, straight scarlet hair reached down to her back and flowed gracefully in the swaying wind. And her amber eyes were something magical and otherworldly.

Sigurd felt something stir in his heart. It wasn't the simple excitement a man feels when he sees a beautiful woman. No, this was something more profound and substantial. He couldn't explain why, but he felt *bound* to this warrior woman. He could feel a tangible bond between them. He first experienced it when Brynhild kissed him on the Bridge of the Damned. Given the dire circumstances, he hadn't had time to think about it then. But now, he realized they shared an emotional connection so strong it went beyond familial ties or love. It was a powerful feeling he had not even experienced with his wife, Gudrun, his mother, or even his children. He felt he was bound to this warrior woman, twined together like threads in a tapestry.

They remained there for a while, silently staring at each other as she cradled his healing body.

"Brynhild," Sigurd whispered, breaking the silence.

"Sigurd," she replied sweetly. She leaned in close enough for their noses to touch. He closed his eyes, succumbing to his emotions, and pressed his lips against hers.

"Hey…um…Brynhild, was it?" Sinfjotli interrupted. "Where *are* we right now?"

Sigurd broke the kiss and sat up. He checked his surroundings and was awestruck by what he saw. They appeared to be standing on top of giant ash-white tree roots. And behind them was the most colossal tree trunk Sigurd had ever seen. The sheer size and majesty of the tree were enough to boggle the mind. Even with his superhuman eyesight, Sigurd could not see the canopy.

There could be no mistaking this mighty tree.

"Yggdrasil," Sigurd gasped. "The World Tree, it's… so beautiful!"

He and Sinfjotli got to their feet and spent the next few minutes basking in the World Tree's glory. High above them, the Yggdrasil's trunk passed through a giant blue sphere. But it was too far away to discern any distinctive details. Sigurd could spot a few other giant planetary spheres nesting amongst its branches.

"Those must be the Nine Realms," Sigurd guessed.

"Then that must be Helheim over there." Sinfjotli gestured behind them to the green planetary sphere connected to the root they were currently standing on.

From the outside, Helheim looked like a giant blue-green gaseous planet. Its atmosphere looked deep, cold, and too thick to see the horrors that lay within. It was one of the more fascinating features of Yggdrasil's roots.

Sigurd's eyes lit up with utter joy and glory. "But if we're standing on the root of the World Tree…and that's Helheim over there…then that means…that we *did it*!"

Sinfjotli clapped Sigurd on the shoulder. "We did it, Sigurd! We fucking did it! We escaped from Helheim itself!"

He raised his arms and howled out a victorious cheer. Sigurd joined him in the glorious victory cry. They had earned this moment of triumph. No one, not even Baldur himself, had ever escaped Helheim's clutches. To be the first to successfully escape the underworld was an honor beyond the power of words to describe.

"You are the first humans to escape Helheim," Brynhild congratulated them when their celebrations ended. But then her tone changed, becoming more serious. "But I fear that this is merely the beginning of your journey. You've climbed out of the boiling pot, but now you may have to lunge into the fire."

"Perhaps, but we wouldn't have made it out of that pot if not for you," Sinfjotli said.

"I see you've become a valkyrie again," Sigurd noted as he turned toward Brynhild.

"Not quite." Brynhild examined her hands and flapped her wings. "I've assumed my true form as a valkyrie and regained my armor and wings. But I am far from whole. The curse Odin placed on me remains active. I'll never be able to decide the victor of a battle again."

"But you're still an amazing warrior," Sigurd reminded. "You were the bane of the undead back there."

Brynhild blushed at his praise. Despite her warrior appearance and austere beauty, she was very adorable when she was shy. Sigurd wanted to embrace her again, but a mistrustful thought crossed his mind, and his feelings of longing turned into suspicion.

"Why did you save us?" Sigurd asked. "Did Odin send you to help us?"

"No," Brynhild assured. "As I told Hel on the Gjallerbru, Odin and the other Aesir had nothing to do with my appearance in Helheim. I went there of my own volition. I was traveling through the Valley of Shadows when I sensed an army amassing on the Bridge of the Damned and carved my way to you as fast as I could. I would have arrived sooner if a stone giant hadn't delayed me."

"But why?" Sigurd asked. "Why would you willingly venture into Helheim?"

"To be with you," she answered.

Something exploded in him. He felt like kissing her again, but another thought crossed his mind, and those feelings of longing and desire turned into suspicion.

"You never answered my question on the Gjallerbru," Sigurd recalled. "Why did you help us even though you orchestrated my death? And what promise to you did I break?"

Brynhild looked deep into his eyes, which evoked a whirlwind of emotions within Sigurd: anger, impatience, pain, joy, sadness, and confusion.

"It seems the potion Grimhild gave you still hasn't worn off." Brynhild sighed. "I suppose that's to be expected."

"What potion?" Sigurd knew Gudrun's mother, Grimhild, was a sorceress, but she had never made him drink one of her potions.

... Hadn't she? Sigurd recalled what Hel had said on the Gjallerbru, "*It seems the potion she tricked you into drinking was so powerful that it continues to affect you even in death. In a way, that woman was the author of all your pain.*" And before they parted forever, Gudrun told Sigurd: "*When you learn the truth about us...please don't judge me too harshly. I did what I did...because I love you.*"

Was this potion what Gudrun was talking about? Had Grimhild and Gudrun's entire family somehow betrayed him?

"I—I don't understand," Sigurd muttered.

"You will soon enough," Brynhild promised. "Look into my eyes, and you'll know the truth."

"Please, just tell me why..." he pleaded.

"Just *look,* and you'll understand everything." she insisted.

Sigurd relented and stared deep into Brynhild's amber eyes. After a while, a part of Sigurd's brain felt like it had caught fire. It did not feel like the concussion he'd suffered after slamming his head against the root of Yggdrasil. It almost felt like a dormant part of his brain was awakening. Nanna told him that there was a magic barrier in his mind, keeping specific memories locked away. But now, that barrier started cracking as he stared into Brynhild's eyes. Soon, the barricade shattered, and all the repressed memories rushed out. Like a flood, the memories came, and Sigurd was drowning in them as they rushed before his eyes.

He saw himself riding his horse, Grani, up a tall mountain wreathed in clouds. He remembered this was Hindarfjall. At the summit, he found a stronghold surrounded by a ring of fire. The lurid flames burned with a roar that would have daunted the heart of any other visitor. But without hesitation, Sigurd rode Grani through the fire without being burned. The fire didn't even feel warm as they passed through.

Within the ring of fire was a great castle with shield-hung walls. The great gates stood wide open, and Sigurd rode through them unchallenged. In the center of the fortress, he found a beautiful shield-maiden sleeping beneath a tree surrounded by red and white overlapping shields. She was armored for battle, and he realized the warrior was a beautiful woman when he removed her helmet. Her chain mail corselet was so tight that it seemed to bite into her flesh.

Sigurd remembered drawing his sword, hesitating briefly, and then slicing open her chain mail armor, which parted like cloth. As her corselet sloughed to the ground, her eyes flashed open. She looked at him and smiled.

More memories came flooding back into Sigurd's mind. He remembered drinking with her, training with her, learning the runes from her, and spending many intimate nights with her. He remembered proposing to her, giving her Andvari's ring, and exchanging solemn vows to marry her when he returned one day. All his memories of Brynhild came back to him in perfect clarity.

Sigurd fell to the ground, clutching his head as the memories flooded his mind. As he struggled to regain his senses, he vaguely heard Sinfjotli asking if he was all right.

"It's done," Brynhild announced. When Sigurd looked up at her, it felt like he was now looking at a different person. Or rather, it felt like *he* was an different person, seeing her from a new perspective.

"Back with us, brother?" Sinfjotli asked worriedly. "I got the feeling you left just now."

"I remember," Sigurd muttered. He stood up and glanced at the ring on his finger. "I remember...finding you at the top of Hindarfjall. I remember training with you and learning the runes. I remember giving you this ring, Andvaranaut, and promising I'd only marry you and..."

Suddenly, it all clicked into place. "Oh...I see. That must be why Hel and Hræsvelgr called me an oath breaker. I vowed I would marry you...but then I married Gudrun instead."

"And you tricked me into marrying her brother Gunnar," Brynhild added.

"What?" Sigurd gasped. "I... how?"

"After you married Gudrun, your Gunnar asked you to help him court me," she explained. "Before you lost your memory, you told him all about me. Since you were now married to his sister, he decided he ought to marry me instead. You brought him to Hindarfjall, but he couldn't pass through the ring of flames because he was unworthy. So you dressed as him and walked through the flames. You then pretended to be Gunnar and courted me on his behalf. We spent three nights together, sleeping with a sword between us. When I agreed to marry Gunnar on the fourth morning, you stole the ring Andvaranaut from my finger before you left and then gave it to Gudrun. Because of your actions, I was tricked into marrying a lesser man and forced into a marriage I hated."

"I don't understand," Sigurd gasped. He felt confused and guilty. "How could I just do that? How could I marry Gudrun and do such a cruel thing to you?"

"Because you had forgotten your promise," Brynhild replied. "You forgot about me."

"But how could I?" Sigurd demanded.

"You have our wretched mother-in-law to blame for that," Brynhild sneered. "Your wife's mother was a sorceress. After you became blood brothers with Gunnar and Hagen, you visited their father's kingdom. When Gjuki saw all the gold you had taken from Fafnir's hoard and heard of your prowess as a warrior, he asked you to marry into the family. You refused, explaining that you were already betrothed to me. But his wife Grimhild would not accept 'No' for an answer. She tricked you into drinking a potion specifically designed to make you forget about me. Once your memory was wiped, you married her daughter. When you tricked me into marrying Gunnar and stole Andvari's ring, you did it thinking that I was a stranger."

Brynhild paused for a moment. "You asked me earlier why I helped you and your brother on the Bridge of the Damned. Why did I help you even though you tricked me into a marriage I hated? Why did I help you despite everything that happened between us? The answer is simple. It's because...I love you, Sigurd."

"If you love me so much, why did you have me killed?" Sigurd demanded. There was no malice in his voice, only confusion and shock. No matter how hard he tried, he couldn't bring himself to despise the woman before him. "And why didn't you mention you were betrothed to me when I saw you again disguised as Gunnar? Everything could have been prevented if you had said something."

"Because the potion you drank affected me too," Brynhild explained. "Our souls are connected, Sigurd, like threads in a tapestry. When you drank the potion Grimhild offered to you, the spell also affected me, and I forgot everything about you and everything related to you."

"However, Grimhild was unconvinced that the spell had worked on me." Brynhild growled. "Her greatest fear was that I would reveal the truth, and then you would slaughter her whole family and raze her kingdom for forcing you to break your promise. So she used you to court me on Gunnar's behalf to ensure that couldn't happen."

"But why would Gunnar do that?" Sigurd demanded. "We were blood brothers! Why would he use me like a cat's-paw to marry you when he already knew how much I loved you?"

"I couldn't say," Brynhild shrugged. "Compared to you, Gunnar was always a lesser man. Maybe he was jealous and wanted a way to feel superior to you. Or maybe he was just following his mother's commands. Regardless, when Gudrun revealed the truth to me while we bathed in the Rhine and showed me the ring Andvaranaut, which you had taken from me, I felt nothing but hatred for you. You had tricked me into marrying a lesser man. Moreover, I was certain you had seduced me. You promised me you slept chastely with a sword between us on those nights you posed as Gunnar. But I discovered my maidenhead was gone on my wedding night to Gunnar. You were the only one who could have passed through the flames and seduced me. I believed you were a scoundrel who had sworn a false oath to a valkyrie, taken my virginity, and tricked me into a marriage I hated. I wanted nothing more than to drive a sword through your heart. But I was powerless to take revenge myself. Odin's curse still prevented me from harming any living creature. I tried goading Gunnar and Hagen to seek vengeance on my behalf, but they refused. They had both sworn oaths preventing them from harming you. But their younger brother Guttorm overheard everything. And he wasn't so reluctant."

Sigurd remembered what Hel had mentioned on the Gjallerbru. She claimed Gunnar and Hagen had built up the boy's courage by feeding him morsels of wolf meat and snake, filled Guttorm's heart with malice toward him, and pressed him to carry out the deed for the honor of their family. Had they done that out of honor or simple malice and envy?

"But after you died, the potion's effects wore off, and I remembered everything," Brynhild continued. "I remembered the day we first met atop

Hindarfjall. I remembered the days we spent training together. I remembered the passionate love we shared each night. And even the child we conceived. It all came rushing back to me in perfect clarity! I was so overwhelmed with grief and despair over what I had done that I didn't want to live anymore. I just wanted to be with you. So I drove your sword through under my arm and asked to be burned alongside you on your funerary pyre."

"Child," Sigurd repeated. "We...had a child?!"

"Yes, Sigurd," Brynhild nodded. "I gave birth to a daughter after you left Hindarfjall."

"And you never told me?!" He shouted.

"I never got the chance. I didn't discover I was pregnant until after you had left to attend your mother's funeral. But I had another reason for not telling you. I learned long ago that we were both destined to die tragic fates. I wasn't sure about the specific details. But I suspected something might happen while you were away, and I worried for our child's safety. Thus, I took steps to protect her from whatever happened to us. I sent her away to be raised by her foster father, Heimir, until you returned. But after you drank Grimhild's potion, I was affected by the spell and forgot about her. In hindsight, sending her away and not telling you about her was the right decision. If Grimhild learned about our daughter, she would have stopped at nothing to kill her."

Brynhild glanced up the trunk of the World Tree. She stared at the realm of Midgard and squeezed her eyes shut. "Our daughter was only three years old when we died. But she still lives, Sigurd! I can feel it."

Sigurd became mired in an amalgam of strange emotions as countless questions raced through his mind. Learning that Gudrun's family had erased his memory so they'd have a claim to his treasure, the reason he'd been murdered, and that he'd had a secret daughter with Brynhild left him utterly dumbfounded. He could only bring himself to ask one question.

"Our daughter...what...is her name?"

"Aslaug," Brynhild answered proudly.

"Aslaug." As Sigurd said the name, courage and joy swelled within his heart. The knowledge that he still had a living child and that the Volsung bloodline endured lit a fire within Sigurd. All the grief and despair he had carried with him since his conversation with Gudrun vanished.

Sinfjotli cleared his throat. "This has been a fascinating tale. But what should we do now?"

Sigurd glanced back at Helheim. Then he looked up at the trunk of the World Tree in deep thought. "Before I blacked out, Hel claimed, 'This is only the beginning.'"

"I'm afraid she's right," Brynhild muttered. "Odin may have given you a second chance at Valhalla. But redemption is something you must earn through epic deeds. You'll have to undergo many arduous trials before the Aesir allow you into Valhalla."

"Odin said something like that when he visited me in my dream," Sigurd recalled. He quickly recounted the details of the dream to them. "He told me: 'Seek out the Norns and receive their guidance.' Do you have any idea what we should do?"

"If you wish to have an audience with the Norns, then you should make your way across these roots until you reach the northernmost root of Yggdrasil," Brynhild instructed. "From there, you must travel down into Niflheim. But whatever you do, do not dawdle! Niflheim is the coldest of the nine realms. Helheim's climate is child's play by comparison. You'll both freeze to death if you linger there too long."

"Aren't you coming with us?" Sigurd asked.

Brynhild grimaced. "...it pains me to say this, but I cannot. While you slept, I received an order. My queen has summoned me to Asgard."

"Which queen?" Sinfjotli repeated. "You mean Queen Frigga, Odin's wife?"

"No," Brynhild shook her head. "*Freyja* is the Queen of the valkyries. She is my true master. And she has summoned me. As a valkyrie, I cannot disobey her. The last time I disobeyed the gods, Odin stripped me of all my power, imprisoned me on a mountaintop in a deep slumber that lasted decades, and leveled so many curses upon me I was incapable of defending myself from any threat. I dare not disobey them a second time. I'm sorry, but I'm afraid we must part ways for now."

"I—I understand." Sigurd nodded.

Brynhild turned to Sinfjotli and smiled. "You are a mighty warrior, Sinfjotli. You bravely held back Hel's undead army by yourself, while Sigurd and I spoke with Hræsvelgr. Please look after your brother. Sigurd means more to me than life itself."

Sinfjotli hesitated for a moment and then grasped her hand. "You have my solemn vow, my lady."

Satisfied, Brynhild turned back to Sigurd. She looked at his golden armor for a moment, then picked up her dragon helmet and handed it to Sigurd.

"You can have this back now, since it was originally yours."

As she held the helmet out for Sigurd, it transformed into an elaborate gold war helmet.

Sigurd's eyes widened. "This is Tarnhelm, Fafnir's Helmet of Dread, which has the power to take on the shape of its opponent's greatest fears. I found this in his hoard, along with my golden hauberk. I wore this whenever I went into battle. But it was missing when I woke up in the city."

"It was with me when I woke up after I died," Brynhild explained. "I can't have you gallivanting around the Nine Realms in an incomplete suit of armor." She handed him the helmet, then wrapped her arms around his neck and pulled him in for a long, passionate kiss.

"Our fates are intertwined, Sigurd," she declared. "My life, my fate is in your hands. I was denied you in life. But I promise I will always be with you in death wherever your soul resides. Whether we are in Helheim or Valhalla is for you to decide. Farewell, my love."

Brynhild spread her wings and flew up the trunk of the World Tree. Sigurd stood there watching the love of his life fly away until she was nothing but a shining star high above them.

Sinfjotli touched his shoulder, which snapped him back to reality. "You heard her. We'd better get moving."

Sigurd nodded. He put on his helmet and looked back at the World Tree's distant canopy, contemplating the daunting journey ahead. His superhuman vision allowed him to see farther than any mortal man, but even he couldn't make out the top of the World Tree. And yet, as he gazed up, a twinkling light caught his eye—Asgard, distant and ethereal, shining like a star in the night sky at the very top of Yggdrasil's branches.

At that moment, he knew their journey to reach the realm of the Aesir and the Hall of Heroes would be nothing short of epic. The road would be long and treacherous, full of obstacles and challenges beyond anything he could imagine. But Sigurd was determined to succeed, to prove his worth and earn his place among the Einherjar. He closed his eyes and took a deep breath, steeling himself for the journey ahead. It would be a herculean test of his strength, courage, and willpower, but Sigurd was ready to face it head-on. And he wouldn't be facing it alone.

After adjusting his helmet straps, Sigurd turned to Sinfjotli and reflected on everything he and his long-lost brother had accomplished recently. Sigurd was grateful to have Sinfjotli by his side, knowing he could not want a better man for a brother or traveling companion. Sinfjotli had proven his worth as a warrior time and time again, and Sigurd knew that he could always count on him when the going got tough.

"Let's go." Sigurd urged.

EPILOGUE

Baldur strode through the City of the Lost, his steps echoing down the Path of the Dead. Signy and Gudrun's spirits followed as they snaked through the crowd of spirits. Every time he passed by one, its misty form took on a corporeal form, allowing them to appear as they were while still alive.

But Baldur was blind to it. His eyes were fixed ahead, watching for any sign of danger or disturbance. And his mind was focused on the battle raging to the north.

"You should go back," Signy urged. "You shouldn't have stopped fighting just to protect worthless trash like me."

Baldur stopped walking. He turned toward her and enveloped her in a fearsome hug before she could react.

"You are not worthless, Signy! You might've had a turbulent past, but that's behind you now!"

It was a half-truth. Signy had endured much suffering in Helheim at Siggeir and Hel's hands for her many crimes. Her trauma was so profound that even his aura couldn't entirely dispel it. It would take a very long time for her psyche to recover.

Still, his warm embrace and heartfelt words moved her to tears as she buried her face in his robes.

"That's righteous of you to say," Gudrun admitted while wiping a tear from her eyes. "But Signy still brings up a good point." She tapped the symbol on her forehead. "You promised this mark would protect us. Signy has it, too. Wouldn't it be more prudent to remain on the front lines instead of escorting us?"

"I won't leave that to chance," Baldur vowed as he broke the hug. He reached up and tapped the brand carved into Signy's forehead. "This mark can only protect you from *physical* harm. But there are many ways to tear apart a tree."

If they tried marching to his ship alone, it was guaranteed that Helheim would conjure a vision. And with Hel's eyes upon them, it would be a vision so traumatizing that their egos would shatter.

"Also," Baldur added, "at this point, continuing to fight the undead army served no point."

The draugs had achieved their mission and kept him occupied long enough for over a hundred thousand undead monstrosities to make it onto the Gjallerbru by the time he made it back. He resumed fighting them, hoping to stem the tide, but it was already too late.

Still, Baldur valiantly continued to hold them off as long as he could to stem the tide or at least halt the flow of undead flooding onto the bridge. Swords shattered upon his invulnerable skin, shields cracked beneath his fists, and countless draughts were felled, but the army was endless. He fought with all his might, hoping to buy some time for Sigurd and Sinfjotli to figure out a way out of this sticky situation.

But he finally stopped fighting when he sensed Signy enter the city with his mark. He knew enough undead on the bridge to trap Sigurd and Sinfjotli in a pincer attack. He resolved himself to protect Sinfjotli's mother and prayed they could hold out on their own.

Sighing, Baldur continued walking south. But as they trekked farther, he couldn't help but notice that the echoes of the battle in the north were growing fainter. That could only mean the Battle of the Gjallerbru was finally ending. And there were only two possible outcomes.

He lowered his eyes. By his very nature, Baldur was incapable of feeling fear. But he could still feel apprehension and worry for those he held dear. He shut his eyes and focused his mind, trying to sense the events unfolding far away on the Gjallerbru. But before he could get a clear reading, an immense power surge reverberated throughout the realm. It was like a colossal gale, capable of obliterating everything in its path. Baldur gasped in shock, realizing Hræsvelgr had roused himself and unleashed his might.

The windstorm descended upon the city, howling louder than the mightiest beasts. The gusts were so powerful that they made the very ground tremble. Baldur gathered Gudrun and Signy in his arms and dove into the nearest building, hoping to shield them from the worst of it. But the winds were so strong that they battered the structure, rattling its foundations and threatening to reduce it to rubble.

The very air seemed to be alive with the sound of destruction as the storm raged on with undiminished fury. The gale roared through the city streets, sending the snow and ice that had accumulated for centuries hurtling in all directions like a furious blizzard. The fierce wind uprooted several of the skyscrapers in the northernmost section of the city, causing them to come crashing down to the ground with a deafening roar. Baldur peered outside and watched in awe as draugirs and other undead were swept and lashed through the streets and sky above like helpless leaves caught in a storm.

"What's happening?!" Signy screamed.

As Baldur opened his mouth to answer, his heart skipped a beat as he sensed something else amidst the chaos of the gale that threatened to tear the city apart. The life forces of Sigurd, Sinfjotli, and the third entity he had detected earlier, which had grown weaker and more distant, had vanished altogether. He felt a jolt of shock and disbelief in the depths of his being, and he knew it could only mean one thing. The three of them had escaped Helheim!

Whirling around, Baldur dashed outside into the raging gale and gazed northward. The hurricane-like winds were so strong they made his long hair ripple like a flag and threatened to throw him off his feet, but he didn't care. Shock, disbelief, and relief flooded through him like a warm tide as he confirmed that his friends, whom he had thought were lost forever, had escaped the underworld against all odds.

And he wasn't the only one who felt it. Every spirit walking down the Path of the Dead stopped in unison and peered behind them. It was as if they also sensed the three of them exiting Helheim, even though that should have been impossible.

"Is everything all right, Baldur?" Gudrun called out.

"They did it," he whispered, still in disbelief.

"What?!" Signy shouted. "We can't hear you over this wind!"

Baldur threw his hands in the air. "They did it!" He yelled jubilantly. "They really did it! They've escaped Helheim!"

"You sound surprised, old friend." A familiar voice noted.

Baldur heard a familiar rattling of bones as Signy and Gudrun screamed. Baldur whirled around, and his mirth melted like ice in a desert. Sitting cross-legged on the steps in front of the doorway was the queen of the underworld. Despite the winds howling through the city at five hundred miles per hour, Hel remained calm and serene. Her braided hair was billowed around her head and shoulders, but she remained seated on the ice-covered steps. Hel's gaze remained unwavering as she locked eyes with Baldur, unperturbed by the tumultuous weather and chaos that was sweeping across her realm.

"Hel," Baldur muttered. "What are...?"

"Just a moment, old friend." Hel interrupted, holding up a finger. "Let me stem this chaos."

She stood up, raised her scythe high above her head, and slammed the butt against the ground. A powerful shockwave emanated from the point of impact. The very air seemed to ripple and distort, and an intense burst of energy surged forth, causing the fierce gale to cease. And not just the windstorm. Baldur could sense the sudden calm that had descended upon Helheim. The River Gjöll, which had been turbulent and chaotic, became still and stagnant. The clouds scattered by Hræsvelgr's winds returned. It was as if all the chaos throughout the underworld had been frozen in place, leaving an eerie and unsettling stillness.

"There," Hel remarked casually. "Now we can hear each other."

Baldur turned back to Hel, glancing over her shoulder as he did so. His shock turned to apprehension as he noticed Signy and Gudrun cowering in abject terror within the building.

"Pay them no mind," Hel urged with a wave of her hand. "Those two aren't why I'm here."

Baldur narrowed his eyes. "You don't care that I've placed them under my protection, even though by all the ancient laws, they ought to belong to you for their crimes?"

Hel shrugged. "Are you expecting me to make a fuss? I'm not a miser like Rán, who gets cranky when she loses something that she's long had but has never before used or paid attention to. What's two lost droplets amidst an ocean? Go ahead. Add them to your menagerie."

Baldur relaxed somewhat but kept his eyes trained on Hel. "Then why are you here?"

"To speak with you, of course. Did you have fun playing with my draugs?"

Baldur lowered his eyes. "'Fun' isn't the word I'd use."

"Oh, don't be so coy. You're an Aesir, remember? Fighting is what you and your ilk live for. I'd go so far as to guess that was the most alive you've felt in centuries...figuratively speaking, of course."

Baldur lowered his eyes. He couldn't deny it. Fighting off Hel's army and battling ten draugs at once was the most fun he'd had in years. Yet, he couldn't bring himself to smile.

"Interesting," Hel muttered. "I expected you to be more boastful, especially after defeating ten of my draugs."

"I'd hardly call it a victory," Baldur dismissed humbly. "All I did was knock them all into the River Gjöll."

"No one has ever defeated that many draugs in a single battle," Hel reminded. "Try to take a little more pride in that. I'm sure Kvasir is already penning an epic poem in your honor."

"The true honor and glory belong to Sigurd and Sinfjotli. They've done what even I was unable to do. Speaking of which, you don't seem very perturbed about it."

Hel grinned. "Oh? What did they accomplish exactly? Sure, they managed to leave my realm. But that's just the first step. The road to Valhalla is long and perilous. One slip up, and they'll return here. It's only a matter of time before they're mine again."

Baldur clenched his fists as he closed the distance between them and stood before Hel. "Give them the credit they deserve! They weathered all those hellish visions you forced upon them. They slew countless draugirs and weathered every undead minion and malediction you unleashed upon them!"

Hel locked eyes with Baldur for a long time. "Oh, I *am* giving them credit, old friend. But I'm giving you the lion's share. They never would have made it this far without you. You stopped them from killing each other in that plaza. You brought them to your ship, fully restored them to life, protected them from me, escorted them through my city, gave them a head start on the Gjallerbru, held off my army as long as you could, crucially told Sigurd about Hræsvelgr." She gestured to the building behind her. "Coincidentally, this place is where you told them about my little pet. If you hadn't put the idea in

Sigurd's head, he wouldn't have enlisted his aid and escaped. Therefore, you deserve more credit than anyone for their escape."

Baldur lowered his eyes. He had no retort to that.

"What's the matter, old friend? You helped two mortals achieve what you never could. Shouldn't you be happier you helped someone escape my realm and relish all the glory you gained along the way?"

Baldur clenched his fists. "The feelings are soured due to all the pain and suffering you put them through. Especially because you forced them to watch Siggeir torment Signy before their eyes!"

"Is that a hint of judgment and anger in your voice? I didn't think you were capable of those emotions." Hel chuckled dryly. "Baldur, I adore you. But you can be so naïve sometimes. You got two things wrong there. First, I never interfere in my draugs' fights. 'Do what thou will.' That is one of the few commandments I give my subordinates when I give them a mission. How they complete it seldom matters. Granted, Siggeir disobeyed my instructions to summon my entire army as soon as he appeared and tormented Signy in front of her son. But he did so of his own volition. Second, I vowed on the Bridge of Judgment that I wouldn't hold anything back. You cannot judge me for trying to destroy them. Must I remind you that you're an Aesir? Battle and war are your family's oldest pastimes. Have you been here so long that you've forgotten what war is like? It's not like those games of Tablut you, Nanna, and Hodr play to pass the time. There are no rules. There are no penalties. Neither side is equal, and there are no forbidden tactics. The only goal in a war is to destroy your enemy. Don't complain or blame your opponent for trying whatever they can to achieve that goal."

She looked away and studied the devastation that had befallen her city. "Having said that, I can see why your father is so obsessed with these two mortals. You made the right choice, giving them your mother's apples and doing everything possible to assist them. Hræsvelgr did quite a number on my city after Sigurd seduced him to his cause. Though I permitted him to act, I suppose I deserve some blame for the destruction."

Hel burst out laughing. "That's the part that humors me the most! Sigurd's ability to talk to birds, something I and so many others dismissed as a trivial power, proved invaluable in letting them escape my realm! I'm so amused by it I may not castigate Hræsvelgr for rebelling against me."

Baldur had stomached all he could. He marched past Hel and entered the building. He helped Signy and Gudrun to their feet, wrapped an arm around their shoulders, and escorted them outside. They each buried their face in his jacket, unable to even glance at Hel as he carried them past the goddess.

"Leaving so soon?" Hel asked.

"You have more pressing matters to deal with rebuilding," Baldur reminded. "Hræsvelgr's gale spread much destruction throughout your realm. The Gjallerbru is destroyed, and the city is even more ruined than before. You have much to do, and I no longer wish to speak with you."

Hel's smile faded. She seemed genuinely hurt by that. Baldur would have usually apologized, but he'd had enough of her for one day. He turned his back on her and continued walking south.

"If you ever get bored on your ship, I can arrange for you to fight against my draugs again," Hel offered.

Baldur paused. Although the offer intrigued him, he chose not to turn and continued trekking the Path of the Dead.

As he walked farther south, Hel heaved a heavy sigh, then raised her eyes to the emerald sky. She snapped her fingers, and a vision of Sigurd and Sinfjotli trekking across the roots of Yggdrasil manifested in the clouds. She grinned as she watched them hop from one root to another.

"The rabbits have been set loose. The hunt begins, Odin. This will be fun!"

ALEX E. MARTIN

END

Did you know? Reader reviews are very important to an indie author's success.

They validate our work and help others find our stories. If you enjoyed Fugitives of Helheim, please leave a review filled with stars.

Click the link or scan the QR Code below:

Don't forget your free gifts! Scan the QR Code to tell me where to send them:

***

Continue the journey on the following pages with a sample chapter of The Frozen God, the next book in this series, compliments of yours truly.

SAMPLE CHAPTER

Sigurd's face burned as if tiny needles were piercing his skin as the wind whipped around him.

"Hold fast, Sigurd!" Sinfjotli urged. "Don't give up the ghost yet!"

Sigurd couldn't reply through his chattering teeth. His breath steamed out of his blue lips like smoke from a chimney as he clutched the giant black wolf's snow-crusted back, desperate for warmth, as another mighty gale descended on them, howling like a leviathan. The wind whipped across the snowdrifts and made everything seem so white that it was hard to tell the sky from the snow.

The sun was gone. Snow and ice devoured everything around them, turning the world gray and pale blue. Each step felt like a battle. Still, the giant black wolf shuffled forward on the ice-coated tree root.

Most of Sigurd's body was numb. Ungodly pain ravaged the few areas that weren't frostbitten. His heart pounded, and his breath came in raspy, panicked gasps.

Sigurd tried to remember the last time he'd felt warm. Was it after they escaped Helheim? When Guttorm murdered him in his sleep? Or perhaps they *had* perished and were *in* Helheim?

No. The realm of the dead's frosty blizzards was a cool autumn breeze compared to Niflheim's unforgiving atmosphere. Sigurd's saliva froze between his teeth with every breath. Everywhere they turned was a mist that froze his blood in his veins. The chill entered his bones as if the fog and snow were creeping through his layers of clothing under his hauberk and armor, through his skin, and wrapped around his bones.

The pain and frostbite became so bad that Sigurd tore off his golden hauberk and plate armor, leaving nothing but the clothes Nanna had gifted him to protect him from the cold. Some might call that foolish, but his armor hurt rather than protected him in these conditions.

Even Sinfjotli wasn't immune to the cold. The giant wolf's fur insulated him, but he also felt like he was simultaneously experiencing every winter he'd lived through throughout his life.

"C-can...y-you...s-smell...an...anything?" Sigurd lisped through chattering teeth.

"The winds are blowing too hard," Sinfjotli reported. "I can't...argh...get a scent."

"W-We...s-should t-turn...b-b-back." Sigurd suggested.

"We've come too far." Sinfjotli insisted. "They're here. They have to be."

Sigurd was too tired and chilled to argue as he buried his face in Sinfjotli's black fur. How had it come to this? How did he go from being a fugitive of Helheim to a scared, frostbitten wreck desperately clinging to his brother's fur for warmth? His mind retreated to the recesses of his memories, desperate to distract himself from this frigid hell.

Their journey to this realm had been perilous and long, but nowhere near as deadly as the situation they were in now. After bidding farewell to Brynhild, Sigurd and Sinfjotli marched north across the World Tree's roots. They trekked across Yggdrasil's twisting roots for two months, though it sometimes felt like an eternity. They'd been attacked by many creatures along the way: insects the size of barns, toothy worms the size of islands, and other nasty beasts that Sigurd's mind was too weary to recall.

He still bore the scars from those battles. They always walked away from each fight with at least a dozen wounds. Yet the Apples of Idun they'd eaten in Helheim healed their injuries and sustained them throughout that perilous journey devoid of food, water, and sleep.

That felt more like a curse than a blessing. Sigurd had been unable to quench his parched throat for weeks. He wished for food, even though his stomach didn't growl. He craved slumber, but his body buzzed with too much energy to permit that.

But more than anything, he sought guidance. That brought them to Niflheim, the coldest realm.

Sigurd remembered how foreboding and beautiful the coldest realm was from afar. Even hundreds of miles away, standing on the ancient roots of Yggdrasil, he felt the mind-numbingly frigid air seep into his bones, making the hairs on the back of his neck stand on end. Niflheim's swirling atmosphere was an ethereal blend of vibrant blues, cerulean, and flecks of white constantly in motion like the sea. Chunks of ice swirled within its atmosphere, a grim warning of the merciless winter that gripped this realm where warmth was a distant memory.

Sigurd glanced up at Yggdrasil's trunk. His home realm of Midgard shone like a star high above him, along with two other bright lights. The distance was so vast that he couldn't make out Midgard's details, even with his superhuman vision.

But he was sure of one thing. Niflheim dwarfed Midgard a dozen times over. Finding three goddesses inside that frigid planet would be like locating three grains of sand at the bottom of the sea. Every instinct warned him to avoid this realm at all costs.

But where else could they go? They couldn't hope to climb the World Tree. They couldn't linger on the colossal roots without getting attacked by other creatures that called these lowest echelons of the universe home. The only other realms they could travel to were Helheim and fiery Muspelheim; both were less viable options than the realm before them.

Sigurd shared a look with Sinfjotli, who shrugged.

"We came this far," his half-brother reminded. "No sense hesitating. We clawed our way out of Helheim. We can surely handle Niflheim."

Gods above, we were so naïve, Sigurd reflected. *We let the glory of escaping Helheim get to our heads. We should have...* His thoughts trailed off into uncertainty. What *could* they have done? What in Ymir's name could they have possibly done to prepare for this journey when all they possessed was a magic sword, a suit of armor, ragged clothes sown by a goddess, and the ability to transform into a wolf?

Baldur's apples and Sinfjotli's shapeshifting power were the only reasons Sigurd clung to life. The snake-eyed warrior had been the first to succumb to the elements after weeks... days...or hours. He honestly did not know how long they'd been in this realm. The Apple of Idun burned within his stomach like coals in a furnace as it struggled to heal him. Every time it healed a patch of frostbite on his nose or fingers, another thirteen patches sprang up somewhere else along his body.

Sigurd soon collapsed face-first into a deep snowbank. The snow enveloped him like a blanket, and to his shame, he wanted nothing more than to go to sleep and never wake again.

But Sinfjotli had other ideas. He transformed into a wolf, dug Sigurd out of the snow, and hoisted him on his back. The soft fur was the first warm thing Sigurd felt in ages.

"You won't die like this," Sinfjotli vowed as he sprinted across the snow-covered branch. "Neither of us will."

Sinfjotli always kept his promises. But honor and courage meant nothing in these inhospitable conditions.

Niflheim grew darker and colder as they traveled further, as if they were sinking toward the bottom of an ocean that light would never reach.

Sigurd kept himself busy scanning the darkness with his snake eyes, ensuring they stayed on the path. Sinfjotli almost slipped off Yggdrasil's branch more than once. If Sigurd didn't notice and warn his brother, they'd fall into a ceaseless abyss from which there'd be no return.

As another bone-chilling gale blasted them, Sigurd wondered what his beloved Brynhild was doing now. She'd flown up Yggdrasil's trunk to Asgard after helping them escape Helheim. Sigurd didn't know what dangers lurked throughout Yggdrasil's trunk, but he hoped she was in a warmer place.

Thinking about her was one of two things that kept him going. The other was their long-lost daughter, Aslaug.

I had another daughter all this time and never knew. After Sigurd learned Svanhild and Sigmund were murdered, his resolve cracked. But learning from Brynhild that he still had a living child convinced him to move forward.

Cruelly, her name was the only thing he knew about her. He wondered what sort of life Aslaug lived. What did she look like? Which of her parents did she resemble more?

Those thoughts were the only things keeping Sigurd conscious as Sinfjotli ventured deeper into the darkness.

But soon, even his half-brother succumbed to the elements. A foot of snow had gathered on Sinfjotli's back before the wolf's legs finally gave out beneath him and slumped on his belly.

The sudden movement sent Sigurd tumbling off his brother's back and rolling on the ice-covered branch.

It's over, Sigurd knew as he sprawled on his back, listening to Sinfjotli's panting. *We gave it everything we had, but this was as far as we could go.*

The blizzard relentlessly pounded them, piling an inch of snow every minute.

The snow will become my burial shroud. But I'll feel warm soon.

Regin taught him long ago that everyone feels warm just before death comes. Sigurd eagerly awaited that feeling, though it saddened him he didn't die bravely on a battlefield.

This would be his second death. His first had been bloody but brief, courtesy of Guttorm. This wouldn't be glorious, but it would be memorable...if there was anyone to witness it.

Snow shifted off Sigurd's forehead and blond hair as he turned his head to the side and peered further down Yggdrasil's root into the abyss.

We never so much as glimpsed the Norns. All our strife amounted to nothing in the end.

It wasn't so bad as bleeding to death in his bed. Besides, Sigurd knew what awaited him. Soon, he'd see Baldur, his aunt, and the others. Hopefully, he'd see his children, too. He hoped Baldur found them by...

A crunching sound cut through the blizzard's shrieking wails. Sigurd's snake eyes noticed three humanoid shadows shifting in the mist. But his body gave out on him, and his eyelids shut before he could wonder if they were friend or foe.

Click here to continue reading or scan the QR Code below:

APPENDIX

HOUSE VOLSUNG

Boasting descent from the youngest son of Odin and Frigga, the Volsung family is one of the few mortal families in Midgard that can truly trace their lineage to the All-Father. They have been kings, conquers, avengers, and heroes. But above all else, they were warriors who carved their names into the annals of Midgard's history. Thanks to Sigurd and Sinfjotli, their story isn't finished yet.

SIGURD SNAKE EYES (slain by Guttorm but resurrected in Helheim),

—his horse, GRANI, roaming free in Midgard,

—his father, [SIGMUND],[1] perished in battle against Lyngvi's forces

—his mother, [HJORDIS], perished in battle against her brother-in-law, Yngvi,

—his children:

    —by his paramour, BRYNHILD:

        —ASLAUG,

    —by his wife, GUDRUN:

---

1   Regular brackets] indicate a valiant death and the charcter became Einherjar.

—{SVANHILD}[2], trampled to death by horses,

—{SIGMUND}, slain by GUTTORM,

—his half-brothers:

—SINFJOTLI, by his aunt SIGNY (poisoned by his stepmother but resurrected in Helheim),

—[HELGI] HUNDINGSBANE by his stepmother BORGHILD,

—his wife, [SIGRÚN], who perished in the Volsungs; last stand,

—[HÁMUNDR] by his stepmother BORGHILD, who perished in the Volsungs' last stand,

—his other kin:

—his aunt, {SIGNY} who died by suicide,

—her children by her husband, SIGGEIR the Beast:

—{RAGR}, her first son, killed by Sigmund at Signy's behest,

—{REKKR}, her second son, killed by Sigmund at Signy's behest,

---

2   {Angled brackets} indicate a character is deceased and possibly ended up in Helheim.

—{AURORA}, her only daughter, killed by Sinfjotli at Signy's behest,

—{HANSEL}, her fourth son, killed by Sinfjotli at Signy's behest,

—by her brother, SIGMUND:

—SINFJOTLI, her third son,

—his uncles:

—[GRÍPIR], a hermit gifted with prophetic visions, perished alongside his sister in battle,

—{ARNE the SWIFT}, devoured by Siggeir's mother,

—{COLDBORN BLOOD AXE}, devoured by Siggeir's mother,

—{FRODE the WISE}, devoured by Siggeir's mother,

—{GERALD the DEVOTE}, devoured by Siggeir's mother,

—{HALVARD SQUINT-EYE}, devoured by Siggeir's mother,

—{JERRIK the UNDYING}, devoured by Siggeir's mother,

—{ORWIG the PROTECTOR}, devoured by Siggeir's mother,

—{THURMOND the MIGHTY}, devoured by Siggeir's mother,

—{ULF the BLOODLETTER}, devoured by Siggeir's mother,

 —his maternal grandfather, [EYLIMI], killed by Hávard,

 —his paternal grandfather, [VÖLSUNG], killed by Siggeir,

 —his paternal grandmother, HLJOD the Valkyrie,

  —his great-grandfather, [RERIR the STERN], who died fighting,

  —his great-grandmother, {BRENDA} who died in childbirth,

   —his ancestor, [SIGI, called THE MAVERICK AESIR], who died slaying countless men.

HOUSE GJUKUNG

An ancient dynasty that ruled over the Burgundians in the land of eternal mist, they played a pivotal role in Sigurd's final days in Midgard. Sigurd's arrival brought great fortune and prosperity to their lands. But after his death, they met a horrific, bloody end at the hands of Atli of the Huns.

{GUDRUN} who committed suicide,

—her father, {GJUKI}, the King of Burgundians who reigned until being slain by Atli's forces,

—her mother, {GRIMHILD}, who was tortured to death by Atli's forces,

—her siblings:

    —{GUNNAR}, executed by Atli,

        —his first wife, BRYNHILD,

        —his second wife, {GLAUMVOR},

    —{HAGEN} brutally slain by Atli,

    —{GUTTORM} slain by Sigurd.

—her children:

    —by her first husband, {SIGURD}:

        —{SVANHILD} trampled to death
        by Jormunrek's horses,

        —{SIGMUND}, killed by Guttorm,

    —by her second husband, {ATLI} of the
    Huns:

        —{ERNAK}, killed by his mother,

        —{EITEL}, killed by his mother,

    —by her third husband, JONAKR:

        —[SORLI] killed by
        Jormunrek's men,

        —[HAMDIR] killed by
        Jormunrek's men,

        —[ERP] killed by Jormunrek's men.

THE AESIR

The gods who created Midgard continue to keep watch over it and the other Nine Realms from Asgard. After the All-Father, Odin, and his brothers, Hoenir and Vé, slew the primordial giant Ymir and fashioned Midgard from his corpse, he and his descendants continue to protect their creation and maintain the stability of the other realms.

ODIN the All-Father, King of Asgard and Chief of the Aesir,

—by his wife, FRIGGA, the goddess of marriage, family, and motherhood:

    —{BALDUR}, the god of goodness, joy, light, and forgiveness, who Hodr accidentally killed,

        —{LÉTTFETI}, his horse,

        —{TWILIGHT}, his pet dragon,

    —{HODR}, the god of darkness and winter, killed by Vali,

    —HERMONDR, the messenger of the gods,

    —[SIGI], the Maverick Aesir, perished fighting and became Einherjar,

—by the Jotun, GUNNLǪÐ:

    —BRAGI, the god of poetry,

—by the Jotun, FJÖRGYN:

    —THOR, the god of thunder,

—by the Jotun, GRIDR:

    —VIDAR, the god of vengeance,

—by the nine Jotun mothers, ANGEYJA, ATLA, EISTLA, EYRGJAFA, IMDR, GJALP, GREIP, JARNSAXA, and ULFRUN:

    —HEIMDALL, Watchman of the Gods and Guardian of humanity,

—by the Jotun, HRÓÐR:

    —TÝR, the god of war and justice,

—Odin's brothers:

    —HOENIR, the god of silence, spirituality, and silence who gifted the first humans, Askr and Embla, with their wit and sense of touch and smell, and later became the temporary regent of the Vanir after the bloody Aesir-Vanir War,

    —{VÉ}, the god of fertility and sensuality who granted the first humans, Askr and Embla, their outward appearances, speech, taste, hearing, and sight,

—Odin's allies:

—The NORNS

—SKADI, the goddess of the hunt and winter,

>—her servant, [BREDI], an Einherjar whom Sigi killed

—the EINHERJAR of Valhalla.

THE VANIR

The other major family of the gods, the Vanir once battled the Aesir in a bloody war. They were the only race in the Nine Realms to force the Aesir to capitulate after many lives were lost in the violent Aesir-Vanir War. They now monitor the Nine Realms alongside the Aesir as equals. Living in Vanaheim and sometimes Alfheim, the Vanir protect the natural world and receive half of those who perish bravely in battle.

NJÖRD, the god of the sea and former leader of the Vanir,

—his children:

    —FREYJA, the goddess of love and war, the current leader of the Vanir, and equal to Odin,

    —FREYR, the god of magic, harvest, and fertility and the ruler of Alfheim,

—SOL, the goddess of the sun, who flees in a chariot from the wolf, Sköll,

—MANI, the god of the moon, who flees in a chariot from the wolf, Hati,

—NANNA, the goddess of cooking, joy, and peace,

—IDUN, the goddess of youth, spring, and rejuvenation.

THE DWARVES OF SVARTALFHEIM

The dwarves are the Aesir's oldest allies, whom Odin created from maggots feasting on Ymir's corpse. Tracing their descent from the first dwarf, Ivaldi, they are hailed as the greatest smiths and craftsmen in the Nine Realms who created Mjolnir, Draupnir, Gullinbursti, and Gungnir. Their contact with humans in Midgard is rare, but always consequential.

IVALDI, The King of Svartalfheim and Father of the Dwarves,

—{HREIDMAR}, murdered by his son, Fafnir,

    —{OTTR}, a shapeshifter Loki, Odin, and Hoenir accidentally killed,

    —{FAFNIR}, who transformed into a dragon and was famously killed by Sigurd,

    —{REGIN}, Sigurd's mentor and foster father, who he later killed in premeditated self-defense,

—{LITR}, Baldur's companion who got kicked into his funerary pyre by Thor and now keeps the Hringhorni in order and builds homes for the righteous,

—ANDVARI, a shapeshifting dwarf whose treasure Loki swiped to pay a weregild to Hreidmar,

—THE HULDRA BROTHERS who crafted Mjolnir, Draupnir, and Freyr's boar, Gullinbursti:

    —BROK,

    —SINDRI.

THE JÖTNAR

The inhabitants of Jotunheim, who trace their descent to the beginning of the world, the Jötnar, or frost giants, are the Aesir's oldest enemies. The fates of the two races have been intertwined for as long as time has turned: by blood, marriage, and their eternal feud, which will culminate in Ragnarök. Giants possess ancient treasure, magic, and knowledge older than the gods and have been as instrumental in shaping the history of the realms as the Aesir.

{YMIR}, the first being, whom all giants, gods, and beasts trace descent from, was mother and father to all before being slain by Odin, Hoenir, and Vé, who molded his flesh and blood into Midgard,

—SUTTUNGR, the giant king who acquired the mead of poetry,

    —his daughter, GUNNLQÐ,

    —his brother, BAUGI,

—HYRROKIN, the giantess who launched Baldur's funeral ship, the Hringhorni, out to sea,

—{FÁRBAUTI}, the father of Loki by his wife, the goddess {LAUFEY},

—{THIAZI}, the shapeshifter who kidnaped Idun and later became a draug,

      —his daughter, SKADI, who became the goddess of the hunt and winter.

LOKI's PROGENY

Loki, the most infamous of the gods, was the son of the goddess Laufey and the giant Farbauti, who became Odin's blood brother. No god in the Norse Pantheon was more notorious or wily than the god of tricksters. Sometimes, he was the Aesir's greatest ally, at other moments the worst thorn in their side, and later their worst betrayer after he orchestrated Baldur's murder. Yet Loki's descendants were just as infamous and reviled as him. All endured tragic fates, and many became the Aesir's worst enemies, destined to battle the gods at Ragnarök.

LOKI

—by his lover Angrboda:

 —HEL, goddess of death and Queen of the Underworld,

  —Móðguðr, the Guardian of Helheim who ensures no one living enters the underworld,

  —her horse, HELHEST,

 —FENRIR, the wolf destined to battle Odin at Ragnarök,

  —by Odin's pet wolves, GERI and FREKI,

—SKÖLL, the Celestial Wolf who chases the sun across the heavens,

—HATI, the Celestial Wolf who chases the moon across the heavens,

—GARM, the Hound of Helheim who ensures no soul may leave Helheim unless his aunt allows it,

—JÖRMUNGANDR, the World Serpent who is so large he encircles the entirety of Midgard and bites his tail. Destined to battle Thor at Ragnarök,

—by his wife, SIGYN:

—VALI,

—{NARFI},

—by the stallion SVANDILFARI (while Loki was in the form of a mare),

—SLEIPNIR, the eight-legged mount of Odin who carries the All-Father on journeys throughout the Nine Realms.

HELHEIM'S DRAUGS

The mightiest entities in the underworld, subordinate only to Hel, Garm, and Móðguðr, Helheim's draugs are among the fiercest foes imaginable. With semi-invincibility, unique abilities, and inconceivable power, they are the mightiest enemies one could face. Only monarchs or generals have the potential to join their ranks. Some were the blackest of villains. Others became corrupted upon their death. Yet all now burn with hatred for the Aesir and their allies.

—SIGGIER the Beast,

—KING DURRAN,

—DONG ZHOU,

—QUEEN TAMARA,

—GOLIATH,

—KING PORUS of Paurava,

—THIAZI,

—YUE FEI,

—ATLI of the Huns,

—GENERAL ANTONY,

—AGAMEMNON,

—ALLANT,

—aspiring draug:

    —HEDRICK the Troublemaker.

        —his father, [HÖFUND]

        —his mother, [HERVOR]

        —his brother, {ANGANTYR}

Other Notable Houses and Legendary Figures

THE VALKYRIES

The valkyries are the winged female warriors who serve Freyja and Odin. They scour battlefields to choose the slain worthy of a place in Valhalla or Fólkvangr and dispatch any restless spirits to Helheim. They are some of the Aesir's most formidable warriors and the bane of the undead.

—BRYNHILD,

—HLJOD.

HOUSE HUNDING

An ancient house that survived the bloody Battle of Frekastein, they eventually defeated Sigmund and his army, destroyed Hunaland, and almost extirpated the Volsung bloodline. Under their king, Lyngvi the Lusty, many ancient families and kingdoms were brutally razed. They were later brought to justice, and their bloodline was wiped out by Sigmund's youngest son, Sigurd the Dragonslayer.

{LYGNVI the Lusty,} the king who brought the Volsungs to their knees, brutally executed by Sigurd,

—his many sons by countless women, all slain by Sigurd during his war of vengeance,

—his father, {HUNDING}, slain by Helgi,

—his older brothers:

    —{ÁLFR}, slain by Helgi,

    —{EYIÓLF}, slain by Helgi,

    —{HJÖRVARD}, slain by Helgi,

—his twin brother {HÁVARD}, the general of army, killed by Sigmund,

—his nephews, called {THE SONS of HUNDING}, all slain by Sigurd.

THE ORPHANS

A group of formidable warriors lead by Sigurd. Orphaned during Lyngvi's bloody invasion of Hunaland, they swore vengeance against the monarch and his entire bloodline. They later perished bravely in battle alongside Queen Hjordis in a civil war against her brother-in-law.

SIGURD SNAKEEYES

—{BIRNA} Blood Tusk,

—{FOLAN} the Fletcher,

—{VAFI} the Loon.

THE THREE EAGLES:

—GULLINKAMBI the Golden,

—FJALAR,

—HRÆSVELGR the Corpse Eater.

HOUSE YNGLING

The oldest and mightiest Scandinavian dynasty. Their prince and future king, Alf, rescued and married Hjordis after Sigmund perished fighting Lyngvi's army and raised Sigurd as his stepson.

King ALF,

—his father, {HJALPREK},

—his twin brother, {YNGVI},

—his first wife, [HJORDIS],

—his second wife, THORA,

{HÖGNE}, King of Östergötland, who perished at Frekastein,

—his daughter, [SIGRÚN],

—his son, {DAGR},

{GRANMAR}, King of Södermanland, who perished at Frekastein,

—his son {HOTHBRODD}, who perished at Frekastein,

{JORMUNREK} the King of the Goth, mutilated and slain by Gudrun's last three sons,

—his son, {Randver}, executed for treason,

—his advisor, {BIKKI},

{HARMUND} the Black, a cruel bandit leader slain by Hjordis,

{BRYNJAR}, brother of BORGHILD, killed by Sinfjotli in an honorable duel,

{SELKIRK}, the general of Siggeir's army, slain by the king,

VOLUND the SMITH, an elven smith who forged the cursed sword Mimung.

THE NINE REALMS

The Nine Realms, a group of vastly distant worlds spread across Yggdrasil's branches and roots, are home to many races and untold wonders. Few can travel between the realms; even fewer dare to journey beyond their home realms. The Nine Realms offer the ultimate challenge to those with nothing left to lose and everything to gain.

ASGARD, the home of the Aesir,

VANAHEIM, the home of the Vanir,

ALFHEIM, the home of the elves,

SVARTALHEIM, the home of the dwarves,

MIDGARD, the mortal realm,

JOTUNHEIM, the home of the frost giants,

NIFLHEIM, the realm of eternal frost

HELHEIM, the realm of the dishonorable dead,

MUSPELHEIM, the realm of the fire giants.

ALSO BY ALEX

ABOUT THE AUTHOR

Alex E. Martin is an epic fantasy storyteller and lover of Norse Mythology. Born in the Northeast United States, Alex is an avid explorer, fencer, aspiring chef, dog lover, gamer, and world traveler with an insatiable thirst for adventure.

Learn more at https://sites.google.com/view/alex-e-martin/home or scan the QR Code Below: